Coming To

Alan Brody

COMING TO

Published by
BERKLEY PUBLISHING CORPORATION

Distributed by
G. P. PUTNAM'S SONS, NEW YORK

For Paula

. . . the beautiful changes
In such kind ways
Wishing ever to sunder
Things and things' selves for a second finding, to lose
For a moment all that it touches back to wonder.

—RICHARD WILBUR

Prologue

———◆◆◆———

Phil

October 19, 1962

PHILIP GAYNOR sat with his fists in the shallow pockets of his leather jacket. His legs stretched straight before him. He was a light-skinned blond, the kind who can go for a week without looking unshaven. He had, in fact, shaved that morning. Philip could never have been taken for one of the other, unkempt, directionless young men who park themselves on the benches along Riverside Drive. There was a restless look of purpose even in the droop of his body, a sense of energy deferred only for the moment. The air of wealth and a family with history clung to him.

He wore his brown lumber jacket as though it were shabby, but it was real leather, thickly lined, with firm, invisible stitching. It had been a birthday gift from his father-in-law. Philip had told him that the one he had would wear another season, but Bernie Kahn insisted, almost pleaded. He even came into the city and took him down to Saks to be sure of the fit.

Philip's features were strong; sharply defined without turning angular. The straight, clear lines on his chin and nose, and his deep brown eyes compensated for his light coloring. They gave him a quality of surprise and hidden resources.

His bench was submerged in a sandbox area across from 115th Street. A few discarded toys lay on the ground, a matchbox truck, a shovel, a cardboard wristwatch. The sand-box was surrounded by a low iron fence. He watched his four-and-a-half-year-old daughter through the bars. She squatted alone, making cakes with an overturned coffee can.

It was a cold, gray autumn afternoon. Even with his hands in his pockets Philip felt his knuckles numbing.

A copy of the *Yale Law Journal* lay on the bench beside him. He always brought books with him when he took Vikki out, but he rarely opened them. It was impossible to concentrate, while constantly keeping an eye out for Vikki. When he did try to read he found later that he had retained nothing. All he remembered was the process of trying. He picked up the *Journal* now, held it open and upright on his thighs, and stared.

"In an earlier article in this Journal, The Limits of Collective Bargaining, (1.78 *Yale Law Journal* 1107 [1969] [hereinafter cited as *Limits*]), we asked whether private sector collective bargaining should serve as the model for collective bargaining in the public sector. . . ."

The arrangements for the day had been complicated. Sheila had insisted she needed a full eight hours alone. She left Vikki at the nursery school and asked Diana Brautigan to pick the child up for lunch. It was Thursday and Phil would be finished with classes at 2:30. He usually stayed in the Law Library until five, then came home for supper and a little time relaxing with the women—they all got a kick out of the way he called Vikki and Sheila "the women"—before he went off to his job at the late-night bookstore. Today he rushed off to Diana's as soon as his constitutional law class was out.

Phil liked being there for Sheila when she needed him. Before he met her he had been only a bright, brash pre-law student at Columbia. His father had been a judge in the Connecticut Supreme Court, his mother the oldest daughter of the Connecticut Harmons. He had packed his valise with all the assurance of his wealthy upbringing and the arrogance of any eighteen-year-old, and brought them to New York. He had refused, in a stormy confrontation with his mother, to accept any of her money. He would make his own way. All his

2

energy was focused on his own future. It was through Sheila that he had learned, to his astonishment, that he was capable of kind ways, and every time he took over for her on days like this he was again aware of how he had changed over only seven years. So many people believed that the added pressures of a family would be too much for a young law student, even one as gifted as Phil. But as he hurried across campus to Diana's apartment that afternoon he marveled at how Sheila—and later Vikki—had brought out unexpected stores of energy in him.

Sheila and Diana Brautigan had been unlikely roommates at Barnard; Sheila studying pre-law and tearing herself apart with social consciousness, organizing activities for ACTION, and then CORE, then SNCC, while Diana divided her time between drama courses at Barnard and feverish trips downtown where she made the rounds. Phil was never quite sure of what "making the rounds" was. It sounded mysterious and faintly compromising. Whatever it was, it worked. Diana constantly got calls to do tv commercials and spots in films being shot in New York. Even after she married and had Donna she kept working and running. Somehow, in the middle of it all, she and Sheila had kept their friendship alive. The proximity helped. They had both married Columbia men and both lived on the West Side. Their children went to the same nursery school and they joined the same baby-sitting pool.

When Phil arrived at the Brautigans' that afternoon he found Vikki perched on a stool, screaming, while Diana washed blood off her forehead. She had fallen against a corner of the coffee table. It was just the forehead, thank God. Another inch and she might have lost an eye. Diana worked quickly and efficiently while Donna stood by with her large, serious eyes and explained to Phil that it was an accident.

Diana wore a blue cocktail dress. She was being careful with the blood. "Oh, God, I'd love to hug her," she said, with genuine but distracted anguish. "Comfort her, will you, Phil?" He took Vikki in his arms. Her crying subsided. "Selma Raskin is giving a cocktail party. I'm having a late lunch with my agent, then we're going over together."

3

"Who's Selma Raskin?"

"The producer for *The Criminals*. I just finished doing a segment."

Phil grinned and shook his head in admiration.

"I'm waiting for my sitter to get here. She's new in the pool and she's never been in this crazy house before. I'll have to show her. . . ." She reached out gingerly and smoothed Vikki's hair. "Feel better, sweetheart?"

Vikki buried her face in Phil's jacket and nodded. Diana made a face at him to show how really scary it was.

The sitter arrived. While Diana swept around the apartment giving last-minute instructions, Phil helped Vikki on with her coat and snowpants.

They stopped at a grocery store on Broadway and bought two apples, then headed for the sandbox. They sat together, munching, for a while. Phil tried to talk to Vikki, but she was in one of her moods. She could sit for hours and refuse to respond to anything. She would pretend not to hear or simply shrug. They had tried smacking her, shaking her, screaming at her. Sometimes it would work. She would suddenly open up and talk and laugh as though nothing had happened. Other times she held immovable. Either way it was always Phil or Sheila who ended up feeling guilty, helpless, resentful, so they finally decided to ignore it and let her pull herself out alone.

Vikki finished her apple and give him the core. It printed a cold, wet shape in his hand as he went to drop it in the sidewalk trash basket. He started to wipe his palm on his jacket, stopped, made a fist instead and tried to work the stickiness out with his fingertips. Vikki wandered into the sandbox and found a discarded coffee can. She filled it, packed it, and turned it over. Part of its lip was bent so the cakes never came out even.

She was dark, like Sheila, with the same wide features. Her eyes were long. They seemed to stretch to the sides of her face and lend her Sheila's exotic quality. Vikki's cheeks were still the chubby cheeks of a child, though, so the eyes looked even narrower. If she was happy they would seem crinkled with silent laughter, but when she was serious or simply con-

4

centrating, they looked mean and calculating. She was concentrating now on her sand cakes, her face framed by the tight green hood of her coat. Phil thought of Donna Brautigan's startling round eyes and tried to check a surge of resentment. He and Sheila had been convinced for a long time that Vikki was something beautiful and special, not just to them, but to the world at large. There had been a fine, almost Oriental delicacy about her as an infant. Strangers would pass them as they wheeled her in the stroller and Phil would always watch for the moment when their ordinary, thoughtless interest would suddenly change to a genuine recognition of her evanescent beauty. Those moments had become less frequent as Vikki grew. They had disappeared altogether over the past six months.

It was over the past six months, too, that the trouble with Sheila had grown.

Phil's fingers were glued to the page with cold. He recrossed his ankles stiffly and went back to the *Journal*.

"In an earlier article in this Journal, *The Limits*. . . ." No. He'd already read that. ". . . We concluded it should not. One argument was, and is, that a wholesale transplant from one sector to the other is inappropriate. . . ."

It felt stupid to even think about it as trouble. That threw it all out of proportion. There were simply changes going on in Sheila, small ones, changes so inconsequential that he might not even have noticed a year before. This year, though, the pressure was on, and he was sensitive to everything. He was coming up for his bar exam in five months. He had already had three tense and disheartening interviews with law firms. The job market was tight, even for Phil, who had the prestige of the *Law Review* behind him. His classmates were becoming tight-lipped. The closest bonds of friendship were starting to fray. Sheila was probably picking up on the charged atmosphere and, God knew, his own nerves were growing more vulnerable as the possibilities for the following year grew more uncertain.

It had started in little ways. When they were first married she would read the paper avidly. Every morning he would

5

leave her with the *Times* spread out on the kitchen table so she could scan it while she nursed Vikki. At dinner she would bubble and seethe with the same fierce concern he had loved when she was in the thick of the action at school. Now she picked up the paper from the front door, barely glanced at the headlines, and transferred it, unopened, to the growing pile in the living room. Mystery novels lay face down and tented all over the apartment. They set his teeth on edge. The half-read novels and the neglected papers were somehow connected with the nights he was not at the bookstore and she would plead with him to go with her to a neighborhood movie. She knew it cut into his studying for the bar exams and there was always the struggle about whether they could afford the baby-sitting hours, but she always won out. Halfway through the film she would grow restless and tell him she was going home. He would leave with her.

So far she had kept the household going. She was always in the process of doing a room. When he came home at five he would find her working feverishly at a late, makeshift dinner. She would explain that she had lost track of the time because she'd been cleaning the bedroom, or Vikki's room, or the living room—but they never seemed to show the results.

She was always tired, and distracted, like a woman living with the vague sense that she'd misplaced something of value, refusing to give up the search even while she met her other appointments.

The night before he had come home from the bookstore as usual at 1:30 and found Sheila asleep with the television on in the bedroom. She was still in her jeans and one of his old white shirts that she wore around the house. Every light was burning except for the one in Vikki's room. The dinner dishes were piled in the sink. Unwashed pans and mixing bowls lay strewn over every surface. She had fallen asleep before she refrigerated the leftovers. The kitchen was thick with the smell of sparerib grease and broccoli. There was one clear space on the counter near the stove. Sheila knew he always unwound over coffee before going to bed. She had left one clean

6

cup with a spoon of instant for him. The pot they used for boiling water was crusted with mashed potato. Phil cleared a place in the sink, scrubbed out the pot, and put on water. While he waited for it to boil he went through the apartment turning off lights.

He couldn't count the number of times he'd casually mentioned the business of turning out lights when she wasn't using them. He had tried to be tactful. He understood how exhausted she was by the end of the day, but. . . . Phil hated this head-of-the-household role she'd been forcing him into more and more. They didn't have a hell of a lot of time together, but it seemed as though lately whenever they did he found himself laying down the law—and angry and frustrated because he felt somehow tricked into it. The worst thing was that it always worked, at least briefly. As soon as he raised his voice and spelled out rules, Sheila would nod, promise to be more careful, and apologize for not taking care of it herself in the first place.

It was partly his fault, too. He knew how edgy he'd been getting. Sometimes he could stand off, watch himself, know his reactions were out of proportion, and still not be able to control his tone. It was the pressure. Once he got past the bar and found a job they would be home free. Then she could lean on him for the rest of their lives.

He had left a small lamp burning near his reclining chair in the living room, and he brought his coffee there. Vikki's tricycle blocked the archway. One of her dolls sat slumped on the sand-colored, circular sofa Bernie and May had given them for their third anniversary. Phil smiled wryly. He could never think of it simply as "the sofa," only as "the-sofa-Bernie-and-May-had-given-them-for-their-third-anniversary." Its history was dyed into the tufted fabric. He pushed back on the chair and closed his eyes. He loosened his tie and collar stud. In the darkness he felt his shoulders relax and he measured how tight he had been from the length of the drop.

Sheila stirred in the bedroom. She usually woke for him so they could sit over his coffee and have some time alone. There was something romantic and New Yorkish about sitting up over coffee at two in the morning, she in her nightgown while he was still dressed for work. It was a young thing to do and it kept them in touch with their undergraduate days. It was also a prelude to lovemaking. If Sheila woke for him it was a signal that she was willing. That was important. Even before they were married, they had made an agreement that each was free to say no. They never actually had to say anything, though. Over the years an elaborate set of signals had grown. When Phil rubbed his eye in a certain way Sheila knew he was too distracted, or when Sheila pressed her palms against her lower back he knew she was tired. They had both been picking up on all kinds of signals lately and Sheila stayed asleep more often until now it had become as much a routine for Phil to sit alone with his coffee as to sit with her. Sometimes, when she did wake, he felt as though she was intruding.

He hoped she wouldn't wake now, at least not right away. He wanted to hold on to the quiet and the drop of his shoulders a little while longer.

"Phil?" Her voice was still thick with sleep. "Honey?"

He kept his eyes closed. "Hi."

"What time is it?"

"Same as usual."

"Do you want me to get up?"

She made it sound like a chore. "That's OK, honey."

"I didn't mean to fall asleep. I just lay down for a second. . . ."

"It's OK. I'll see you in the morning."

There was a silence. "Maybe I should get undressed."

"Whatever you want."

"I should." There was a pause. "I'm too tired."

He smiled indulgently and pictured her lying there with her own eyes closed like his.

"Phil?"

"Hmm?"

"Which?"

"What?"

"Should I undress or not?"

8

"Whichever you want." He laughed, but the words were edged with impatience.

"Are you all right?"

"Fine."

"I'm going back to sleep."

"OK."

The sheets rustled. Everything turned quiet. He drank his coffee slowly. In the heart of the stillness and dark he felt a sudden, inexplicable rush of tenderness for Sheila, tenderness and an odd, indefinable sense of loss. He wondered if she were deeply enough asleep for him to clear up the kitchen without waking her. He had a vision of her walking into it in the morning, the look on her face when she found it clean. It would be like a gift and her own surprise would make her know the same astonished love that had prompted him to give it. He turned off the lamp and went to the kitchen. It would have to be a surprise. He surveyed the clutter. He could never be quiet enough. Even if Sheila slept through, there was always the danger of waking Vikki. He carefully put his coffee cup on the counter where she'd left it for him and turned out the light. He crept down the hall to the bedroom and undressed in the dark. Before he got into bed, he gently undressed Sheila, rolled up her clothes and lay them at the foot of the bed. He kissed her once on the forehead and went to sleep.

That morning she had wakened him cheerfully and announced the day's arrangements. Vikki was already at school. Diana would take her until Phil arrived. She hated to kill the afternoon for him, but she simply had to have it. She wanted to pull things together, to clean and rest and get things back on an even keel. He was not to come home until five. That was all she asked. She wanted to be sure to have enough time to do a thorough job.

Phil said nothing about the lights. For an instant he had a glimpse of the old Sheila. He had forgotten how clear and bright Sheila's eyes were, how smoothly she moved when she worked. He had not realized how much she had been dragging her body through the apartment, how seldom he had

9

seen her with her hair brushed and pulled back, and how little she smiled. She seemed positively renewed, as though something had happened, perhaps in the deepest part of the night, to break an enchantment.

The cold made Phil's eyes tear. He glanced up at the number on the top of the page. Twenty-four. His eyes had traveled over every word for three pages but he'd lost the sense after the second sentence.

He checked his watch. 3:30. His heart sank. He had been sitting in the cold less than an hour. He had promised to keep Vikki out until five. He dropped the *Journal* and put his fists back in the pockets. His eyes still smarted. He blinked. There were cold tears behind the lids. This was the part he always forgot when he agreed to take Vikki out. The sting in the eyes, the tears, the exhaustion that spead thrugh his body like a slow poison. He could go for a whole day of classes, sometimes get in a handball game at the gym before supper, work through the night at the bookstore, and still need to unwind over coffee. But afternoons like this drained him. He could feel it beginning now with a gnawing fatigue below his chest. His eyelids became heavy. He let them close, but the tears seeped out and forced them open.

Vikki's cheeks were bright with the cold. Her gloves swung loosely from the safety pins on her cuffs. She would not hold out for the hour and a half. Phil would have to stall her. That was when even the seconds would crawl, while he sat shivering against the cold trying to convince her she was playing. As long as the sand and the coffee can held her attention he was still free and alone. He tried not to look at her and kept himself very still.

Across the Drive on 114th Street, a wrecking crew worked on an old apartment house. The steel ball cracked against the top floor and released a shower of plaster and brick. The cold air muffled the crashes.

He shot a quick look at Vikki. Her hands were still working but she had raised her eyes to survey the empty sandbox.

Phil was determined to stay out till five this time. These

afternoons were the only times Sheila had to herself, besides the three short mornings Vikki was in nursery school—and even then they often asked her to fill in for absent staff. Phil knew, too, that when she finally got around to asking him to give up an afternoon she needed it. That was why he gave them so willingly.

Once he had suggested that he and Vikki stay inside and Sheila get out, take advantage of the city, meet a friend, and do something. They couldn't afford anything extravagant like lunch or a matinee, but there were the free museums, window-shopping, or just plain visiting in somebody else's apartment. None of her friends was free, so she started out at the Metropolitan. Before they were married Sheila could sit alone for hours in front of El Greco's "Toledo" or Rodin's "Orpheus and Eurydice." Now, they didn't seem to hold her and she ended up wandering down Fifth to Saks, buying two dresses at discount, and putting them on her mother's charge. This time it was she who came home early.

She never wore the dresses.

The steel ball swung against the loosened bricks. Vikki went back to her sand play. Phil tried to decide if it was time to look again at his watch. He glanced at his wrist while he thought, and looked before he decided. Less than five minutes had passed. He sank lower on his spine and tried not to think.

Vikki plunged her hands in the sand and scooped it into the coffee can, still too engrossed to notice the cold. It would hit her at any moment. If he told her to put on her gloves he might just call attention to it; if he didn't, she might notice only when it became painful. Then he would have to take her home anyway. He hoped Sheila had been out at least once. He wanted her to have some idea of what it was like in case they did have to leave early.

"Vikki, honey. Come here. I'll help you get your gloves on."

She looked up from her work. Phil knew he had made the wrong decision. "Is it time to go?"

"Not yet. But I'll help you put your gloves on. It'll make your hands warmer."

11

She stood up, a patch of frozen sand on each knee of her snowpants.

"I want to go home," she said as she climbed out.

"We're going to stay a little longer."

"I'm cold."

"That's why I want you to put your gloves on."

"I'm cold all over."

"Mommy wants us to stay out till five today." He took her hands to work the fingers in. He kept pleading with Sheila to get mittens, but she insisted that regular gloves gave more freedom. "If you're bored in the sandbox—" As soon as the words were out he knew he shouldn't have used them, but he continued without a break: "—you can watch them tear down the house over there."

"I see that every day."

"Well, find something to interest you. We're staying out." He tugged at a woolen finger. "Hold your thumb straight, will you?"

"Why are you mad?"

"I'm not mad. We're just staying out, that's all." He finished with the gloves. "There. That should make you feel better."

"I'm still cold."

"I tell you what. You go back to play for another ten minutes or so, then we'll go get a treat on Broadway."

"A Coke?"

"A hot chocolate."

"I want a Coke."

"You just said you were cold."

She looked at him blankly.

"All right. We'll see how you feel. But give it another ten minutes."

She wandered away from Phil, but she did not return to the sandbox. She slipped her shoes between the bars of the railing and gripped the spikes at the top. She leaned away at arm's length, her head thrown back, and stared at the gray sky. For a while she swayed on her outstretched arms, then slowly circled the sandbox. When she'd made a full revolution she pulled herself up. "Is it time yet?"

Phil shook his head.

She started around once more, taking the spaces two at a time. Phil picked up the *Journal* and pretended to read. With his head lowered he could glance from his watch to Vikki's feet. They moved around two, then three, then four spaces at a time. The minute hand crept up the side of the watch. Phil held his stomach and jaw tight. If they held out for ten, he might stretch it to fifteen or twenty minutes. He looked up once and found Vikki's eyes firmly fixed on him as she moved. "Now?"

He looked at his watch as though for the first time. "Another five minutes." He lowered his head again quickly. This time he tried to read.

"In an earlier article in this Journal, The Limits. . . ." He might as well start from the beginning again. If he really applied himself he might follow the thread, work himself into it, and forget the time. Perhaps if she saw he was really engrossed, she would give up and find something to occupy her, too. He checked himself on the first sentence. Yes, he understood. It was all introductory.

"We concluded it should not." He frowned. *What* should not? He went back to the first sentence.

"I have to go."

Vikki stood next to him, her thighs crossed. It was the one thing he'd forgotten before they left Diana's.

"Where does Mommy take you?"

"She makes sure I go before we leave."

He shut the *Journal* and stood up, looking helplessly around the Drive. "There must be a place on the campus. Can you hold it in?"

She shrugged.

"Well, try." There was no choice now. They had to leave. They started up toward 116th Street, caught between trying to hurry and holding back so Vikki could keep control.

13

Phil was furious at himself for forgetting. Now that they had put some distance between themselves and the sandbox it seemed as though he might have found a way to keep them going until it was time. He had just begun to apply himself to the *Journal*. Next time he would bring the right kind of book —and start reading sooner.

There were public bathrooms in Dodge Hall next to McMillin Auditorium. They crossed the Drive at 116th Street and headed for those. At Broadway they had to wait for the light. Phil searched Vikki's face anxiously. The light changed. As they crossed he tried to decide whether to send her alone to the women's room upstairs or take her down to the men's room.

They hurried into the building. "I'll show you where it is," he said. She kept his hand firmly in hers.

"Come with me."

"I thought you were a big girl."

"I can't get my snowpants off."

"I'll take them off here."

"Come with me."

"I can't go into the ladies' room, sweetheart." He started up the stairs.

"I can't reach."

They stopped at the top of the flight. Her face had a look of serious inward concentration.

"OK." He swept her up in his arms and clambered down two flights to the men's room.

It was empty. He hurried her past the rows of gleaming sinks and put her down in the first stall. As he fumbled with the strings of her hood he glanced at the walls. They were covered with drawings. There was no sense moving her now and, besides, the other stalls would be just as bad. He stripped off her coat and hung it up. He kneeled and tried to work off her snowpants. Vikki put her hands on his shoulder for balance.

"All you have to do is pull them down," she said. "I'll be careful."

"You're sure?" Their voices echoed in the high-ceilinged room.

14

"Yes. Just hurry."

He pulled the snowpants, Danskin slacks, and underpants down to her shins and started to help her on to the seat. She wriggled out of his grasp. "I can do that myself."

"I was only—"

"I'm not a baby." Vikki stared at him.

"Well, get moving, honey," he said impatiently.

"You can leave me alone now."

"What?"

"Daddy. *Please.*" Her tone was haughty and urgent.

Phil blushed unaccountably and backed out of the stall. She closed the door after him, her snowpants like shackles.

"Don't lock yourself in," he said. The lock snapped. "And be careful."

He leaned against the book rack near the urinals and waited. The large clock over the door clicked up to 3:45. His watch had been running ten minutes fast all day. He set it back.

The toilet flushed. Phil rushed to Vikki's door.

She stood before him with her pants crushed own around her ankles. Philip kneeled, half out of the stall, and pulled them up.

He put his hand into the underpants. "You're damp." He felt the slacks. "You're soaked right through."

"I had a little trouble."

"Oh, for Crissake! I offered to help you."

Vikki's face puckered.

"All right. All right," he said quickly. He finished pulling the pants up and worked the suspenders over her shoulder. "It's just that it's cold out and I don't want you getting sick. Mommy's got enough on her hands . . ." he muttered.

"Can we still get a treat?"

"Hot chocolate."

He slipped on his lumber jacket, then helped Vikki on with her coat. "You don't need your gloves," he said. "Just keep your hands in your pockets."

It was still not quite four o'clock when they started down Broadway. There were a couple of places Phil knew with counter service. He headed toward one at 112th Street.

15

Their faces were flushed with the heat from the bathroom, and the cold air licked at them. At 113th Street Phil fished in his pockets to check his change. It was a habit. He always checked his change before he went down the subway steps or into phone booths, just as he always took out his keys before he got to the front door of the apartment house. He hated fumbling. He liked transactions to work smoothly, with a certain amount of dignity and expertise. His pockets were empty. He stopped and rechecked his lumber jacket, then his back pockets. He pulled out his wallet. He'd spent his last bill on lunch—and his change on the apples.

"I don't have any money," he said abruptly.

Vikki's eyes opened wide. He stood indecisively.

"Daddy?"

"I completely forgot. It's all in Mommy's wallet."

"What about my—"

"I don't have any money."

"Could you charge it?"

"A hot chocolate?"

"Mommy does sometimes. At the place near us."

That irritated him. He had no idea Sheila was charging fountain drinks at the little drugstore near 120th Street. It was one thing to run up a monthly bill on medical needs, but there was something degrading about putting those little cash register tabs on a charge.

"I tell you what. We'll go home just to pick up some change and then go right out again to Hundred Twentieth Street."

"But you said Mommy wanted—"

"She won't even know we're there. She's probably napping or vacuuming. If she's vacuuming she won't hear us and if she's napping we'll tiptoe. I know just where her wallet is. It'll only take a second." He turned her around and they started back.

The clock over the First National Bank said four o'clock.

Phil knew that Sheila would hear, whether they tiptoed or not, but he would announce they were on their way out again before she had a chance to move. He would reassure her that he was still in control, still coping, and leave as swiftly as he

16

planned to arrive. Later, when they returned triumphantly at five, he would breezily apologize for their brief appearance. They turned into the campus at 116th Street. The cold seemed less bitter now they were headed home. Perhaps they could really slip in without her noticing. Maybe if they were quiet enough he might even manage to change Vikki to dry pants before they slipped out. That would be what he called coping—and he would not have to apologize at all, not even playfully.

Phil's mouth tightened against a familiar wave of resentment. It always came about this time, as he passed the steps of Low Library. Up ahead, across Amsterdam Avenue, was the Law Building. From the corner of his eye he caught glimpses of bundled children riding their bicycles around the Library fountain. There was something wrong with the whole business of having to make elaborate apologies for going into his own home. It didn't make sense. Whenever Sheila sent them off like this, whether it was for housework or just to get some time off, she gave them a deadline. He always accepted it cheerfully, promised to comply, and never remembered how much he hated it until they approached Amsterdam and the last leg home—always too early. Then he would buck against the stupid sense of humiliation and wonder what would happen if Sheila didn't name a specific hour. It was the very act of naming the hour that defeated him.

They turned up Amsterdam into the imaginary warmth under the Law School Bridge.

"When we get home you tiptoe right into your room," Phil said to Vikki. "I want to change you into something dry."

She looked up at him questioningly.

"It's all right." There was a trace of defiance in his voice. "We're going out again."

One Hundred Eighteenth Street was a ragged corridor that began at Amsterdam, ran for just one block, and opened out onto Morningside Heights. Its sides were a gray patchwork of apartment house walls.

The inner door to Phil's building was always locked. There was a buzzer system with two verticle rows of buttons. The numbers beside them faded into the brass. The speaker was broken.

Phil and Vikki swept into the little alcove. He had his key ready. They passed through the inner door and on to the elevator in the middle of the dim hallway. The walls on the fifth floor were beige, with a texture like laminated stucco. Vikki pulled her hands across it as she walked. A little rectangular name-strip that Sheila had inked in fancy lettering identified their apartment: PHILIP B. GAYNOR. They paused for a moment and Phil put his ear against the door. There was no sound.

"She must be napping," he whispered to Vikki. "Now, remember. Scoot right into your room. I'll come as soon as I've got the money. OK?"

Vikki nodded.

"I hope she didn't put the chain on." Nothing irritated Phil more than the jerk and thud of the door when it opened against a chain. When they were first married he would arrive home exuberantly, go to swing open the door, and come flat against it. It was like having his nose punched. Sheila had learned to leave it unchained when she was expecting him. When he came home at unusual times, though, he would find it chained, and lately she had been forgetting to release it even when she did expect him.

Phil eased the door open, bracing himself for the resistance, but it swung past the chain length and he ushered Vikki in.

She disappeared into the first room off the long hallway. Phil tiptoed past it. Through their half-open bedroom door he could see Sheila on the bed. Phil stopped and tried to close the door noiselessly. He slowly pulled it to, then released the knob. It clicked. He froze, straining to hear if Sheila stirred. There was no sound. He backed off and stole past the kitchen—it was immaculate—to the living room at the end of the hall. It, too was clean and free of clutter.

The pocketbook was not in the living room or the kitchen. He would have to sneak into the bedroom. He crept back to

18

the door he had just closed and eased it open. Vikki peered out of her room and he waved her back in. The pocketbook was on his desk. He crossed the room, hardly daring even to look at Sheila. Out of the corner of his eye he saw she had showered. She was wearing a light-yellow terry cloth robe and had turbaned her head in a towel. He smiled. Long, hot, needly showers were one of Sheila's great luxuries. He could imagine how, after she had finished working, she decided she had earned the longest, hottest, needliest shower she'd ever taken. He knew just the set of her jaw, the smile and the way she stretched her neck in a defiant gesture of self-indulgence. Phil was careful even to mute his smile, though, as though afraid it might wake her.

He lifted the pocketbook from the desk without a sound and turned to take it out with him. It was opened. One of the handles slipped. The insides clattered to the floor.

He leaped to one knee, furious and ashamed, collecting the lipsticks, compacts, keys. "I'm sorry, honey." He still whispered as though somehow he could recapture the spell of silence. "Go back to sleep. We're going out again. I just had to get some—" He stopped, then wheeled toward Sheila. She had not moved. She lay on her side, facing the night table as though she were sniffing the empty bottle and the glass, still damp, beside it. They were Phil's pills, the ones he'd gotten when the tension of interviews started. He sprang to the bed and shook her. "Sheila!" The first cry was still a whisper. Then, as though he had been released, he shouted, "Sheila!" He slapped her, but he could not tell if she stirred or if he made her inert body move with the strength of his blows. He flung her on her back and ripped open the robe to listen to her heart; all he could hear were the rushing sounds in his own head.

The towel had fallen away from her head and her hair lay spread out, damp, against it. He pulled her up by the arm and grabbed it over his shoulder. With his free hand around her waist he forced her up, kicked open the door, and dragged her down the hall. The phone was in the kitchen. He stumbled against the walls with the weight of Sheila's limp body. Her cold hair brushed his neck. As he turned into the kitchen he saw Vikki behind him.

He readjusted Sheila's weight to free one hand and phoned for an ambulance.

St. Luke's was only five blocks away. He had barely put down the phone and started walking her when he heard the siren on Amsterdam Avenue. He pulled Sheila back down the hallway to buzz them in and wondered if she could have known he would come home early.

Part One

Coming To

1

Sheila

October 20-

November 17, 1962

EVEN BEFORE she opened her eyes Sheila Gaynor knew she was still alive. She was neither relieved nor disappointed. She simply noted it. She knew she had been unconscious and that meant she was not unconscious now. So she was alive.

They had used a stomach pump. She remembered that. She remembered the tubes that pushed through to the back of her nose and forced their way down her throat. She remembered the drawing and the way she tried to vomit the rubber out. She could hear her own belching sounds, as utterly disconnected from her as the splash of the stuff they were pulling out. She lay on her back examining her own consciousness like a curious, exotic object, interesting but absolutely incomprehensible, nothing she would seriously think of owning for herself. Still, she turned it over in the darkness and puzzled, trying to understand how she could remember all those sensations so vividly, yet not be able to remember experiencing them. It was as though this present memory were both the memory and the experience, that the pumping itself had and had not happened. It must have happened because she remembered it, but she could not remember its happening. Then she realized it was not a memory. It was happening now, the tubes and the choking and the chaos of straps and sheets in the darkness and her hair, still damp, but tangled now and matting on her forehead and neck, and while it happened, even now, she knew what it would be like to remember later and her eyes flew open to stop it.

Late morning sunlight streamed through the window of the hospital room. Phil sat in an armchair looking down at the street. He did not know she had opened her eyes. He had taken off his jacket and loosened his tie. Sheila studied his neck. She could see the straight line that emerged from his shirt collar and rose diagonally to his ear. She noticed the curve of his ear and the way the close-cropped hair behind it curved away in a graceful line neatly defined by the barber's razor. She noticed the arc that his collar made. It seemed to Sheila she had never before been able to see the truth of detail with such clarity. Phil was a cluster of lines and arcs suspended impossibly before her in space. She wondered if she might not really have been dead some time during the night and if that might not account for this new ability. Perhaps she was, after all, on the other side of death, perhaps she had made herself immortal and now she saw only the present moment, uncluttered by past or future. She thought of all the times she had touched Phil's throat, its graininess at night when it brushed her shoulder, its astonishing smoothness when she grazed it with her fingertips after he'd shaved. All her love and desire for him had always focused there. She remembered how many times he would think he was making love to her while all the time it was only she there, alone, gently tracing the line of his neck from its base at his shoulder up to where it disappeared into a little hollow below his jaw. And it was only his ignorance of her own, secret ritual, finally, that stirred her. She could remember all that now, while he sat there, as unaware of her gaze as he had always been of her gentle touch. She could remember and wonder dispassionately how she had ever invested so much in that absurdly formal arrangement of hair, creased skin, and bone.

If she had to wake up at all, it was best that it happen like this, on the other side of death and of time, where she could

24

remember without need, without any sense of urgency, and without passion. What a release to remember without fear of future confusion!

Phil turned to glance at her as he must have done a thousand times while she'd been asleep. He turned away mechanically until it hit him that her eyes were open. His head jerked back. If Sheila had cared she might have laughed at the helpless spontaneity of his double-take, but she simply stared at his drawn, clouded face as impassively as she had stared at his neck.

With a single movement he glided from the armchair to the side of the bed and stood over her. A tentative, tender smile hovered over his face. He wants me to tell him what to do, she thought and once again she was pleased with her newly found clarity. An uncertain moment passed, then Phil sat at the side of the bed and fumbled for her hand. She let him take it. He raised it to his lips and glanced up worriedly to search her face. This time she did release a laugh, but she could tell from his face that her expression had not changed. Laughter was still an idea.

He leaned over to kiss her forehead. The closer he came the more detached Sheila felt. If he had been just an idea inside her, like laughter—or a physical presence a thousand miles away—she might have been able to feel something for him. The dryness of his lips, though, and the thick, white linen-sweet smell of his shirt only took him farther away from anything to do with her.

He let go of her hand and she used it to brush some hair away from her forehead.

Phil smiled. "Let me." He reached out to smooth it back. He kept his eyes fixed on her forehead, stroking it gently long after all the hair was gone. Sheila turned slightly to face the window. Phil drew his hand back. From the bed she could only see blue sky, filtered through the thin veil of grime on the other side of the glass. The room must be high, she thought. She wondered why they had given her a room so high. She glanced up, without moving her head. There was no curtain around the bed. Why had they put her in a private room?

25

Maybe they thought she was dangerous. The idea amused her. She began to ask Phil, but stopped before she had even turned. She was not ready to speak. To speak, to use even a single word, might break her tie with death, distort her vision, and implicate her in life. Only a moment before she had dropped a sack she'd been struggling with for hundreds of years, one she had started by holding in her arms before her, then, as it grew heavier, shifting on to her back—until it occurred to her to let go, simply let it slide. She had just begun to feel what it was like to stand up straight, to arch her back without her burden pulling her down. One word would be a movement toward hauling it up again. She could let her questions wait.

"Sheila? Honey?"

She examined the sky, then the film on the outside of the window, then the cream-colored molding around it.

"It's all right, sweetheart." His voice was soft, reassuring, but there was a plaintive note she had never heard there before, like the overtone on a piano. "Everything's going to be all right."

She wondered what he could think might not be all right. She had let the sack slip; she was free to choose whether or not to pick it up; for the first time she had found that power, so what on earth could he possibly think was wrong?

"Honey? Can you talk? Can you look at me?"

If it had been anyone but Phil he might have taken pity on his confusion. She might have turned to him, smiled to reassure him, maybe even touched his cheek. She knew how helpless he felt and how he hated to feel helpless. But it was too dangerous. If she helped him she might confuse the memory of her love for him with the real thing. That would endanger her young freedom. Later, perhaps. When she was ready. When she chose.

The bed gave as he leaned closer.

"I understand," he whispered. "You don't have to look at me. I just want you to know it's all right."

She listened carefully, trying to hear his words with the same detached precision she had found when she looked at

26

him. She couldn't. The pure sound of his voice became muddled with meaning. The words tried to pull her down. She struggled against comprehension. It was no good. She had already understood. He was telling her he forgave her, sure that she must feel guilty. It had not occurred to her that she'd done something wrong. Wrong meant an act with responsibilities attached and she'd never committed an act like that. Every decision she'd ever made had sprung from necessity. You didn't stop to think about right or wrong when your action sprang from necessity. And you didn't feel guilty afterward.

She glanced from the molding to the folded beige coverlet at the foot of the bed and wondered what it must be like to feel guilty. How beautiful to believe that you've made a choice that has made you responsible. What a luxury to carry around inside you; a constant, inescapable reminder of your own, flawed identity. She knew other women had felt it. They'd tried to tell her what it was like to know they'd betrayed a friend, destroyed a lover, cheated on a husband. "It's a terrible thing to know you're a bitch," one of them said once. Now Sheila thought, How wonderful it must be to know you're anything at all. Guilt was the one thing she'd never felt. Perhaps it was her yearning for it that had sustained her so long and finally led her back to consciousness.

"Vikki's fine," Phil said, still searching for a way to reach her. "She had a bit of a scare at first, but she knows you're all right now. She's with Diana. Bernie and May are coming in. I didn't call them." He laughed nervously. "I don't know how they manage it. They picked last night to call to say hello. When there was no answer they got worried and called Diana. She tried not to tell them, but they must have heard something in her voice. They kept pushing until she had to. She feels terrible about it."

Sheila listened carefully, trying to help a sense of guilt fill her like an emotion.

"Honey? Do you want me to stop talking? Do you want me to leave you alone?"

She turned. His whole face pleaded with her to answer.

"Just tell me," he said as though he were admitting defeat. His eyes were rimmed with concern. For one instant she saw them flash with anguish. I caused that, she told herself. She had chosen to remain silent. Phil was suffering. She was responsible. That choice of silence, the first she had made since her new life began, the one she perpetuated every moment that passed, she had seen the result of that choice flash across his face. Her choice and its consequences were hers now, and they made her inviolable. She tasted what it was like to inflict suffering, to know that only she could soothe it, to choose not to and to loathe herself for the choice. She embraced her selfishness and felt herself float off once again. I've been resurrected mad, she thought, I'm a goddamned nut. But if she was not responsible for her madness, she had, at least made the guilt her own. Phil thought she was guilty of suicide; she knew she was guilty of silence. Whatever happened from now on, she would carry that inside her like a memory of grace.

A rustling nurse swept into the room. She was a dumpy woman underneath all the starch, in her late fifties, with close-cropped kinky hair and rimless glasses.

"You're awake," she said cheerfully. "I expected you'd stay asleep for another two hours or so." She approached the bed and took Sheila's wrist.

"She won't talk," Phil said.

The nurse remained silent while she took the pulse. She replaced Sheila's arm just where it had been. The sheet was still warm there, and the offhand tenderness of the gesture shocked Sheila.

"How long have you been awake?"

"Only a few minutes," Phil answered for her. "Mrs. Wheeler, she won't talk."

Mrs. Wheeler worked around the room, straightening chairs, rearranging the water tray, opening the window, more like a fussy housewife than a nurse.

"Of course not."

"Is that . . . usual?"

Mrs. Wheeler shrugged and returned to Sheila. "I don't

suppose I'd much feel like Madame de Staël if I woke up after swallowing a bottle of sleeping pills and having my stomach pumped. Sit up for a second, sweetheart. You've made pancakes out of your pillows." Mrs. Wheeler lifted her from the back before Sheila could resist. She held her firmly by the shoulders and whispered in her ear. "Just stay there for a second until I can get you comfortable." She chuckled. "He wants to know if it's usual." She stood up and left Sheila sitting. "You could have wakened babbling," she said chattily as she fluffed the pillows. "I bet he still would have asked if it was usual." She turned to Phil and hed the pillow suspended in the air before her. "What if I said yes? Would it make a difference?" She replaced the pillows and guided her back.

Sheila closed her eyes as she sank. When she opened them she was sitting up. Mrs. Wheeler had arranged the pillows to support her.

"Don't you think we ought to let Dr. Rankin know she's awake?" Phil asked.

"Oh, I expect he'll look in before long. Why don't you go downstairs and get yourself something to eat. Mrs. Gaynor and I can hold the fort together."

"I don't think I should leave."

"You've been sitting here five hours straight. You must be starved."

"It's not me—" he began.

She touched Phil's shoulder confidentially. Sheila could tell it irritated him. "It's all right, Mr. Gaynor. It's a myth that people aren't hungry in a crisis."

"But I want to help."

"How?"

"I thought just being here might—"

"You weren't doing such a hot job when I came in."

"I don't want to leave her with a stranger. Especially now."

"It's conceivable that she might be more comfortable with a stranger. Especially now. And I don't think we ought to keep talking about Mrs. Gaynor in the third person."

"Look, Mrs. Wheeler—"

"You're hungry and you're tired," she broke in. "I understand your concern." She nodded. "I really do. If you stay here now, you'll only be making yourself more comfortable."

"You mean uncomfortable—"

"I mean comfortable. You'll get more hungry and more tired and you'll feel better and better about yourself, because it'll feel as though you're doing something. You might think for a minute about how you'd feel if you just woke up after trying to commit suicide." Phil started. "It's all right. We all know why we're here. You might think how you'd feel," she continued.

He looked at Sheila. She could see the eagerness to escape in his eyes, muted by a look of concern. It was a familiar look and Sheila could remember all the times she had felt it was up to her to resolve it for him, all the times she had reassured him as though all she saw was the concern. "Maybe I ought to check on Vikki," he said. "And Bernie and May should be there by now. I'll have to figure out what to do with them. It'll all be OK, though," he added quickly. He shot a look at Mrs. Wheeler. She turned away discreetly and rummaged through a shopping bag full of books. He approached the bed. "I've got everything under control, sweetheart." He stroked her cheek. His hand trembled almost imperceptibly and the truth of that made Sheila close her eyes once in acknowledgment. He smiled. "And I am starved," he whispered. "I'll be back as soon as I can."

He gathered up his jacket quickly and headed toward the door.

Mrs. Wheeler settled into the armchair with a book on her lap.

Sheila watched him leave. Mrs. Wheeler was already engrossed in her reading, probably a professional talent from years of returning to interrupted sentences. She sat with one elbow on the arm of the chair, her head tilted slightly. She rubbed her own forehead gently with her fingertips. For the first time since she had wakened Sheila thought it might be safe to speak.

"Not yet." Mrs. Wheeler stopped her without looking up from her book. "There's plenty of time. No need to force it."

She turned to her. She was unsmiling but her eyes were clear with understanding. "It's work once you give it up. I know that. You've got time and nobody's pressuring you." Sheila closed her mouth slowly. She did not take her eyes from the nurse's. Mrs. Wheeler smiled and shook her head. "No, I'm not your fairy godmother and I have no mystic abilities. I've just been in this chair so many times."

She took off her glasses and rubbed her eyes. Her cheeks were full and unlined, but when she dropped her hand Sheila noticed how the skin beneath the eyes fell in deep, tired folds. She put her glasses back and turned to the book.

Sheila tried to recapture the sense of detachment she'd wakened with. It had vanished. Some time after the nurse had arrived she had fallen back into time.

Phil had gone to check Vikki; Bernie and May had called Diana; Mrs. Wheeler was reading; and yesterday she had tried to commit suicide.

They had snapped a plastic bracelet on her wrist. "Gaynor, Sheila Fraidele. Fem. Cauc." The bracelet was where her watch had been yesterday. The memory ran through her like a small shock. She had just finished working the vacuum cleaner back behind the galoshes and luggage in the hall closet when she noticed it was one o'clock. It was then she had thought, I haven't much time, without understanding what she meant by that.

She went back to the living room to check her work. She was glad she had. The furniture polish and dust rag were still on the coffee table. It would have been stupid to leave them there after the care she had taken. She could not understand why her heart beat so loudly as she calmly picked them up to put in the kitchen. On the way she stopped and held out her hand to see if it trembled. It was steady. All her movements were calm, deliberate. She shook her head at the mysterious pounding and tried to find some explanation for the sense of pressure she felt. She could find no reason to rush. She'd finished the house in record time. The morning had whizzed by. Phil and Vikki would not be back for another four hours. Her system

31

speeded again at the thought. It took control to keep from dashing to the kitchen, flinging the polish under the sink, and then rushing off to . . . what? This simple task of clearing the polish and rag seemed to lead to a great, urgent blank. She followed it out curiously, listening to her heart pound and watching to see what she would do after she opened the cabinet, replaced the polish on the lower shelf, and spread the rag on the windowsill to dry. Each step after that seemed inexorably right, but she could not see beyond one to the next. It was only after one was completed and she found herself in the middle of the next that she understood the act before. She went to the bedroom and undressed. As she unbuttoned Phil's shirt he realized that was why she had left the kitchen. She took off the shirt and her jeans and hung them up carefully. She noticed she wore no underwear. That puzzled her, too. She knew she had purposely put none on that morning and she vaguely remembered deciding it was important to keep the hamper empty. She stood naked at the closet door for a moment, feeling more and more split off from each of her own decisions. It was sweet and a little frightening to realize what a tenuous thread held them to her, how easily it could snap. Perhaps that was why her heart beat so fiercely. She glanced up at the terry cloth robe on the door hook, and that was the moment the objects outside her took over. Her body drained and went limp. There were no more decisions to make. The robe told her she must slip it on and she obeyed without question. Her slippers took her to the bathroom. The silver faucets demanded turning. The hard spray soothed her. It reassured her she was right to submit and helped drain away any last thoughts of resistance. The towels were there to dry her and wrap her wet hair. As she gave her head to the swathes her eye lit on Phil's pills and she saw all the fragments of action come together and crystallize with the crackle of a sudden freeze. The robe, the slippers, the faucets, the soap, the shampoo, and the towels—even the polish and rag in the kitchen—all had betrayed her, and as she began to flip the pills back in her throat one by one, she enumerated all the other objects that had led her to this. The dresses, the canned goods, the books and the diapers, the hair bands and theater tickets, diaphragms, telephones, linens, and glasses. She worked her way slowly to the bedroom, ticking them off in her head with the satisfaction of a spy unmasking the enemy, swallowing two, now three at a time, each with a little sip of water. She sat on the edge of the bed. The bottle was still half-filled. She sighed and was glad she had learned how to press on through even the most boring task. She finished it off and lay back, dizzy and bloated. Just before she went blank she thought of the chain on the door. She could not remember if it was hooked. Phil would be furious. . . .

"I didn't plan it." The sound of her own voice shocked her. She had expected it to quiver, but it was sharp. The tone was steady. She had no idea how long she had been alone with her thoughts.

Mrs. Wheeler looked up from her book.

"Yesterday morning when I woke up I thought everything was all right. I was sure I'd worked it all out. I had no idea. . . ."

Mrs. Wheeler nodded. "I was on duty when they brought you in. You looked like you'd meant it."

"How do you mean?"

"It's the ones who plan it that don't really mean it. They always leave a dozen holes in the job so they're bound to be discovered. The ones who mean it just suddenly discover themselves in the act, too late to plan the failure. They tell all of them they were lucky, but most are just good planners. You really were. Lucky, I mean. Your husband told me how he found you. It didn't sound like you planned it."

Sheila was silent a moment. Mrs. Wheeler had been right. It was comforting to have a stranger there. The need and confusion in Phil's eyes demanded too much of her. Mrs. Wheeler was impersonal, and it left her free to speak. There was no danger that her words would be jumbled up in a clutter of shared memories.

"I'm sorry," she said tentatively. "I didn't mean to interrupt your reading."

"You did so. Besides, it's an Agatha Christie and I was just about to decide I'd read it before." The nurse put the book aside. Sheila looked down at the sheet border folded over her blanket.

She smoothed it with her fingertips and gave a nervous little laugh. "I guess I'm trying to figure out how I feel," she said.

"What on earth for?"

She groped for an answer, then shrugged. "I thought it was a good idea a minute ago." Sheila hesitated. "Do most patients talk like this?"

"You and Mr. Gaynor are positively gung ho for the usual, aren't you?"

"We're very conventional people. We went to conventional colleges, had a conventional wedding, a conventional baby."

"Now you want to know if your suicide was conventional."

"I'm also consistent. It's all so scary. I mean, I must be a very different person than I thought I was, but"—she made a small, helpless gesture—"I don't know how to act like some other person."

Mrs. Wheeler smiled. "I wouldn't rush things."

There was a loud knock at the door. It swung open before either of the women could answer.

"Mrs. Gaynor? I'm Al Rankin." The doctor moved to the bedside and glanced at the chart. "How are you feeling?"

"A little tired."

"I'm not surprised. You're a very lucky lady."

Mrs. Wheeler looked up innocently to meet Sheila's glance.

"I just saw Mr. Gaynor in the commissary. I'm not sure who's in worse shape. He said you weren't talking."

"I'm talking now."

Dr. Rankin was in his mid-forties. He carried himself like a middle-aged man who was also a young doctor. His smile was warm and tolerant, but the set of his shoulders was aggressive. His wrists were covered with dark hair down to the knuckles. His eyebrows, too, were thick and the ends of hair tufts sprouted over the top of his buttoned shirt collar. He could not help looming.

"Anything in particular you want to talk about now?"

34

"You mean like, 'What's new?' " she said dryly.

He laughed. "I didn't think so. I just wanted you to know I'm around if you do want to talk things out. I'll be dropping in each day while you're here. Then we'll start having regular sessions when you leave."

"How long am I going to be here?"

"As long as you want. Your husband told me he's got everything under control at home. You need rest. That's the most important thing right now."

"Rest?" He hovered above her, still smiling. His eyes were dark brown and impenetrable; his beard line was heavy. His whole face merged for an instant with the faces of all the professional men, the teachers, the lawyers, the doctors, the rabbis, the organizers, who had ever told her what she must do, all the men who had recognized her promise, urged her to action, and then left her to work it out on her own. He was all of them, but now instead of prodding, instead of urging, he was telling her to rest. She tried to keep back tears of gratitude, angry that she should have to be grateful. The tears sprang up in spite of her and blurred her vision.

"Oh, shit!" she cried, furious. The word broke apart in the air. All the fatigue, all the despair and frustration heaved up from her stomach and forced their way out. Sobs racked through her. "Oh, shit! Oh, Christ!" Waves of exhaustion and anger sprayed out. She banged on the mattress with hard, closed fists. The broken cries forced their way out. She opened her body to let them through. It was like diving into darkness. "Now! Now!" she was shouting. The words were barely intelligible. "You bastards! Sons of bitches! Why now?" Tears and sweat and mucus flowed out and smeared her face. The sobs came more slowly and rhythmically. The nurse and the doctor remained still, waitng. She lay back, breathing hard and gulping. She tried to wipe her eyes with one hand.

"Kleenex?" Dr. Rankin held the box out for her imperturbably.

"How about a towel?" she said, catching her breath.

"Use as many as you want."

35

Sheila pulled one out and ran it over her cheek. Dr. Rankin kept the box available and took the used ones from her with his free hand.

"It's all right, Mrs. Gaynor," he said gently. She stopped wiping and looked up at him curiously. He was the second man to reassure her about something for which she had not felt guilty. She finished wiping her face and wondered if other women cried and committed suicide because they had to, or only to be pardoned after. "If you need anything you can count on Mrs. Wheeler. And if you need me, I'll be on the floor for another couple of hours."

Sheila nodded.

Phil burst into the room, red-faced and out of breath. He took a moment to pull himself together.

"I'm glad I caught you," he said to the doctor. "How is she?"

"It's all right, Phil," Sheila said. "She's talking now."

The men exchanged quick glances, Dr. Rankin stepped aside. Phil slipped beside Sheila. She let him embrace her.

"I was so worried," he whispered.

He held her with her arms pinned to her sides and kissed her cheeks.

"Be careful. I've still got dragon breath."

"I don't care."

"Did you get something to eat?"

"A little." He let go and she settled back on her pillows. His face was still wrinkled with concern. It puzzled Sheila. She'd already wakened, began talking, even had a good, hard cry. She was ready to begin, but he was still responding to the preliminaries. "Tell me what you ate," she said.

He looked at her blankly, then turned red. That was why he hated awkward situations. His light coloring made him so vulnerable to a blush. "It's not important."

"A sandwich?"

He waved it away.

"A full dinner?" His blush deepened. "It's all right. You heard Mrs. Wheeler. You're allowed to be hungry."

"I'm going to run along," Dr. Rankin broke in. "I told Mrs. Gaynor I'd be on the floor for another couple of hours if she

36

needs me. I think things are going to be fine." He looked at Sheila. "You just get plenty of—" He paused. "Take it as easy as you can." He turned to Mrs. Wheeler. "I'd like to see you outside for a minute."

Sheila watched him curiously as he ushered Mrs. Wheeler out. It had suddenly become so easy to wield power over these men. She began to understand the weakness of other women, the tears and breakdowns. How seductive it all was. She could keep them running and blushing and watching their words as long as she wanted. All she had to do was lie there, wrapped in a hospital gown and a little plastic bracelet and let them think she felt guilty.

Phil fumbled for her hand, but she drew it away. After a moment he said, "We've got a lot of talking to do."

Sheila nodded. "I suppose so. But I need some time on my own. I'm not ready for the touching and the looking and the holding yet."

"I understand."

"Do you?"

"I think so."

"Because when you said we've got a lot of talking to do, it sounded like you meant the old kind of talking."

"What kind was that?"

"Oh, you know," she said. "The kind where we both sit down and calmly, rationally, and with all the best intentions in the world, share our ideas about what's wrong with me. And for God's sake don't blush again," she said quickly. "It's painful to look at. Even out of the corner of my eye." She shook her head slowly and smiled. "You must have been pissing in your pants last night."

"Terrified."

She raised her arm and showed him the bracelet. "You told them my middle name."

"They needed it for the forms."

"I'll save it for my mother and father. They'll be pleased to know you remembered my heritage when it counted. It might give you points."

"They're here, by the way."

37

"At the hospital?"

"At Diana's. May answered the phone when I called."

"I don't want to see them yet."

"I know. I told them to stay with Vikki and I'd come over as soon as I could."

"Was that why you ran up from eating?"

"How could you tell I was running?"

"I've had second sight since I woke up. When are you going over?"

"As soon as I'm sure you're OK."

"I'm OK."

"Mrs. Wheeler isn't giving you any trouble, is she?"

She shook her head. "She's probably waiting for us to tell her it's all right to come in. Why don't you go see Mom and Dad? They might decide to come up if you take too long."

"Should I leave orders that no one's to see you?"

"It won't do any good if he decides to come up."

Phil started toward the door.

"Phil?" She stopped him. "What's today?"

"Wednesday."

"What time is it?"

He checked his watch. "One thirty."

"You've got a three o'clock class."

"Oh, that's not—"

"It's all right if you try to make it."

"I don't think—"

"It's all right." She paused. "It really is."

He murmured something noncommittal. Sheila knew he would find himself in class at three.

She lay back and closed her eyes. Her own crying had surprised her. She was still not sure of where it had sprung from. The Sheila Gaynor she knew did not cry out of gratitude or anger—and she did not try to commit suicide. The Sheila Gaynor she knew coped cheerfully. She frowned. Then what the hell was she doing here? She tried to summon up a picture of what she had been before yesterday. She tried to see a young woman in starched shirtwaists, smiling and smelling of soap. It was a picture she had never consciously

38

tried to summon before, but she realized now that whenever she'd felt herself slipping, beginning to question and slipping into the void, it was there for her—everything she was supposed to be. A young lawyer's wife, bright, inventive at making do during the early difficult years, proud of her husband's promise, proud of the daughter she'd given him, proud of her own luck at finding herself safe—and so soon. It was a woman who never existed, but Sheila had believed in her. Now the suicide made that impossible. Behind her closed lids she looked back on the months before with astonishment. She could see herself sitting alone with her baby in a cluttered apartment, pretending the phone would ring to fill the next minute. She remembered how she would pick up a brush to pull her hair back and her arm would turn leaden. Or how she would stand in front of the cans of corn at the A & P, paralyzed over which brand to choose. She remembered how one day, a month before, Vikki had been playing with the knobs of the television set and switched on a game show. Sheila had snapped it off, trembling. Having the set on in the middle of the afternoon meant utter defeat. But the next day she sat down in front of it as soon as Phil left and watched all day. She told him about it that night as though it was a bizarre joke, but as she told him she also felt a perverse sense of triumph. She remembered avoiding her own eyes in the bathroom mirror, and the time only a few weeks earlier when she had wandered halfway home from Riverside Drive before she realized she'd left Vikki playing in the sandbox. She didn't tell Phil about that. "Oh, my God." She opened her eyes. Everyone else must have seen what was happening. Why hadn't anyone told her? She laid her wrist across her forehead as though she was shielding her eyes. Maybe they had, and she hadn't heard because it was the other Sheila who listened, the imaginary one who was coping. Even now, until this instant, somewhere in the back of her mind she had been sure the suicide was a mistake, some kind of a crazy fluke, like a germ she'd picked up on the subway. Now she was only surprised at how late it was in coming. No wonder I've been so goddamned tired, she thought. I've been dead for a year without the sense

39

to lie down. She let her arm fall away from her head and turned to look at it. She had tried to lie down, though, and it landed her here, alive. She could still remember the emptiness of the past few months, but now it was only a memory. Now, at least, she was conscious. The emptiness was still there, still dark and limitless, but now it was something that stretched away outside her and she was alive enough inside to be frightened.

Mrs. Wheeler returned, smiling mischievously. "How did you like Dr. Rankin?" She settled into her chair again.

Sheila hesitated. "Not very much."

She nodded. "He's a bit tense."

"I thought it was me. I mean, I thought maybe I was just being hostile because he's a shrink and . . . you know, defensive reaction and all. . . ."

"For God's sake, don't get on that merry-go-round. If you let a psychiatrist get you into that kind of bind you're through."

Sheila stared at her. "You're positively subversive, aren't you?"

Mrs. Wheeler nodded. "I like psychiatrists," she said. "As long as they remember they're only Band-Aids and not the elixir of life. Some of them tend to be dreadful bullies. Especially the young ones."

"Dr. Rankin?"

"He's growing up. But he still tends to push a little. Don't let him."

"What did he want to talk to you about?"

"Oh, the usual instructions. Drugs and gentleness. It's routine in mental cases."

"Mental?" She paused. "Of course," she said quietly. "I hadn't really thought of myself as a case before. I mean, I thought of myself as crazy, but not with all the trappings—the nurse and the private room on the psychiatric floor." She shook her head. "Crazy, but not insane. Do you know what I mean?"

"Do you think you're insane now?"

"I did something insane. I must be."

40

"The suicide? Why is that insane?"

"Because. . . ." Sheila took a minute. It still seemed such a necessary act, yet she knew now there was something wrong about it. "Because you just don't—"

"What?"

"—act on binding decisions?" she asked slowly. Sheila put her head back on the pillow. "Oh, God, I am tired," she said. "It's been a heavy morning."

"It's afternoon."

She closed her eyes. "It feels like morning."

She woke briefly to find a strange nurse knitting in the armchair, a tall, stringy woman with an oval face. It was dark outside.

"Where's Mrs. Wheeler?" Sheila asked drowsily.

The nurse smiled a great, toothy smile. "Oh, good. We're awake."

Sheila sat up. The night made a faint mirror of the window. It took her a minute to recognize her own reflection. The hospital gown drooped from her shoulders. Her hair hung in strands and her features washed together. "I look like the goddamned first Mrs. Rochester," she murmured.

"Can I get you anything?"

"Where's Mrs. Wheeler?" Sheila repeated.

"Oh, she's been off duty for hours. I'm Miss Sprigge."

She stared at the flying needles in Miss Sprigge's hands, then fell back to sleep.

A young, black nurse was on duty the next morning. She sat very straight and starched, cutting little figures out of construction paper with a large scissors. The sky was light again.

She looked over as soon as Sheila stirred. "Good morning."

Sheila tried to return her smile. "You are not Miss Sprigge."

"I am not Miss Sprigge. I am Mrs. Booker."

"And you are cutting out paper dolls—which is a very strange thing for a nurse to be doing, Mrs. Booker."

The woman laughed and held up the orange silhouette of a Pilgrim woman. "It's for the children's ward."

"I can't tell you how relieved I am."

41

Mrs. Booker put down the paper and scissors. "They should be coming around with the breakfast tray any minute. You must be starved."

Sheila sat up. "Do you think you might help me get to the bathroom first?"

Mrs. Booker took a bedpan from the night table. Sheila stopped her.

"Please. By the time I'm finished arching and positioning and getting used to the cold metal on that thing I could crawl to the bathroom three times. Just help me up."

Sheila swung her legs over the side of the bed and put her arm around Mrs. Booker. She was shakier than she had thought. The sudden shift in poition made her dizzy and she had to let the nurse do more of the work than she'd planned.

"I'm sorry. I didn't think I'd be this wobbly."

"It takes getting used to."

She expected to go down the corridor to a patient's room. Instead, Mrs. Booker led her to a door Sheila thought was a closet. It was a small, gleaming private shower and bath. She helped her get settled. "I'll just straighten your bed while you're here."

Sheila surveyed the bathroom. She was still a little puzzled by all the privacy. There were simply too many suicides going on all the time for each one to be taken care of like this, she thought. Phil certainly couldn't afford this kind of setup. It felt as though she were being positively rewarded with a stay in a luxury hotel.

Her toilet things lay spread on the surface of the sink. Her toothbrush had never looked so appealing. There was a bar in the wall beside her. She pulled herself up and make her way to the sink. The water shocked her as she washed her hands and face. She fought it at first and tried to hold on to the drowsiness. Finally she gave in and even splashed herself with cold water.

Mrs. Booker came back while she was brushing her teeth. "Oh, Mrs. Gaynor, why didn't you call me?"

Sheila waved her away. "It's all right," she said through the

42

foam. She rinsed and when her mouth was clean she said, "There. I'm beginning to feel human again."

"Let me take you back to bed."

Sheila could feel her knees weaken. "Just a second." She hung onto the edge of the sink and looked at herself in the mirror. It had been a long time since she'd done that. Lately she'd been simply glancing at it long enough to believe she had seen the same, scrubbed, bright-eyed face she'd graduated with five years before. Now she looked hard. She was surprised to find it had not changed that much after all, and she realized with a curious relief that she had expected to see her mother's face staring back at her. She ran her fingers over her forehead and cheeks. They were still cool from the water. Her eyes were long and dark. As her fingers approached the corner of one eye, the lid shuddered slightly. It was more clearly veined than before. That and a slightly deeper hollow in her cheeks were the only permanent signs she could find.

She picked up her hairbrush.

"Why don't you do that in bed?" Mrs. Booker led her back gently. Sheila sat on the edge. She worked at the tangles on the bottom, then slowly moved up until the brush ran smoothly. She shook her head once, then dropped the brush on the night table and swung back. The sheets were tight and cool.

"I feel like I've just done a year's hard labor."

Mrs. Booker laughed. "You've got more energy than most."

A nurse's aide came in. She wheeled a large cart behind her.

"Here's breakfast," Mrs. Booker said.

"That'll be along in a minute, ma'am." The aide swung the cart around. It was covered with flowers—gladiolus and roses, gardenias, zinnias, a Japanese plant, a dwarf tree with a plastic figurine meditating beneath it, and one large arrangement with fruits and candies wrapped in yellow cellophane.

Sheila gaped.

"They're all for you, ma'am."

The aide brought the cart to Sheila's bedside. "There's a card with each one."

They were all from Bernie and May.

To brighten the day. Mom and Dad.
Because we love you. Mom and Dad.
Couldn't resist these. Mom and Dad.
These are from the garden at home. Dad.

Sheila glanced at them. She shook her head sadly. Nobody nurtured a garden like Bernie. She could imagine him settling in the car beside May, ready to drive north to visit their suicidal daughter, then jumping out to cut the last of the season's flowers. What greater proof of his love? She even knew how he spread the damp newpaper in the trunk and laid them on top.

The note with the plant was the only one in her mother's handwriting. *I'm sorry, darling. I couldn't stop him. Enjoy them anyway. Love, Mom.*

She smiled indulgently. The smile froze as she read the last note. *Hope you like your room. Best in the house. Mom and Dad.* She closed the note quickly and crumpled it.

"Somebody sure does think a lot of you," Mrs. Booker said brightly. "Shall I arrange them around the room?"

Sheila shook her head.

"You shouldn't just leave them all bunched together on the cart."

"Well, then, could you see your way clear to flushing them down my fine, private toilet?"

"Mrs. Gaynor!"

"Or just wheel them down to the ward for the peasants."

"You're acting like a child."

Sheila nodded. "A spoiled brat. I know. I don't deserve to have such goddamned nice things. Get them the hell out of here, will you?" She shoved the cart away. Mrs. Booker took it while it was still rolling and wheeled it out.

Sheila glanced around the room. The walls had grown uglier, the sheets had lost all their luxury, and even helpful, crisp Mrs. Booker had turned oppressive. Sheila was sorry now she had sent her out wih the flowers. She would have liked to send the meditating plaster figurine sailing through the window.

44

Mrs. Booker returned. "You ought to be ashamed of yourself."

"I know," she said tightly.

"That people care so much about you. . . ."

"I know, I know. I've heard all that." Her eyes flashed at the nurse.

Mrs. Booker returned to the chair and resumed work on the silhouettes. Her silence was an angry one.

A familiar, gnawing resentment was working hard, just below Sheila's chest, like a hooded worm. She wanted to reach inside, to pull it out and fling it away. It had fastened itself tightly, though; there was no way to get in—and it had enough food for a lifetime. She should have known the private room and the round-the-clock nurse were her parents' doing. What could have made her believe they would let her have even suicide to herself? She remembered the simple house wedding she and Phil planned, with only a few of their closest friends, and how it had mushroomed into a ceremony and dinner in a Woodview hotel. She'd felt the same gnawing then, but she thought it was joy at Bernie's pride. When she was pregnant with Vikki, Diana had sent her to the clinic at New York Hospital. She began taking classes in natural childbirth. Phil came with her, but Bernie and May did not trust clinics. They discovered that this one was allied to the Cornell medical school and begged her to go to a private obstetrician. They could not bear the idea that their grandchild would be in the hands of students. They would pay, of course. Bernie got the name of a doctor from friends in Woodview and May came into the city to accompany her on the first visit. Sheila felt the gnawing then, too, but that time she thought it compassion for May's concern. Vikki was born in a twilight sleep.

And always the same shame and disgust with herself for feeling ungrateful. Never guilt. She thought back on the day before when she realized she'd never felt guilty. Perhaps if she'd chosen, just once, to do what she planned for herself, at the cost of Bernie's pride or May's concern, she might have known guilt. It must have occurred to her. She knew it had, because when it did, that was the cue for a realistic discussion with Bernie or May or Phil, one when she had to agree she was being childish, as childish as Mrs. Booker told her she was now.

Breakfast arrived, but Sheila had lost her appetite. When the aide returned, the tray was untouched.

"Don't you feel like anything at all?" she asked sympathetically.

"Have you got a cigarette? If you've got a cigarette I'll take some coffee."

The aide shot a look at Mrs. Booker.

"What's the problem? Aren't I allowed cigarettes?"

"I'll check your chart," she said. She had taken on a cool, impersonal manner.

"Well?"

"It doesn't say anything."

"Then, please can I have a cigarette," Sheila said patiently.

"I don't have any," the aide said.

"Did my husband leave my handbag?"

The nurse nodded toward the night table. Sheila's handbag was on the lower shelf. She wondered if Phil had left her cigarettes in it. He did not smoke and the way she had been going through two packs a day for the past few months had been the source of an ongoing struggle. Every time she drew deeply Phil winced. "It's killing you," he would say. "You wheeze all night and you cough all morning. It's just a stupid, infantile oral need." She could not make him understand that her pleasure and comfort came from her lungs, the sting and constriction that was finally better than breathing. It reminded her she was alive. That was why she smoked them down to the filter.

She rummaged through the disordered bag. It was a large carry-all that she used for her daily outings with Vikki. Phil had not touched anything. Loose napkins lined the bottom. There was a Dr. Seuss book, a small brown bag with an apple core and Oreo crumbs, Vikki's cracked plastic sunglasses, and a small rag doll. In a side pocket she found a paperback mystery and a half-empty pack of Viceroys.

46

"You can leave the coffee," she said to the aide.

The first puff was a disappointment. It made her dizzy and promised nausea, but Sheila persisted. She inhaled almost defiantly. When she was finished she knew, with relief, she would want another one soon.

Phil noticed the stubbed-out cigarette when he arrived an hour later. Sheila saw his eye go to it before the door was closed.

He looked rested and crisp. There was a little red shaving nick at the side of his chin. She was surprised at how glad she was to see him.

"I brought you these," he said. His voice was unnaurally cheerful, with the pointed disregard of circumstances people reserve for hospital visits. He flipped open his briefcase and hulled out some magazines, fresh copies of *Harper's Bazaar, Better Homes and Gardens,* and *McCall's.* "Oh, and this." He took a *Superman Comic* from the pocket of his topcoat and grinned at her. "It was this or *Classic Comics* and I knew you wouldn't want anything heavy."

She smiled.

He took her hand. "How are you feeling?"

"Do me a favor," she said quietly. "I'm going to be in here for a couple of weeks. Don't ask me that. OK?"

He nodded.

"Why don't you take off your coat?"

He let go of her hand and dropped his coat on the foot of the bed. He was wearing his brown wool suit.

"You look very nice."

"Thanks." There was a pause. "You brushed your hair."

"I did indeed."

"Do you have everything you need?"

She nodded. "Except for a nightgown. Do you think you might bring me a nightgown or a pair of pajamas or something so I can take off this tent?"

"I'll bring it this afternoon."

"Thanks."

There was another long silence.

"Do you have a class today?"

47

"In an hour."

She nodded. He put his hands in his pockets and smiled at her.

"Diana sends her love."

She nodded again. "Thanks."

"And Bernie and May."

"Do they?"

"They said they sent flowers." He looked around the room.

"They arrived." She looked past Phil. "Mrs. Booker, do you mind if Phil and I have a little time alone?"

She dropped her paperwork.

"Seems nice," Phil nodded after her. "Conscientious."

"Good with her hands, too," Sheila said flatly. "Who hired her?"

"What do you mean?"

"How come I've got round-the-clock nurses, Phil, and a private room?" He looked down toward the bed crank and touched it absently with the toe of his shoe. "Did you think I wouldn't notice?"

"Are you uncomfortable?"

"I wasn't until I found out why I'm in here."

"I don't know if this is the time to talk about it, honey."

"How could you possibly let them?"

"Maybe we ought to talk with Rankin first."

"Who hired him?"

"He's a staff doctor."

"Why do I have to talk to him first? You're my husband. I can talk with you."

"Sheila, try to be reasonable."

"That's not unreasonable. Please, Phil." Her voice sounded peculiarly young in her own ears. "Please don't think we have to consult with professionals before you can talk to me. I'm still a person. Honest to God. And all I want to know is how you let me end up in here with Bernie and May paying for it."

"You've taken things from them before."

Sheila nodded. "But you knew how I felt about it, didn't you? You must have known."

His tone was patient, careful, but it stung like a slap. "I really

48

didn't have time to think about nuances. Finding you first, then sitting there with Vikki in the emergency room for a quarter, a half, three-quarters of an hour without any idea of what was going on on the other side of the door. Do you know what that was like?"

"I think so," she said quietly.

"I didn't even know whether you were still alive. Then the relief, and the confusion with Vikki and bringing her up to Diana's."

"I said I think I understand."

"Bernie and May called here right after they spoke to Diana. They kept asking me why it had happened and I couldn't tell them. Then Bernie made me promise to get you a private room. You know what he's like in situations like this."

"I know."

"They were having trouble finding a bed in the ward for you, anyway, and I wasn't in such great shape myself—so I just switched Bernie over to the admissions office and let him take care of it."

"OK. All right." She tried to match his clear, reasoned tone. "I understand. Just get me changed now, OK? That's all. No more questions. I'm not upset. I'm not angry with you. Just get me transferred."

"To a ward?"

"Whatever we can afford."

"But that's the point. We can't afford—"

"Then whatever's cheapest. We'll go into debt. OK? As soon as I'm better I'll get a job to pay it off. It's my fault, anyway. So let it be my debt, too. All right?" Her jaw was tightening. "*Mine.*" She bit the word off.

"You're not making sense, Sheila."

"I know that, too, darling. I really do. It's stupid and it's childish and i's all the things you've told me it was. Just humor me. This once."

"The main thing is for you to get better," he said tenderly. "It doesn't matter where that is or who pays for it."

"It matters to me."

"But you're still not thinking clearly."

49

"I can't breathe in here."

He sat beside her and reached out to stroke her face. Sheila slapped his hand away. She drew a shocked breath. "I'm sorry, Phil," she said quickly. "I didn't mean to . . . I'm trying. . . . It's just that you're not listening to me, darling."

"I'm listening," he said coolly.

She covered her face with her hands and held them there. "Let me get hold of myself," she said from behind them. "Just give me a second. OK?"

He waited.

She dropped her hands and nodded to reassure him. "OK. Now I'm going to explain why I've got to get out of this room." She did not look at him as she spoke, but her whole body leaned toward him, reinforcing her words. "I tried to commit suicide the other night—"

"Sheila—"

"—it's all right. I know what I'm saying. I understand it. I tried to commit suicide. I can't tell you why yet. I only know that there wasn't just one reason. That much I do know already. And that's really interesting too, you know? I used to think that people committed suicide because one thing finally happened an that was how they reacted to it—like in the movies. But that isn't how it is. The market crashes, your husband dies—or your kid—or you lose your job, or your arm or a breast, you go a little crazy for a while, but you don't commit suicide. Not like I did. When you do what I did there's no one thing you can point to comfortably and say, 'That's why.' " She smiled a little sadly. "You know, like my father wanted you to do and you couldn't. Because there is no one thing—and if you try to pick one of the hundreds of little things it seems so stupid, carping. But they pile up—without your even noticing, they pile up until even things that aren't problems become impossible. Like deciding what pair of socks to wear or how to part Vikki's hair. You can't decide because they're not yours to decide about. The socks aren't yours, or the little girl, or the brain that's supposed to be doing the deciding. They're not yours because there's no you to own them. But that's what's so terrible. You see? Because even though there's no one there, you can still hear someone, somewhere, screaming with boredom. So you shut her up." She shrugged. "You just . . . put her away. . . . Where was I? Shit, I've lost my point."

"Why you need another room," Phil murmured. He was looking down at his hands.

"Right. Good. Thank you," she said with determined reason. "You see? I haven't lost my point at all. The suicide was mine. That's the point. If nothing else in my whole life was mine—"

"You know that's not true."

"Of course it's not true. But it's what I believed—and no matter how many times I told myself it wasn't true I couldn't stop believing it. Nothing was *mine*," she said slowly. "The suicide is. This room isn't. And I can't start all over again, darling. One way or another I'm going to have to build on my own suicide. I know that much. I'm going to have to start there and you can't let my mother and father take it away from me before I've even begun. So please, please get me out of here."

She waited.

Phil noded without looking up from his hands. "All right." She let out a breath. "I'll ask Rankin what he thinks."

Sheila stared at him.

'What's wrong?"

"I didn't ask you to consult."

"What else do you want?"

"Get me out of here."

He raised his hands helplessly. "I can't. I don't know what's right." He looked at her for the first time. "I want to do what's best for you."

"I'm telling you."

"I'm not an expert," he said, pleading. "And you're in no condition—"

"I'm your wife and I'm telling you that I need something . . . badly. . . ."

"And I said I would do what I can."

"No," she said incredulously. "You said you'd consult, as though I were some strange case. Don't. Just tell them you want me changed out of here into the ward where everyone else who does what I did. . . ."

"Sheila, you're too tired and troubled to start all that now."

"All what?"

"All that business about being middle class and privileged."

"Oh, dear God," she whispered.

"I just need somebody who can think objectively. You can't now. I certainly can't."

"What did I give up when I took those goddamned pills?"

"If you'd only stay calm I'd be able to trust you, honey. But look how emotional you're becoming. How do you expect me to believe you're thinking clearly—"

"I'm not thinking clearly. I told you that before. I'm being irrational and infantile. But I'm telling you what I need to survive."

"OK, OK," he said soothingly.

Sheila stared at his profile. He held very still. Then she lay back and tried to understand why he was making her beg. Even if he did get her transferred now she could never be sure that he understood. An old sense of doubt began working on her. Maybe he was right. Maybe she wasn't thinking clearly and he was right to hesitate. She had tried to control herself to explain as calmly as she could, but she had botched it, so maybe he was right and her own confusion was blowing the business out of proportion. But she knew, too, that the urgency was real. She had somehow maneuvered herself back into a corner. She was helpless again. If she was seeing things clearly and getting out of her father's room was really crucial, then she had to make Phil see her as clear-headed, reasonable. The only way to prove that was to give up trying to change rooms. She stared up at the ceiling. It was unlined and white.

Phil coughed uneasily. He went to the window.

"Have you seen the view from up here yet?"

Sheila shook her head dully.

"Spectacular. You can see right over Morningside Park."

"Phil?"

"Hmm?"

52

"I'm . . . I'm sorry I lost control." She tried not to sound humiliated. He turned toward her, his face suffused with tenderness and relief. She sat up.

"I'm really going to try to make it as easy as I can for you. I really am."

He made an uncertain movement toward her. She held out her hand and he came back to her side.

"I'm sorry." Her voice was very small.

"It's all right," he whispered. "I told you that before. Do you remember?"

She nodded.

"Yesterday when you woke up. I told you it was all right and I meant it." His voice, his whole body had suddenly turned soft and protective. His eyes shone. She put her arms around him and buried her face in his shoulder. Phil stroked her hair.

"I love you, Sheila."

"I know."

"I didn't want to lose you."

"I know that, too."

"I was so frightened." He laughed softly. "Isn't that a terrible thing for a man to admit to his wife?"

She shook her head.

"All I could think of was everything good we had together and how we had to get it back—any way we could."

"We will, darling. I promise."

"I'll help you."

The sleeve of her gown had fallen back and the wool of his jacket scraped her bare arm. "I am a baby sometimes."

"I wouldn't have it any other way."

"I put you through such hell."

He lifted her head and kissed her on the forehead. Sheila lowered her eyes. "Honey?"

"Hm?"

"Would you not get mad if I asked you again?"

"Asked what?"

"To have my room changed?"

"I won't get mad." He kissed her again.

"Soon?"

"Do you want me to go down and check now?"

She looked up at him gratefully. "Oh, darling, would you?"

He smiled, closed his eyes lightly, and nodded. "If you still want it now that you've calmed down." He shook his head, grinning. "You should have seen your eyes flashing before. You were really something."

"I bet I was."

"Now you're my old Sheila again. Aren't you?"

She pulled his head to her and kissed him on the mouth. He tried to keep it light, but she held him there, then moved closer in to him.

Phil broke away. "Hey, steady. Mrs. Booker might walk in."

"Let her. She might learn something."

He disengaged himself gently. "Let me go down and see what I can find out about the room. OK?"

"You sure you want to? Now, I mean? I was just starting to feel like a foreign movie."

He stroked her face. "You really are a nut."

She grinned impishly.

"I'll be right back."

"OK. But it won't be the same."

His light skin betrayed him again. He went to the door, adjusting his jacket. Before he left he turned to her. "Jesus, I'm glad to have you back."

She nodded.

He left and her eyes went as hard as a whore's.

He came back a half hour later with nothing definite to tell her. They would put Sheila on a waiting list. The ward beds were filled with patients from the clinic, patients, Phil explained, who had no way to afford anything else. Sheila thought of suggesting she switch places with one of them and let Bernie and May keep paying for the room. Instead, she said she hoped something would open up. It seemed stupid and unimportant now, anyway, and she wondered bitterly whether that was because she had won by getting him to try to do something, or because she had lost by humiliating herself in order to get it. Whatever it was she had struggled to make a

54

coherent choice and once again the point had disappeared in the struggle. She lay back uneasily, listening to Phil's explanation. He was sympathetic. His eyes were full of apology, but she had the sense that she was slipping back. Nothing had changed. There was still no way to break out because she still could not find the limits of her trap. Every time she came up against a wall she had only to follow Phil's lead, be cool, reasonable, realistic, and it would open out. It was, after all, an irrational act that had landed her here in the first place. Now the best thing was simply to bow to necessity.

Dr. Rankin came for his visit in the afternoon. Sheila said nothing about the room. She talked, instead, about inconsequentials, history which seemed to satisfy him. She told him about how she and Phil had married right out of college, how she had gotten pregnant with Vikki almost at once, and how Phil had had to work at an insurance company for two years to save up enough to start law school. His mother had wanted to give them an allowance, but Phil had refused. He accepted tuition from his father's trust fund only because his family's wealth disqualified him from fellowships. He had applied, though, just to be sure he could have gotten one on his ability. For the rest, he had to prove his independence.

Through the week she sketched in details. She talked of Phil's family. He was the middle child, between Renata, the older daughter, and Paul, the youngest. Phil's mother was a widow who ruled her other two children with an iron bank account. That was another reason for Phil's refusal to take any money.

She talked about Bernie and May. He was in real estate in Woodview, New Jersey. Bernie's mother Doris, a once-vivacious woman whom Sheila loved particularly dearly, lived in Woodview, too, in a residential hotel. She spent most of her time playing poker with five other women, though she was beginning to seem feeble and very old.

Sheila told all the details as though she were telling someone else's story. She used the first person: "It was hard for me, but I was proud of Phil's independence." "Even with all the scholarships my mother and father had to knock themselves out to get me through college. I've always been grateful for that." "I

55

love Vikki. I guess that's why I get so overprotective." But all the time she stood apart, like an author who had simply chosen to tell a story through a first-person narrator.

Rankin said little. Sometimes he sat in the armchair while she lay in bed; sometmes they both sat by the window and Sheila stared out at the river all the time she spoke. She talked more and more, not only to Rankin, but to Mrs. Wheeler and the aides who passed in and out with her meal trays, even to Mrs. Booker, who gradually thawed. She spun her story out for anyone who would listen and sometimes, even when she was alone, she would keep the narrative going silently, like a movie inside her head. She never dared stop to question what had released the flood of words. They were safe. Concrete facts, anecdotes, detailed memories of scenes and faces. She kept them in front of her and clung to them by talking. Her voice grew more lively, her eyes steadily brighter, until the vitality behind the words turned unnatural, her enthusiasm edged with desperation. She had to cling to the words outside her because as the days passed the horror of what she had tried to do grew more and more real. She remembered the silence she had wakened with, how she had welcomed it, held it there, and even wielded it as a weapon against Phil. The truth of that grew sharper, more monstrous as she watched it move farther back in the past and with all the logic of nightmare, the greater the distance between her and the memory, the more terrible and immediate it grew. Sheila was afraid it would overwhelm her. So she talked.

Phil came in every day between classes. She was quieter with him. He was cheerful but the strain was beginning to show. The lines in his neck grew tight. The skin on his cheekbones and forehead showed signs of breaking out. Bernie had gone back to Woodview. May had stayed in the apartment to look after Vikki. Phil was sleeping on the sofa. He had signed up for a bar exam cram course downtown. That would start in a week and gave him still another schedule to juggle. Two of his friends had taken jobs with the district attorney's office, but he was still holding out for a private offer. He had been through two more interviews that week. His mouth grew tense when he told her about them.

Sheila could not tell him of the fear that was growing inside her, and she could not chatter brightly. Their sessions remained tentative. After a while they both began to welcome the nurse's presence.

At the beginning of the fourth week Dr. Rankin told Sheila they would be able to let the nurses go. She ought to think about going home. Sheila agreed, but the knot of terror inside tightened. She wanted, God knew, to get out of that room as soon as she could, but she felt her jaw go hard and her limbs go weak whenever she thought of returning to the apartment. If she remained in the hospital, though, she remained alone. Mrs. Wheeler, Miss Sprigge, and Mrs. Booker would no longer be there, and it was only they who stood between her and the horror of darkness still growing inside her.

The next morning she dozed off after breakfast. Phil had told her he would not be in to see her the next day. His work had fallen behind and he simply had to spend some time in the library. Neither of them would admit it, but his visits had become grueling. It was a relief to have a morning free of fumbling conversation and the strain of trying to make the silences seem relaxed. Their life together was in a state of suspension while Sheila remained in the hospital.

Mrs. Booker was making artificial flowers out of colored tissue paper and pipe cleaners. Sheila could hear the rustle and snap as she dropped off to sleep. It was a curiously soothing sound. She concentrated on it, and the room and Mrs. Booker slipped away. Yet the farther away they moved, the more distinct the sound of the paper and scissors grew. Soon it was no longer soothing, but insistent and vaguely irritating. She tried to open her eyes, to sit up and ask Mrs. Booker to stop, but the nurse was already too far away and the noise was growing too loud to shout through. Phil burst into the room, breathless. He was wearing a white hospital coat over his brown suit and he had dyed his hair and eyebrows black. He rushed to the bedside and Sheila could see his lips

57

moving. "I can't hear you," she shouted. "Talk into the rustle." He turned his head toward the sound until his voice came out of it. "They told me I could watch. I brought you these." He held out a bouquet of orange and red paper flowers. "Take them." The noise grew louder as he pushed them toward her. She shrank away. "No, Phil. Please, I don't want them. It's very sweet of you, darling. It really is, but I don't want them." Phil brought them closer, but there was still a long way to travel. Sheila knew if they ever reached her, if she ever touched them, something terrible would happen. She turned to Mrs. Booker for help, but the nurse had found Sheila's government Honors Thesis and was cutting out silhouettes from the pages. The flowers were at her fingertips now. Phil grabbed her wrist. "No, Phil. Please. I don't want to." He pulled her toward him. She lost her voice and watched as he put the bouquet in her hand. It stung once and she felt herself swept into the noise. Phil's head was still turned. The line on his neck stood out sharply. She focused on it from inside the flowers and watched it grow larger as she traveled toward it on the current of sound. She tried to pull back but there was nothing to pull against. She gave in, let go and closed her eyes. Darkness scooped her up. The noise stopped. Everything went still and silent except for a distant, slow throbbing somewhere below. The sound was familiar. She tried to place it in the darkness. Then she looked and saw herself on the other side of the room, lying on the bed in a hospital gown, staring back. The throbbing was Phil's heart. He sat in the armchair looking out the window and she was the curve of his neck, a thing, without emotion, without meaning, a formal arrangement of skin and bone. She struggled to transform herself, to merge with the woman on the bed who stared at her so impassively, but she was trapped. She could not even scream and she knew that Phil had only to turn his head and she would disappear completely. The heartbeat slowed and grew louder. It changed to a voice. Now that she was a thing she could understand the language of things. The heartbeat spoke to her. It repeated her name. "Mrs. Gaynor. Mrs. Gaynor Mrs. Gaynor." She listened carefully. It seemed to hold out the hope of release. It grew more distinct. Then it turned into

Mrs. Wheeler's voice. "Mrs. Gaynor." Sheila found her eyes. She opened them and looked up. The nurse stood over her. It took a moment to feel relief.

"Must have been a whopper," Mrs. Wheeler said gently. She nodded. "Remind me never to take morning naps again." She sat up, relieved to hear her own drowsy voice. "I can handle nightmares. At least at night you know you're asleep so you try to wake up, but the damned daymares. . . . You're sure you're awake and there's no way out." She shuddered.

"How do you feel now?"

"Better. I'm better." She laughed. "You know, I used to have a friend at Barnard who said that all the time. Harriet Spiegelman. You'd meet her on Broadway or in the john or at a theater or a rally and say, 'Hello, Harriet. How are you?' and no matter where it was or when you'd seen her last, she'd nod very seriously—like that—and say, 'Better. I'm better.' Diana and I used to talk about how reassuring it was to say 'Hello' to Harriet." She shook her head. "God, the things you remember when you've just been scared out of your wits."

Mrs. Wheeler laughed. "Anyway, you're better."

Sheila nodded seriously. "I'm better. And hungry. How long have I been asleep? I didn't miss lunch, did I?"

"It'll be along. I've come to say good-bye."

"Oh, no," she said softly.

"I walked from Eighty-ninth Street this morning."

"It must have been freezing."

"Glorious. Crisp and clean. I could feel my cheeks and see my breath for the first time this season. It's going to be a good winter."

"I hope so," Sheila said softly. "I can't remember when I was so hungry."

"It's a good sign."

"Is it? Then why am I so scared?"

"Are you?"

"Terrified."

"As scared as you were a little while ago?"

"When?"

"Before I woke you?"

Sheila took a minute. She shook her head.

"You're on the road then."

Sheila extended her hand. She took it and held it until Sheila matched its grip. "Good luck, Mrs. Gaynor."

"I've got lot of hard work to do."

Mrs. Wheeler nodded.

"Thank you for all your help. I'll think of you often."

Mrs. Wheeler laughed. "I hope not. That's a dreadful burden to put on anyone—being thought of in all kinds of odd moments. I'll never know when I'm safe." She brought up her other hand and covered the handclasp. "I promise I won't think of you at all."

She let go. An aide brought lunch and the two women left Sheila alone. It was the first time she had been alone since she had wakened almost four weeks before. Sheila poured some coffee from the carafe into her cup. Her hand was trembling. If I get this in without spilling it will be a sign, she said to herself. I'll be all right. She filled the cup halfway. A few drops spilled on the saucer as she turned the carafe upright and she tried to decide if that counted. Her eye went to the buzzer on the night table. She could find some excuse to call in the aide. Sheila looked at the door where Mrs. Wheeler had just disappeared. No. It was too soon. She couldn't give in that quickly. She would wait.

She ate her lunch and tried to smoke a cigarette with her coffee. It tasted harsh and boring. She stubbed it out after a few puffs and wandered to the window. Her cup rattled in the saucer. The view was too familiar to absorb her. She had already flipped through all the magazines. The articles on how to stretch your house space and grow your own herb garden were stupid and irritating. She drained her cup and went to the bathroom. She was only going to brush her hair, but she ended up showering, too, and putting on some light makeup. Her tray was gone when she came out.

An hour later Dr. Rankin found her sitting on the edge of the bed in her yellow terry cloth robe. Her hair was pulled back in a pony tail.

"I want to go home," she said.

60

2
Phil
November 17, 1962

PHIL WAS not in the library that afternoon as he told Sheila he would be. Eleanor and Fred Ryan, old friends of the Gaynor family, had called to invite him to lunch at home and spend the afternoon at the Athletic Club with their grandson. Phil thought it best not to tell Sheila. She had met the Ryans only once and she did not like them.

They lived in a brownstone in the East Sixties. Phil liked visiting there. It was one of an unbroken row of town houses. Some were diplomatic headquarters and professional offices now; others, like the Ryans', were still private homes. The stone walls were sandblasted clean every year, the wrought-iron grillwork freshly painted. In summer the street was vibrant with flowers in great, baroque stoop urns, and carefully manicured hedges ballooned over low cement walls. Now the bushes were bare, the urns emptied and hosed down for the winter. Behind them the heavy doors of brass and leaded glass and oak seemed even more impregnable.

Phil liked the ease he could show to the street as he mounted the stairs to the Ryan house, and the way he could wait in front of the cut-glass doors with the assurance that he would be welcomed.

Wealth like Ryan's was still an awesome thing to him. His own family was rich but it did not have the Ryans' hereditary power. Philip Gaynor, Sr., and Frederick Ryan had been friends since before he was born, but Phil had never had the sense they were equals. Phil's father was a brilliant lawyer. Many had considered him a great judge and part of the aura about him sprang from the fact that he had worked his way out of the middle class. He was different—only very subtly, at least by the time he had become a judge—but different from men like Ryan. Phil's father had worn his accomplishments with calm confidence, the way Phil wore a new set of clothes, knowing he was handsome, knowing he belonged in them, and that they fit as they could fit no one else, yet always fatally aware that he had changed out of something else to put them on.

For Phil the house off Fifth Avenue was the greatest symbol of Ryan's position and history. It had been the family home since the nineteenth century, even while the Ryans built their empire in Connecticut. For legal and political reasons there was a Ryan estate near the Gaynor house in Northfield, about sixty miles outside Hartford, but the house in Northfield was always a second home. Phil became aware very early of how many of the people who moved from New York lived in Connecticut. It made the Ryans, who moved from Connecticut and lived in New York, that much more legendary.

Phil saw the house for the first time when he was eighteen, beginning at Columbia College. It was freshman week. Eleanor Ryan had invited him to dinner to welcome him to the city. He could still see her coming toward him noiselessly across an Oriental rug. She wore a violet chiffon dress. Her gray hair was swept up from behind and held in place with a comb. She extended her hand just as Phil wondered how he should greet her. He put out his own. She shook it firmly and he knew, for the first time, what it felt like to be graceful.

She led him across the room to a large couch upholstered with tapestry material. Behind the couch, in a small area all to themselves, stood an antique harp, a velvet-covered stool with a low back, and a music stand. There was music on the stand.

"I used to play," Mrs. Ryan said and smoothly guided him down. She was in her sixties. Her body was small and sturdy, her face like porcelain, a few lines there, seemingly at her sufferance, placed where she wanted them. "Frederick will be along soon. He's been in New Haven all day, but he's looking forward to seeing you. Can Todd get you anything?" The butler was still at the door. "I'm going to have a Dubonnet. It's very light and nice, but if you want anything else. . . ."

"That's fine," Phil said.

She nodded to Todd.

Frederick Ryan never showed up that evening. Phil and Mrs. Ryan had drinks and dinner alone. She kept up a steady flow of conversation, asking all the right questions to get him to talk and listening with a care and interest he had never known before.

He had always admired Frederick Ryan. That night, sitting at one end of the mahogany table with his wife, eating poached salmon and talking about himself as a man with a future, Phil fell in love with him. Even his absence fed that love. As he passed from the dining room back to the living room for brandy and coffee, he felt as though he were moving through the man's body. The air was sweet with tobacco and tweed; the solid furniture, the heavy hangings, the bronze sculpture, even the effortless charm of Eleanor Ryan made the man's physical presence unnecessary. Phil's head swam like any young man's the first time he falls in love. His father had taught him what it meant to be his own man, how important it was to work out his own destiny. He had learned confidence, tenacity, the right to take what he earned with pride and dignity. The one thing his father could not give him was an ideal, an unattainable identity with which he would long to merge. Now he had found it. Frederick Ryan's absence was the greatest sign of his power. He yearned to be absent the way Ryan was that night while Phil moved through his house, talked to his wife, sat in his furniture, and thought of no one but him.

It was warm outside when he left. He walked down Fifth Avenue, filled with th Ryans and the feeling that he had made a momentous decision. He would never leave New York. If his father's Connecticut was green and expansive and the air thin and clear, Frederick Ryan's New York was red and polished brown, arranged, and the air was pipe smoke and brandy.

63

Connecticut, especially Northfield, was windows that looked out on history. New York was the great sliding doors to the Ryan living room that shut time out.

That had been ten years before. The Ryan house had remained the still point in his life while he went through Columbia, married, battled with his mother about working for two years, had Vikki, and now was about to finish law school. He could trust it to be as he had seen it the first night, right down to the music beside the harp.

He had thought about the house a great deal during the past three weeks. He needed something steady to hang on to. His own feelings were still in flux. He would be in the Law School library, so engrossed that he would seem to have forgotten all about Sheila, when a great surge of love and concern for her would break through his work and leave him useless. In class, at odd moments, the horror and confusion of what had happened would suddenly make his skin tingle; he would play throuh the whole scene again until his body went limp with relief that she was safe. He knew they were having trouble. He wasn't home as much as he ought to be; Sheila was tired; Vikki was going through a difficult stage. These were all the common kinds of problems his friends were having, and Sheila was as strong as any of their wives. But they were moving in the right direction. The end was really in sight and she knew that. Once the bar exams were out of the way and he was settled with his first job, they could coast for as long as they wanted. He wondered if perhaps that wasn't really the reason behind it, Sheila couldn't take the pressure of their success. Those were the times his jaw would go tight and he would imagine how much more smoothly and quickly his career might be moving if it weren't for the constant preoccupation with her and Vikki, the number of choices he had simply ruled out because of them, the number of times he had glanced at his watch and irritably closed up his books because he was expected. Then, just as swiftly, he would grow angry at himself, flush with guilt, and remember that it was only Sheila and Vikki who gave it all meaning in the first place.

Behind all the constant, shifting feelings toward Sheila stood the Ryans, as powerful, as stable, as ideal as ever.

The inner door moved and Todd's shape swam toward him from behind the cut glass.

"Hello, Mr. Gaynor."

"Hello, Todd."

"They're in the living room."

"Hello, Phil." Frederick Ryan came across the living room to meet him. He had the walk of a man who had never lost the impulse to action, but whose body refused to respond with its former bouyancy. He wore a tan leather sport jacket with cowhide patches at the elbow. His head was bald, with great freckles. The white fringe around them stood in a determined crew cut. He was not much taller than his wife.

Eleanor Ryan was just coming through the door from the dining room. She carried a bowl with a single, floating water lily. "Philip. How are you?" She was as cordial as ever, but he saw a brief question flicker in her eyes.

The strain of the past three weeks must have shown on his face. Phil had told the Ryans Sheila was out of town for a while. It was the only time he had felt that there might be something shameful in what had happened. He could talk about it easily with Diana Brautigan and some of his closer friends at school. All of them seemed to hve a reference point he could depend on without fear of moral judgment. The idea of having the Ryans know made him uneasy. They had always regarded Sheila as some kind of subtle weakness on his part anyway. That was why he had avoided contact with his mother, as well, since it happened.

"You're looking tired." Ryan searched his face less subtly as they shook hands.

"I am." It was lame.

"How are Sheila and Vikki?" Mrs. Ryan placed the bowl.

"Fine. Just fine."

Ryan reached up and put an arm around him. "Come on in and sit down. Do you drink this early?"

"If you're having something. . . ."

"Don't worry about us."

"All right, then. Bourbon on the rocks."

Mrs. Ryan nodded at Todd.

Phil sat down.

"It seems ages since we've seen you." She sat on the sofa across from him. Her smile was as open as ever, but Phil was certain she knew something was wrong.

"How are they treating you at the mill?" Ryan jerked his head uptown.

Phil grinned. "I'm almost ground out."

"Not too fine, I hope."

"I'm doing what you told me three years ago. Learning it all, believing half."

"Good. From what we've been getting out of New Haven this last couple of years they're doing just the opposite up there. I hope *you* don't want to be a storefront lawyer."

"I may have no choice."

"Troubles?"

"It's a buyer's market. There's always the district attorney's office."

"Storefronts and d.a.'s. We've spent a lot of money turning out more good lawyers than we need." He smiled. "That's the only reason we've got so many idealists on our hands."

"I don't think that's fair."

"It's easy to keep from selling out when nobody's buying." Ryan's eyes twinkled. Tangling with the young was his favorite sport.

"That may be true in my case, but some of my frieds have already had some big offers. What about them?"

"What about them?"

"They're thinking of turning them down."

"What are they thinking about?"

"Alternatives."

"Alternative offers? Or alternative ideals?"

Mrs. Ryan laughed.. "Fred, you're being a sophist."

He chuckled. "Phil knows that."

"Of course I do." His smile was less easy.

"You're both decadent."

66

"Eleanor thinks I snap words the way boys in the locker room snap towels. How come your friends are getting all the offers? With your background they should be clamoring for you—even in a tight market."

"I think I may have limited myself too much."

"How?"

"I've only applied to New York firms."

"That's a hell of a provincial thing to do."

"I don't want to leave the city." Ryan studied him silently.

"Have you heard from Sheila?" Mrs. Ryan asked.

Phil shifted in the chair. "Yes. She's fine."

"That was her mother I spoke to on the phone, wasn't it?" Mrs. Ryan turned vague as she asked it. She grew absorbed in the position of the lily bowl.

"Might have been. She's taking care of Vikki."

"I told you, Fred. I thought I recognized her voice from the wedding. I have a gift for voices and Sheila's mother had a very distinctive one, with a good sharp edge. That's how I remembered it. Anyway, Fred said it was impossible because Sheila was visiting them."

"She is. I mean, she's down in Woodview, but that's mainly to get a little rest, not to visit the . . . her parents." Mrs. Ryan nodded. "It's hard work, with the house and Vikki and so little of me around." He tried to keep it chatty, but he always sounded defensive when he mentioned Sheila to them. Even the most casual reference felt like a betrayal.

"I know," Mrs. Ryan said softly. "I had four daughters."

"Yes, but—" Phil stopped, about to say, "It was different for you."

She smiled and shook her head almost imperceptibly. Her eyes went vague again. "Here's Todd," she said, more to herself than the men. As she turned away from him, Phil noticed how deeply the lines had embedded themselves in her face over the last ten years. She seemed no longer quite in control of them, though she had not stopped struggling for ascendancy. Her moments of vagueness were like rests, while she searched for something to take the place of the struggle.

Todd served the drinks.

67

"We were up to see your own mother last week," Ryan said. He settled back with a glass of sherry.

"How is everybody? I've been meaning to get in touch for the past—"

"Your sister's getting married," Mrs. Ryan said.

"Renata?"

She nodded, amused at his open surprise. "It was bound to happen sooner or later."

"It was never as sure as all that, Eleanor," Ryan said. He winked at Phil. "We'd all pretty much given up hope for the sooner, and even the later was running out."

"Fred, she's Phil's sister."

"But he's right. Renata's thirty-five. I really did figure—"

"Well," she said lightly. "You were wrong."

"He's a fellow from my firm. A hell of a nice guy and a hell of a good lawyer, too." Phil remembered what the young Fred Ryan had been like when he heard him describe someone as "a hell of a nice guy." He remembered playing on the fringe of the grown-ups who were having drinks on the club terrace, or watching through the stair railings while groups formed at the party. Ryan was always there, casual and low-voiced, leaning into a circle of people, talking about someone who was a "hell of a nice," or "a hell of a good," something. "His name is Ed Ronstein." He pronounced it "stine." "German fellow," he added.

Phil tensed. Ever since he had known Sheila he had to work not to hear the nuances.

"When is the wedding?"

"Two months."

"So soon?"

"They've known each other for a year or two," Mrs. Ryan said. "And it's going to be a small wedding. In the house. What's wrong, Phil?"

"Nothing. Nothing at all." But he fowned. It had been years since anyone in the family had expected Renata to marry. She had been nineteen when thir father died. He had always been unreasonably strict with his only daughter and she had seemed to welcome it. Their mother was a driving force

68

in her husband's career and while Constance Gaynor organized her life from political event to political event, from dinner party to dinner party, Renata was left to organize the family from day to day. It was she, more than Constance, who was a mother to Paul, the youngest of the Gaynor children, and while Paul hated her for depriving him of his real mother, he remained dependent on her. Within the household Renata was aggressive, efficient, tender to Paul, and respectful to Phil. Phil was younger than she, but he was the older son. Outside the family she was shy. Her voice barely rose above a whisper. If there were men present she did not speak at all. People who did not know her well politely suspected her of being deficient. People who did, simply thought her dull.

"Tell me more about Ronstein."

"A very bright guy," Ryan said. "He's been with us for eight years. Came from Huntles and Latham. Do you remember that big tobacco case I told you about two years ago? He handled that one. Did a beautiful job. Got a precedent decision out of the judge, to boot." Ryan filled a pipe. "He's loyal to the firm. To me." He smiled and nodded to Phil. "You can be sure he'll be loyal to Renata, too."

Phil nodded.

"He's had his offers. From every big firm in Connecticut. Told me about every one of them before he turned it down. That kind of loyalty pays off." He said it as though he were telling a cautionary tale. Phil got the uncomfortable feeling that his sister might have been part of the payoff.

"Sounds like Renata is lucky."

"He's fifty-two," Mrs. Ryan said.

"I'm working him into a partnership," Ryan added.

Phil waited for Mrs. Ryan to continue. "You're looking at me like a lawyer, Phil."

"What's the fuss about?" Ryan said softly. "Ronstein's age isn't a problem."

His wife smiled wryly. "Not to you, Fred. You're on the other side of it."

"That's where youth can learn from age. We know what it feels like to be fifty. They only know what it looks like."

"I suspect that's just what Phil's worrying about. Ronstein's feeling while Renata is still looking." She turned to Phil. "It's not a stunning match. You're quite right about that. But it will do. He's a widower. He has three children in school. They haven't had a mother for five years and it's beginning to tell on them. Ronstein is an excellent lawyer, but he's not the genius Fred is or your father was. He was never handsome and he looks his age now—however he feels. He does have money from both sides. His own family is in import-exports. His wife's father owned the Northeast Insurance Company. Renata will be more than comfortable and she will have a sure future. As it is, the situation in your mother's house is degenerating and it will be just as well if she leaves."

"What do you mean?"

She paused. "Whatever the dawbacks you think the marriage may have for Renata, her leaving can only help Paul."

Phil nodded. "How much did you two have to do with it?" he asked cautiously.

"Quite a bit. Fred and I arranged their first meeting at a dinner in the Northfield house. We encouraged it along with your mother."

"How much encouragement id it take?"

"Less than we thought. It finally did seem so natural and right."

"I'd like to meet him."

"Why don't you go up for a weekend?" Ryan suggested. "It shouldn't be too omplicated with Sheila out of town."

"I might do that," Phil said quickly.

Todd appeared at the door. "Your grandson is on the phone in the study."

Ryan and his wife exchanged a quick glance. He nodded to Todd and pushed himself out of the chair. "This shouldn't take long. Why don't you both have another drink?"

"Not for me, thanks. I've got to be in some kind of shape if I'm going to play ball this afternoon."

"I'm fine, too, Todd," Mrs. Ryan said. She turned to Phil when they were alone. "Well, Phil. How long has it been since we were alone like this?"

70

He smiled. "I was thinking the same thing."

She laughed. "I doubt it. Ten years ago was a good chunk of your life. For me it was yesterday." She ltoked at him curiously. "Did you have any idea of how furious I was with Fred that night?" He stared back, astonished. "And how impossible it was to keep the evening going?"

He shook his head slowly.

"No. I didn't think so, but I wasn't sure. Good. That's a load off my mind."

"You haven't been thinking about it for ten years?"

She surveyed him with amusement. "You were an insufferably dull young man, then." He blushed past his ears, but she could not offend him. Her eyes were warm with the most tender tolerance. "I can only tell you that now because you're turning out fine—just fine. And because I'm old enough to have license." She shook her head slowly. "Will I ever forget you in your three-piece suit—and the fresh creases in your white shirt. You'd had a haircut that afternoon, too. Hadn't you?"

He lowered his head, trying to hide a grin.

"I suppose that was why I was so furious at Fred. Not for leaving me alone to entertain a college boy—he'd done worse than that before—but because you'd broken out a new shirt and gotten a haircut for him."

"You were incredible that night. I never dreamed—"

"Oh, Philip, Philip." She reached out and touched his hand. "I don't know how any of us ever made it past twenty."

He wondered if he should be hurt or offended. All he could feel was a confused happiness. With her candor, her amused tolerance, her sharing of the other side of his memory, Eleanor Ryan seemed to welcome him deeper into the bosom of the family. "Did you have me here to tell me about Renata?"

"Only in part. Frederck has some other things he wants to discuss with you. It's going to be a busy afternoon." She paused briefly. "Your sister's fate always seems to be sandwiched in between other matters." She sighed. "Besides, I wish your mother would get over her aversion to using the telephone and communicate those things herself instead of asking us to be go-betweens. I can't imagine Frederick agreeing to do things like that for anyone besides your mother."

"It is an unpleasant task for you, then."

"You know very well it is."

"Why is Renata being pushed into this marriage?"

"Nobody said she was being pushed." She looked at him curiously. "You know, Phil, it seems to me you've asked everything about the marriage except one question. I've been waiting for it, but I'm beginning to suspect you have no intention of asking." She waited. "Why haven't you asked how your sister feels?'

He lowered his eyes. "I guess I thought I knew."

She nodded. "People always seem to think they know what Renata feels. How did you think she felt?"

He shrugged. "Resigned? Obedient?"

"To whom? Do you think the *entire* thing was engineered?"

"It crossed my mind."

"You're right. It was. But that doesn't necessarily make the marriage evil."

"I didn't say—"

"Ronstein was beginning to feel far too isolated in Northfield. It's difficult for a widower to find anyone in a society as closed as that. He was becoming restless. Fred was sure he was starting to look around seriously for a chance to move. Renata's prospects were already somewhere appreciably below zero and it was telling on her."

"Telling?"

"She was drying up," she said flatly. "It shows on a woman. It shows all over. Her neck gets stringy. Her voice turns thin and her silences become hostile. Renata is more than resigned to marrying Ed Ronstein."

"Grateful?" he asked with distaste.

"The girl is exhausted. She's been holding on to fraying hopes for a good, long time. She's finally able to let go with someplace to fall, someplace secure, someplace comfortable. So the marriage will do. It will do very nicely."

"And with a little luck she may be happy."

"Not luck. Practice. Your sister is thirty-five years old. Leave it to the teen-age brides to be radiant and white. They can afford the schooling time. Renata's beyond that." She paused. "I'm always puzzled when husbands, sons, and brothers begin to worry about a woman's happiness. What's your idea of a woman's happiness?"

"I don't know."

"Yet you're worried about your sister's."

"I mean, I don't know specifically. I've seen happy women. . . . I've always thought of you as a happy woman."

"I am. And it's taken work. More than it will take Renata."

He looked surprised.

"Her alternatives are more limited than mine were. She has no skill, no . . . art." She made a vague gesture at the harp behind her. "No prospects. And she's plain. She knows already how exhausting it is to work at your own happiness. I've talked with her. People tend to underestimate your sister. I was guilty of that myself. She's a hardheaded young woman. Her situation has taught her what it takes other young woman years to learn."

"What's that?"

"How to compromise. How to face what it is that you can't have and then . . . will your own refusal of it." She paused. Her eyes clouded and turned vague, then snapped back into sharp focus. "Your sister knows the traps of hope. How debilitating they can be." She looked at Phil without blinking. "I can assure you your sister will never have to feel grateful. She'll be happy. your sister will never have to feel grateful. She'll be happy.

"Then maybe she'd be better off unhappy," Phil said drily.

"That's not for either of us to decide."

He nodded and sat there feeling he had been convinced, but still trying to figure out what he had been convinced of, and why, if it were all so clear, he still felt uneasy.

"Is your wife ill?"

Phil raised his head sharply. "Why do you ask that?"

She waved the question away. "I'm on the other side of fifty, too—indeed, I've been a hostess for nearly that long. If you'd heard as many men make excuses for their wivs as I have, you wouldn't need to ask. What's wrong?"

73

"She's just very tired."

"Did she collapse?"

"I suppose you might—"

"She's not in Woodview at all, is she?"

Phil blew some air out of his mouth and shook his head.

"In the hospital?"

He nodded.

"Don't worry. I'm not going to pry into details."

"You don't seem to have to," he said with a wry smile.

"I'm not going to pretend I'm surprised, either." Phil was sitting forward on the edge of the armchair, his knees apart. His hands hung loosely clasped between them. She leaned back on the sofa and surveyed him. "And here we are worrying about Renata's happiness and a compromise match while anyone would have believed your wife made an ideal one."

"What do you mean?"

"Happy people don't collapse."

"But we are happy," he said quickly. "Or were, before—"

"You don't have to defend Sheila to me. I don't judge her when I say she's unhappy."

"I think you do." He looked up, surprised at his own response. He held her eye for a moment and realized he had to follow through. "I think you and Mr. Ryan have always judged us by each other. And I've never thought you approved of Sheila."

"Does she approve of us?"

He blushed.

A smile played around her lips. "I'm going to tell you something you won't believe now. I don't dislike your wife." He started to respond. "No. Let me finish. I've never felt anything for her and I've always believed that a great deal of your decision to marry had to do with a need to rebel against your own background, that for you, there was something exotic about a girl like that."

Phil's face tingled. He could not tell if it was anger or shame. And if it was shame, it was, perhaps, shame at not being angry. "Like what?" he asked softly.

74

Mrs. Ryan was unruffled. "A Jewish girl from the middle class. I'll tell you something else. Right now I feel very deeply for her. I believe I know what she's going through. Better, perhaps, than you."

"She tried to committ suicide."

"Why do you tell me that? Do you think it will shock me?"

He shrugged. "I just thought you ought to know."

"If she's lucky she'll learn from it. It's not easy to be a lawyer's wife, especially a successful lawyer—which is what you're going to be. I've only met Sheila once and the time I did she was well-mannered but somewhat sullen. She's also clearly a new breed and there's a great deal about these young women I simply don't understand. They're bright, indulged, demanding, with expectatons I would never have dreamed of. But then I had expectations, too, that Sheila could never have dreamed of. I'm old. I come from a different time. I suppose I would be less sure of myself if I didn't see them going through the same unhappiness, the same confusion, that I and my friends did, and my daughters and their friends did. She has my compassion."

"But you did"—he hesitated—"come through it."

"Most of us." She closed her eyes lightly and shook her head. "I don't envy the young a thing."

Frederick Ryan came back from the study.

"I think we can go in and eat now." Phil thought it sounded a bit too hearty.

"Everything all right with young Fred?" Phil asked.

"What do you mean?" The sharpness surprised him.

"I only—I thought maybe he was calling off the handball game."

"He'll play."

Phil followed Mrs. Ryan into the dining room. Just as they passed the sofa, she stopped and turned back to Phil. "I—" It startled him. He fell back clumsily and had to regain his balance on the back of the sofa. "I'm sorry," she murmured. "I didn't realize you were so close. . . ."

He stepped back toward her and his shoulder brushed the

75

harp. It was untuned. She winced and covered it quickly with a vague gesture toward her hair. "I just wanted to tell you I won't say anything to Fred about Sheila."

Ryan questioned Phil about school and his prospects more closely over lunch. By the time they were ready to leave for the club, Phil was sure there was a job offer waiting to be sprung. He wondered why it was taking so long for Ryan to come to it. He knew that private offers like this were handled differently from the standard law school interviews. Perhaps Ryan was putting him to some kind of test. For an instant he wondered if it didn't all hinge on whether he won the handball game that afternoon. That was crazy, he knew, but once the idea entered his head he couldn't get rid of it.

Before they left, Eleanor Ryan asked if he could come back for dinner. He tried to figure out the right answer, finally said "Yes," and muttered something about having to call home.

"You can do that when we get back," Ryan said.

Todd drove them to the club. In the car, Phil wondered if there might be an even subtler test and the right thing would be to lose. He tried to shake free of the whole idea but whenever he tried to think about something else, he thought of Sheila.

"How long since you've seen Fred?" Ryan asked.

"Two or three years."

Ryan nodded. "I don't know what kind of shape he'll be in. You were right. He did call to cancel the game." His mouth went tight. "I wish I could still play myself."

"If he wanted to cancel—"

"I want him to play," Ryan said, then fell silent.

The club was on East Fifty-fifth Street. Todd held the door for them as they got out. Phil followed slightly behind as they mounted the stairs. At the top Ryan stopped.

"He hates to lose," he said, as Phil came up beside him. "Beat the hell out of him."

Young Fred was waiting for them in the lounge. He sat sprawled in a great wing chair, facing the door. He did not move as they came to greet him.

"Good morning, eminent grandfather."

"It's three in the afternoon."

76

"Morning is a state of mind." He nodded at Phil. "Phil. You're looking fit."

Phil smiled.

"Well, shall we play? Or would either of you like a drink first?"

"I've got the court reserved," Ryan said flatly. "You two get changed. I'll meet you there."

Fred unfolded himself from the chair. He was two years older than Phil, short like his grandfather. Standing between them, Phil felt as though he should hunch. Young Fred had the same loose walk as Ryan, although now it seemed a little more tentative than Phil remembered. He was perfectly groomed—his dark business suit was meticulously tailored to his small body, his hair trimmed short, his rep tie flowed over his collarpin and lay flat against his chest—but underneath it all was a sense of neglect. It showed in the faint pink rim around his eyes and the slackness of the skin on his jaw. Phil had never been so aware of how fleshy his lips were. He had always envied young Fred. Fred's father had died in 1943, at Okinawa, when Fred was seven. Ryan took him and his mother to live in the town house. Ryan raised the boy and Phil had always been jealous of young Fred's life with his grandfather. Now, as he opened the door to the locker room, Phil noticed that his fingernails were manicured like a corpse's.

Thick carpeting muted every sound inside except for the click of billiard balls that came through an arch at the far end. Two older men were playing. They worked around the table with their drinks and cigars, setting them both in special trays as they lined up their shoots. They played naked. Other men sat naked in lounge chairs scattered through the billiard room: some read magazines, others watched a football game on television or dozed. A black uniformed steward passed through noiselessly, delivering drinks and taking orders. He was the same age as the loungers.

Phil had been in the locker rooms of clubs like that before. His father had belonged to one in Hartford. None of them ever as exclusive as Ryan's. This was the only one where the mirrors gleamed over sinks that were dark, polished wood,

77

not porcelain, and where there were no phones for business calls. The naked loungers possessed the room like high priests. Phil's step became light on the carpet. He felt he should whisper.

Fred led him to a closet stocked with athletic supplies. "Just take what you need and meet me at locker twelve." He glanced around the room. "Are you sure you don't want a drink while we're changing?"

"No, thanks."

Phil pulled out a T-shirt, shorts, white sneakers and socks, and a jockstrap. As he left the closet he glanced at the sinks. Each one had a new razor, comb, and brush. Everything in the room was ready for use, yet nothing seemed like a luxury. He felt like a guest in a world of absolute necessity, run by men who understood, as artists understand, the way things must be arranged.

Fred was taking off his shoes when Phil found him. He undressed slowly. There was a drink on the bench beside him. "All set?"

Phil nodded.

"You're going to need a pair of gloves. I'll show you where they are when we're dressed." He nodded at his drink. "You don't mind, do you?"

"No. Not at all." Phil still had trouble getting his voice above a whisper.

"I don't really like the stuff. It's just that it bugs the hell out of eminent grandfather."

Phil smiled weakly. "Do you always call him that?"

Fred disregarded the question. "Well, how have you been, Phil?" He rolled off his socks and stuffed them in his shoes. "When was the last time we saw each other?"

"Two—three years ago? At your wedding."

Fred smiled. "That's all over." He shook his head. "Bad, bad move. After the honeymoon we found out we only liked each other in hotels. How's your wife? Sandra?"

"Sheila."

"Sorry."

"She's fine. A little tired. . . ." His voice trailed off.

78

Fred took off his shorts and pants. He hung them on the thick, molded hangers in the locker.

"Has eminent grandfather sprung his offer yet?"

Phil was taking off his own pants. He could concentrate on the process to mask a reaction. "What makes you think he has an offer?"

"Come on, Phil."

He looked up. Fred held his stare. "No."

"He will. After the handball game. Has gracious grandmother invited you to dinner?"

Phil nodded.

"There will be a crème de menthe thing for dessert. Eminent grandfather will taste it, nod approval to gracious grandmother, who will lower her eyes with an ambiguous mixture of pleasure and contempt. Then he will proceed to offer you a job."

Phil smiled. "Can I count on that?"

"Call me tomorrow if I'm wrong. Like a ritual. It's all ritual."

They were both naked. Phil was aware of a quick glance from Fred, sizing him up as an opponent. He was surprised at how hard Fred's body was. He had not expected it from the slackness in his face. The hair on his chest and stomach was thick and curly. "My brother Esau is an hairy man and I am a smooth one," Fred said. "Let us now don our ritual jockstraps and ritual sneakers and ritual gloves and shorts and shit, all purified by the eunuchs of the Central Athletic Club in the holy sterilizing machines and play our ritual game of handball." He unrolled his jockstrap and stepped into it. "Don't tell eminent grandfather I warned you about the ritual. He'd be crushed."

"Is it really that much of a routine?"

Fred nodded. He did a little knee-bend as he adjusted himself. "He even went through it with me—when I was sixteen. Only then he was still playing himself and it was only an office boy job—but it was exactly the same. I didn't know it then. I only figured it out later, when he couldn't play anymore and I took over the game. It's just as well. It's my only justification for being on the payroll. I was a lousy office boy,

79

bad clerk, inept junior lawyer—but I'm 'a hell of a good handball player,' " He imitated Ryan's voice. "So welcome to my office."

"Does it matter whether you win or lose?" Phil asked.

"To him or to me?"

Phil shrugged as he pulled on his shorts.

"It matters to me." The edge to his voice made Phil look up. Fred's face and body changed as he put on his outfit. The faint, wry smile that had hovered around his lips was gone. His eyes were steady. The muscles in his legs were tight. "It's all I've got," he said simply. "I've never figured out if it matters to him."

Phil could feel his own face go hard in response. "Why the ritual, then?"

Fred put his foot on the bench and leaned toward him. "You don't want to know whether it matters if I win at all. You want to know whether it matters if you lose."

Phil looked down at the sock he was rolling.

"Are you feeling tested, Phil?"

Phil sat down and put on the sock.

"He's got you if you're worried." Fred sat beside him. "You start feeling tested by him and you'll never stop." He lowered his voice. "You know what's the smartest thing to do? You want me to tell you what the smartest thing you could do would be? Tonight, when he makes his offer, in the nicest, boyish way you can, thank him and suggest that perhaps he ought to take the offer and the crème de menthe thing and his compliments to gracious grandmother and insert them. Then go back home and tell Sandra—"

"Sheila—"

"Right. Go home and tell her what you've done and that you're on your own. I know the offer he'll make you. I guarantee you don't want it."

"Why not?"

"The testing never stops. Believe me. Turn it down."

Phil bent over to lace up his sneakers. Fred watched him closely. He shook his head.

"What's wrong?"

"You think this might be a test too, don't you?" Phil shrugged. "It's too late, then. You're already jumping through the hoop."

Phil was growing irritable. Ever since they had arrived at the club he was having trouble matching young Fred with his memory of him. He had always admired the assurance and the polish of the memory; he did not like the man he was now. There was a bitter edge on the most offhand word. His smile was oblique, and Phil hated the uncomfortable feeling that, like the razors and combs and brushes, young Fred was ready for use.

"What do you say we play a little handball?" Phil said flatly.

"Sure thing, champ."

Phil stood up and started toward the courts, getting used to the spring in the sneakers. Fred kept his foot on the bench. As Phil passed he gave him a light, locker-room slap on the buttocks. Phil spun around. The two men held each other's eyes for an instant, smiling tightly. "You forgot about the gloves," Fred said softly. He took his foot off the bench and gestured to the other side of the room. He led Phil to a locker full of gloves and balls.

Phil pulled a pair over his hands and buckled them at the wrist. Fred bounced a small, black ball against the floor once. He flipped it to Phil.

There was a small window with shatterproof glass built into the top of the court. Phil could not see Ryan but he knew he was watching.

Young Fred had said nothing more since they left the clothes locker. His face went tighter, his eyes harder as they approached the court. Phil tossed the hard little ball from hand to hand, determined to keep loose. Fred slammed the door to the four-wall court. Phil jumped and turned it into a limbering movement. He thought of saying something casual: "Nice court," "It's been a while," "Hope my arm holds out." Before he could choose, young Fred's voice rang out from behind like an order. "Visitor's serve!" He sprang to a ready position in front of Phil.

Phil put his hands on his hips. He stared incredulously. For

81

the first time all afternoon he wanted to laugh. Every muscle in Fred's body was tense. His face, even in profile, was savage. He looked more like he was waiting to scrimmage than return a handball.

"Volley for serve?" he asked softly.

"Visitors!" Fred barked without moving.

Grotesque as it was, the stance made Phil nervous. Somewhere above them Ryan was watching. He wondered what he thought of his grandson's attitude, if that was, perhaps, the attitude he should be taking. He hunched his shoulders experimentally and tightened his thigh muscles. It was no good. Phil was used to going limp and loose-jointed before play. He took a deep breath. His heart was beating fast and he pulled in breath to push against it. He glanced at Fred once, wondering how long he would be able to hold that frozen urgent position. Then he dropped the ball and let his own body go as if he were falling after it. He swung. His hand smacked the ball. All the loose, separate limbs pulled together. He lost consciousness of everything but the ball. Fred sprang into action. The ball leaped from wall to wall and Phil met it each time with all the force of his back and shoulder in his hand.

He danced around Fred, oblivious to everything now but the ball. He gave himself up to it, let it lead, sensitive to its rhythm, shifting direction against it, meeting it, and, for an instant, working his own will on it with a stinging palm. Phil loved the game. He loved the speed that forced his concentration on the single, hard, black object as it ricocheted around him; he loved the way the closed court magnified the smack of his own gloved hand against it, and the deeper smack as it hit the wall, and his own grunts as he put his whole body into each swing; he loved the smells of leather and sweat and wax as they grew sharper, and his breath coming more and more quickly. It took only two returns. Everything flew from his consciousness—Sheila, Ryan, his sister, school, his career—all the separate, confusing decisions, the incomprehensible demands for understanding and the urgent, conflicting needs spun together into a ball as tight, as hard as the one he danced

82

against now—and he resolved them all each time he met it in the bright, tingling center of his palm.

The game moved quickly. Even the interruptions when one of them scored a point or they exchanged serves became a part of the flow. Phil's arms began to ache. His lungs strained to pull in air. Sweat plastered his hair against his forehead and trickled down the sides of his face and neck. He rose on the buoyancy of his thighs and embraced the power, the exhilarating sense of power over the ball and his own body as he drove it harder.

His T-shirt clung to his back and his shorts to his buttocks. His sense of time came only from the heat as it intensified the flow of sweat. He was absolutely alone in his concentration on the game. He knew where Fred was every instant, and where he would be the next. He could feel the impact as clearly on Fred's hand as his own. He could measure, as finely as the finest measuring device, every arc of the ball.

Once as they exchanged serves he found himself turned around, facing the back wall. He glanced up and saw Ryan's head in the window above. The old man's face was impassive. His mouth was tight and his yes hard as they had been in the car. Phil looked away quickly and pretended he had not seen him at all. He was embarrassed, as though he had caught Ryan spying. His face flushed even hotter for an instant. He turned toward the front wall, trying to look unconcerned, but he knew the man's eyes were on him. The back of his neck went tight. He worked his shoulders to loosen it. Fred served and Phil lost the point on the first return. He fumbled the next two. He wants to see how I play under pressure, Phil thought. He knew I'd spot him sooner or later. He was just waiting. . . . He could feel his whole body tighten. He tried to break through and recapture the freedom and absorption in the sheer joy of the game. It was turning into a hands-down match for young Fred. Phil could sense him loosening and driving in as he tightened. He lost the next volley. As the ball sped past him he spun around and glanced up again. Ryan was smiling. This time Phil did not turn away. He stared up trying to figure out if the smile was one of encouragement or triumph. He drew his wrist across his forehead to wipe away the sweat. His arm was as wet as his face. He breathed heavily; his shoulder helped his lungs work.

"Let's play!" Fred's voice was sharp and impatient.

"Just hold it!" Phil shouted angrily. He dropped his arms to his side and remained looking up at the window. Ryan's face never moved. After a long time Phil nodded and returned a smile as hard, as uncompromising as Ryan's. It didn't matter anymore whether Ryan was testing him. He lowered his eyes to Fred. His T-shirt was gray against the wet, black hair on his chest. His face was red and his whole body heaved while he waited to serve. Fred was feeling tested, too. But Fred hated the test and Phil loved and welcomed it. The idea of test had leaped into his head at the Ryan's house because he had wanted the game to be one. Every game was a test for Phil. That was why he loved playing so much. He never felt more alive than when he met that kind of challenge, and proved himself against someone else—and, even more exhilarating this time, proved himself under the eyes of a man like Ryan. Even if Ryan hadn't intended a test, even if the old man had told him he hadn't, Phil would have made it one, just as he made the man's ambiguous smile a challenge by returning it.

He nodded once at Fred and leaped to position. He'd have no more trouble. He understood why Fred was such a good opponent, yet so grotesque. Ryan's grandson played his game as though winning meant an end to the test. It made his play savage and desperate. Phil played his game as though it were his first, and winning meant a chance to play more, to prove himself over and over.

Fred served and Phil returned it with a new, triumphant drive. He new he would win and he knew, as well, that Ryan would offer the job and that he would take it and join the world of men like Ryan and all the others lounging in the locker room—and he'd meet every challenge they threw at him with the same force he put into this swing, the same endurance and pride in his own power. His hand met the ball and sent it back fair and far out of young Fred's reach.

84

It was still a hard victory. By the end of the game Phil was wrung out. He made the last point and turned automatically toward the window. Ryan was not there. Phil turned to Fred.

"Great game." He unbuckled his right glove to shake hands. Fred left the court before it was off. Phil stared after him. He finished getting out of both gloves and followed him to the showers. Fred was already peeling off his T-shirt.

"You all right?"

"Great. Why?" It was muffled as he pulled the shirt over his head.

"You walked off the court so fast."

"Had to get out of this outfit before I drowned or stank myself to death." He braced himself against the wall with one hand and pulled off his sneakers.

Phil relaxed. "I was afraid that something was wrong."

"Nothing wrong." He said it heartily and smiled at Phil. The smile was broad and open at the mouth. The eyes flashed bright and cold from behind it. Phil froze. "Good game." Fred slapped him on the back. It stung against the damp shirt. "Do you think you passed?" He stripped off his socks and shorts.

"Come on, Fred," Phil said gently.

"I mean it." He maintained his aggressive cheerfulness. "You really won it. Hands down."

"You gave me a run for it."

"No contest. *Triomphe. La gloire.*"

"OK," Phil said uneasily. "Thanks."

"But did you pass?" He pulled off his jockstrap and flipped it to Phil. "That's the question." He stepped into a glass-enclosed shower booth and turned on the water.

Phil threw the jockstrap in the laundry chute, stripped off his own outfit, and got in a shower. He started with warm water and slowly let it go colder. This was always one of the best parts for Phil, letting the sweat wash away, then soaping himself and letting the cold spray work like a massage. Now, though, he could not enjoy it. He was still tense and angry. He wanted to get clean and dry and away from Fred as fast as he could. Ryan had told him Fred hated to lose, but he hadn't expected the viciousness. Phil's jaw clenched when he thought of Fred's eyes. The hatred unnerved him—even more the intensity behind it—and behind that something so desperate it frustrated Phil's anger.

"Say, Phil." Fred called to him from the next stall. His voice was casual, as though nothing had passed between them. Phil wondered if he might have imagined the hostility. Perhaps he had simply braced himself for it because of what Ryan had said. "About the job."

Phil smiled. "I know. I'll call you tomorrow."

"It's not for the New York office, you know."

"What do you mean?"

"It's Connecticut. He wants you near Northfield." Phil stopped smiling. "Can you hear me?"

"Sure can." He lowered his head and let the water work on the back of his neck.

"Your mother called last week."

"I know. Renata's getting married."

"They've known about that for a couple of months. She called to get e.g. to give you a job near home." Phil raised his head sharply. "Can you hear me?"

"Sure can." He said it more softly.

"I guess with Renata moving out and all. . . ."

"How do you know about all this?"

Phil heard him turn off the water. His voice came through more clearly. "How do I know about the crème de menthe thing? Another tradition. Your family. Mine. And the way they look after their young. It's enough to break your heart." Phil was finished with his shower but he kept the water on. "Besides, they'll probably tell you your mother's involved. Maybe even without your asking. If there's one thing you can say about my grandparents it's that they're candid. They can afford to be. Right? With the world by the balls? Anyway I thought I'd give you a chance to ask if they didn't volunteer the information."

"Thanks." Phil turned off the water and stood in the silence a moment. On the other side of the glass Fred dried himself.

Phil slid back the door. Fred grinned up at him. His face was open and friendly. He nodded toward a cupboard. "Towels," he said.

Phil took one out.

"Can I challenge you to a game of pool and a drink before we get dressed?"

"Your grandfather's waiting."

"We can invite him in."

"No, thanks."

Fred shrugged. "Well, look. I'm not eating with you, so I think I'll see if I can drum up a game. You don't mind, do you?"

"No. Not at all."

"You know where to find everything. Combs, brushes, razor. . . ."

"Sure."

Fred extended his hand. Phil shook it. "Good game. Thanks." He disappeared into the lounge.

Phil finished drying as the billiard balls started to click.

3

Sheila

November 17–
November 18, 1962

PHIL HAD left a five-dollar bill with her earlier that week. Sheila had spent it all on cigarettes but she found a dime wedged in a corner at the bottom of her pocketbook. Dr. Rankin had told her to call Phil to pick her up. She would have liked to leave on her own, but she needed something to wear. The only things Phil had brought were fresh nightgowns and pajamas. At first she had thought, I'll wear what I came in. Then she realized she was wearing that.

There was a pay phone at the end of the corridor. Sheila felt out of place as she walked to it. She ought to have been limping or bending over some fresh incision. She felt positively aggressive as she walked upright past half-open doors. Faces turned toward her and she wished her robe were not quite so yellow.

Phil would not be home now. Her mother might be. That would be an ordeal, but she did not want to wait until dinnertime. Now that she had asked to leave and Rankin agreed, she was impatient. Besides, it probably wouldn't be any less of an ordeal with Phil. Only different.

She closed the door to the phone booth, dropped in her

dime, and dialed. The main thing now was to avoid any awkwardness. She prepared her greeting. She had a flow of directions ready for May when she answered. The phone clicked.

"Hello?" The piping voice on the other end was Vikki's, slightly muffled because she still forgot to speak into the mouthpiece.

Sheila had wanted longer to prepare for Vikki. She covered the phone.

"Hello?" Vikki repeated it.

Sheila took a breath, then spoke through her fingers just as she'd seen it done in the movies. She raised her voice and affected an English accent. "Hello. Might I speak to your mother, please?"

There was a short silence.

"Grandma's taking care of me." Sheila heard fumbling on the other end, then the outlines of her mother's voice. Vikki said, "Somebody wants Mommy." May's voice came into focus. "Hello? This is Mrs. Gaynor's mother. Can I help you?"

"Mom? It's Sheila. Don't let Vikki know it's me."

"Yes? What is it?" May said it in the same tone of voice. Sheila sank onto the little bench, relieved. "One moment, please." May said something to Vikki. When she returned to the phone her voice was low and trembling. "Freddie? How are you, darling?"

Sheila smiled. Her mother hadn't called her Freddie since the wedding. "I'm all right. I want to come home."

"Is it all right? The doctor, I mean. Did he say it was all right?"

"Everything's fine."

"Oh, Freddie, honey. I'm so glad to hear your voice."

Sheila nodded. "I know. Now, listen. Can you come and get me? I wanted to go home alone but I don't have anything to wear. There's a blue knit dress in the closet that I know is clean. Bring that one. Leave Vikki with Estelle Donado. She's got two kids close to Vikki's age and she's always home. On the fifth floor. OK?"

"Of course, darling. The blue knit."

"And there's a pair of black low heels, probably under the bed."

"I put them away."

"And my medium-weight coat. How is it out? Will that be enough?"

"It should be. Oh, Freddie, I'm so glad."

"Look, Mom, don't tell Vikki where you're going. OK? And don't rush her off to Estelle. Just take her down and once she's settled in and playing go back up and pack."

"All right."

"I'm in room—" She paused. "I don't know the number. It's the fifteenth floor. Just ask the nurse at the hall desk. All right?"

"Fine."

"I don't want to stay on the phone any more, in case Vikki comes back."

"I understand."

"I'll see you soon, then."

"Yes, darling."

Sheila hung up. The dime fell in the collection box but she still automatically felt in the return. She closed her eyes. It would not be easy. She thought she'd be able to plan all her greetings, map out responses. There would always be the surprises, the challenges and measures of how far along she really was. And aftertastes. She had gotten through that one. No one was hurt, but now she had to admit to herself she had panicked when she heard Vikki's voice.

May arrived a half hour later with a shopping bag full of Sheila's things. The bag said, DON'T BUY JUDY BOND BLOUSES. They were the only kind May used.

Sheila sat on the edge of the bed with one knee up and her arms around it. She had hoped to be able to tell how she looked from her mother's face, but May registered nothing. She paused in the doorway, smiled, and came over, quickly kissed Sheila on the forehead.

"I brought everything you asked for," she said and got to work unloading the bag. Her voice was a familiar mixture of warmth and efficiency, but Sheila knew she was controlling it.

May Kahn had turned fifty the April before. She was a sturdily built woman, just beginning to spread around the hips. She wore her husband's plaid car coat, the same kind Sheila had seen her in every autumn since she could remember, with the sleeves a little too long and the shoulders at a comic droop. May believed autumn and spring coats were extravagant. A heavy winter coat made sense, and sweaters when it was chilly, but to spend all that money for the two or three weeks in between was outrageous. So she used Bernie's cast-off car coats and somehow managed to find herself in them all the way from October to January.

Her hair and skin were dark like Sheila's. Her lips were small and delicate, and the nose, which had been fixed, was straight. Only the forehead and the skin around the eyes had prominent lines, as though age were seeping down from under her hair.

"I couldn't find the blue knit, but I brought this one." She unfolded a cream-colored wool dress with a white leather belt. It was the one Sheila bought at Saks on the afternoon she had started for the museum. "It looked new. The tag was still on it."

"I never wore it."

"I also brought a skirt and blouse in case you—"

"It's all right." Sheila stood up and took the dress. "I'll wear this."

"Here's the underwear. I brought a slip, too. I know how you are with wool."

"Thanks." She started into the bathroom.

"Freddie?" May went to Sheila and took her daughter's face in her hands. "You look fine. You look just—" She pulled Sheila toward her and lightly kissed her cheek. Sheila went into the bathroom to change.

She slipped on her panties and hooked her bra clumsily. Her impatience had been mounting since she'd spoken to May on the phone. The room had become intolerable, not so much because it was Bernie's anymore, but because she was finished with it. She hated hanging around.

91

She put on her slip and worked her way into the dress. It had been snug in the dressing room at Saks. Sheila hadn't cared. She had even been amused at the lifeless way the salesgirl admired it when she realized Sheila would buy it. Now it hung a little loose. She surprised herself in the mirror. She had got used to the woman in pajamas and a yellow robe. The dress made her a stranger, drawn and tight-mouthed.

"Freddie? Is everything all right?" May called from the other room.

Sheila wondered at the idea that anyone could call that middle-aged stranger Freddie. "I'll be out in a second." She could not reach the back to zip it all the way. "Can you give me a hand?" She left the bathroom. May was collecting things for the shopping bag. When Sheila came out, May quickly crumpled a Kleenex and dropped it in the wastebasket. Her nose was red.

"These dresses were not designed for people who live alone." She turned her back to her mother. May zipped her up. "Thanks. You can leave the magazines."

"Are you sure? There might be some recipes. . . ."

Sheila slipped into her shoes, went back to the bathroom, scooped up the toilet articles, and brought them back to the bag. The sound of her shoes was loud and her body felt funny on top of them. May had wedged the magazines in with the clothes. Sheila pulled them out.

"I think that's it." She surveyed the room without really looking.

"Was the room all right?"

Sheila tightened. May looked away. "I'm glad to be finished with it." She bent to pick up the shopping bag.

"Let me." May got to it before her. "You take your pocketbook."

In the elevator Sheila concentrated on the arrow of the floor marker. May darted quick, worried glances at her. Halfway down, May laughed tentatively. "I was so angry at your father. Can you imagine the spectacle he made of himself at the florist's? Every time he ordered another arrangement the salesman's eyes got wider. He's such a baby. Of course, I'm used to it, but I was so worried it would upset you."

"Why did you think that?"

"Oh, I don't know." She fumbled with the paper handles of the shopping bag. "He just doesn't know when to stop. And I was afraid you'd be upset at the expense—even though you never have to worry about that," she added quickly. "Anyway, I guess it was all right, after all. Wasn't it?" She threw another quick look at Sheila. "You'd think after all these years I'd have learned that people love your father just as he is—and that they understand that he means well. . . ." She laughed nervously. "And I certainly should trust you to understand. After all. . . ."

Sheila nodded and smiled. She kept her eyes on the arrow.

"I used to die a thousand deaths until I realized that."

"Realized what?"

"That everyone loves your father. They all understand it's his nature to give like that. Give. Give. Give. I used to just fall apart until Freda Rempel said to me one day, she said, 'May, it's just that his heart's so big he has to do that to relieve the pressure.' After that I realized that everyone understood." They reached the lobby. Sheila started out. May kept pace without breaking the flow. "Still I sometimes just get so embarrassed with strangers." She shook her head. "He's such a baby. Where are you going?"

Sheila had started toward the desks at the far end of the lobby.

"Have to check out."

"That's all taken care of."

"When?"

"Before I went upstairs. I took care of everything, darling."

Sheila nodded and took a deep breath. "OK." She marked it off in her mind as a stopping place. It was a natural part of the flowers and the room and the nurses, and she had already conceded those to Bernie and May. Besides, she had not signed herself in. Maybe it had been a little presumptuous to look forward to signing herself out.

She stood a moment, still nodding at her mother. May smiled back at her. "Was that all right, darling?"

"Fine. Just fine."

"I just thought it would be easier."

"It is. It's fine." But as she buttoned her coat and they started for the main door, Sheila marked it as the time when the refusals would begin.

She braced herself for the shock of the cold autumn air. She had forgotten how deceptive the city weather was. It was manageable at first, like a lightly chilled blanket, and the mildness surprised her. Sheila relaxed and started up Amsterdam Avenue. It was only when they hit the corner that the wind came up from 112th Street and she remembered the treachery of the cross-streets. It doused her awake.

Late-afternoon crowds clustered around the bus stop near the Columbia dormitories. At the main campus entrance on 116th Street the ragged traffic was starting to get heavy with students, clerks, and women with carriages and children in tow. A young man in a T-shirt dodged cars against the light and disappeared into John Jay Hall. From the window on the fifteenth floor the street had looked still, as though the whole city had taken time out with her. She had carried the stillness from the room, but there was nothing in the street to match it. The buses had been picking up the crowds, the mothers had congregated around the plaza fountains, and someone had been dodging traffic every afternoon. She had been alone. Leaving the hospital meant rejoining the others. Everything turned familiar—her shoes pushing against the pavement, the smell of the mysterious steam that rose from the manhole covers, the set of her own shoulders against the cold as she approached the big intersection at 116th Street. They passed under the Law School Bridge and she recognized the tightening just below her stomach. Before it had simply been a part of her life on the street. She had taken it for granted. Now she knew it was a sign of how much she dreaded going back to the apartment. She slowed down, wishing she could stay on the street, suspended between the hospital room and 118th Street. She stared up through the end of the tunnel.

"We're almost home," May said. She shivered. "Maybe I should have brought you a heavier coat."

94

"Let's go get a cup of coffee."

"I'll make you one as soon as we get home."

"There's a little place on Amsterdam," Sheila said. She tried to make it sound casual. "I just feel like getting something before we go home. Do you mind?"

"No. Not at all. Are you sure you don't want to—"

"It's just a little past a Hundred Eighteenth."

The drugstore had a small fountain with three narrow booths across the aisle. It was overheated, but every time the front door opened, cold air puffed on their necks.

Sheila and May crowded into a booth. They kept their unbuttoned coats on. Sheila leaned her shoulder against a Formica wall at the inside end. They had hit the afternoon lull. A policeman waited near the register for a take-out order.

The counterman smiled at Sheila as he whipped out his check pad. "Haven't seen you around in a while."

Sheila smiled back in confusion. For a moment she thought he would use his pad to take notes on her absence. She also remembered that she used to know his name. The smile went on a little too long.

"What are you going to have, darling?" May prompted gently.

Sheila sat up. "Oh, just a cup of coffee. I only want something to warm up with."

"I'll have tea," May said.

"There's a fifty-cent minimum at the booth."

"That's all right," Sheila said quickly.

"Oh, Freddie, get something else. We've got to pay for it anyway."

"No. That's OK."

"An English muffin or something. We can bring it home to Vikki."

"You can move to the counter if you want to, ma'am," the counterman said to May.

"Just bring us coffee and tea. OK?" Sheila said.

"I can't stand it. Fifty cents for a cup of tea. I'll never get it down." May looked at the counterman. "Bring us each a

95

Danish." She leaned toward Sheila. "For me, darling. All right? You know how I am."

"Just coffee for me."

"Then bring two Danishes for me," May said. "And put one on her check." She patted Sheila's wrist. "Vikki will like it."

The counterman held his pencil suspended. The policeman at the register called, "Hey, Kim, those burgers are frying up!"

Sheila's jaw tightened at the back. She closed her eyes lightly and nodded, thinking, Yes, that's his name. Kim.

May leaned back as he left. "I'm sorry, darling. I—"

"Don't be."

"What?"

"Don't be sorry."

"It's just that I know how you hate it when your father makes scenes in a restaurant."

"That's different." It was true that she hated going to restaurants with Bernie. He always managed to find a reason for sending food back. Even when he was justified Sheila would sit there ashamed at the clumsy way he handled it. She would end up angry at him and angry at herself for being ashamed of him. May never humiliated her in quite the same way, but she did hate the way her mother hung on to everything she did by apologizing for it.

"Tell me about things at home. How has it been?"

May flicked her wrist to dismiss it. "Vikki and I are pals. You know that. And Phil's never home, so there was plenty of time to take care of everything. Phil wanted to give me the bedroom and sleep on the couch but I wouldn't let him. So Dad bought a cot before he went back to Woodview and we put it in Vikki's room. It's marvelous. It folds up into practically nothing. You can keep it in a closet or just any old corner."

"I'll let you take it back to Woodview with you."

"We'll see. It's yours now. And it's good to have for emergencies."

Sheila smiled. "I'm not planning any more emergencies."

"Oh, I didn't mean that," May said, flustered. "I just meant unexpected guests and things like that. Anyway, it made it all

96

much easier. When Vikki woke up in the middle of the night I was right there for her."

"She woke up?"

May hesitated. "Every night. She doesn't for you?"

Sheila shook her head.

"That's funny," May said. "I guess I just took it for granted she did. You know why? Because you used to. Every night until you were six or seven, you'd wake up at least once a night. Don't you remember?"

"No."

"When you were still in a crib you'd call out and I'd weave down the hall and hold you for a couple of minutes, then weave back again. By the time you were two and a half I could do it without waking up. Then, when you were out of a crib, you'd come down the hall yourself and get into bed with Daddy and me for a couple of minutes, then get out again and go back to your own bed. You don't remember? We used to call you our night spook."

"I bet I was asleep, too."

"I never thought of that. I bet you were." She laughed. "Anyway, the first night I was there and Vikki called out, it was like being twenty-six again. Daddy and I were in your room. That was the first night. He had to go back toWoodview the next afternoon, but we spent the morning getting the cot for me and the flowers for you. Anyway, it was the most natural thing in the world. Vikki called out. I was up like a shot. And you know how long it usually takes me to get out of bed." She paused. "I sat there holding Vikki and I was so groggy from the day I forgot all about what had happened or why I was there and it just might as well have been you in my lap."

The counterman came with the order. May straightened up and rested her fingertips on the edge of the table. She looked like a curious child when waiters served her.

"Are you sure you don't want anything?" May asked. "It's on me."

Sheila smiled and shook her head.

May poured sugar and stirred the tea with her left hand.

97

Her wedding ring made a little arc. Sheila stared at it, then at her mother's face. She tried to disentangle the face and hands from the thousands of memories and assumptions she had invested them with over so many years, to see the woman as someone detached from her. It was impossible. The skin around the ring was mottling and crosshatched with tiny lines. The hair was graying. But even while Sheila recognized the specific signs that May was a person apart, as subject to time and change as herself, she could still only see her as she always had. There was still no difference between the body of the woman who sat there stirring her tea and the one who held her when she woke at night; between the face that smiled at her now, edged with concern because she had tried to commit suicide, and the face that smiled in open approval when she brought her report cards home. Sheila was convinced that she had only to cut the tangled threads to extricate the image of her mother from the woman who sat there, staring vaguely at the paperback book rack as she spoke, and she would be able to see, as she had never been able to see before, her mother on one side, herself on the other.

"Diana Brautigan came over a couple of times," May said. She shook her head. "Do you know she doesn't look older than she did when you two were roommates? How does she do it?"

"I wouldn't know," Sheila said dryly.

"And her little girl. Dana?"

"Donna."

"Donna. I knew it was some peculiar name. She's as pretty as her mother—only in a different way. She and Vikki play beautifully together. Don't they? Diana's girl tends to be a little pushy, though. Have you ever noticed that?"

Sheila did not respond.

"But she's a dear child," May said quickly. "And I suppose she's good for Vikki. Vikki's such a little lady. I suppose she needs someone strong like that to draw her out. Her mother's a pretty strong woman, too."

"Diana?"

"She was telling me about how she got the role in a television show. *The Outlaws* or something."

98

"*The Criminals.*"

"She really is amazing."

"She just knows what she wants to do."

"Could you do that sort of thing?"

"If I knew what I wanted."

"But you do know." May paused. "Oh, I suppose if it came to protecting Vikki or standing behind Phil you could do just about anything. I guess I could, too, if it came to you or Daddy."

Sheila stared at her mother, still trying desperately to make the separation. If only she wasn't wearing that damned car coat, she thought. It was so much a part of May it was hard for Sheila to tell whether she ever responded at all now to her mother or just to the coat. She picked up the coffee cup and held it tightly in both hands trying to control an impulse to tear through the red and black plaid and touch the wrinkling skin on her mother's neck. Anything to break through and find some fresh way to look at the woman.

"Daddy called last night to find out how everything is. He calls every night, but last night he sounded especially lonely. Everyone in Woodview's been having him to dinner." She clicked her tongue. "He's such a babe in the woods when he's alone. I know he wanted to ask how much longer I'd be staying, but he didn't—and I couldn't tell him. Your phone call was such a surprise. He's going to be happy when I come home tonight."

Sheila looked up, startled. She had known May would leave as soo as she was well enough to come home, but she had never allowed herself to really examine the prospect of that first night alone. Phil would be working and she would be home with Vikki like all the other nights. For an instant she wanted to plead with her mother to stay, at least until morning. Until this moment she had been able to disregard the small, spinning ball of panic in her stomach. Just being near her mother had kept it under control, and even while she knew it was an illusion she could rest secure and believe that May would be able to take over if her own fear got out of hand. Yet at the same time that she frantically searched for some graceful way to keep her mother with her, she knew that she mustn't. This was her chance to recognize May as a woman with her own life, her own obligations, and to let her go without adding the burden of a concern that should not be hers.

Sheila remembered all the times before when, exhausted, she would find some way to get May into the city to take over for an afternoon. She would never ask for help outright. Sometimes she would suggest to Vikki that they call, just to talk. Other times she would come across a dress or a bag she thought might be right for May and buy it with May's charge card. Then she would call and ask when May was planning to be in the city again and explain that if it were soon she wouldn't bother to mail it out. May always understood and arrived before Sheila had to admit what she really needed. It was always just before she went over the edge of exhaustion. Sheila would stand on the brink, carrying Vikki, the apartment, Phil, and the extra weight that she could not even identify, her arms aching, until May came into view. With one last effort she would fling them all on her mother before she dropped. Then, even while she was falling into the weightless afternoon, she would wonder if perhaps she might not have been able to wait it out another day, or week, and that would bring with it a sense of failure. Sheila would shower and lock herself in the bedroom to sleep on those afternoons. When she woke May would be there, waiting for her, ready to dump it all back in her arms, and after her mother was gone Sheila felt abandoned, cheated, thinking, If only she'd given me one more hour. Then she burned with humiliation.

Sheila remembered it all as she stared at May over her coffee cup. This last time, though, May had not arrived in time. That was why now she could not feel cheated or abandoned. All she could do was to concentrate on the ball of panic, knowing it was she, and she only, who must carry the weight.

"And Vikki," May was saying. "I can't wait to see her face when she sees you."

100

Sheila put down the cup and fumbled in her bag for a cigarette.

"You're still smoking?"

She nodded.

May laughed a little shrilly. "I don't know why I thought they might have cured you of that in the hospital."

"What bus do you want to make back to Woodview, Mom?"

"Oh, I don't know. I thought I'd make sure you were settled in first, maybe cook dinner for all of you. That is, if you want me there when Phil comes home," she said quickly. "Of course, it would be a treat if I get back in time to make a late dinner for Daddy. I could do that if I caught the five-thirty." She hesitated. "Whatever you'd prefer, darling."

For the first time she looked directly at Sheila. Her eyes were determinedly wide and cheerful. Her mother was desperately casting about for the right thing to say, torn between her and her father. May had been carrying her own weight, with her own aching arms, and Sheila was still as much a part of that weight for May as Vikki was for Sheila. She wondered whose arms May relied on to carry the burden through her own short, impossible respites.

"You want to get home, don't you?"

"It honestly doesn't matter. The main thing now is what you think would be best. Daddy doesn't know you're home yet, so he won't be waiting for me. . . . I'm free as a bird."

Sheila smiled. "Me too."

It stopped May. She burst into a surprised laugh. "That's right. No one else knows you're—"

The little ball of panic turned to a giggle. She reached across and touched May's arm.

May sputtered. "But that's—"

"Absurd," Sheila said and the laughter burst out of them both at the same time, an explosion of relief and a compassionate exchange of the incomprehensibility of both their situations. "Fugitives! We could skip the country."

"Or go to a movie."

They stared at each other, then let it bubble out again.

101

"That's what I love about you," Sheila gasped. "You think so big."

"We could put on disguises."

"Mustaches." Both women shrieked. "And hijack a shopping cart."

"Stop," May pleaded.

"Hide out in the dressing rooms at Ohrbach's." Sheila barely got the words out.

May wiped her eyes with a napkin, squealing and sighing. "Oh, God. That's enough."

Sheila calmed down, too, in little flurries. They lapsed into silence, punctuated with small, reminiscent laughs. May turned back to her teacup and stirred it distractedly. Sheila finished her coffee. She concentrated on the burning end of her cigarette. The silence turned awkward. The intimacy of their laughter embarrassed them.

"Are you going to eat your Danish?"

May jumped. She seemed to notice the pastry for the first time. "I'm not really—" But she broke one halfheartedly. "Maybe Vikki and Phil for dessert, darling."

Sheila shook her head.

"Well, then." She pulled some napkins out of the dispenser and spread them on the table. "I'll take them on the bus with me." She wrapped the napkins around them and dropped them in the shopping bag.

"We'd better get going if you want to make the five-thirty." Sheila adjusted her coat over her shoulders. "You've probably got to get your things together."

"There's very little."

Sheila caught the counterman's eye for the check. It was $1.03. May glanced at it as she slipped out of the booth. "Taxes. Taxes. Taxes. City. State. I'll never get used to it. You never know what you're going to pay."

Sheila shrugged. "You just always plan for things to be a little more expensive."

They went to the register. May put down the shopping bag while she paid. Sheila watched the hastily wrapped napkins unfold on the top of the pile.

102

The front door of the apartment opened onto a long, narrow corridor. At the far end was the living room. Sheila usually left Vikki's tricycle and wagon, her doll carriage, and the family's boots and rubbers against the hallway walls. She used a collapsible shopping cart for trips downstairs to the A & P and up to the washing machines on the roof. She kept that in the corridor, too. It was always filled with clothes she had just brought down or was getting ready to take up. Vikki's coat usually hung on the closet doorknob. Sheila draped hers over the cart. She was constantly losing gloves and finding them, days later, freshly laundered.

Over the three years they had lived there, Sheila had come to think of the corridor as an extension of the apartment house hallway. Sometimes she would even let some of the clutter spill out on the other side of the front door.

She stood behind May as she unlocked it now. It swung open on a clear view to the living room. May had waxed the wood floor and washed all the fingerstains and wheel scars off the walls. Soft light came through the living room windows at the far end.

Sheila stood outside while May went in and took off her coat.

"Come on in, darling."

Sheila shook her head. "Wrong apartment."

May blushed. "It was empty so much of the day, I used the time to do a little work. Vikki helped."

"It's a goddamned bowling alley."

May smiled.

Sheila followed her mother in. She stood behind May as she hung up her coat. "Let me take yours." Sheila kept her hands in her pockets. The coat hung loosely from her shoulders.

"Let me leave it. A little chilly." She avoided May's eyes. Her jaw really did feel tight as though she were just about to shiver against the cold. "Where is everything?" she asked as she wandered from room to room.

"The rubbers and the shopping cart are in the closet."

"How did you fit them in?"

"Well, you know there was a huge empty carton taking up half the closet."

"That was my closet carton."

"I asked Phil about it but he didn't even know it was there."

"It's been there three years."

"Oh, dear, were you saving it for something?"

"No. I guess I just thought it was too big to throw away. I was always afraid I'd throw something valuable out with it."

"It was empty. I made sure of that."

Sheila nodded. "It always has been."

The Formica play table in Vikki's room gleamed white. Someone had stacked her coloring books on one side with a plastic box of crayons beside them. Toys filled all the shelves. A stuffed dog lay on Vikki's pillow. Sheila walked to the middle of the room and revolved slowly. The doll carriage stood near the door with three dolls asleep inside. Behind the doors was a folded cot.

Sheila nodded. "This is what I meant."

"What, darling?" May looked alarmed.

She smiled. "Everytime I tried to clean up. This is what I meant."

May followed her to the other rooms. They were all the same. Whenever Sheila tried to do a job like that it always felt as though she had simply forced all the confusion behind some imaginary barricade, a shaky barrier between herself and chaos. After a couple of hours she could see it all seeping out from underneath. But this was the real thing. Nothing was hidden. It was all there. The pans on the kitchen wall, the stacks of magazines, the throw pillows that had always seemed covered with cat hair even though they did not own a cat. They were all open, available, but tamed somehow. Sheila stood in the middle of the living room. She dug her hands deeper in her coat pockets. Nothing threatened her. There were no webs to avoid in the corners of the walls, no streaks on the molding.

"Well, well, well."

"I thought it could be like a fresh start," May said shyly.

Sheila took off her coat and started to drape it over the sofa arm. She stopped herself. "I'll go hang it up."

"Maybe I should get Vikki," May said.

Sheila's rhythm barely broke as she went to the closet. "Good idea."

May passed her. "I'll only be a second."

"Mom?"

May stopped at the door.

"Thank you for doing all this. I really did need your help."

May stammered. "That's what mothers are for."

"Is it?"

"I'll get Vikki."

Sheila wandered back to the living room. May hadn't left out ashtrays. She found them stacked in a kitchen cabinet and scattered them around on all the surfaces. She sat with her feet tucked underneath her at the far end of the sofa. There wasn't much time to prepare for Vikki. Sheila had been avoiding the thought of that first meeting. Vikki would be bigger. That was the way it always worked. Even after those day-long separations when May took over, Sheila would always feel a little shock at how much bigger Vikki was when she saw her again. She always remembered her six months younger. That did not bother her now. That same little shock would probably be there no matter how much she prepared herself. What frightened Sheila was the terrible, empty indifference she felt. If she had been able to lie to herself she might have simply latched on to the fear and tried to convince herself it was that first awkward moment between mother and daughter frightening her, but she knew it was not that. Her own indifference came first and that was what terrified her now.

She ran her fingers over the coarse, sand-colored upholstery. Before today, if there was one thing she could never have accused herself of it was indifference to Vikki. From the moment she suspected she was pregnant her child had filled her consciousness. She was determined to do it right. Everything else in her life had happened before she could make her own choice. With her family, her school, even with Phil and

105

her marriage she was never conscious of a beginning. She was always finding herself in the middle of a situation. Only then would she start to work back to the first decision that led her there. When she found it she could never believe the choice was hers. They were all like her father's presents, the electric can opener, the unbreakable amber glassware, the fiberglass shower curtain. She could use them all, but they were never what she needed and never quite right even for what they were.

Vikki was nobody's gift. She was Sheila's and Sheila cherished that knowledge even while she carried the baby inside her, not yet knowing what it was that her body was making, knowing only it was she, now, and she alone who shaped it. After Vikki was born, and in spite of the fact that Sheila had not been awake at the birth, she was still sure she could make her daughter's childhood clean, painless, filled with joy. Her own might have been like that if only May and Bernie had been as conscious as she and Phil. When Sheila thought back on her own childhood she remembered only ambiguity. She remembered May, always so cheerful and busy, with periodic migraines when they had to turn off all the lights in the house, unplug the phone, and walk on tiptoe. She remembered Bernie, bursting in the front door with his arms full, dropping all his packages to sweep her up, cover her face and stomach with kisses, then leaving after supper and before her bath for a gin game. She remembered playing happily in her own room and wondering why she made her mother have headaches and her father leave the house every night, and why they never told her outright it was her fault. She remembered confusion and she was determined to make Vikki's memories clear ones. Vikki would remember safety and unclouded love. No one could have been more supremely conscious of what she was about than Shiela. The infant was fed on demand. Sheila slept with her ears cocked. There was one night when she had fallen asleep after making love with Phil. She heard Vikki whimper for a feeding. Sheila could feel the sperm dripping down her thigh as she stumbled to the nursery and undid her top. Vikki's gums had stopped hurting her and she felt as though love were streaming out of her everywhere. It had been like a sign that she was right and she imagined that Vikki was sucking in that sense of well-being.

There were other signs as Vikki grew. Her delicate beauty, her laughter, and, as young as she was, the clear evidence of her gentleness and sensitivity. Vikki walked at ten months; she spoke in sentences before she was two. It all confirmed Sheila's devotion to the course she had chosen. She took Vikki out to play where all the mothers congregated—at the Riverside sandboxes, around the fountains in front of the Low Library, near the sprinklers on Morningside Drive. She talked brightly with the other women, but she kept her attention on Vikki. If there was a sign of trouble she moved in, calmly, unobtrusively, and simply maneuvered Vikki out of it. It was a talent she had with adults as well. Sheila hated scenes. They were stupid, unnecessary, and even if the rest of the world thrived on them, she would teach her daughter to hold scenes in the same contempt she did.

When the trouble with Vikki began, Sheila's devotion grew confused and resentful, yet she still could not conceive of a time when she would think of her daughter with indifference. Phil began to question the way Sheila treated Vikki. He wondered if, perhaps, she was not too concerned, too protective. Sheila dismissed it. Phil persisted. She grew irritable. One morning the fall before, they had taken the Sunday *Times* to the plaza in front of Low Library. The plaza was deserted. Vikki played near the dry fountain. Phil and Sheila sat on a little strip of grass with the paper spread around them. Sheila was just about to pour some coffee from a thermos when Vikki scrambled up on the fountain and tried to walk around the rim. Sheila dropped her cup and started toward her.

"Leave her alone." Phil grabbed her arm and pulled her down.

"She'll get hurt."

"Let her."

"It's all concrete around there."

She tried to pull away but Phil held her firmly.

"If she hurts herself—"

107

"If she hurts herself she'll find out what it's like to hurt herself."

"Do you want her to?"

"It wouldn't be a bad idea."

The rim was four feet high. Vikki slid one foot next to the other in a slow, little Chinese shuffle. Sheila stayed in Phil's grip, her eyes riveted. Vikki moved toward the far side of the fountain. Her feet slipped. She teetered.

"Vikki!"

She turned toward Sheila and lost her balance. Sheila pulled out of Phil's hold as Vikki disappeared. When Sheila reached her, Vikki was screaming. Blood covered one side of her face. Sheila scooped her up and carried her back to the grass. She rocked her and made low comforting sounds.

"You're getting blood all over you." Phil took out a handkerchief. Sheila pulled it out of his hand.

"I'll do it." Her eyes flashed.

"She took a bad fall, Sheila. That's all that happened."

Vikki's wails grew louder. Sheila tightened her hold. "She didn't have to."

"She would have been all right if you hadn't called."

"What are you, suddenly? The big, stern father?"

"Let's find out how bad it is, at least. Why don't you use that?" He waved at the handkerchief.

"Let her calm down first."

"You're only feeding it."

She clenched her teeth. "Leave us alone." She ran her hand over Vikki's head in nervous, tender little circles.

"For Christ's sake, Sheila! Let the kid breathe!"

"She's been hurt!"

"Like any other kid. What are you trying to do? She already thinks she's too goddamned special and delicate for this world."

"Not now!"

Phil sat back on his knees. "At least get rid of all that blood before it dries," he said quietly. "She may need stitches."

Sheila dabbed at Vikki's face. "It's all right, sweetheart.

108

Everything's all right." Then, to Phil, "She might have lost an eye."

"She didn't."

It was a superficial cut. She sent Phil to get Band-Aids and Mercurochrome. Vikki's cries had subsided. She lay nestled against Sheila, looking after Phil as he ran toward Amsterdam Avenue. Her eyes were narrower than usual. Perhaps that was from crying, but when Sheila looked down, Vikki's face was a mixture of triumph and helplessness Sheila had only seen in women far older.

That expression haunted her. All through the next year she watched Vikki's face as it seemed to coarsen into it permanently. She watched, too, as Vikki turned moody. She remembered how curious and talkative she used to be with strangers. Sometimes it would worry Sheila. More often it was a source of embarrassed pride. So charming, so alert, so delicate and lovely, people would say. Sheila would nod and blush. Now, when she introduced her to friends and relatives, Vikki turned sullen and answered their questions with shrugs and grunts. Sheila told herself it was a stage and consulted Gesell, but she also found herself smiling apologetically and jumping in to answer for Vikki.

"How do you like nursery school?" a baby-sitter might ask.

Sheila would glance at Vikki for signs of withdrawal. "Oh, she loves it. They're absolutely marvelous over there. How old are yours? When they're ready you've simply got to check it out. Just enough freedom and just enough structure to give the kids a sense of security. Vikki's used to a lot of freedom, but they introduce the kids to limits and routines so beautifully. . . ." She kept the sitter's eye while she chattered and held Vikki close against her thigh, stroking her face and shoulders.

Once they had been up to Northfield to visit Phil's mother. Mrs. Gaynor kneeled down to greet Vikki. "Let's have a look at you," she said. "How was the trip?"

This time Sheila did not even stop to look. "Marvelous." Her hand shot out to Vikki's shoulder, but she did not look down at Mrs. Gaynor. "Phil's such a good driver. And the thruway was empty."

109

Mrs. Gaynor smiled. "You're wearing the dress I sent you. I suppose it fits all right."

"It's just fine, Mother Gaynor. I didn't know you had a Bonwit's up here."

Mrs. Gaynor looked up. "I got it in the city."

"It's adorable."

She made a little nod of acknowledgment and turned back to Vikki. "How is nursery school?"

"She's doing beautifully—"

"For God's sake." The woman looked up sharply. "Will you let the child speak for herself?" Sheila froze. "I already have a relationship with you." She glanced at Phil, then rose and held out her hand. "Come along, Vikki. You and I will see how things are going along in the kitchen." Vikki shriveled into Sheila's side but Mrs. Gaynor took her hand and firmly led her away.

Sheila winced now as she remembered it. She stubbed out her cigarette and got up from the sofa. The threads of love, concern, and resentment had grown more tangled over the past year until the very thought of unraveling them had drained her. So she'd simply cut them. She stood now, looking out the window at the late-afternoon street, with the limp end of indifference dangling between her fingers. May would bring back Vikki any moment. There was no way to convince her she had not been abandoned, that Sheila's love and concern was enough to keep her from choosing suicide. Sheila had, for all her care and consciousness, supplied her own daughter with far more dreadful ambiguity than any she had ever known. There was no way to undo it. It would be too cruel to admit her indifference, a lie to disguise it. Sheila, herself, was the one thing she could not protect Vikki from.

The lock on the front door clicked. From the window she could see down the hallway. Sheila turned to brace herself. Vikki rushed in before May. She wore navy blue play pants and a yellow pullover. A pocketbook hung from her wrist. She looked no bigger than Sheila remembered, but her hair had been cut in a pageboy and that changed her face. Her cheeks looked fuller. The bangs accentuated the slant of her eyes.

Sheila glanced at May. They've been to Best's, she thought. "Hello, darling," Sheila said and blessed her voice for not shaking. She did not know whether to open her arms. She held them ready.

Vikki stopped at the archway. May stood nervously in the background. Vikki said, "Did you know that Emily Donado has her own telephone in her room? Is that because she's ten?"

There was a short silence. Sheila nodded. "It may be," she said, and she kept nodding.

May's bags were already packed. They helped her into the elevator but she would not let them come down. "You're in your stocking feet," she said, holding the button. "There's a draft downstairs." She kissed them hastily. "Good-bye, darlings," and she let the door shut.

Back in the apartment, Sheila moved into action. The trick was to keep things going. "It's almost five. I've got to get supper ready." She glanced at Vikki. The child still showed no signs that her absence had affected her. Sheila had read enough to expect some kind of punishment. There simply wasn't any. From their first greeting until May's departure, Vikki had chattered about everything she had done while Sheila was gone, about her friends, and how she had had to show Grandma the way to nursery school and where they kept everything in the house. Sheila waited, almost hopefully, for the familiar signs of withdrawal.

"How would you like to help me make it?" she asked.

Vikki nodded.

The refrigerator was crammed with supplies. "Grandma must have spent all her time shopping."

"Grandpa brought a lot."

"Did he come every weekend?"

"Uh-huh. His beard scratches more than Daddy's when he kisses."

"Does it?"

"But his head is smoother."

Sheila laughed and ran her hand over Vikki's head once. "I just can't get used to you with your hair like that."

"It's just like Donna's."

"Is it? I hadn't realized."

"That's where Grandma got the idea."

"How about a salad? You can shred the lettuce." She took out a fresh head. "And what else? Something fast and easy. It's getting late." She glanced over all the containers and packages. The old panic at making decisions moved in. "Hamburgers and French fries," she said quickly. "For a treat. You can make the patties, too." She brought over the kitchen ladder and set Vikki up with a salad bowl. She stood over her as she slowly pulled the leaves apart. "Here, I tell you what, honey. Why don't we get the hamburgers ready first, then while I'm frying them, you can do the salad." She pulled the bowl away and gave her the hamburger. "Do you know how?"

Vikki picked up a scoop of meat and shaped it with splayed fingers. It came out the size of a silver dollar. Sheila hovered behind, torn between watching and wanting to jump in and finish the job efficiently. She glanced at the clock. Phil would be home in fifteen minutes. "Do you want some help?" she asked tentatively.

Vikki shook her head. She clapped out another pattie.

"I'll set the table then. Daddy should be home any minute. Unless you'd rather set the table and let me do the hamburgers."

"That's OK."

Sheila watched a moment longer, then broke away. She set the table quickly and started the potatoes frying. Vikki had made five little patties. She was less than halfway through the meat. "Oh, that's swell, honey," Sheila said brightly. "I'll finish it up now. It's getting late and I want everything ready for Daddy when he gets home. You go back to the lettuce now."

She replaced the salad bowl and brought the meat to the stove. She shaped the rest and quickly put it up. She felt better now that she was in action. No one was more efficient in the kitchen than Sheila. She loved the feeling of control and pace she could generate as she juggled preparations. She put up one part of supper after another, she adjusted flames with one flick, stirred, lidded, lowered a boil, salted, raised an oven reading, all without a break in rhythm, without a wasted trip from refrigerator to stove. She had made a science of it during her first few years of marriage. All her training in SNCC and CORE, where she constantly prepared rooms and agendas for meetings, typed, mimeographed, collated, one hand always holding the phone—it had served her well.

The phone rang while Sheila was turning the French fries.

"Let me," Vikki said quickly.

"Can you reach it?"

Vikki got on her knees on the top of the ladder.

"Be careful."

She worked the phone off the hook. "Hello?"

"Talk into the mouthpiece, honey," Sheila said automatically.

"Hello? It's Daddy." Sheila lowered the flame. "Mommy's home. We're making dinner. . . . What? Mommy called and Grandma brought her home." Sheila turned quickly. Vikki played with the telephone wire. She could not tell if Vikki had actually recognized her voice when she'd called earlier. Sheila went to her. "Fine," Vikki said. She listened. "Fine." There was another pause. "Fine." Sheila went to take the phone, but Phil was still talking to Vikki. "Fine," Vikki said. "Do you want to talk to Mommy?" She waited again, then, "Fine," she said. She nodded this time. "Fine." She gave the phone to Sheila.

"Phil?"

"Hi. Sheila?"

"Yes. It's me."

"You're home."

"Yes."

There was a brief pause. "How's everything?"

"Well, I guess it's fine," Sheila said. She looked at Vikki. "Isn't that right?"

Vikki shrugged.

"You get six fines. I get one shrug."

"You sound OK."

"I am."

"Is your mother there?"

113

"She's gone home."

"You're alone?"

Sheila closed her eyes lightly and smiled. "No, honey. Vikki's with me."

"I didn't mean that."

"I know."

"Sheila? How come you decided so suddenly?"

"I ran out of magazines."

"Honey, I didn't know you were going to—I called to tell Mom I wouldn't be home for dinner. I'm downtown. . . ."

"Already? I thought you were in the library."

"Something came up. I'm having dinner with the Ryans."

"The Ryans? What's going on?"

"What do you mean?"

"Dinner with the Ryans doesn't just suddenly come up."

"No. You're right. It's a long story. I'll explain when I get home. Look, do you want me to cancel and come home instead?"

Sheila wanted to say yes. She wanted to beg him to tell the Ryans to go to hell and quit the bookstore for good and come home to be with her. She started to speak, but she also wanted to hear him tell her that he would come home without her having to beg.

"Sheila? Honey?"

"I'm here," she said softly.

"Do you want me to come home?"

"It's up to you. I'm only making hamburgers." She put one hand against the wall. It was too soon to start that business again, anticipating whatever it was that he wanted and giving him reasons to choose it.

"Will you be all right if I stay down here? It'll be late, you know. With the bookstore and all."

"I know."

He gave a short, soft laugh. "I'm really surprised. I just wish you'd have let me know, honey. I never would have gotten into this bind if I'd known. I really feel terrible." He waited.

Sheila's grip on the phone tightened. She would not tell him it was all right, and she could not be angry and disappointed.

114

Then he would treat her as though she were still sick and make her believe she'd been wrong to come home.

"How are the Ryans?"

"OK. Renata's getting married."

"Renata?"

"That's one of the reasons they had me down. They wanted to tell me."

"Did you say anything about me?"

"No. . . . Well, yes and no."

"Yes and no? How did you manage that?"

"I wasn't going to, but Eleanor Ryan asked how you were and she saw something was up. She even seemed to know what it was."

"A rich, wrinkled sibyl," Sheila said. "I've always said it."

"I only told her, though. Fred Ryan doesn't know." There was a pause. "Would you like me to come home?"

"Of course." She said it casually. "Are you going to?"

"Honey." His voice turned into a whisper.

"I can't hear you."

"I think Fred Ryan has some kind of offer for me," he said, a little more loudly. "That's why I'm. . . . Honey, can you get along without me then?"

"I have been known to."

"Is Vikki all right?"

"Sensational."

"The two of you?"

He was working her into a corner where she'd be forced to absolve him. "Look, Phil. I'm leaving the door unlatched for good now. I'm home. There's enough food here for three of us. You decide what you want to do. OK?"

"You sound upset."

He had her. If she said no she'd be reassuring him. If she said yes he could make her responsible for his decision to come home. How did he manage it? She glanced at the stove.

"Phil, the dinner's burning up and Vikki and I are starved. We'll either see you in a little while or later tonight."

"Are you sure?"

"Of what?" She said it flatly, but she was pleased. She'd

115

maneuvered herself out. It was an important triumph. There was a long silence. This time it was up to him. Vikki watched Sheila. She was still shredding the lettuce. In the middle of the silence Sheila smiled at her and nodded encouragement.

"Isn't Daddy coming?"

Sheila opened her eyes wide and shrugged.

"Well, OK, then," Phil said.

"Fine, dear." She hung up.

"Is Daddy coming?"

"I don't know, honey. I don't think so." She raised the flames under the two frying pans. She was trembling and a little frightened. The telephone was not being kind to her today. It seemed determined to rush things, first with Vikki, now with Phil. Phil hadn't taken her by surprise the way Vikki had, though. After all, she'd set herself up for something like it with the sudden decision to leave the hospital. What took her by surprise this time was the way she handled it. Phil would not be home till late. She knew very well she would have had to throw a scene to get him to leave the Ryans and make the trip uptown. She had not done that. But she had not made it easier for him, either. That was new. She could see herself being worked into the same old impossible position, like the game of Dr. Nim that Phil liked so much. No matter how many marbles you chose to release, the machine was always a move ahead and you were left with the responsibility for releasing the last. She was trembling now, not because she'd finally won, but because she'd refused to finish. That possibility had never even occurred to her before. It brought its own, new kind of consequences that Sheila would have to sort out. For the moment, though, as curiously frightened as she was, she was also sure that she'd done the right thing. She turned over the hamburgers. Or that she could make it right.

Vikki had shredded the whole head of lettuce by the time the rest of the dinner was ready. It flowed out of the bowl onto the counter.

"Now, that's an enthusiastic salad," Sheila said.

"Is that good?"

116

"Great." She went to bring it to the table.

"I'll do it." Vikki clambered off the stool.

Sheila handed the bowl down to her. "Be careful." She watched her carry it across the room, leaving a trail of shreds. Sheila stood tense, ready to run if she dropped it. She didn't. As soon as it was on the table, Sheila thought, What if she had?

Vikki ate all the little hamburgers she had made and filled up on lettuce. When she asked for fourths, Sheila said, "You've already eaten enough roughage for a constipated army."

"I made it."

Sheila smiled. "This'll be your last, then. OK? I don't want you waking up in the middle of the night with a tummyache." She glanced at her daughter quickly. "In fact, I don't want you getting up in the middle of the night at all anymore. Grandma told me you woke up all the time. No reason for that kind of silliness anymore, is there?"

"Grandma slept in my room."

"I know. That was because you woke up."

Vikki picked up a piece of lettuce. She shook her head.

"You didn't wake up?"

She nodded.

"You did wake up. That's what I said."

"Grandma's so noisy."

"What?" She gave a surprised laugh. "You mean she woke you up?"

"Her bed goes *squeeklunk*."

"What?"

"*Squeeklunk*."

Sheila stared blankly.

"Like this. *Squeeeeak. Clunk.* Whenever she got in."

"And that woke you up?"

She shook her head.

"That didn't wake you up."

She nodded.

"It did."

"The first time Grandma woke me up, not the *squeeklunk*."

"Vikki," Sheila said slowly. "This conversation is not making sense."

"The first time Grandma was in your room," Vikki said. "She came into my room in the middle of the night and woke me up."

"What for?"

Vikki shrugged.

"Well, what did she say to you?"

"She just put me in her lap."

"Didn't she say anything?"

Vikki shook her head. "I think she was crying."

"Then what happened?"

"Grandpa bought a new bed."

"The next day, you mean."

Vikki nodded.

"The one that goes *squeeklunk*?"

Vikki looked at the piece of lettuce she'd just picked up. "Do I have to eat the rest?"

"Don't tell me you're tired of it?"

Vikki looked up at her seriously. "You're different," she said.

"Am I? How?"

She studied Sheila carefully. "Your dress."

"Is that all?"

"I don't know."

Sheila put her elbow on the table and leaned her cheek on her fist. "You know what? You're different, too."

"How?"

"I don't know either. But I tell you what. Let's promise to tell each other as soon as we figure it out. OK?"

Sheila left the dishes in the sink after dinner. While she was clearing, Vikki said, "Play with me."

Sheila felt a momentary tightness. Before, when Vikki asked her to play, she'd always end up romping wildly, tumbling and tickling. It was the only way Sheila knew to get the free, delighted response from her that play was supposed to give. They would start with make-believe games, but neither

118

of them really liked that and Sheila would grow tired of prompting and jacking up enthusiasm. She would finally challenge Vikki to catch her and they would run through the apartment. That would turn into a game of hide-and-seek and Sheila would be reassured by Vikki's shrieks when they discovered each other. It would end with the two of them laughing determinedly on the floor and Vikki crawling over Sheila while Sheila tickled and hugged and swung her. She did not have the energy for that now.

"What would you like?"

"Whatever you want?"

"Well, let's see." She dropped the last few dishes and spoons in the sink and went into Vikki's room.

"Everything's so neat in here." Her eye lit on the stacked crayons. "How about coloring?"

Vikki looked mystified.

"We've never done that before, have we? Here, I'll show you." She pulled out the two children's chairs from the play table and opened a coloring book. "You take one page and I'll take the other." Her knees rose slightly higher than her stomach. "This chair is low, isn't it?" Vikki sat next to her, slowly.

"No Princess?"

Sheila shook her head. "I never really much liked that game. Did you?"

"Hide-and-seek?"

"I'm tired of that one. I feel like something quiet. Here. Let's share the box." She pushed it between them and started rummaging. "I want the Burnt Sienna. That was always my favorite. I even liked how it sounded. Burnt Sienna." She found it and showed her the label. "See? Burnt Sienna. Yummy. Now, which page would you like?"

Vikki shrugged.

"Well, at least let's find a clean one."

She found a page with a round-faced boy on one side and a round-faced girl on the other.

"Here we go," Sheila said.

Vikki started halfheartedly on the girl's dress. After a mo-

119

ment she dropped her crayon and watched Sheila give the boy a Burnt Sienna jacket.

"What's the matter?"

Vikki shook her head. She covered the page with her hand.

"What is it?"

"I can't stay in the lines."

Sheila lifted Vikki's hand. The yellow dress bled out to the white sky around it. She smiled and nodded. "I used to have the same trouble. You don't have to."

"You're staying in."

Sheila laughed. "Let me tell you, it took years."

"Why do they put them there if you don't have to?"

"What?"

"The lines."

Sheila shrugged. "For the people who want to, I guess. I tell you what. Let's find some empty paper and draw our own pictures. OK?"

She found some typing paper on Phil's desk and brought it back to the play table. "Now we can do whatever we want."

"What are you going to make?"

"I don't know yet. But it'll be all Burnt Sienna." She made a few light curves on the paper. Vikki tentatively picked up a blue crayon. She made a line and the crayon snapped.

"Here. Why don't you use one of the fat ones?"

"It's not the right color."

Vikki's mouth set in a tight line. It was starting. Sheila knew the signs of the struggle. It was almost with relief that she recognized the narrowing eyes, the shoulders turning rigid. She held her crayon suspended, wondering if somehow she, herself, had forced the moment, just to reassure herself that her absence had mattered. They held each other's eyes. Or did this mean that it hadn't mattered? Everything Sheila felt now was familiar—the surge of resentment, the anger rising in her throat, the urge to smack and smack hard. The very meaning and purpose of her absence seemed to hang in the balance as they stared at each other. She could play the same old scenario of frustration or she could disregard the challenge, smile cheerfully, and go back to her drawing. That would leave the tension unresolved. She could turn petulant and withdrawn herself, or she could try to cajole Vikki out of it. Any one of those meant a resumption of the struggle. Before, for whatever reasons, she had needed that struggle. Now it held nothing for her.

She reached over and took Vikki's mean little face in her hand. She kissed her on the forehead and shook her head gently. "No more of that for me, thanks. I've got things to do." She got up and went to the kitchen.

It was impossible to hear anything else in the apartment while she washed the dishes. Sheila usually left them until late at night. It was too hard, straining after every sound behind the running water to hear if anyone needed her. It was only after Vikki was asleep and Phil was gone that she would wander into the disordered kitchen. Then she would be too tired and leave it all till morning. Now she turned on the water and let the sound surround her.

She was still feeling her way. It was all new territory. All the old maps had led her through the route of the last two years. When she woke in the hospital she knew only that she had survived the trip. Now she was beginning to understand how tortuous it had been. She was still too close to see it clearly. Perhaps as she moved farther away in time it would come into focus. All she really knew now was how natural, how safe and normal it had all seemed while she was still on the other side. She remembered looking at everyone else's life, the divorces, the bitterness, the miserable children, and thinking, How mad, how unnatural—and how lucky I am to have found my own, clear way. Now she knew that her own, clear way was as clouded as theirs and that if she were to follow it again it would lead back to suicide.

She turned toward the doorway. There was no telling how long Vikki had been standing there. The narrow-eyed meanness was gone. She watched Sheila with the look of a puzzled animal.

"Would you like to dry?"

Vikki did not respond. Sheila smiled and turned back to the sink. When she looked again, Vikki was gone.

That morning, when she had told Dr. Rankin she wanted to go home, he said he thought she was ready. She needed rest. She needed time for herself. She understood that now, didn't she? She would see him once a week as an outpatient as long as they thought it necessary, until she was back in the swing of things. He was reassuring. She had a task and a purpose to bring home with her. She would find a way to readjust. She had only been home a few hours, though, and Sheila knew already that her real work was different from the sensible, reassuring project Rankin had offered. Readjustment meant finding her way back to the old safeties, the ones that had betrayed her in the first place.

Her arms felt light as she scoured the hamburger pan. She felt uneasy, vaguely distrustful, the way she sometimes felt at the dentist's when he began to assemble his drill and she was not sure the Novocain had really worked. What she had to do was expose those old securities and reject them, one by one. They were dangerous. She knew that now. But before she could expose them she had to search them out and recognize them when she found them. That would be harder. That meant touching nerves.

She finished the dishes and snapped off her rubber gloves. The apartment was quiet. She strained her ears toward Vikki's room. There was no sound. It was one of those deep silences she had learned to distrust since there had been a child in the house. She made her way noiselessly down the hall and stopped at the side of the doorway. Vikki sat at the play table, drawing circles with a fat, blue crayon. Her head tilted low toward the paper. The tip of her tongue worked in and out slowly, helping her concentrate. Sheila folded her arms and leaned against the doorjamb. For the first time she was able to look at her daughter as a person apart, imperfect, vulnerable, as impenetrable as any other human being. It was her own admission of indifference earlier that had freed them both. She studied Vikki's astonishing separateness. How could it be that she had never noticed how irregular and faintly comic her face was, how genuinely graceful her neck, and how ungainly her wrists? Was that possible? Could wrists be ungainly? Of course. They were Bernie's, thick and barely differentiated from where the hand started. She had never realized that. She had never dared to look. Before now any irregularity in her daughter had to be just another unique version of her own. Sheila's wrists were thin and tapered. She could never afford to notice Vikki's. Even the withdrawals and the temper tantrums had been Sheila's. That was why she had needed them. They were familiar. Every time the two of them played out one of their anguished scenes, with Sheila secretly welcoming them, this was what she'd been avoiding, this recognition that Vikki was not hers or anyone else's, but already a person apart. Incomprehensible, yes, but on her own terms, not Sheila's.

Vikki looked up from the funny, shapeless circles she drew and for the first time Sheila did not look into her own eyes.

"It's bedtime, honey. Get your nightgown on." Her voice was matter-of-fact and she wondered if Vikki could hear any of the amazed, new tenderness beneath it.

She put Vikki to bed and wandered into the living room. It was 7:30. Phil would not be home until 1:00. Usually she spent the time avoiding the dirty apartment. Tonight it was clean. She was on her own. She made herself a cup of coffee and settled into Phil's recliner with a cigarette. She sat for a long time. Vikki was asleep. Phil was at work. Her mother had gone back to Woodview. She felt as detached as she had when she woke in the hospital. There had been nothing to avoid then, either. This time, though, Sheila wanted to talk.

She went to the kitchen and phoned Diana Brautigan.

Donna answered. "Brautigan residence. This is Donna Brautigan speaking. Who's calling, please?"

"Hello, Brautigan residence. This is Sheila Gaynor."

Donna dropped her professional answering voice. "Hi."

"How are you, sweetheart?"

"Fine. Mommy's not here. She's at a party to watch herself on television. That's why I'm up so late. I got permission to watch, too."

"She's on tonight?"

"It's her dayview."

123

"What time?"

"Nine o'clock. And it's a whole hour."

"Oh, great. I'll have to watch. Listen, honey, will you leave a message that I called?"

"OK. Do you have a television in the hospital?"

"I'm not in the hospital anymore. I'm home."

"Are you better?"

"Better and better."

"Vikki was good while you were away. I promised I'd tell you that."

"Thanks. Don't forget to tell Mommy I called. OK?"

"OK."

"Well...." There was a short pause. "How have *you* been?"

"Fine."

"Good. Any exciting things happen lately?"

"No. Same old rat race."

She laughed. "You're insufferable."

"Is that good?"

"It's you."

"Well, it's almost time for Mommy, so I'll hang up now, OK?"

"OK, honey. And don't forget to tell her. Write it down."

"OK." Her voice turned professional again. "Thank you for calling."

Sheila turned on the television in the bedroom. She took a pack of playing cards from the drawer in Phil's desk and propped herself in bed. Solitaire was a habit while she watched televison. She had begun playing one he year before when she decided to give up smoking and wanted something to do with her hands. Her abstinence lasted two shows, but she had, in the meantime, found a new addiction. It became a kind of fortune-telling for her. If the solitaire worked out four times in one evening the next day would be a good one. If it didn't there would be trouble, something unpleasant in the mail, a scene with Vikki, Phil in a foul mood. This time it came out on the first try. She collected the cards and reshuffled, wondering if that was just a come-on or if she could really

124

even control the course of her cards now. Coming out on the first try like that—it would not be easy to sustain that pace.

Sheila's grandmother had taught her to play solitaire. Doris Kahn had come to live in Woodview when her husband died. Sheila was ten; Doris was in her fifties. Both were just discovering what it meant to feel lonely. They could spend time with each other and never feel they were being dependent the way they felt with May and Bernie. She lived in the Paradise, a Woodview hotel with two floors and an elevator. There were other women like Doris there. Every afternoon the women gathered in the solarium and played poker late into the night, breaking only for dinner. Doris consistently won, and would save her winnings all winter to blow at the track over the summer.

It was during the holidays, when the other women were visiting with their own families, that Sheila spent most of her time alone with Doris. She would sit with her in the solarium learning dozens of variations of one-, two-, even three-pack solitaire. Once she asked Doris to teach her to play poker. "You don't want to learn that," Doris said, waving it away. "It's an old woman's game."

The second deal was a short one. Sheila uncovered only three cards, no aces. The third was close. She laid out all the spades and diamonds up to the queens. The four of hearts and the three of clubs stayed buried.

She wondered if May and Bernie had told Doris about her. Probably not. She was over seventy now and Sheila's parents had been braced for her heart to give out for years.

She glanced at the clock. It was nine. The women would still be up in the solarium. She could call just to say hello.

The credits for *The Criminals* faded in on the television screen.

The next game of solitaire came out.

Diana played a rich, bored heiress who steals Monet's "Water Lilies" from the Museum of Modern Art just for the hell of it. Most of the show was devoted to the two men sneaking through the deserted museum at night while Diana draped herself around sculpture. She was terrible. Sheila was sorry she had called. Donna knew she was watching and there was no way to avoid saying something when she saw Diana.

She kept playing solitaire through the next show and the 11:00 news. Once she went into the kitchen to make coffee. She sat on the kitchen ladder while the coffee perked and took the Manhattan phone book on her lap, thumbing absently through it. She stopped at the W's and noticed the Wheelers took up three pages. She wondered how Mrs. Wheeler was listed, if she used her full name, her initials, if there was an RN after it. Over the whole month in the hospital Sheila had never learned her first name. What would happen if she tried a couple? If just by chance she found the one she was looking for? It might be a nice gesture, just to let her know she was back on her own and happy—and, honestly, just to talk, because she was thinking about her. Mrs. Wheeler might be touched, or she might interpret it as a call for help. Sheila would not want her to misunderstand in that way.

The coffee finished perking. Sheila closed the phone book and put it away. She left a low flame under the pot to keep it warm for Phil.

There was a Barbara Stanwyck movie after the news. The solitaire had come out four times, but on one of them she was not sure whether she had turned over an extra card by mistake. A fifth time would be reassuring. She could feel herself getting drowsy but she was determined to be awake—and dressed—when Phil arrived. She flipped off the set and left the bedroom.

There was a faint smell of gas as she passed the kitchen. The flame under the coffee had gone out. The pot was cold. She emptied the grounds and readjusted the burner before she went to the living room.

Phil came home a half hour early. She was on the verge of cracking the *Times* double-crostic when the front door clicked. She filled in the word she had just found as his footsteps came down the hall and she figured out the author and title of the

126

quotation. There was no time to write them in. He paused at the bedroom and hurried on.

"Sheila?"

"Hi." They always called in whispers when Vikki was asleep. She put aside her magazine and pencil.

He still had his coat on, unbuttoned. At the archway he stopped and put down his briefcase. Sheila stayed in the chair a moment. He straightened up and stood hesitantly.

"You're dressed," he said.

She started to answer, but instead of speaking she found herself up and crossing the living room to him. It was not until she had seen him that she realized how lonely she had been all night, how desperately she had been waiting to talk to someone, to touch with nothing between, no telephones, no television screen, no plaid coat. Phil put his arms around her. His face was cold and his clothes smelled of the winter street. She kissed him.

"I left the bookstore early. I would have been home even sooner, but I was trying to find a florist open on Broadway."

She shook her head. "I'm glad you didn't."

"You know what it's like? Trying to find a florist at—"

She kissed him again. "No more flowers."

"You look fine."

She nodded. "And no more apologies."

Phil frowned.

"What's wrong?"

He waved it away. "Nothing." But his face stayed clouded.

She stared at him, puzzled, then closed her eyes and let out a deep breath. It turned to a laugh. "You thought you smelled gas."

His face flamed.

"You did. I was keeping the coffee warm and the burner went out." Her hand trailed down his coat front. "I'll pour some."

Phil looked tired. The skin on his jaw seemed tight and the corners of his mouth, even when he smiled, worked up hard. Sheila guarded against letting her body fall into old positions

127

as they settled in across the kitchen table. Her shoulders set forward, eager to possess his day, to fill up with his events. She forced them back. She crossed her legs against the impulse to spring up and do—anything—refill his cup, get him a napkin, put back the milk, wipe the table—anything to prove that she was capable of action, too. She kept her finger looped in the handle of the coffee cup and the other hand tight around the side.

"How are the Ryans?"

"Good."

"You look a little tired."

He nodded. "It was a hell of a day. A lot of things at once." He looked up sharply. "I didn't mean—"

"It's all right. What happened?"

"Well, first they told me about Renata." He gave her all the information he had from Eleanor and Fred Ryan. Sheila said nothing. She let Phil recite the details as though he had rehearsed them. Those were the times when the cool, clear-eyed reason of the Gaynors came through in him, that same ability to cover all the angles that would make him such a first-rate lawyer. "A fine sense of balance," they called it in recommendations for law school, while hers, she knew, always talked about "energy and infectious enthusiasm." She listened carefully now, as he explained all the advantages for Renata. He described Ronstein as "a hell of a good lawyer," and she heard Fred Ryan. He explained how tough Renata was. She heard Eleanor Ryan. Sheila wondered what that steel-backed woman in chiffon thought when Phil told her about the suicide. The words sprang easily to Sheila's mind. Gutless, indulged, Jewish. She could see the wrinkled neck extend, the lips widen and clamp.

Phil said something about his brother.

"How's he taking it?"

"They didn't say. It'll be good for him, though, in the long run. He's twenty-two. He's got to start growing up."

Sheila nodded absently at the words. She concentrated on his voice, trying to locate what she heard that was so new and that chilled her. It was in the tone. It was something familiar.

128

That was why she had trouble pinning it down. It had been there for eight years, but she had never before noticed. He spoke slowly. His words were considered. She always recognized that. The sound came from a little too high in his throat. She'd always known that, too. It gave his voice a disarming, boyish quality. This new thing had leaped out and caught her ear when he started to talk about Paul. Somehow it implicated her as well, and it colored everything he said as he explained the bloodless arrangement for his sister's marriage.

"You're not happy," he said, and smiled at her gently.

She started to reassure him. Before she could speak she found it. It was his assurance. She clasped her cup tightly and took a sip. He was still smiling, but as Sheila glanced at him over her cup, she saw it was not a gentle smile at all. He thought it was. She saw that, too. He thought he understood her affection for Renata and her anger at the manipulation of her life, but the tone of his voice was in his smile and it wasn't gentle. He and the Ryans had considered all the aspects —some were unpleasant of course—but resistance was out of the question. That was the key. No resistance. For Renata. For Paul. And as he explained it to her, she realized that his smile and his voice showed there was no fear of challenge from her, either. There never had been.

"When is the wedding?"

"January. It'll be small."

She wondered what would happen if she did offer a challenge. How? This was not even her affair. The Ryans and Mrs. Gaynor may have made the arrangements. Phil may have gone along with them, but Renata was finally responsible for herself and there was nothing across the table to challenge except the smile and the voice. Perhaps, after all, she imagined it. Maybe there had simply never been any decision to challenge, never any affair that was hers, and that was why she had never tested resistance. That was more puzzling still. With six years of marriage had there really been nothing that was her affair?

"Did Ryan make you an offer?" she asked after a short silence. Phil looked up startled.

"About what?"

"I'm changing the subject," she said dryly. "On the phone you said you thought Ryan was going to make you some kind of job offer. Did he?"

Phil made a noncommittal gesture. "A feeler."

"And?"

"I don't know yet. He's got something in Connecticut."

"Near home?"

"Very."

Sheila sat back, relieved. "You discouraged it."

Phil did not answer.

"Phil?"

"I left it open."

"Working for Ryan? In Connecticut?"

"With the way things are going I can't afford to be a big shot." He waved it away. "Anyway, it's silly to speculate. It's all so tentative."

Sheila got up. "Do you want another cup of coffee?" The idea that Phil would even consider moving back near his family was going to take some time to assimilate. He knew what it would be like for her. Was she being selfish, or childish, to expect him to reject it out of hand?

Her hands automatically started up to massage the small of her back. She stopped them midway and pretended to adjust her belt. She had not thought about making love, until her hands moved into that familiar signal of rejection. Phil had probably been waiting for some sign from her since he had come home. "Or do you want to go to bed?"

He looked up at her with a hint of strain in his smile. "Bed or sleep?" That was another signal. Somehow they had never been able to come out and ask each other for sex. Over the years they had developed all these elaborate codes. Gestures and words that played around the edges of intimacy.

"Whichever you want."

They held each other's eyes a moment. He looked at the clock on the wall behind her. "It's already one thirty."

"I'm not tired." He looked up at her again. "I'm all right, Phil." It was hard for him to hold her gaze and that brought

130

out all the tenderness she felt in spite of her resentment over Renata and the forebodings about Ryan's offer. She extended her hand.

Sheila lay in bed and watched Phil move around the room as he undressed and got things in order for morning. Stripped down to his underpants and watch, he was laying out his clothes for the next day on the chair by the desk.

"You know something? Of all the men I ever slept with, you're the only one that ever wore jockey shorts. Why is that?"

"Maybe they had different tailors."

"You remember Richard Greene? The coordinator from NYU?"

"No. What did he wear?"

"Whaddayacallem? Boxer shorts. He said jockey shorts were for kids."

"Did you make it a habit to discuss underwear?"

She laughed. "I wonder why I thought of that. I'll have to tell Rankin about it."

Phil stacked the next day's books on his desk. His skin was very white. She watched his muscles move as he arranged his things. He had been thin seven years before. That had been one of the things about him that intrigued her. He had been so slim and firm. He was still well-built, but over the years she had felt him thicken under her touch. The boy's body had gradually turned to a man's. He became heavier on her, slower. His waist gave out slightly over the elastic on the top of his shorts. Not a lot. Just enough to remind her that it hadn't before. She wondered how her body was changing and if he noticed.

He took off his shorts and undid his wristwatch as he came to the bed. There was a small lamp on the night table. He laid the watch out beside it. His chest and stomach were smooth and the light caught him at an angle that made him look hard and young again. He switched off the light.

"Is the alarm set?" he asked in the dark.

"Yes."

The bed heaved as he got in beside her. Sheila waited for his

131

touch. She was tense. She tried to let her whole body relax back into the bed. Since she had gone into the bathroom to put in her diaphragm, half her attention had been on this moment. She wanted it to be all right. She knew she could not expect too much of herself all at once, but she also knew that if it wasn't all right here, nothing else would work, either. That had made her even more tense.

She felt his face over her in the darkness. His lips fumbled over her cheek, trying to find her mouth, and she gave a little laugh. He kissed her. She put her hands on his head. His hair was fine. For an instant she thought of faking pleasure. She'd done it before when she was nervous or depressed. Perhaps just to get past this first time, she might go through the motions. It would at least allay his fears about her and leave her free to pull herself together without his hovering behind. She let her fingers trail down to her secret place on his neck, trying not to examine how she felt as she tried to respond. The trick was to get out of herself, to pay attention only to his body. She started to turn on her side, to get him to lie on his back so she could concentrate on him, but he gently forced her back. "Take it easy," he whispered. He took her breast in his hand and kissed it. She tried to give herself to it, but she could feel herself resist. Her own hands moved down over his shoulder to his side and hips. His skin was cool. He was sitting up on his side and she did not like the creases it made at his waist. She thought of imagining he was someone else. Perhaps that would excite her. She thought of what he had looked like as he leaned over the lamp. Dozens of other men tumbled through her mind. Richard Greene, who had small, dark nipples; Dr. Rankin, who had hairy wrists; a redheaded student who had once talked to her in the park and whom she had wondered about even as they were talking; her first political science professor, who had silver-white hair and a deep voice; Joe Brautigan; Paul Newman; an intern who wore a white uniform she had seen at the hospital; the boy in the T-shirt on Amsterdam Avenue; Rodin's "Orpheus"—but it was too late for any kind of elaborate fantasy.

Phil brushed the inside of her thigh. Her legs moved apart automatically. She raised her head to kiss his neck and he

132

made soft, reassuring noises. "It's all right," he whispered. "Relax." It made her feel like a virgin. She remembered the first time, something she had not thought of in years. He was a young, married instructor at Barnard. He had taken her up to a friend's apartment for a drink and when she found herself in bed her only thought was at least to be good. She could still feel his grip on her hips, pinning her against the mattress. She could still hear him laughing. "Take it easy. It's simpler than that." He tore into her, still whispering instructions to calm down and not work so hard.

Phil took her nipple in his mouth. She had to use all her energy to keep from giggling. She arched slightly and she knew he thought she was excited. He rolled on top of her. She was not ready for him, but she reached down and opened herself to let him penetrate. He ran his tongue over her breasts and held her buttocks tightly. His breathing changed. It turned to soft moans. She decided to fake it, but just as she did she felt her body respond. She lay beneath him an instant, suspended between choices. She could still hold back, keep control, and only pretend to pleasure, or she could give herself up to it now that the impulse was there. It was only an instant of real choice. If she held back too long, the real response would be gone; it she let go she would not be able to turn back. She shuddered and gave in to the pleasure. Everything turned warm. She surrounded him with warmth inside and her hands pressed against the small of his back. She tilted her pelvis to feel him more sharply. Her whole body started to crest. Perhaps it was just relief or perhaps it really was the beginning of something new, but it had never promised to be so full, so sharp and total as this time. Phil's rhythm speeded up. She pressed more firmly on his back to stop him. It was no good. He stopped sharply himself—too soon—and she felt him pulse inside her. She lay still a moment, her hands still pressed around him. Then he lowered his head and kissed her gently on the neck.

He gave a soft, tender laugh. "You really made it this time, didn't you?" he whispered. Her eyes flew open in astonishment. He brushed her ear with his lips. "Didn't you?"

She closed her eyes again and nodded, ashamed of the lie.

133

4

Phil
November 18-
Thanksgiving, 1962

THE HOLIDAY season was coming up. Phil would have liked to fall into the old day-to-day routine for Sheila's sake. She needed the stability of that. Besides, he was sure she wanted to test her own strength and prove to him and Vikki that the whole affair had been a momentary aberration. The holiday schedule was part of an even larger, annual routine, though, and this year, more than any other, it would be unwise to break it. Bernie and May did not celebrate Christmas, so the system had worked itself out naturally: Thanksgiving in Woodview, Christmas in Northfield. Easter was a problem, but they never worried about that until March.

May had called to make arrangements the day after Sheila got home. They were to rent a car and drive down Thursday morning. That meant laying out a deposit, but Phil could expect Bernie to take his hand some time during the afternoon and fold in some cash. The money would cover the car and leave about twenty dollars extra. He could accept those kinds of gifts from Sheila's family while he agonized over taking Christmas presents from his mother if they seemed too useful. Bernie's money was so clearly marked for Sheila and Vikki that it would have been cruel and selfish to refuse it.

Besides, Phil never had the sense, as he did with his mother, that the gift was a criticism.

Sheila had come home on the Thursday before Thanksgiving. That gave them less than a week to get the old rhythm going before it was interrrupted. It was enough for Phil to see the change in Sheila. There was nothing he could point to directly. That made it even more unsettling. On the surface everything seemed restored. If anything, it promised to be better. Sheila flung herself back into the business of living with an energy he had not seen in years. The morning after her return she was awake before him, showered and dressed, with breakfast on the table. Vikki was still asleep. His place was set with a napkin in a ring.

"My body's still on hospital time," she said, but her cheer and efficiency seemed far less casual than she suggested. "Did you sleep well?"

"Great."

She set a cup of coffee in front of him and turned away to scramble some eggs. Her arm worked vigorously from the shoulder. "Me, too. What a relief to be back in my own bed."

"Is Vikki still asleep?" He asked it softly, expecting her to lower her voice at his reminder.

"I'll wake her as soon as you're out." There was no change in the volume. "Did I tell you I saw Diana on television last night?"

"No."

"She was awful. I don't know what I'm going to say to her."

"Don't tell her you saw it."

"No good. I called and spoke to Donna before I knew she was on. That was how I found out. She'll tell Diana she told me." She brought the eggs to the table and scraped them into his plate.

"Aren't you eating?"

"I did already." She took the pan to the sink and scoured it. "It was really weird seeing Diana like that. The first time they showed a close-up I had to turn away. Isn't that peculiar? You know how when you're describing someone in a dream you say things like, 'I was in this car with so-and-so, only it wasn't

135

so-and-so'? That was how I felt when I saw her on the television screen. It was Diana, only it wasn't. And she wasn't as gorgeous as she is offscreen. No. That's wrong. She looked just like she always does, except her hair was done up and they had her in this high-fashion coat-suit. But I began to think that we only think she's so gorgeous out here because there are so many ugly people on the street to compare her with. But on television, with all those model types, like, you know"—she sucked in her cheeks and lowered her eyelids—"she didn't look special. I felt absolutely disloyal."

Sheila dried her hands and brought a cup of coffee to the table. She told Phil the whole plot of the television show. She made him laugh at some of the absurdities. She imitated Diana draping herself over the Brancusis. She talked brightly, stopping only to light a cigarette or take a sip of coffee. If Phil tried to speak she jumped in before he could finish.

He did not know if he should encourage her animation or plead with her to calm down. He searched her face for signs of hysteria. Her eyes were clear; her smile was quick and open. She had pulled her hair back into a bun as tight as a ballerina's. The last time he had seen her so much in control was the morning she tried to commit suicide.

He still had no idea of what to expect. He wished he had found some time to talk with Dr. Rankin and ask what signs of trouble he should look for. He would have felt more sure of himself. Even if he had found the opportunity, though, he probably wouldn't have taken it. There was something wrong, something shameful about asking a professional man for advice like that. If anyone should have known about his wife it was Phil, and if anyone should have recognized danger signs it was he.

He had been expecting her to come back from the hospital like any other convalescent, moving slowly, quiet, a little depressed perhaps. He had prepared himself for a test of his own patience. He would train himself to be doubly sensitive; he would make as many solicitous phone calls as he thought he should from the library, the bookstore, between classes. He would help her through another difficult period until she was back on her mental feet again. More than anything else she would need his support. In spite of the difficulties that might make for him—especially now—he had almost looked forward to giving it. It would be a sign, for one thing, of his genuine love. Sheila seemed determined to show she would not depend on him.

She was laughing now as she described May in the drugstore, falling apart at the fifty-cent minimum. Her legs were crossed and she leaned forward to flick her cigarette ash on the impulse of laughter.

"Can you imagine her giving my father those two sticky Danishes with the gas fumes from the bus and little bits of napkin stuck to the icing?"

Phil smiled weakly. She was trying to show him she was all right. How could he let her know she didn't have to, that he wouldn't mind her dependency, that he understood she was still not well enough to carry her own weight? He pulled his napkin out of its ring.

"To celebrate?" he asked, holding them up.

"Every morning from now on."

He forced an approving face. He remembered all the mornings he had tiptoed around the kitchen trying to give her an extra half-hour's sleep, pleased with himself, yet vaguely resentful. If he was in a rotten mood he would sit over his coffee and nurse that resentment, thinking what breakfast must be like for the Brautigans—or the Ryans.

"When is your first appointment with the doctor?"

"Monday."

"Do you want me to come home for Vikki?"

"It's for three o'clock. You're in class." Phil felt another odd stab of resentment. "I'll use the pool."

"How many hours do we owe that thing now?"

"I'll figure it out. Don't worry, though. I'll make them up."

"Why didn't you make your appointment for a time when I was free?"

Sheila looked at him quizzically. "I purposely didn't. I didn't want to have to ask you—"

137

He checked a gesture of irritation.

"Would you rather?" she said quickly. "I can change it this Monday if you want. I just didn't want to interfere with your schedule if I could help it."

Phil was puzzled at his own discomfort. He knew how to deal with the old Sheila. He knew how to control his resentment at her dependency. Now she was telling him he no longer had to. She was removing the cause, and if he was going to be supportive, here was a genuine struggle for him to support. It only seemed to unnerve him more, as though he were being asked to give up something even more important than his study time.

Sheila rolled some crumbs together with a matchbook. She swept them off the table into her hand and dropped them in the ashtray.

"The apartment is really incredible, isn't it? Sometimes my mother's compulsions really pay off. How did it feel coming home to a commercial every night?"

"I would rather have had you here."

Sheila laughed. "And both were out of the question."

"I didn't mean—"

"It's all right. I could never do what my mother does to a house."

"But you did."

"What do you mean?"

"The day you . . . left. The whole house was spotless." Sheila stared at him blankly. "Don't you remember?"

He could see it come back to her. "Son of a bitch! You're right. I cleaned the whole place. I'd completely forgotten. I was expecting to come back to the same old clutter, but I'd already started cleaning it up. Isn't that weird? I blocked it out." She smiled the way she did in public when they shared a private joke, only this time Phil felt left out of it.

"I think I'll go see Diana this afternoon if she's free," she said.

"Good idea."

"I'm not going to sit cooped up in the house anymore. You know, I'm beginning to think the only reason I tried to commit suicide was to get a little change. It may have been all I needed, like staying in a hotel. I think I can even cope with getting Vikki's snowsuit on now—or, better still, with her getting it on herself."

"I wish you wouldn't talk like that."

She turned to him, genuinely surprised. "Like what?"

He made a troubled, inarticulate gesture. "I don't know how you can say it so easily."

"That I can cope?"

"No." He hesitated. "You talk about what you did so lightly."

"Trying to commit suicide? Does that really upset you?"

"The words don't upset me." He played with the napkin ring. "It's your attitude." He was having trouble getting the thought out. "You just don't seem to realize how important—"

"Yes, I do." She leaned against the sink. "You bet I do. That's exactly why I'm not going to indulge myself anymore." She drew a mock-tragic face. "I tried to doooo awayyyy with myself. No more Anna Karenina. None of that. I'm not going to be satisfied sprinkling my hair with ashes."

"You know I didn't mean that." He was not handling it well at all. The very first morning and he was blowing all those plans about how careful, how tolerant and understanding he would be. Incomprehensible anger kept rising in him, the worse because she gave him nothing to pin it on.

"Are you sulking?" she asked incredulously.

"Of course not." He dropped the ring on the table. His lips felt tight and he could not look at her. There was a long silence while she studied him.

"I'm trying very hard, Phil." Her voice was lower. It quavered slightly and Phil felt reassured.

He nodded. "I know."

"I don't know how long this is going to last. You know what I mean? I feel rested and I feel like I can cope. With Vikki. With the house. With you." She looked away for an instant. "I'm trying to hold on to it."

He nodded again. "It's just that—"

"What?"

He thought of what Sheila had been like in bed the night before. Her body had felt hard and knotted. It might have finally been satisfying for her, but he'd had to work to control her skittishness, her tense, random movements. When he came it was more a relief than a climax and he'd had to pretend real pleasure for her sake. "Maybe you're trying too hard," he said gently.

She shrugged. "Maybe I am."

He felt better. He'd been afraid his irritation was a sign of selfishness and insensitivity. It wasn't. It sprang from concern for her.

Sheila was half turned away. He got up and took her by the shoulders. His thumbs worked between the spine and the shoulder blades and he gently massaged her. There was enough time to feel how tight she was before Sheila pulled away.

"It'll make you feel better."

"It makes me feel tired. Do you want another cup of coffee?"

"I've got to get going. Corporate law."

"Oh, yes. Professor Rambeau." She exploded the b.

He grinned. "You know more about my day than I do."

"How come all your other teachers call themselves 'Mister' and he calls himself 'Professor'?"

"He's having an identity crisis."

"Who isn't?" She opened the refrigerator and took out a brown bag. "Here's your lunch." She held it back for a moment. "What do you say I meet you for lunch today?"

It took him by surprise. His face fell before he could control it. He pulled it back and tried to look as though he were considering the offer.

"It's all right," Sheila said. "I'll bring my own paper bag."

"What about Vikki?"

"I could bring her. We could come over to the lunchroom right after nursery school."

"Sounds like a great idea." It was not convincing. "You don't think she'll get bored?"

Sheila smiled tolerantly. "No. Will you?"

140

"No," he said quickly. "I'd really love it." Then he realized he should have heard the joke. "It's just that some of the guys use the lunchroom to study. If she got restless—"

"It was just a thought."

"A good one. Maybe some time when you don't have Vikki."

"Maybe."

"I'd really like that."

She gave him the bag.

He took it tentatively. "Well. . . ." Phil kissed her. "What are you going to do now?"

"First I'm going to read the paper."

"Great."

"Isn't it?" she said dryly. "Sensational. Then I'll wake Vikki and take her to nursery school and spend my free time trying to figure out what to say to Diana. Should I expect you home at the regular time?"

"Sure." He did not move right away.

"I'll be all right," she said.

"Listen, about lunch—"

"We'll work it out for some other time."

"I'll call you this afternoon."

"Don't be late for your class."

Phil put his lunch in his attaché case. He wedged it tightly between *Labor Law* and Allyn and Whitehead. He put on his jacket and topcoat. At the front door he picked up the *Times*. He folded it in thirds automatically, the way he did when he took it with him every morning, and offered it to Sheila.

"Such service."

"Be good." He kissed her again.

Phil always used the elevator ride to make the transition from his private to his public life. When it shut on the fifth floor, it shut out the apartment and Sheila and Vikki, the monthly bills, the disordered rooms, May, Bernie, Paul, Renata, or whoever else had called the night before. When it opened on the lobby, it opened on corporate law, his classmates, his professors, job interviews, the glass walls of the Law School Building.

He had never realized how much he depended on that

141

brief, vacant period between floors to set up his day. He realized it this morning because he missed it. His uneasiness over Sheila stayed with him after the doors shut. He carried it through the lobby and out to the street.

He had bungled the business about lunch. Nobody really used the lunchroom to study, even though everyone talked around tables with open books in front of them. Sheila knew it, too.

Phil loved that hour with the other law students. They talked about bar exams, the job market, or the day's political news. They all read the New York *Times* as though they were preparing an assignment for the hour. Phil would sit with his jacket unbuttoned, his tie loose at the neck, and his ankle crossed over his thigh. He tilted his chair back on two legs. Even when Sheila was in the hospital that hour was golden to him. He could be absolutely in control, casual and open, one of a group of leaders who could bat around politics, their careers, sometimes even personal problems with ease and humor. He loved the vending machine coffee with the synthetic cream and bits of cup wax floating on top. The idea of Sheila's joining him for that time was unthinkable. He knew, for one thing, that the other students felt the same as he about the hour. To bring a wife to the table would be disloyal, the violation of a society as closed as the lounge at Frederick Ryan's club.

Phil had never thought of being unfaithful to Sheila. It was not out of any moral conviction, or even out of the intensity of his love for her. His imagination simply did not run in that direction. Still, when Sheila had suggested that she meet him for lunch, Phil understood what other men felt like when their wives found them out in an affair.

He replayed the scene in his mind again as he walked down Amsterdam Avenue, and winced.

Three charter buses stood parked at the corner of 116th Street near the law school. Students with knapsacks and canvas hand luggage milled around the doors. They were mostly undergraduates, although Phil recognized a few scattered law students. Everyone carried mimeographed instruction sheets.

Some scanned them with serious faces; others held them rolled in their fists or crammed in pocketbooks. The crowd had a curious mixed quality, solemn and exuberant, like celebrants at a tense festival. The buses were marked for Mississippi.

Three years before, when the freedom riders had started organizing and before the first bus had gone south, Sheila had wanted to join them. It was impossible, of course. Vikki was just two years old and Phil was starting law school. She had heard about the scheme from a friend who had married an instructor at Harvard. Phil liked the idea behind it but he wasn't convinced it could work. It smacked of a public relations gesture and a lot of people involved seemed a little hysterical. He and Sheila had talked about it. She had agreed there was no guarantee, that it might even be dangerous, but it was something she could do. After all the meetings and forums and hot debates she had organized, this was a chance, at last, to act. Phil was proud of her conviction and, as the movement grew, he was once again amazed at her prophetic instincts. There was more than one way to act, though, and that was what he had finally brought her to understand. His work in law school might not have the same glamor or immediacy as the buses, but in the long run he would be in an even better position to help. Phil understood the way power worked. You gained it slowly and you used it rationally. As the oldest son in the Gaynor family he had been trained to it.

The lecture hall was big enough for three hundred students. The seats of the amphitheater fanned out around the speaker's platform. They rose steeply. When students stood to answer questions—and Professor Rambeau insisted they stand—it was like calling down a well.

The sides and the back of the room were already filled. The buzz of voices and the rustle of the *Times* and *The Wall Street Journal* filled the room.

Phil spotted a single seat halfway up at the side. He climbed the center aisle and pushed through. He snapped open his attaché case and pulled out his text on corporate law, careful not to dislodge his lunch. Rambeau's daily assignments were brutal. Phil had been planning to read all night after the Ryans and his shift at the bookstore, but Sheila had surprised him. He wasn't ready for class. He flipped the pages, skimming for key phrases and bold-faced precedent decisions.

A heavy young man looked over his shoulder. His face was pink from shaving and he wore a wool jacket that scraped against Phil. "Just remember *Freeman versus The State of New York*. The State of New York won. The decision was based on the mutual obligation of the institution and the individual."

"What was the case?"

"I don't know. My brother took the course five years ago. He told me it's Rambeau's favorite decision, but that's all you have to know about it."

Professor Rambeau demanded perfect attendance at his lectures. He had a determinedly thick French accent when he lectured and a soft, monotonous delivery, the kind that encouraged daydreaming. Every five minutes he would shoot out a question and choose a name at random from his roll book. If the student could not answer, Rambeau's accent would fade, each word turn crystal clear, and he would cut the student down where he stood.

Everybody hated him. He was the sourest topic in the lunchroom and the one most often brought up. Phil could never be quite as violent about him as the others. The man knew his field. If his methods were a little terroristic, they, too, were a part of the training. A successful lawyer had to know how to hold up under that kind of fire.

A nervous spurt of voices filled the hall as Rambeau appeared. Phil tightened, too, but in his own way he welcomed it. It was another kind of challenge to measure his ripeness.

Rambeau was a squat, thickset man with a small mustache that looked penciled in. He mounted a small box behind the podium and began speaking before the sound of shifting bodies subsided. He leaned over the podium with his hands dangling over the front end. He never moved from that position.

Phil tried to listen carefully and pick up some clue to the

144

questions Rambeau might ask, but the man kept making references to reading Phil hadn't done. His mind wandered —first to Sheila, and then, as if to avoid the confusion she'd brought home with her, to the Ryans.

Dinner had happened exactly as young Fred predicted. After the main course, the serving woman brought out a tray of fruits in aspic and a decanter of crème de menthe. Eleanor Ryan said, "Shall I serve?" Fred Ryan nodded. She cut into the aspic and brought out a perfect square. She covered it with crème de menthe until it just dripped over the sides and gave it to the serving woman, who brought it to Phil. All conversation stopped. Phil watched, fascinated and excited. He could be sure, now, the offer would happen. He caught Ryan watching him. It occurred to Phil that young Fred had purposely prepared him so Ryan could watch how he handled his excitement. He forced his face to look noncommittal and thought he saw Ryan's flicker of approval.

The grandson had treated the tradition with contempt. Phil liked it. He liked the idea that Eleanor Ryan had learned to slice out those perfect squares by doing it for all the other top men who worked for Ryan, that she was doing it now for him, and he might be one of the last. He liked the way they acted as if this were the first time it had ever happened and he liked being able to act that way, too—even while they all might know that he, too, recognized it as ritual.

Ryan tasted, nodded approval, and turned to Phil. "Let's get down to business."

Phil shot a look at Mrs. Ryan. She had lowered her eyes.

Ryan laid out the terms. He needed a junior lawyer in his Connecticut office. The work would be all research for the first couple of years; he couldn't expect to plead. That would be standard operating procedure no matter where Phil went, unless he was planning to chase ambulances. The salary would be good, better than anything he'd be able to find in the city, and the chance for advancement a hell of a lot better than that. Naturally.

Ryan spoke the way his wife had sliced the aspic. His precision riveted Phil. Constance Gaynor knew about the offer. She approved. She would be delighted to have him and his family close to home.

Phil asked if there were openings in the city.

Ryan nodded. "A couple. But they're not what I'm offering you."

"Can I ask why?"

"I need you in Connecticut. There are plenty of your caliber lawyers who'll take a job in New York. I need someone like you, who's comfortable in Connecticut. You've been around tobacco most of your life. Your father's name counts for something. Don't get the idea I'm offering you a free ride." He smiled coolly and shot a look at his wife. "Those are reserved for the immediate family. I want you in Connecticut because I want someone good. The Surgeon General is going to be coming out with a report on cigarettes sometime next year and the tobacco industry is going to be hopping. You'll be right at the center of all the action." Ryan lit a cigar. "Besides," he said vaguely. He puffed a few times. "I want to see what kind of a team you and Ronstein make."

Phil's head shot up. The old man's tone was casual and, at the same time, suggestive. He left no way for Phil to ask what he meant, even while he silently smoked his cigar. "I'll have to know if you want the job no later than Christmas. You'll be at your mother's, won't you?"

"Yes." He glanced at Eleanor Ryan. "We'll all be there."

"Good. We can get more specific then. I think you'll be with us. What's this business about your wanting to stay in the city? Is that something Sheila's cooked up?"

"No," he said quickly.

"She's a city girl. It shows all over her. She'll have to adjust to Northfield."

"She might be able to better than me."

"What's your special love for New York?"

Phil lowered his eyes.

"Fred," Eleanor Ryan broke in softly. "I think that's Philip's business, don't you?"

146

Phil was relieved, yet his face stung. Eleanor Ryan knew his secret. She knew how much he loved Fred Ryan and that her husband and the city were one in his mind. The prospect of giving up the city meant giving up the chance to build a life like the old man's, to earn his strength, his quiet, unquestioned power, the admiration of young men like himself.

It might mean giving up the chance to use that power for social change in the way he had assured Sheila he would. She might see it as a contradiction anyway, and claim that power like Ryan's could only work to preserve the past; but that was wrong. He could do both. When he had Sheila and Vikki as secure, as invulnerable as the Ryans, he would be able to take the risks he wanted to. If he could work for Ryan in New York he could work toward that. He could contain them both, just as the city itself could contain the Ryans' unchanging brownstone and the freedom buses. But working for Ryan in Connecticut meant a return to the past, to his father, his family. It would mean safety, security for Sheila and Vikki, but maybe not invulnerability, not the greatness of Frederick Ryan, not so much freedom to take risks.

Maybe that was what growing up was all about. Ryan seemed to demand an impossible decision. It wasn't impossible, though. Just difficult. Until he'd confronted Fred Ryan's hardheaded realism, Phil had thought of his future as all or nothing. Power, ideals, security for Sheila and Vikki. He'd seen himself as a hero. Maybe he should start thinking of himself as a man. That meant compromise. Perhaps it only meant giving up dreams of glory.

"A good lawyer's like a good scientist," Ryan said. "You work with the evidence. You build your case on what you have, not what you wish you had."

"I understand that."

"That's not advice from an employer; it's a friend of the family speaking."

"I appreciate it."

"Here's more. Don't commit yourself until you have to."

Phil nodded.

147

"But when you do it, do it. There are some people who think they never have to. They're wrong. Besides, you're lucky. You know when you have to."

"Christmas," Phil said.

Ryan nodded once.

Phil had still not touched his dessert. He scooped up a spoonful. It tasted sharp and minty at first, then bland. The fruit center, sweet, almost overripe, surprised him.

"Mr. Gaynor?" Professor Rambeau's voice cut through his thoughts. Phil rose in confusion. He had not heard the question. The heavy young man beside him smiled and surreptitiously nodded encouragement. Phil clutched at it.

"*Connecticut versus The State of New York*," Phil said.

There was a short silence. Someone across the hall coughed. Phil heard what he'd said. "I mean—" His authority failed.

"What do you mean, Mr. Gaynor?" Rambeau's voice was ice. "It's best to say what you mean, don't you think? Decisions, after all, are based on what we say, not what we mean, when we practice corporate law. That might not be true in philosophical law or bus-riding law or cloud-cuckoo-land law, but we're not training you for those. Are we?" He paused, then insisted. "Are we?"

"No, sir."

"No, sir. That's an intelligible answer. I'm reassured. I was afraid you'd taken to speaking in tongues."

The young man beside him sank in his seat.

"*Connecticut versus The State of New York*" Rambeau said. "Now that you've given us all a glimpse of the battle of the titans shall I repeat the question?"

Phil had heard the stillness that filled the hall before. It was tense, breathless, ashamed. He had never stood in the center of it, though. It made his head swim.

"That won't be necessary, sir. I haven't prepared the reading."

Rambeau glanced down at the podium briefly. "Mr. Sanitelli, would you care to do your heritage proud by telling Mr. Gaynor the decision we've been discussing?"

148

A tall stoop-shouldered student stood in one of the front rows. He wore a dark-blue suit. The edges of his jacket was rumpled. *"Freeman versus—"*

"Please turn and address Mr. Gaynor. He's the one who needs your help."

Mr. Sanitelli hesitated, then turned toward Phil. Neither looked at the other.

"Freeman versus The State of New York. The State of New York won the decision."

"Based upon?"

"The mutual obligation of the institution and the individual."

Rambeau looked at Phil.

Phil nodded. The professor said nothing. He waited.

Phil said, "Thank you."

Mr. Sanitelli turned forward.

"Be seated, gentlemen."

Phil eased back into his seat. The heavy young man shifted to give him room.

Phil's head spun. He kept his eyes turned forward. He did not dare look around the amphitheater for fear of seeing someone look at him. He could not tell how long he sat, absolutely still, unable to focus on anything. Rambeau was a blur. His mouth moved but it had nothing to do with the drone that accompanied it. Phil's back and shoulders ached from holding them rigid.

It wasn't over yet. It wouldn't be until after lunch. No one would bring up what happened until Phil did. He had to find the right balance of concern and indifference to carry it off. It was another initiation. It would not be complete until he had proven himself with the others.

There was a stir around him. The heavy young man wriggled in his seat and Professor Rambeau collected his books and papers. The session was over. Phil pulled his attaché case from under his chair and snapped it open. As he laid his book in it he went limp with relief. It occurred to him that sometime in his life the same thing had happened to Fred Ryan. All he had to do was figure out how Ryan had handled it.

149

Lunch was touchy, but he carried it off. Some time during the hour Mr. Sanitelli came in. Phil smiled and nodded to him across the room. That clinched his success and brought him home free.

The strain left him useless for work, though. He cut his class in labor law and stayed in the library. He called home twice during the afternoon. Sheila was out. He let the phone ring a long time before he remembered Diana. He started dialing the Brautigans once, but hung up before he had finished and went back to his books. For the rest of the afternoon his mind wandered from Rambeau's assault to Sheila, to Christmas, to his sister, his brother Paul, his mother. Wherever it went it hit an impasse. He dozed part of the time with his elbow on the library table and his head on his fist. When it was time to go home he felt restless, incomplete.

All he wanted this year was a steady routine that would help him make it through classes and the bar exams. So many of his friends were in just his position, strapped for cash, with wives and kids and uncertain prospects. At least he had an offer to consider—an attractive one, too, even with its drawbacks. Yet Ryan's offer was turning out to be as much of a distraction as anything else. He could not understand how all the others were able to manage a steady schedule while his, ideal as it seemed, kept breaking apart. Even before Sheila went to the hospital he could remember settling into a rhythm, coming home with a sense that he'd really done a day's work, and that if he could keep it up he'd be ready for all the final hurdles. The feeling would last for a week, then Vikki would get sick, or Sheila show signs of exhaustion, or his brother would descend on the apartment and camp out in the living room for a couple of days. It always meant juggling study times and distraction even while he was at his books.

It was the same today. He'd left the apartment for a day that should have been a setup for real accomplishment, but he'd brought Sheila and the Ryans to it. That left him open to Professor Rambeau. The scene in corporate law, on top of everything else, tore the whole day apart.

Sheila seemed determined it would not be she who got in his

way and just as determined that he know it. When he got home for supper she was as energetic and self-sufficient as she had been at breakfast. He was barely through the door when she said, "Cuba's been under blockade for three goddamned weeks!" She was incredulous. "Why didn't somebody tell me?"

She had just got to the paper before he came in. It seemed that Diana had called right after he left that morning so she didn't get a chance to look at it before it was time to wake Vikki. She and Diana agreed to meet when they picked up the kids at nursery school, have lunch, and spend the afternoon together.

"I don't know what's more terrible," she said. She handed him a glass of grapefruit juice while she put the dinner together. "The blockade or my not knowing about it. Why didn't it ever come up?"

"You were in the hospital." He stood in the doorway with the juice and watched her work. He could not remember the last time he'd seen her move so fast. "How did you handle Diana?"

"The business about the show?" Sheila laughed. "I didn't have to. I love that girl, I really do. The phone rings, I pick it up, and this voice says, 'You know what's funny?' No 'Hello. How are you? How was the hospital? Are you still alive?' Nothing. 'You know what's funny?' So I say, 'No.' And she says, 'The only thing that worried me was the idea that you might have been up all night trying to figure out a way not to tell me I stank up your screen.' "

"What did you say?"

"I said, 'You stank up my screen.' "

Phil smiled. Sheila chattered on as she worked. He did not hear everything she said. Her eyes sparkled every time she looked at him. She seemed to be signaling she was all right. Phil remembered that morning, how he'd wanted to calm her, to plead with her not to try so hard. He was still convinced she was moving too fast.

"Dinner's ready." She called Vikki and Phil realized his daughter hadn't run to meet him when he arrived. It had left him feeling he wasn't home yet.

151

"Where is she?"

"Donna taught her how to make flour paste and showed her a scrapbook she was making of all Diana's clippings. So she decided to start her own."

"Of what?"

"I have no idea. Blue Cross notices, maybe."

Vikki appeared behind Phil. Globs of paste covered her hands to the wrist and droplets dotted her arms to the elbow. Bits of newspaper and magazine clung to her shirt and pants. Phil backed into the kitchen.

"Donna showed me how to make paste."

"You look like the abominable snowman," Sheila said.

"I'm hungry."

"Go into the bathroom and wash. Then come for dinner."

"Shouldn't somebody help her?" Phil asked.

"Daddy, help me."

"Don't be silly," Sheila said. "You're old enough to wash yourself."

Vikki hesitated.

"Here, I'll help." Phil started toward her.

"No. She can do it herself."

"I don't mind."

"I do. And when you're not here, I'm the one who has to help. Vikki's big enough to wash herself."

Vikki looked at Phil.

"Sheila?"

"Go on and do a good job," she said. Vikki went to the bathroom slowly.

"New regime?" Phil asked. They sat down.

Sheila nodded. "While Donna was showing her how to make paste, Diana taught me a thing or two."

"Since when is Diana the ideal mother?"

"She's not. Neither am I. And what a relief it was to find out that little bit of information."

Vikki came back quickly. Her palms were clean but the backs of her hands were still lumped with paste.

"How the hell did you manage that?" Sheila laughed. "Go back and finish, darling."

Vikki's face puckered.

"Aren't you changing gears a little fast?" Phil asked cautiously.

"The backs of your hands and all the spots on your arms." Sheila disregarded Vikki's puckered face. "Go on."

Vikki backed off slowly. She looked from Sheila to Phil, then made her decision. Her face crinkled like foil. She let out a sustained wail. Sheila shot from the table. She whirled Vikki around and smacked her three times. Phil flinched. She took Vikki by the back of the neck with one hand, forced her into the hallway, and shoved her toward the bathroom. Vikki's wailing grew louder as she moved farther away.

"Don't worry," Sheila said when she came back to the table. "I haven't turned into a child beater."

"Wouldn't it have been easier to go with her?" he asked a little sullenly.

"For who?" Sheila was calm, good-humored, but her hand trembled when she picked up her fork. "That's the exhilaration of battle," she said.

He started to speak, then hesitated.

"What?"

"She hasn't seen you for almost a month."

Sheila nodded. "And I'll be damned if I'm going to let her rest on feeling deprived."

Vikki came back, silent and cautious. Her hands were clean but wet. "Good girl." Sheila pecked her on the cheek. "Now dry them with a dish towel and sit down." Vikki went to the sink without a word. Sheila's eyes opened wide. She shot a look of surprised triumph at Phil.

Vikki sat quietly through dinner, throwing occasional puzzled glances, first at Sheila, then Phil. He wondered if she were reassessing his power.

He was tired. The day felt as if it had started the morning before. He still had six hours to go at the bookstore. Sheila wanted to talk about Cuba. Phil and his friends had hashed that out over lunch for over a week when it first happened. It was stale now and he answered her questions laconically.

"It doesn't look dangerous anymore," he said, finally.

153

"But the implications, Phil. Don't you realize what it means? That kind of unilateral decision? He didn't even go to Congress." It was irritating to hear her press a dead issue so hard, and her tone suggested they really ought to do something about it. He shrugged and made a helpless gesture to close the conversation.

Sheila maintained her pace and energy for the rest of the week. She was up for him every night when he came home from the bookstore and awake every morning before him. She was learning how to really take naps, she told him. Every night after Vikki was asleep she would lie down for a couple of hours. She had started lying down in the morning, as well, during nursery school hours, but she quickly found she did not need that.

"You know why I used to be tired all the time?" she said one time early the next week. "Because I wanted to be."

Phil tried to dismiss it.

"It's true. I could always find a reason not to get enough rest. Vikki needed attention, I had to do the laundry, I had to make a phone call, take the garbage out. . . . You see? So I wouldn't rest. Then I would be tired—and that would give me a reason to avoid all the things I had to do that were keeping me from getting enough rest. Isn't that insane?"

She seemed to be wildly rooting around in their life before as though it were a rummage drawer, pulling out piece after piece, examining, discarding, replacing. She was judging it all but Phil could not see where the judgment came from. It was all too haphazard. There was no difference between her determination to be awake for him every night and to get the newspaper read every day. Her anger over the blockade was as intense as her anger at the rising price of bacon, or a casting director who made a pass at Diana.

What alarmed him most was Sheila's exuberance. Even when she was outraged he could see such delight beneath it, such an astonished joy at her own vehemence that it made him apprehensive. She committed herself to the business of challenging the pattern of her life the way she used to commit herself to political causes before they were married—and the

154

way she had later committed herself to the marriage. That ability to barrel into any new situation had always been one of her most endearing qualities. Phil had almost forgotten it. He recognized it again, though, quickly enough. Now it seemed dangerous. It was one thing to jump into an ACTION project or a love affair with both feet and no safety rules. It was another to tear into the fabric of their whole life together. He was afraid her own enthusiasm would betray her.

He did not want to say anything about his concern until she saw Dr. Rankin. The psychiatrist would be able to spot the trouble and handle it. Phil was sure, too, that if there were any immediate danger Rankin would contact him. He didn't. When Phil asked Sheila about the first session she said, "We talked about Cuba. And Thanksgiving." She chuckled. "He's got in-law problems, too."

Phil felt betrayed and wondered if he should question Rankin's professional ethics. Of course, he could not be sure Sheila was reporting accurately. It might not really have been so casual, after all. That made it worse. There was no way he could find out and that left him feeling excluded and helpless.

He called home after every class and two or three times from the library. If she was home she would answer brightly, sound genuinely puzzled about why he called, then reassure him. She was just on her way out, or she and Vikki had just come in from shopping, or the park, or Diana's, and wasn't it cold out? Most of the time there was no answer. That was when Phil would panic and the image of Sheila unconscious in her yellow bathrobe would flash through his mind. He would not be able to study until he'd called again and found her in. Twice during the week the fear became so real he left the library and went home to be sure she was really out. Then he hurried back down Amsterdam Avenue, afraid of running into her and Vikki, ashamed of his mistrust.

They were to drive to Woodview on Thursday. On Wednesday night he came home from the bookstore and found the house empty. It was one in the morning. He ran into Vikki's room. Her bed was made and her clothes lay on the chair by the play table. He raced through the apartment

155

looking for some clue, furious at himself for not admitting his worst fears sooner. He shouldn't have waited for Rankin's advice. He should have trusted himself, but he'd been too afraid he was being irrational. He ran from bedroom to bedroom, trembling and trying to think straight. He pushed through all the clothes in the hall closet. Vikki's snowsuit was there. So was Sheila's coat. He imagined her running out in her yellow bathrobe in the November night with Vikki in nothing but her nightgown.

He thought of calling Bernie and May. If Sheila had run off they would be the most likely people to run to. But if she hadn't gone to Woodview he did not want to alarm the Kahns. He was about to call the Brautigans when the front lock clicked. He tore from the kitchen and flung the door open.

"Jesus Christ, you scared me," she whispered. She held Vikki asleep in her arms. "What's wrong?"

Phil could not speak right away.

"Phil?" she asked quickly. "What is it?"

"Where were you?"

She looked at him blankly. "Didn't you see my note?"

"What note?"

"I left it with your coffee," she whispered. "I was sitting for Estelle Donado." She searched his face. "You didn't see it. Oh, you poor baby." She bit her lower lip and winced as if to show him she knew how he must have felt, then she signaled him to be quiet. She tiptoed into Vikki's room and eased her into bed.

Phil followed Sheila to the kitchen. "I was afraid you might be worried at first, but I was sure you'd see it there." His cup, with coffee powder at the bottom, stood on the stove near the kettle. The note lay beside it.

His shame and relief must have shown. Sheila's face turned suddenly gentle. She went to him and stroked his head. "Oh, sweetheart, you must have been out of your mind." She laughed softly and her voice was tender with concern. "I'm sorry," she said. "I'm so sorry. I can't see how you missed it."

Phil put his arms around her and pressed her to him tightly. She kissed his cheek. "Shall I make some coffee now?" she said in his ear.

156

He lowered his face to her shoulder and nodded.

"I can't."

"Why not?"

"I'm a prisoner in your viselike grasp."

He pulled her tighter, then released his grip slowly. "Estelle called about seven," Sheila explained as she got the coffee ready. "She had some kind of affair to go to. Her sister had to cancel out at the last minute so I said yes. Besides, she's in the pool and that meant more sitting hours. Did you know I've racked up about fifteen already since I've been home? And poor Estelle. She's got about forty hours' credit. She keeps sitting for everybody and hoping someday she'll get a chance to use them for herself. She's got eight brothers and sisters and Tony's got six. The only time she ever uses the pool is when somebody's either getting married or hemorrhaging."

Phil was still too ashamed to speak. Sheila knew it. Her chatter was a kindness. He hadn't seen the note because he did not believe it would be there. The moment he found the apartment empty all the week's tension had broken, all the mistrust he'd been fighting since she came home had burst out. It was almost as though he'd been waiting for a catastrophe that would vindicate his fears. Sheila knew now that he doubted her ability, that over the whole week he had not believed in any of her discoveries or accomplishments.

The kitchen table was set for breakfast. Sheila brought his coffee and stood over him. She had not said anything for a while. "It's all right, Phil. I would have been scared, too. Especially if I'd been scared before."

He nodded.

She turned to get her own coffee. Phil looked up at her back. She was wearing a green cotton dress with a thin belt. The belt accented her tiny body. Phil loved to take her waist in his hands and marvel at the way his thumbs almost touched. She was never more fragile than at those times and he never felt more proud and protective. She turned to him. Their eyes met. Hers always turned soft, serious, as vulnerable as her body when that happened. This time they stayed serious, but clear and steady. She was not conscious of being looked at. She

157

looked very hard at him, and Phil recalled, for the first time since he could remember, that they were the same age. For an instant it was Phil who turned frightened and young.

She smiled and his sense of loss and humiliation grew sharper. There was a security in her smile more painful, more desolate and confusing than all the apprehensiveness and doubt of the week before. Then he had been afraid she was not as capable and strong as she thought. Now he knew she was.

He turned away. Her face was new, her smile so frank that it forced him to look at their life through her own relentlessly tender eyes. He found it unthinkable that he had not really wanted Sheila strong, independent, healthy. Yet if she were all those things he would not be able to show his concern, to practice his kind ways—and over the past three years that had been the only way he'd known to express his love. Now he would have to find another way. He did not even know where to begin.

Woodview was an hour and a half from New York. With holiday traffic and stops for Vikki they could figure on an extra hour's traveling time. Phil went downtown early to pick up a car. Bernie insisted on an Impala from Hertz. Sheila was ready for him when he got back. She had packed a small suitcase for Vikki with a change of clothes, pajamas, and a blanket so the child could sleep in the back on the trip home. There was also an A & P bag with Vikki's dolls, an extra sweater, Kleenex, a couple of bananas, a hairbrush, and another A & P bag for garbage. They put the suitcase in the trunk and the bags in the back seat. Sheila ran upstairs for the crisper from the refrigerator. She had promised to bring the salad for May. When she came back she also had a cosmetic bag.

"Mom left it in the bathroom. I'm so glad I remembered."

They put the crisper near Sheila's feet in the front and the bag in the glove compartment.

"Are we ready to go now?" Phil asked, a little impatiently.

"Would you go up and bring down the cot from Vikki's

158

room?" He started to protest. "I don't know when we'll have a car again, and it's just cluttering up the apartment."

"We might be able to use it when my brother visits."

"He's always managed on the couch. I want to give it back to my parents. Just roll it down. It'll fit in the trunk."

He blew some air from his mouth and worked his way out of the car.

The cot didn't fit. They had to force it into the back seat. Phil almost tore the upholstery, but they finally managed to wedge it and still leave half a seat for Vikki. Phil had to crane his neck to see through the rearview mirror.

"This may be the first time in history that we go to Woodview with more than when we come back," Sheila said as they started off.

"I wouldn't count on it." Phil smiled wryly. He remembered the wonderful, expansive feeling of driving alone up Riverside Drive from the Hertz office as he stretched to check traffic behind him. He turned off 118th Street.

Vikki got on her knees. She set up her dolls on the shelf beneath the back window and blocked the rest of Phil's view. He thought of telling her to sit down but he did not want to take a chance while she was busy. He rolled down his window to adjust the side mirror.

The day was cold and overcast and they all wore bulky coats. Every year Phil looked forward to the Thanksgiving trip as their autumn jaunt. He had visions of romping with Vikki through thick, brilliant leaf piles. He was always surprised by the gray, flat ground and the trees already naked and brittle-looking. He rolled up his window and turned on the heater.

They passed the city of huge oil drums near Secaucus. Vikki leaned over the front seat.

"I'm getting sick."

"That's the smell, honey," Sheila said. "We'll be out of it soon." She maneuvered around in her seat and rummaged through the bag on the floor. "There's an empty bag here just in case." She found it and handed it to Vikki. "Use this if you have to throw up. And unzip your snowsuit. It's warm in the car." Sheila settled forward again. Phil wondered if he would

159

ever again take a car trip that wasn't a series of constantly shifting, bundled bodies.

Sheila lit a cigarette and stared out the window. Smoke filled the car.

Phil glanced at her. "Honey?"

"Hmmm?"

"Your window?"

She snapped to. "I'm sorry." She rolled down her window halfway. "Zip up again, sweetheart," she called in back. "How are you doing? Feeling better?"

"I'm fine. Marie threw up."

Phil looked in the mirror. Vikki was replacing a doll on the back shelf. "Here's the bag." She handed it to Sheila.

"I don't want it."

"It's dirty."

"It's your kid."

"Then I'll get sick."

"Sheila," Phil said quickly. "Take the bag."

"What if one of the others gets sick?" she said to Vikki.

"They're all right."

"Give it to me, honey," Phil said. He raised his hand for it. She gave him the empty bag and he saw Sheila's lips twitch against laughter.

The cold air knifed in on Phil's neck through the open window. "Sheila? Honey? Maybe the side vent would be better."

She rolled up the window and opened the little sail-shaped panel on the side. It didn't clear the smoke as efficiently, but at least the draft was not as direct.

Phil darted another look at her. She hadn't been so calm since she came home. He wanted to talk with her about Fred Ryan's offer. Ever since that first night when he'd treated it so casually he'd been looking for a way to bring it up again. There were a couple of opportunitites during the week. Each time Phil found a reason to avoid it. He was still not sure she was rational; he was tired; she was reading; he wanted to make love and it would distract her. Now there were no excuses but he still could not open it up with her.

160

He was acting like a kid, carrying around a guilty secret, trying to find a way to get rid of it and afraid, at the same time, of being caught with it. That was stupid. There was no secret. Sheila knew about the day he spent with the Ryans, and she knew about the offer. He hadn't made a decision yet. He didn't plan to until he had talked it out with her. There was no reason to be nervous about a discussion. Sheila was sharp. When it came down to serious business he could count on her to be realistic. He had never before been wary of leveling with her and he couldn't avoid the knowledge that he was wary now, not for her, but himself. He was trying to protect something. He had never thought he had to protect anything from Sheila. They had both always prided themselves on their intimacy and mutual trust. He could not remember a time he had been ashamed to broach any subject, his family, her family, sex, fear, God. This wasn't even as delicate as any of those. This was practical business. Yet there was something about it that touched the outside boundaries of their intimacy. He knew, for one thing, that he never wanted to have to talk about his love for Fred Ryan to Sheila.

He told himself he wouldn't have to. All he had to do was begin by speaking, get her attention. They could discuss the offer without going near that privacy. Her name stuck in his throat. He was even afraid she might hear him struggling with it.

He cleared his throat.

Sheila turned. "You know what I did yesterday?" she said. It was as though his cough had startled her into speech first. Phil wondered if she had been struggling with his name.

"I had lunch at the men's faculty club. With Leo Kauffman. Do you remember him? The political science teacher?"

"Poli sci?" He tried to think.

"Political science." Sheila clicked her tongue. "Honestly, Phil. Only fraternity boys call it poli sci. Anyway, the whole thing was spooky. I bumped into him on the street the first day I was back and we must have stood and talked for about an hour."

"What about?"

"I don't know. Yes, I do. We were near the campus on a Hundred Sixteenth Street. I was just going home from dropping Vikki and I was watching them load up the Freedom bus. Did you see it? You must have."

Phil nodded.

"Wasn't it gorgeous?"

He smiled briefly.

"We talked about that. At least, we started talking about that. Or, anyway, I did. That was what was peculiar about it. He was crossing Amsterdam Avenue and he slowed down to look at the crowd. I walked over to him and started talking. He remembered me. I shouldn't have been so surprised. I only took about thirty-two courses with him."

"What was so peculiar?"

"That I went to him at all, for openers." Sheila smiled. "Even while I was doing it I knew that if it had been two months before I would have run and hidden behind one of the pillars under the Law School Bridge. Can you imagine that? I would have been absolutely terrified to have him see me. Like if he glanced at me I would have disappeared. Whether he recognized me or not. Just *pffft*. Demolished. I was nervous enough last week, but I was just so goddamned excited at seeing the buses I had to talk to somebody—and he was there. Once I started talking I couldn't stop. All this stuff kept coming out of me. Things I'd forgotten I knew. I started talking about the buses and all of a sudden I was quoting Veblen's theory of the leisure class, and *Plekhanov*, for God's sake! And I was talking about Bernstein and Jaurès' revisionism and Edmund Burke." Phil could hear what she must have sounded like. Even as she told him about it the words were tumbling out so fast they barely made room for each other. She laughed. "The poor man stood there in the cold, all stooped over with this huge, black briefcase that must have been loaded with books, nodding." She imitated it, working her head from the base of the neck. "Well, finally, he asked me if I'd like to have lunch some time and we made a date for yesterday."

"How come you didn't tell me about it?"

162

"I don't know." She stopped abruptly. There was a long silence. "That's a lie." Her voice was softer. "I didn't tell you because I didn't want you to spoil it."

Phil frowned, puzzled.

"Is that a terrible thing to say?"

"No. No. Not at all. I just don't understand. . . ."

Sheila shrugged. "I made the date without even thinking. All this stuff had been coming out of me and I was so excited that I just didn't want it to end. So I made the date and we shook hands—" She hesitated.

Phil understood. "And he held your hand a little too long and pressed it."

Sheila turned quickly and studied his face. "That's right."

He smiled sympathetically. "Did he make a pass at you?" He was glad for the opportunity to reassure her.

"No. He didn't. He pressed my hand because he liked me. He's been a widower for three years. He's lonely and he loves his students. But that was exactly what I thought as I was walking home. And I thought, Should I be running around having lunch with old professors when I've got responsibilities at home, and what if he turns out to be a dirty old man, after all? And who's going to take care of Vikki and what about the laundry and getting ready to go to Woodview?—and all the other reasons I would have found two months ago to kill the opportunity. I guess that's why I didn't tell you. I was afraid you might think of all those reasons, too—and maybe even find a better one. I didn't want to risk it."

"What kind of opportunity?" He tried to make it an honest question, but it came out like a retaliation.

Sheila flinched. She looked down at her lap and absently adjusted her coat over it. "Maybe just to have lunch with an old professor."

Phil shrugged.

"You see? It is bothering you."

"Not at all." He searched for a way to prove it. "How was lunch?" he asked, finally. It was a little too flat. He glanced at her to show he meant the question.

"Fine."

"What did you talk about?"

"Everything. Politics, theory, what's been going on at Berkeley, who the Republicans are going to put up against Kennedy in sixty-four, students he's kept in contact with. I felt like Rip Van Winkle." She shook her head and smiled. "He kept calling me Miss Kahn."

"Did you tell him you were married?"

"No."

"Why not?"

She opened her hands in her lap and made a helpless gesture.

"I was afraid he'd take it the wrong way. That he'd think I was warning him off or something. Besides—"

"What?"

"Nothing. It was stupid."

"Besides what?" Phil was stung enough to insist.

"I was afraid he'd stop talking seriously." She looked down at her hands. "I even kept my gloves on."

"Didn't he ask what you were doing?"

She nodded. She was growing uncomfortable.

"What did you tell him?"

She answered so softly he couldn't hear.

"What?"

She raised her head. Her eyes were closed when she repeated it. "I told him I was going to law school." She gave him a second to respond. He didn't. "It was dumb. I don't know why I did it. I just did." She turned quickly to Vikki. "How are you doing, honey?" she said brightly. "There are bananas in here if you get hungry. Would you like to play a game? Let's see how many blue cars we can find."

The Kahns' house had started off as a white frame crackerbox fifty years before. Bernie and May had bought it after the war. Sheila was eleven when they moved from Brooklyn, where Bernie had been making a lot of money with a small wholesale dress business, but with the postwar boom he had overexpanded, hired a high-fashion designer, three more cutters, live models, and gone bankrupt within the year.

Sheila had told Phil about the fat years in Brooklyn and the shock of the move to Woodview. Eleven was old enough to have become a staunch New Yorker. Her memories were New York memories. Before they were married she would regale Phil with them. *Oklahoma!* was her first Broadway musical, October 18, 1944, at the Majestic. Every Sunday Bernie would take them to Lindy's for dinner. Once she got Pee Wee Reese's autograph. May campaigned for Henry Wallace when she wasn't having migraines and Sheila took the subway alone for art lessons at the 92nd Street Y. Phil would listen, rapt. If he felt like a guest in Frederick Ryan's world, he was an utter stranger to Sheila's. Ryan's New York was as exotic as Morocco; Sheila had the key to the Casbah.

The house the Kahns moved to stood on the edge of the woods that gave the town its name. Land was cheap. Bernie was able to borrow enough to buy fifty acres of wood and field. He went into Real Estate.

Bernie never managed to get rich in Woodview, although everyone around him made money hand over fist. The big deals always seemed to happen somewhere else. He was never able to climb back to where he had been for six years in Brooklyn. Still, he and May were never again as pinched as they had been when they first came to Woodview. They got along. Year by year Bernie expanded the house, partly with the money he earned in the business, partly by selling off his own original acreage. By the time Phil saw it, the house was a substantial one with glassed-in extensions on two sides, a carport with a guest room above, and a quarter acre of lawn ringed by Bernie's flowerbeds.

Phil had never seen the original, four rooms and a rickety garage, but Sheila had made it vivid to him. There were two bedrooms upstairs, a living room and a large, all-purpose kitchen below. The cellar was unlivable. They used it to store everything they had brought from the duplex in Brooklyn. Sheila told Phil how she would sneak down and wander in the jumble of boxes and furniture. She would look at herself in dusty mirrors and remember how they looked when they hung in May's dressing room, pick through boxes of beaded

165

dresses with huge shoulder pads, and run her hand over couches upholstered with brocade. Once she found a box filled with photographs and papers. She sneaked it up and hid it in her room. There were pictures on stiff cardboard of relatives Sheila had never seen. Each was identified on the back with neat printing, but the ink was fading on the oldest and she could not make those out. There was one of a young girl Sheila thought was herself in front of a small Russian synagogue with a young man of about sixteen. It was Doris Kahn's wedding picture. There was a brown newspaper clipping with a picture of May in an ILGWU picket line. The ends broke in Sheila's hand. There were piles of letters in Yiddish, some from Russia, and one huge pile from Germany and Poland dated 1939-42. Years later Sheila discovered Bernie and May had sponsored over forty refugees. One day the box was gone, back in the clutter of the cellar. "I never found out who put it back," she told Phil.

Two years later May's father came to live with them. He could not climb stairs. Bernie tore down the garage to build a small apartment for the old man. There was room in the house for some of the old furniture then. The rest went into a toolshed hidden just inside the woods behind the house.

Phil and Sheila arrived a little after noon. Bernie came out the kitchen door, zipping up his lumber jacket, as they swung into the driveway. Phil smiled broadly at him and automatically assumed a holiday jauntiness. Greeting Bernie was one of the most difficult parts of these visits. Neither of them was ever quite sure of what attitude to take. During the first years of the marriage Bernie would hug Phil and kiss him on the cheek. The first time it happened, Phil went rigid at the feel of his father-in-law's rough cheek on his. Later he grew to accept it. Once he tried to reciprocate by going out to greet him, but by then Bernie had realized Phil's discomfort. He backed off formally and put out his hand. After that they were like two people trying to maneuver through a narrow doorway in opposite directions.

Bernie was in his mid-fifties. He and May were short, and

166

Bernie was thickly built and barrel-chested. His face was round and virginal. His age showed, not so much in lines, as in a faint slackness of his jowls, accentuated by the determined firmness of his cheeks. His eyes were blue.

He took off his glasses and cleaned them, peering in through the car window as they pulled to a stop. Phil always had the feeling he was checking in with borrowed property when he brought Sheila and Vikki to Woodview. Bernie backed off a step to let Sheila open the door. She got out.

"Hello, baby." His voice was cautious and quizzical. Before she could respond he pulled her to him. Phil looked away.

Vikki scrambled out of the back seat and stood far enough back for Bernie to see her new snowsuit. He had sent money for it. He let go of Sheila and squatted. "You look beautiful, princess." He opened his arms. Vikki went to him and he scooped her up.

Phil took the bag from the trunk. He approached Bernie while he still held Vikki. The two men fumbled heartily with each other's free arm.

"Can I help you with anything?"

"No. This it is."

Sheila brought the crisper into the kitchen.

May was working frantically. Serving bowls covered all the surfaces. The oven was on and the smell of roasting turkey was just beginning to fill the house.

"Hello, hello, hello," she said brightly as they trooped in. She pecked Sheila on the cheek and went to Vikki. "How's my roommate?" She took her from Bernie. Phil closed the door behind him. "Everybody looks so wonderful," she said without looking. Then to Vikki, "Come say hello to Esther."

Esther was in the dining room, polishing a stack of dishes and setting places. She had worked for the Kahns' for thirteen years. Her usual day was Tuesday, but she always helped out on holiday gatherings. Phil could never get used to May's familiarity with Esther. He always remembered his own

167

mother's crisp, professional tone with the black domestics from the agency.

"Look who's here, Es." May carried Vikki in.

"Hello, hello." There was a faint, absent echo of May in Esther's voice.

Vikki lowered her head into May's shoulder.

"Haven't we gotten big?" May said.

Sheila stood in the doorway. "Hello, Esther."

"Hello, hello."

Phil came up behind Sheila.

"Vikki, honey. Get out of your snowsuit," she said.

"Here, let me do it." May put her down. "You're getting so big."

"Big enough to take off her own snowsuit, Mom."

"Oh, I know, darling. But let me do it this time. Soon she'll be too big to even let me spoil her and that's what grandmothers are for." She kissed Vikki on the forehead. "Right, sweetheart?" May frowned and kissed her quickly again. "You're not getting a fever, are you?"

"I'm hot," Vikki said.

"That's because she's got the goddamned snowsuit on, Mom."

May shot Sheila an apologetic look. "You want her to take it off herself?"

Sheila flapped her arms once. "Right now I just don't want her to get overheated."

May turned to Vikki. "I tell you what. You take it off and I'll help."

"Are you sure you don't want to bring it to the U.N. first?"

Bernie came in from the kitchen. "Vikki's got a fever?"

"No, Dad."

"You feel her, Bernie." May held Vikki still as she stripped off the snowsuit.

Bernie kissed the child on the forehead. "She feels hot."

"You've been outside. Your lips are cold."

"Then why did you ask me to feel her?"

"Don't be smart."

168

Sheila went past Phil to the kitchen. "Down the rabbit hole," she said from the corner of her mouth.

Phil stayed at the arch between the two rooms. He could see Sheila casually examine the pots and bowls. She seemed relaxed, but the tone of her wisecrack made him look more carefully. Ever since she had talked about her lunch and the silly lie she had told Professor Kauffman her spirits and good humor seemed forced. After last night he knew better than to jump to conclusions. Still, it was possible that this trip would be the hardest test yet for her. He was on guard for signs of jumpiness.

She lifted the top off a steaming soup pot. "Mom?"

"What is it, darling?"

"Who's coming this afternoon?"

May got involved in the legs of the snowsuit. "What?"

"You said on the phone it would just be us and Grandma this year. Who else is coming?"

"Oh, just a few people. You know, dropping in."

"You've got enough soup to flood Woodview."

"You've got to feed people something."

Sheila looked at Phil, then closed her eyes lightly. "Cheese and crackers," she called.

"What?"

"You feed cheese and crackers to people who drop in. You feed soup to armies and dinner guests. Who's coming?"

Vikki was stripped. "There," May said. "That was very good how you did that. Feel better? Look at that gorgeous outfit." She called to Sheila. "Those Danskins are marvelous, aren't they?" Then, to Vikki. "You're so skinny. I can play the xylophone on your ribs."

"Give her something to eat," Bernie said.

She handed him the snowsuit. "Hang it up, will you?"

Bernie shuffled off to the closet, holding the snowsuit like the grail. Sheila replaced the lid on the soup and came back to the dining room. She touched Phil on the shoulder reassuringly as she passed.

"You know how these things happen," May said before Sheila could repeat her question. "I wanted it to be just us. I really did. But then everyone wanted to get to see you. They were all so worried and so wonderful to Dad while I was away. Jack and Alice kept calling from New York. And Edith and Arnie had him to dinner twice a week."

"Edith and Arnie Kaprow are coming?"

"And you don't invite them without Sally and Merv."

"Of course not." She turned to Phil. "You've met the Kaprows."

"I don't remember."

"He's a doctor who believes in euthanasia for patients who can't pay their bills."

"Sheila," May said apprehensively.

Sheila sighed. "Don't worry. I'll be good. Anybody else?"

"Not for dinner."

"After?"

"A few people."

"Who?"

"I really can't think right now." May made a vague gesture as she went back into the kitchen. "Everybody."

"Do you mind, honey?" Phil asked softly.

Sheila took a deep breath. "It's going to be a little like a viewing." She shrugged. "What can I do? We're here."

He touched her hair.

Bernie came back. "Have you people eaten? Are you going to be able to hold out to dinner?" he asked Phil.

"We stopped on the road."

"I had a Coke," Vikki announced.

"That's not enough."

"Are you hungry, Bernie?" May said.

"I could manage a little something."

"Go sit in Poppa's room. I'll bring some soup and bread."

May's father had been dead seven years but they still called the converted garage Poppa's room. They used it now as a family room, with a television set, a bridge table, and a recliner that Bernie sat in to look out at his flowers. There was a pair of binoculars next to the recliner. Bernie used them to study the birds that his feeder attracted.

May put out soup, pumpernickel and butter for them. She gave Vikki a glass of milk. Bernie held a slice of bread in the palm of his hand and buttered it for Vikki.

"Freddie? Can I you make something?"

"No, thanks, Dad. I can manage."

He buttered a piece for himself, tore it in pieces, and dropped them in his bowl.

The soup was thick and meaty. The bread was warm. Phil liked the snacks that Bernie and May brought to Poppa's room better than the regular dinners. They were a routine part of any visit to Woodview and they always appeared spontaneous. Bernie seemed to enjoy the idea that it was Phil and Sheila who were hungry, that he was able to supply them without difficulty, and that whatever he served was right. He showed his pleasure in the way he ate.

Phil had always had great difficulty pinning down his feelings about Bernie. He liked him, certainly, but oddly enough, those qualities that made Bernie attractive were the very ones Phil had disliked in his own father. Bernie had built a comfortable middle-class life for himself, yet he seemed to enjoy retaining his immigrant habits in the midst of it. Phil's father had risen out of his class. He was the son of a Hartford insurance salesman and had married into the aristocracy when he married Constance Harmon. They had been married twenty-three years when he died; he had been a Connecticut supreme court judge for eight; yet Phil would never forget the night before he died, when they were alone in his sickroom, and Philip Gaynor had grinned and said, "I guess I haven't done too badly for a cockney salesman's kid." Phil still believed it was a sign of failure that his own father had never let go of the past, even while he enjoyed watching Bernie eat the bread he had broken into his soup.

May sat down with a bowl of cottage cheese. "It's a quarter to one," she said. "This works out perfectly. Alice and Jack are coming in on the one-thirty bus. Somebody can go pick up Bernie's mother and then meet them."

"I'll go," Sheila said. "Are they bringing Greta?"

"I don't know." She sighed. "They've got their hands full with that kid."

"What's the matter?"

"The usual business. She's involved with a boy."

"What are you talking about? She's twelve years old."

May smiled and shook her head. "Sixteen."

"You're kidding."

"I wish I were. Anyway, he works at a gas station and she's spending all her time with him. She runs over after school and sits in the garage all weekend while he fixes cars or plays his guitar. Who knows what they do. If he's working today she's not going to come."

Sheila smiled. "Sounds like normal kid stuff."

May darted a look at Vikki. "He's married."

"I thought you said he was a boy."

"He is," Bernie said angrily. "Anybody who's married and fools around with a sixteen-year-old is a boy."

"All right, Bernie," May said calmly. He went back to his soup. She signaled Sheila not to pursue it. May was a veteran at deflecting sensitive subjects from Bernie.

"How old is he?" Sheila asked across the table noiselessly.

May held up three fingers, then two.

Sheila's eyes went wide. May shook her head and jerked it toward Bernie. She flicked a warning hand.

"Don't keep trying to protect me, May," he said into his soup bowl. "I know these things go on. It's just that it's my own brother's kid."

"I know, Bernie."

"Any man takes advantage of a sixteen-year-old kid—"

"All right, Bernie."

"Are you sure he's taking advantage of her, Dad?"

"What do you mean, am I sure?" He exploded. "What else is he doing with her? The son of a bitch."

"Vikki, Bernie. . . ."

"Am I sure? What are you going to do? Excuse him?" He was shouting now. "What if it was Vikki? How sure would you have to be? Answer me that with your Barnard education.

172

What the hell good was that education in the first place when you can ask a question like that? What good when you can't think straight and you do crazy things?"

"Dad, you're not talking sense."

Phil put down his soup spoon. At least once every trip they could expect an outburst from Bernie. It never came from the same direction, but the routine was as standard as the one for snacks in Poppa's room. May would bring up a subject, notice Bernie, and signal Sheila to drop it. Sheila would carry it one step further. Bernie would explode and both women would go into action to soothe him. Bernie would leave and sulk for ten uncomfortable minutes, then snap back as refreshed as if he'd napped for an hour.

"Am I sure?" he muttered. He shook his head. ". . . sixteen-year-old kid." He made a disgusted sound, dropped his spoon in the soup, and went to the living room. Nobody watched him leave.

Sheila's face was tight and angry. May worked her spoon in the cottage cheese without eating. She looked up at Sheila. Her own face was a mixture of tenderness and apology. "It's all right, darling."

"It's not." Sheila made a fist to bang on the table. She held back. "I hate it."

"All right."

"Why do you let him get away with it? Every time."

"What should I do? You know how he is."

Sheila glanced at Phil. "You wonder why I hate scenes?"

"Leave him alone, darling. He'll be all right. "

"Sure," she said bitterly. "Now that he's made everyone else miserable, he'll be all right."

"You shouldn't be so sensitive."

"When's the last time you told *him* that?"

"Sheila," Phil said softly.

"Don't shut me up, Phil."

May turned nervously to Vikki. "Go into the other room and see if you can cheer up Grandpa, sweetheart."

"No!" It made May jump. "Don't you dare pull her onto this

merry-go-round." Sheila fixed her eyes on Vikki. "You stay right where you are. Grandpa's had enough little girls running to indulge him and soothe him and cheer him up." She turned back to her mother. May focused on Bernie's abandoned soup. "You don't explode about a thirty-two-year-old boy when you're a fifty-five-year-old infant."

"You know that's not what he's upset about," May said ruefully.

"Then what?"

May looked back at her without speaking. Phil watched Sheila closely, ready to jump in. She held her mother's eyes for a moment. Her own flashed. With an effort she looked away and pulled her pocketbook onto her lap. She rummaged for her cigarettes. "Sensational," she murmured nodding. Her voice was low, but edged. "Back to Lulu McConnell."

Vikki had been watching Sheila, fascinated. She turned to look at May as she reached for her milk. Her hand hit the rim of the glass. It fell and shattered. Vikki froze.

Sheila's head shot up. May jumped from her chair. "It's all right, darling. It's all right. Phil, get a sponge and paper towels." He was already in the kitchen. He could hear May as he searched for the towels. "Did you hurt yourself? It's all right. It's not your fault. We upset you. It's all right. . . ."

He brought back a roll of towels and squatted to soak up the milk.

"Don't get cut," May said.

Vikki wriggled out of her arms and went to Sheila. She buried her face in her mother's chest.

Sheila stroked her hair once. "Hey," she said gently. "You crying?"

Vikki shook her head without raising it.

"That was pretty clumsy, wasn't it?"

She nodded.

"You're too big for that kind of baby stuff now, aren't you?"

Vikki hesitated before she nodded again.

"Be more careful next time?"

Vikki hugged her tighter.

174

"Good girl."

May got up. "I'll get a broom."

Phil was still on his knees, sopping up the milk. He looked up at Sheila.

"Don't you get sore now," she said to him over Vikki's head.

"I'm not." He tore off a dry piece of towel. "It's not your fault."

"Nothing's ever anybody's fault in this house. It's a wonderful thing."

May came back with a broom and dustpan. "I'll do the rest, Phil. It's just about time to pick up Grandma."

Sheila shifted Vikki off her lap. "I'd better get going."

"Can I go?" Vikki asked.

"Get your snowsuit."

May stopped sweeping. "You think she should? I heard her sniffle before."

"It'll be all right."

"Maybe Phil should go. You're upset."

"I'm fine. I'll take the rented car."

"It's in Phil's name, isn't it?"

"I'll avoid roadblocks. Besides, Grandma's terrified of Phil."

"She isn't." May was shocked.

"She thinks I'm Catholic," Phil explained.

"You're not Catholic."

He shrugged. "That's what I told her."

"As far as Grandma's concerned," Sheila said, "if you're not Jewish you're Catholic."

"But she adores Phil."

"She's also terrified."

"I never heard of such a thing."

Sheila turned to Phil. "You'd better get the cot out of the car if I've got to pick up the others, too. We brought the cot back, Mom."

May looked away from her. Her voice turned unnaturally bright. "Fine, darling." She glanced toward the kitchen door, then knelt to pick up a stray piece of glass. "You don't need

175

any help with it, do you, Phil?" she asked casually. "Just put it in the toolshed. I'm sure there's room. Do it quickly, though, will you?"

Bernie came in with a brown paper bag. "Isn't it time to get Grandma?"

"Sheila was just going, darling."

"Good. Bring this to her, will you?"

"What is it?"

He held it back. "Just a little something. For the holiday. She knows what it is."

"Dad always sends a little something," May explained.

"Can I look?"

"What for?"

Sheila took the bag without opening it.

"What's this about the toolshed?"

"Phil's got to store something in there," May said.

"We brought back the cot Mom used when she stayed in the apartment," Sheila said.

"You couldn't use it?"

"You know how small the apartment is, Bernie," May said quickly. "It's just for storage." She braced herself.

Bernie shrugged. "Let me help you with it. I'll have to find a spot in the shed." May went back to her sweeping, relieved.

Vikki came back with the snowsuit and went to May. "Oh, here, darling. Let me help you." She went to put down her broom but pulled back. "Why don't you show me how you do it yourself?" She glanced triumphantly at Sheila.

"Hurry it up, honey. I'll wait for you in the car."

Sheila and the two men went for their coats. Outside, Bernie crawled into the back seat of the car and guided the cot as Phil worked it out. Bernie followed it through the door. Sheila was just getting into the driver's seat. She threw Bernie's paper bag on the seat ahead of her.

"Dad?" She took the bag and pulled back out. "There's chocolate in here."

Bernie waved it away. "It's just a little something."

"It's chocolate."

He turned to Phil to explain. "Doris likes a little once in a

176

while." He made a face as though he were indulging a child. "But she's diabetic."

"She knows how much she can take. It won't hurt her. Besides, you can't go empty-handed. It's for all the women at the hotel. It's a holiday. You'll see. You'll see their faces."

May and Vikki joined them. May had not put on a coat. She hugged herself as she came around the car. "I didn't realize it was so cold," she said. "What a beautiful car."

"Go on back in the house, May. You'll freeze."

Sheila turned to her. "Mom? Dad's sending chocolate to Grandma."

"It's just a little something." May grinned guiltily. "You know your father. You can't go anywhere without bringing. Besides, it's for all the women."

"But—"

"It's all right. She only takes a little nibble once in a while." May put a hand on Sheila's shoulder and guided her into the car. "You'd better get going. It's late."

"I'm not going to bring them to her."

"Darling, I'm freezing," May said. She took the bag from Sheila and threw it on the front seat. "You men take the cot in."

"Can I sit in the front seat?" Vikki asked.

Sheila let Vikki in ahead of her as Phil and Bernie rolled the cot to the edge of the driveway. It was wobbly. Phil looked down and discovered a caster missing.

"Wait a second," he said. "We've lost a caster. Let me see if it's under the car." He got down on his side to look under the car. The caster lay against the back tire. As he stretched for it, he heard May.

"Just take it with you," she said patiently. "Then throw it away if you want to before you get to the hotel. That's what I do. Most of the time."

The toolshed was long and low. Bernie had built a work-table the length of one side. He had hammered nails in the wall above to hang his tools and outlined each with black paint. The outlines stood empty, and the table surface was covered

177

with drills, wrenches, and screwdrivers. At the far end sat a hand vacuum cleaner Bernie had ordered from a Sunday supplement ad. There was no electricity in the shed. Piles of furniture and boxes lined the opposite wall, crammed tight to leave a central aisle. A wheelbarrow stood upended against the back wall. It cut off half the light from a dusty little window. A chainless bicycle lay on its side blocking the aisle.

Phil rolled the cot to the shed. Bernie went ahead to clear a space. When Phil arrived, he was trying to force the bicycle under the workbench. The room smelled of mildew and sawdust.

"You can roll it right to the back as soon as I get these wheels out of the way," Bernie said.

"It'll block your garden tools. Don't you need to get to them?"

"It's OK. I change the damn place around every season." He dropped to one knee and peered under the bench. "It's the handlebars. I'll have to take them off." He rummaged through the litter on the workbench. "Do you see a wrench?"

Phil spotted one. He left the cot in the doorway and brought it to Bernie, who pulled the bike out. "One of these days I'm going to clean up the mess. You want to hold the bike steady?" Phil grabbed the handlebars, careful to keep his pants free of grease.

"Your tires need some air." They were squashed against the floor.

"Some day," Bernie said. "When I get a chain."

The room was too low to let in much light. From where Phil stood he could see Bernie's few wisps of hair silhouetted against the window. He gripped the handlebars hard as Bernie yanked with the wrench. The nut was rusted tight.

"Do you want me to give it a try?"

"That's OK, son." His concentration had allowed the name to flow freely. Phil flinched and focused on his own knuckles. Bernie made a straining noise. It turned into "There!" The nut gave.

They freed the bars and stored the bike.

Phil rolled the cot in and packed it tight against the rakes.

He turned and found Bernie with the wrench, peering at the worktable wall. Bernie looked for the outline and hung the wrench up. "That's a start, I guess," he said absently. He picked up a hammer and searched again. "You let things go, this is what happens. You know what I mean?"

"Sure."

He hooked the hammer in its place. "It's hard to stay on top of everything all the time."

Phil laughed self-consciously. "I know what you mean." There was a silence. Bernie took an awl and found its wall fitting. Phil wondered if he wanted privacy. Bernie might still be troubled by his outburst in Poppa's room. He almost hoped he was. Then it would be all right to move away gracefully and leave him alone. If not, it meant that Bernie was trying to find a way to talk to him. Intimacy was always an embarrassment.

"Can I help you with that?" Phil asked hesitantly.

"Sure. If you'd like."

Phil's heart sank. Bernie wanted to talk.

"That goes over there somewhere," Bernie said as Phil picked up a drill. He waved while he scanned the wall himself.

"Well, how have things been going for you, Bernie?" Phil's voice was too public for the little room.

"Fine. A little slow, but I can't complain. You?"

"Great. Maybe a little too fast, though."

They chuckled together. It went on a shade too long.

"You have—any—uh—prospects? For next year, I mean."

Phil found the drill space. "Couple of things. Nothing definite. I don't know if I ought to talk about them yet."

"Superstitious?"

"No, no. Nothing like that."

"I suppose you won't have too much trouble. Your family probably has some connections."

Phil frowned. It had never occurred to him that people took his future for granted like that. All the time he had known the Kahns he had worked to keep himself separate from his family. Working his way through school was just one way of announcing his independence. "I'm not really counting on that kind of thing." His frown deepened. He stole a look at

179

Bernie. His eyes had adjusted to the gloom in the shed. Bernie's face looked soft. The way he peered at the wall made him seem old and wise. He might be just the person to tell about Ryan's offer. All that week Phil had been wanting to talk it all out. His friends at law school would never have taken the dilemma seriously. They would have told him to jump at the chance and sneered at his hesitation. Sheila had a way of looking at important decisions from such oblique angles that conversation with her might leave him more confused and vaguely guilty. Bernie would be interested, sympathetic, but he would offer none of Sheila's challenges. He might even be grateful for the confidence. In some ways Bernie really was the child May made him seem. It was so easy to please him with a little warmth, a glimmer of intimacy. Phil could offer that now and use him as a sounding board at the same time.

"It's really a coincidence that you should mention my family, though," Phil began. "I was just talking to Fred Ryan last week and he came up with a kind of interesting proposition. You met the Ryans at the Northfield wedding."

"I met a lot of people." Bernie smiled. "It's the first time I ever stood in a receiving line."

"Well, they remember you. Mrs. Ryan spoke to May on the phone and"—he trailed off slightly—"recognized her." He wondered if May hadn't told him of the phone call. The two might have already speculated about the possibilities of an offer from Ryan.

"I think she said something about it," Bernie said vaguely.

Phil smiled to himself. Maybe the son-of-a-gun was more subtle than he gave him credit for. If he did have an inkling before, he'd certainly got Phil to commit himself more than he'd planned. Still, Bernie was the right one to talk to.

He told him all about Ryan's proposition. He said nothing, of course, about his private feelings for Frederick Ryan, only that work with a New York firm would probably take him more in the direction he wanted to go. Besides, he'd already started a cram course for the New York bar. Connecticut looked attractive, frankly, because good starting jobs were more scarce then he'd anticipated. Connecticut would pay well right from the start and he would be working in familiar territory. At the same time, it was hard to tell how far a Connecticut license would take him, if it would allow him to practice the kind of law he wanted to. "I guess it boils down to whether I can afford to make a long- or short-term decision." He was pleased with that characterization. It hadn't occurred to him quite in those terms before. He was glad he'd chosen to talk it out with Bernie.

His father-in-law sorted his tools as he listened. When he finished there were only a few tools scattered over the table. Bernie hung them in silence, then swept the counter with a whisk broom.

"What does Sheila think?"

Phil flushed. "We haven't really— There's still time on all this, you know. I want to give her a chance to get back in the swing of things before—"

"Uh-huh." Bernie relieved him of finishing.

"Besides, you know how adaptable she is."

"Uh-huh. How is she, Phil?"

"She's fine. She really is." He was grateful to Sheila for making him able to say it with conviction.

"She looks all right. A little thin."

"She is all right. She's been resting, taking care of herself and Vikki and the house." He gave a short laugh. "She's really better than she was before, if that's possible."

Bernie did not return the laugh. There was an awkward silence. "Do you know why she did it?"

"Oh, that's pretty complicated," Phil murmured.

"I think I'll be able to follow it."

Phil looked past him to the window. It was the first time he had ever felt intimidated by his father-in-law. Phil could ride out Bernie's temper; he had been able to deal with his frantic concern at the hospital; but he had never before seen him so calm. When he looked at Phil it was with a new mixture of directness and reassurance. Sheila in crisis had given him an excuse to indulge himself. Now he asked about her after the fact and now he seemed to recognize the need for control, for serious consideration, and respect for both her and Phil. The

181

last was what threw Phil. Bernie had never before confronted him so frankly and, at the same time, with such an assurance of compassion. He dug his hands in his jacket pocket and leaned against the work table.

"I'm not sure I really know yet."

"Have you talked about it?"

Phil shook his head. "She's seeing a psychiatrist, you know."

"You think she'll tell him?"

Phil shrugged. "Maybe he'll tell her."

Bernie finished sweeping. He laid the whisk broom beside the vacuum cleaner. "You want to hear something?" he said after a moment. "I never really understood your mother-in-law, either."

"I understand Sheila," Phil said quickly.

Bernie held up his hand and made a calming motion. "It's all right. I'm not blaming you. I'm not contradicting you. When I was your age I understood May, too. Inside and out. I had to. I didn't know anything about myself. I had to know about someone. I knew about my wife. I knew just what she wanted, what she needed, what she was afraid of. She wanted a duplex in Brooklyn; she needed a lot of money to keep her happy; she was afraid of never having a son." Bernie made a funny sighing noise. "Ay, ay, ay, ay. What I knew about her." He turned to face Phil and leaned one elbow on the table. "Did you know your mother-in-law had two years of CCNY?"

Phil was too slow to hide his surprise.

"What we think we know, huh?"

Phil tried to find a response. "I guess that was really an achievement for that time."

"It still is."

"I didn't mean—"

Bernie gripped Phil at the back of the neck and grinned. "Relax." He let go. "I met her there."

"You—"

"I was sweeping floors. In 1934 that was an achievement, too. There was a meeting of the Trotsky reading group one night. That was when janitors and students went to the same meetings. That's where we met. We were both going to go to

182

Spain and work in the medical corps." He nodded. "We almost made it, too."

"What happened?"

"I got a steady job on Seventh Avenue."

"And May?"

"She campaigned for La Guardia and helped organize the ILGWU." He raised his shoulders in a helpless gesture. "We were in love. We wanted to make babies who thought the right way, like we did. Babies who *knew*, you know what I mean? So babies had to eat. Besides, I understood what your mother-in-law secretly wanted. She wanted to get married and get rich. So we did. She stopped going to meetings and started going to luncheons." He smiled wryly. "So when she got what she wanted she got migraines, too, and I said to myself one day, I said, 'Bernie, how come if May got what she wanted and you still want to go to Spain—'" He interrupted himself. "That was over by then, but you know what I mean. I said, 'If May got what she wanted and you didn't, how come you're not getting migraines and she is?' That's when I thought maybe I didn't understand her after all." He took off his glasses and cleaned them with a handkerchief. "So I went bankrupt. I didn't connect it like that at the time. You know what I mean? I just figured I was a born loser. But May stopped having headaches." He shrugged. "Who knows. Maybe when you stop understanding people is the time you start loving them."

"I love Sheila," Phil murmured.

There was a pause. "Maybe it's different for Christians."

Phil looked up, startled. Bernie's eyes twinkled. Phil kept his mouth tight, but he smiled and shook his head. His own father had had the same knack for deflating him. The two men stood quietly in the dark, musty shed a while longer.

Bernie picked up a hoe and tapped it absently on the seat of an old upholstered chair. Phil stole a look at Bernie. Before, in Poppa's room, his face had been sullen and defiant like a child's. Now, in the half-light, as the men concentrated on the aimless tapping of the hoe, Phil could imagine what he had looked like when he was young. Sheila told him Bernie had been handsome, with a strong mouth and serious, searching

183

eyes. Phil could never put together the tired, puzzled man he knew with Sheila's memory. He could always afford to like his quaintness, put up with his quirks, and dismiss him as a failure. He had never before thought of failure as an act of love. He shifted his weight and cleared his throat.

"Maybe we'd better get back to the house."

Bernie nodded. He replaced the hoe. "Phil? About Freddie. . . ." Bernie turned. "We. . . ." His arms hung loose at his sides. "You try to do the right thing, you know what I mean? But sometimes you don't know. . . . She's so. . . . May and I. . . ." He stopped, confused. He tried to begin again. "You and Freddie mean so much—" He looked down. "Oh, I almost forgot." He fished in his pocket. "You might need this for the car." He pulled out some bills and pressed them into Phil's hand.

5

Sheila

Thanksgiving, 1962

THE DRIVE to Doris' hotel took less than ten minutes. It was a relief to be out of the house and alone with Vikki even for that short a time. Bernie and May seemed to be training for the world hovering championship. Everywhere she turned she found one of them, ostensibly busy, but always with one eye on her.

The day would not be easy. Sheila was still not sure that her rediscovered energy and control were permanent. They had taken her by surprise in the first place, and now she could look forward to a day of scrutiny from Bernie, May, Phil, and the entire congregation of Woodview's Temple Israel. Her poor mother had boxed herself in again, trying on one hand to keep the day small and exclusive, and wanting, on the other, to make sure all of Woodview knew her daughter was not mad. The best thing would have been to build a glass case for Sheila, put it in the center of the living room, and lead the guests in one at a time. Sheila could sit there like one of those mechanical gypsies at Coney Island, stamping out tickets that said, "I'm all right. Mom's fine, too." She wondered what they would look for. Trembling hands? Dilated pupils? Wasted shanks? Her shanks had been wasted since she was twelve. Sheila smiled and shook her head. What had really happened, and especially what had happened over the past week, could not possibly show.

185

It had begun when she woke that first morning home. Phil lay beside her. She had gone to sleep ashamed of her failure to give herself up in their lovemaking soon enough and ashamed of her lie afterward. The night had turned the shame to anger. She woke up hating Phil. It came with her morning consciousness, before she had even opened her eyes. There was no time to block it out or turn it into something else. She could not panic about money this time, or the fantasy of Vikki being molested. She could not resent her parents for taking her out of art lessons when she was eleven. She had to recognize that she'd been waking up for years filled with inexplicable rage at Phil. It frightened her at first. She tried to push back into sleep. Then she could wake again and dismiss the anger as a dream. It was no good. Her eyes defied her and opened. She turned her head. Phil's mouth hung slack; his breath was stale. Clumps of hair stuck out where he had slept on them. Sheila rolled on her side and studied him. She wondered if she looked so relaxed, so grotesquely satisfied while she slept. She searched his face for someplace to pin her hatred. The feeling was real. It was terrifying for her. If it had been there all this time, she thought, what business had she lying beside him like this? It meant their marriage had never been any different from those casual affairs she had been through before she met him, complete with that terrible, inevitable moment after sex when she would turn hostile. The boy would be attractive, except for one flaw. It might be a mole on the cheek, or crooked teeth, or a less than strong chin. It would never bother Sheila until after. Then she would fix on it, use it as a focus for all her contempt and resentment. She looked for that weakness in Phil now.

He lay on his side, half out of the blanket. The top of his arm pressed his chest and made it look flabby. His shoulders were freckled. Even Sheila's secret spot below his ear looked slack, and the smell of his night's sleep wafted from under the blanket. It was impossible to find one particular place to focus her contempt. Her husband's whole body was ridiculous. That was the moment when the second shock of the morning

186

hit her. She realized, with the same irresistible force she had realized her hatred a moment before, that she loved him. The first had happened out of sleep, the second out of waking. She tried to think how long it had been since she'd felt anything near the rush of tenderness that took her by surprise. How long had it been that all her energies were so committed to denying her anger that she had no more left to affirm her love? It must have been years. She'd been so afraid to look, to really look at Phil for fear that she would see him as she saw him now—absurd, vulnerable, stupidly aging. Instead, she had frantically clung to an image of him seven years younger, harder, flawless. Yet that was the image she'd awakened hating and this peaceful lump that she'd been so afraid to see was the very thing that rekindled her love.

The love grew warmer, and as it did, the anger grew, too. She lay there, paralyzed, incapable of choosing whether to kiss his dry, puffy mouth or brain him with the alarm clock.

It was 6:30. The next minute she was on her feet, astonished at her own speed. She remembered how she had pulled herself out of bed every other morning, rolling onto her stomach, peeling off like a dry sock on a nylon slip. She looked down at Phil once more and left the bedroom.

She went through the rest of the week no less confused about him, but freed at last by her honesty about the confusion. She no longer had to work to make everything outside conform to some mad idea she carried around inside her, some idiotic, timeless idea of Phil, of herself, and Vikki, and the life they had together.

All through the week she followed the clue of that morning. She could keep the cramped apartment clean now that she did not need to polish it into a penthouse. Her day-to-day routine—the shopping, the laundry, the sitting, and the pick-ups and deliveries—were commonplace, mindless. She no longer had to let them overwhelm in order to convince herself they were affairs of state.

She was still uncertain how long she could maintain her pace or even whether, in the end, her new reality might betray

187

her. That doubt hung in the back of her mind. So she picked her way through the week more carefully than if she had been absolutely sure of her new discoveries.

The lie she told Leo Kauffman was a danger signal. She still could not find the courage to look at that directly. Out of the corner of her mind she could see the vague shape of an irony. Now that she'd stopped lying about the world outside, she lied about herself. But she would look no more closely than that. At least not yet.

The Paradise Hotel was on Woodview's main street, sandwiched between a grocery store and a children's boutique. Sheila parked in front of the hotel. Before she got out she looked at the bag of chocolate on the seat beside her, hesitated, then took it with her.

"Are you going to bring it to Nanny?" Vikki said.

"What would you think of me if I didn't?"

There were loungers on the porch of the Paradise even in the coldest weather. Sheila and Vikki passed three women bundled in coats and blankets. One held a reflector under her chin.

The lobby was deserted. Most of the guests were gone for the holiday. Sheila led Vikki through to the cardroom.

Doris was playing gin at a table near the window. She did not look up when Sheila appeared. The woman with her was frail. She picked nervously at her cards and darted quick, worried looks from the pack to Doris.

An ashtray at Doris' elbow overflowed with tiny butts; two packs of Camels sat stacked beside it. Doris had once been as small as Sheila. Relatives would marvel at how much Sheila looked like their memory of Doris. But some time before Sheila was born, the woman had thickened. Sheila had always known her as she was now, solid and squat, with a walk that looked as though she were still surprised by all the new weight she had to balance. She wore a beige, crepe de Chine dress that stopped a little below the knee as she sat. She kept her feet squarely on the floor, a little apart; her ankles and calves looked like thick tubes. The shape of her face was Ber-

nie's, but the cheeks had given way and the skin beneath
the eyes seemed to hang suspended from them. Her hair was
red. A cigarette dangled wet-tipped from her mouth as she
arranged her hand. She took the cigarette in her thumb and
index finger, drawing even as she pulled it out and extending
her lower lip after it. She kept the smoke in while she examined the cards, then discharged a great cloud through her
mouth and nose.

Sheila approached the table. "Hello, Grandma."

Doris cocked her cheek without looking up. Sheila kissed it.

"Wait a minute." Doris had a chesty voice an inch ahead
of a cough. "She thinks she's got me on a *schneid*. Play,
Millie."

Sheila worked her way behind Doris to look at her hand.
She touched her grandmother gently on the shoulder,
amazed, as she was every time she saw her, at how much she
loved her.

Millie picked up Doris' discard and pecked uncertainly at
the top of her hand.

"I couldn't get a poker game. Everybody's gone for the
holiday. Millie only plays gin. Who's that with you?"

"Vikki."

"Wait a minute." Doris put her hand down on the table. Her
pocketbook leaned against the leg of her chair. She pulled it
onto her lap. "Come here." She pulled out a dollar and shoved
it into Vikki's hand. "That's for growing." She picked up her
hand again. "Play, Millie."

Vikki looked at her mother uncertainly. Sheila smiled and
nodded.

Vikki said "Thank you," and Doris waved brusquely. Vikki
brought the bill to Sheila.

"You want me to hold it for you?"

Vikki nodded. She stayed close to her mother, but Sheila
did not put her arm around her.

"Jack and Alice are coming on the one-thirty bus."

Doris nodded. She picked up a card, barely glanced at it,
and dropped it on the discard pile. Millie went for it like a
squirrel.

189

"Gin. That's my *schneid.*" Her eyes gleamed with triumph and relief.

Doris sighed. "Next time it's poker."

"I only play gin."

"How much do I owe you?"

Millie scratched on a gin pad. "Ten dollars and forty-eight cents."

"Round it out."

"Ten-fifty."

"All right."

Doris pulled a crumpled bill and two quarters out of her bag. "This is my granddaughter." She jerked her head in Sheila's direction.

"Pleased to meet you," Millie said in a little girl's voice.

"You ready to go?" Doris pushed her chair back and noticed the paper bag. "What's that?"

"Your loving son sent it. For all the women."

"What is it?"

"Don't you know?"

"Why does he keep sending me that crap?" She dropped her cigarettes in her bag and raised herself slowly from the chair. "He knows I'm not allowed."

Millie drew a sharp, shocked breath.

"I'm not allowed, Millie," Doris said pointedly. She avoided looking at Sheila. "Give it to Millie."

Sheila put the bag on the table.

"You want a piece?" Doris said to Vikki.

Vikki shook her head.

Sheila helped Doris with her coat. She did more of the work each time she visited.

"Where's the car?"

"Out in front."

Doris pulled her coat around her as though she were already cold and started out. Sheila paused behind her. She could never decide whether Doris looked like a peasant disguised as a queen, or a queen disguised as a peasant.

Mrs. Levith sat alone at the table. She fingered the deck and

190

stared after Doris. The bag of chocolate stood like a holiday centerpiece.

"Good-bye, Mrs. Levith," Sheila said. "Nice meeting you."

The little woman looked startled. "Thank you."

"Have a nice holiday."

"I will. I will." Her tone was obedient.

Sheila took Vikki's hand. They caught up with Doris in the lobby.

"You didn't even say good-bye to Mrs. Levith," Sheila said reproachfully. "It doesn't look as though she's got anyplace to go for the holiday, either."

"Don't feel sorry. She's got five married children and no-place to go because they all hate her."

"Grandma!"

"What, 'Grandma'? She's a nasty old bitch."

"You're just saying that because she got you on a *schneid*."

"Of course. She never loses. She cheats."

"Oh, for Chrissake."

"It's true. She can't stand to lose. She thinks God doesn't love her if she loses. So she cheats to make sure."

"Why do you play with her then?"

Doris shrugged. "She needs to win more than I do." She stopped before they reached the door. "I forgot something."

"What?"

"My lighter. I left it."

"I saw you drop it in your bag."

"I left it. You meet me in the car." She wheeled and went back to the cardroom.

Sheila looked after her puzzled. Perhaps she had shamed her into saying good-bye. She led Vikki out to the porch.

"Why did Nanny give me a dollar?" Vikki asked.

Sheila snorted. "She needed the ten for the gin game."

Vikki climbed in the back of the car and Sheila started the motor to get the heat going. Vikki leaned over the front seat to talk while they waited.

"Why does she paint her hair?"

Sheila leaned her head against her window. She smiled at Vikki. "She thinks it's pretty."

Vikki nodded thoughtfully.

"Do you?" Sheila asked.

"Yes."

"Would you like me to?"

"No. You don't talk loud enough."

Sheila laughed. "Do you like Nanny?"

Vikki considered it a moment. "I think so."

"You're not sure?"

"She's big."

"Yes, she is."

"I think I like her."

"I think I do, too. Very much."

"Why?"

It was Sheila's turn to consider. She closed her eyes. "Maybe because she wouldn't teach me to play poker."

"Were you ever scared of her?" Vikki asked tentatively.

"Never." She opened her eyes. "Were you?"

Vikki looked away. "A little."

"Today?"

She smiled and shook her head proudly.

Doris appeared at the window. Sheila got out and ran around the car to help her in. She took her pocketbook.

"Did you find the lighter?"

Doris nodded. Her mouth seemed tight.

Sheila gripped her arm and eased her into the front seat. Doris held her breath, then let it go as she settled in. A thick puff of chocolate hit Sheila's face. She flushed angrily.

"You went back—"

"It's cold. Shut the door."

Sheila stormed around to the driver's door and got in. She slammed it shut and sat behind the wheel without moving.

Doris stared stonily through the windshield.

"Infants," Sheila said.

"What?"

"Two of them. The one who sent it and the one who took it. Infants."

192

"Jack and Alice are waiting."

"That didn't bother you before."

"What do you want from me?"

"You went all the way back there—"

"For my lighter." Doris arranged herself with dignity and pulled the lighter out of her bag. She dropped it back and snapped the bag closed with finality.

"What's the matter with you?" Sheila's voice was a mixture of frustration and concern. "You want to kill yourself?"

"Ha. Look who's talking." The laugh was mirthless at first, but a real smile played around the edges of Doris' mouth as Sheila remained silent. Sheila put the car in gear and eased out of the space.

"Who told you about it?" Sheila asked once they were in the flow of traffic. Her voice was more subdued.

"Word travels."

"It wasn't Mom and Dad, though."

The old woman made a derogatory sound. "They don't even know I know. They probably thought I'd drop dead if I found out."

"You didn't."

"It would take more than that. I got mad, though."

"But you're not now."

"That I can't afford."

There was a pause. "Do you want me to tell you about it?"

"You want me to tell you about my bad hands?"

Sheila laughed shortly. "You think they're the same?"

Doris gave one vigorous nod. "All bad things are the same. I can't even remember my bad hands. They're all so alike. Good things are different from each other. Tell me about good things. You want to hear about my good hands for the past month? I can tell you every one of them. Every card."

"You knock me out."

"It's not such a big deal. I only had five good hands the whole goddamned month."

They were late for the bus. Jack, Alice, and Greta Kahn stood on the curb near the terminal watching for them. The father and daughter were hunched with the cold, their hands in their pockets. Alice carried a shopping bag in each hand. A pair of large hoops dangled from her ears. She wore a homespun cape of brown wool. The hem of a green dirndl skirt showed underneath.

"There they are," Doris said.

"I hope they haven't been waiting long."

"Don't worry about it." Her mouth went tight. She shook her head. "What a group."

"Grandma—"

"That woman's got no chin at all. How could she have two husbands and no chin? She looks like Zasu Pitts."

"Grandma!"

"My son doesn't look like anything. A vanilla milk shake."

Jack was Bernie's younger brother. Sheila could remember a time when her father and Doris adored him. She could even remember being a little jealous of him. He was only eight years younger than Bernie, but it seemed to Sheila that they treated him more like her brother than his. He was still unmarried, then, a scholarship student at Juilliard. He lived in a small apartment in Greenwich Village.

Whenever Sheila thought of her uncle in those days she thought of his tantrums. He was always at odds with Doris or Bernie, one minute overflowing with gratitude for a cash advance on his allowance, screaming at them the next for destroying his soul, denying him freedom, castigating their coarse, material lives. Now he taught music at a high school in Syosset, and conducted the marching band.

They pulled to the curb beside the three travelers.

Vikki clambered into the front as Jack opened the back door.

"Be careful of Nanny."

"I'm all right." Doris avoided Vikki's feet.

The car was alive with activity. The new passengers piled in the back, their breath still making smoke in the cold. Alice shoved her bags ahead of her, then ducked in, kissing Doris' cheek on her way.

"Hello, Momma." Doris received it without comment. "Hello, Sheila." Alice gave her a brief, penetrating look. Sheila

194

smiled as though she were responding to a flashbulb. That was the look she could expect for the rest of the day.

Greta followed. She was a round-faced, sullen girl, with long, coarse hair. She let it hang over the front of her shoulders and cut off half her cheeks. She plumped down silently next to her mother.

"Hello, Greta," Doris said loudly.

Alice jabbed her. Greta stirred forward as Jack pushed in. She kissed her grandmother and settled back to make room for Jack.

"Hello, Momma." He kissed her. Sheila was startled at how gray his temples had gone. On a more successful man it would have looked distinguished. It gave her uncle the faintly seedy look of a reformed alcoholic. His face and his voice were mild and bemused.

He turned to Sheila. His eyes were a weaker blue than her father's. She thought they were welling up with tears. "Hello, Freddie." Sheila had forgotten what an impossibly sentimental man he was. She smiled and responded with calculated cheer.

"You look wonderful," he said intensely. His voice almost broke at her bravery.

"Sit back," Doris said. "Close your door. I'm getting pneumonia."

Jack settled back and closed the door. Sheila threw Doris a grateful glance. Her grandmother rolled her eyes up in commiseration.

"I sat next to the most wonderful man on the bus," Alice said as they started off. Her voice had a faintly spiritual quality that suggested profundity. "It was jammed. We couldn't find any seats together. Did you see him, Jack?"

"Who?"

"The man I was sitting next to."

"Dark-skinned fellow?"

"He's an Indian." There was a tone of reverence in it. "A specialist in transcendental meditation. I've never met anyone so"—she searched for the words carefully—"so at peace with himself. Do you know what I mean? It's so hard today to find someone really at peace with himself. We rush. We hurry. But what does it all mean if we're not at peace? Don't you think so?"

Sheila looked up and smiled noncommittally through the mirror. Her uncle sat hunched back in his overcoat, holding on to the passenger strap.

"If people could only pay reverence to the spirit. If they could find their spiritual selves. It was so wonderful to talk to him. I've thought about that kind of thing so often, but there he was, saying what I've thought of, only quoting it from the *Bhagavad Gita*. I quoted from Erich Fromm and told him it was a miracle that I happened to sit next to him. By the time we left I felt as though I'd known him all my life."

"What does he do for a living?" Jack asked.

"I didn't ask him." There was a hint of indignation in it. "His name is Krishna. After the god." She laughed. "I told him how we always used to do Yoga together, Greta. He was very impressed by that. A mother and a daughter doing Yoga together."

"I don't do Yoga."

"We used to. Don't you remember. I taught you the breath exercises and the lotus position. Every night when Daddy was at the high school for band rehearsals."

"I was a kid then."

"It wasn't so long ago."

"I'm not interested in that now."

Doris shifted her legs irritably. She rearranged her coat and fumbled with her bag. Once Sheila thought she heard her muttering.

"What *are* you interested in?" Sheila asked cheerfully. She glanced up at the mirror. The girl shrugged and brushed some hair from the side of her mouth. "The last time I saw you it was Elvis Presley," she said, bantering.

"I was a kid then."

"You're graduating high school this year."

"Uh-huh."

"Any plans?"

"I don't know."

196

Sheila kept herself from speaking sharply. The girl's dullness made her own bright smile feel sticky. She tried once more.

"You once told me you'd like to be a nurse."

"I was a—"

"—kid then," Sheila helped her finish. "I never thought growing up could be so boring."

Doris' hands were working nonstop. They all fell silent until Jack said, "There's the house."

"Thank God!" Doris shouted.

There was an extra car in the driveway. The Kaprow's had arrived while they were gone.

Sheila pulled up behind it. All four car doors opened at once. Jack ran to Doris and helped her out while Alice struggled with her shopping bags. Sheila left the driver's seat and called Vikki to follow her.

"I didn't realize she was so big," Alice said, looking after Vikki.

"Could I get out, Ma?" Greta said.

Alice pulled the bag out and started toward the house. Jack had Doris standing outside the car. He went to take her arm, but she slapped his hand away and marched alone to the kitchen door. Jack closed both doors on his side and followed his mother in attendance. Sheila waited to close the last door until Greta came out. She lumbered out, then stood hesitantly. Sheila swung the door forward. It left them facing each other. Sheila smiled briefly, determined to be civil.

"I've got to talk to you," the girl said darkly.

"OK."

"Alone."

"Not out here," Sheila said. "It's freezing."

"It's very important."

"Are you pregnant?"

Greta looked startled. It was the first sign of life Sheila had seen. "No."

"Then it can wait." She finished closing the door. "It could wait if you were pregnant, too, come to think of it."

Greta gazed at her intensely, trying to look deep. She was

197

too hulking a girl, though, and it only made her look duller. "It's about suicide."

Sheila let the handle of the shopping bag slip to her wrist and put her hands in her pocket. She surveyed the girl. Greta's coat hung open. She wore a dark mohair skirt and white cashmere sweater. She was big-breasted and soft. Sheila wondered if that was why she hunched so much. "You want instructions?" she asked sharply. "From everything I've heard you're doing all right on your own."

"I thought you would understand." She started to walk away.

"Greta," Sheila called her back. She held out the shopping bag. "Help your mother. It's nicer if you don't go in empty-handed."

Sheila watched her go off toward the house. Her impatience with the girl's dead eyes and voice in the car had turned to fury at her stupidity. "It's about suicide." The girl had said it like a code, as though Sheila had won membership in a secret society of people as self-absorbed, self-indulgent, and dull as herself, as though Sheila were nothing but her suicide. She wanted to run after her and shake her by the shoulders and smack her the way they smack infants into life.

May appeared at the kitchen door. She kissed Greta in and called to Sheila. "The Kaprows are here, darling. Come on."

Sheila squared her shoulders and went toward the house. The day was starting. It was too soon to let anger run away with her. Perhaps she'd been wrong about Greta. Maybe the girl had genuinely come to her for help. She would get hold of herself, she decided, and find some time in the day to let the girl talk.

Everyone was in the living room. Phil was helping Bernie make drinks. May alternately spread chopped liver and cheese on Melba rounds. Doris was ensconced in the straight, high-backed chair with her ankles crossed, her two packs of Camels stacked on a side table next to her. Jack and Arnie Kaprow sat opposite each other in easy chairs near the fireplace. There was a fire going. Greta had taken one of Doris' cigarettes and was sitting on the floor near her father, staring

198

into the fire. Alice was on the sofa with Edith Kaprow. She had just pulled a box of colorforms for Vikki out of her shopping bag when Sheila walked in.

"These are very creative," Alice was explaining. "You can put the pieces any way you want."

Edith Kaprow was the first to notice her. "Hello, Sheila." It was cordial but she did not smile. Edith seldom smiled. When she did, it was a very efficient statement, with a marked beginning and end. Sheila thought she detected judgment in Edith's greeting, and just the faintest challenge to her to justify her behavior. The quick, appraising look came with it, far more expert than Alice's.

Sheila flashed back her smile. "Hello, everyone."

"Hello, hello," May said, as though she were surprised to see her. She gave Edith a Melba round. "Can I make one for anyone else?" No one responded. She started making another.

Edith and Arnie were in their mid-forties. She was a broad-boned woman, not particularly tall. Her face was long, though, and she wore her hair swept high so that Sheila always had the feeling she was straining to look up at her. Her face was leathery from the golf course.

"Where are the twins?" Sheila asked.

"Away for the holiday. With friends from school."

Alice looked up surprised. "Your children aren't in college already!"

"Prep school."

Arnie stirred in his armchair. "It might as well be Harvard for what I'm paying."

"Arnie, please. He's still the same tightwad, Sheila." She laughed. Edith laughed easily, even though she seldom smiled. "Money, money, money. He'd love to take it all out of the bank in coins and store it in chests so he could play with it. It's his toilet training."

Arnie shrugged. "You're the one who does my billing." He was as dark as Edith, but it was his natural complexion. His body had just passed the point where he could explain it away as middle-aged spread. It was turning soft and fat. He wore a sport shirt with a sheen finish that turned green or blue depending on the light, sharkskin slacks, and woven Italian shoes. He sat slumped and heavy-lidded, as though his clothes were putting him to sleep.

Phil brought Sheila a drink.

"What's this?"

"Scotch and soda." He hesitated. "That's what you usually drink, isn't it?"

"Fine." She saw Edith take it in and wished Phil had asked her before he mixed it. She liked him better when he wasn't so public about being a good husband.

"Your daughter's a doll," Edith said.

Doris went for a cigarette. "She looks like me."

"And she's so bright." Alice was sitting back, looking radiant with her hands folded under her drink. There was a napkin wrapped around the bottom of the glass. "Remember how Greta used to love those colorforms, Jack? I once bought her a set with a staff and musical symbols. She picked it up so quickly. I tried to find one of those for Vikki but they don't seem to stock them anymore."

"What time is the football game on?" Arnie asked.

"You're not going to watch football today."

"I can go upstairs. Bernie? You know what time it's on?"

"Two thirty, I think."

"That's what time I planned dinner," May said softly.

"You follow football, Jack?"

Jack crossed his ankle over his thigh. "A little."

"You do not," Alice said blandly.

"Green Bay Packers today."

"No kidding." His enthusiasm wasn't convincing.

Sheila sat in a rocking chair near Alice. "I never understood the fascination of football."

"We need more chairs, Bernie," May said.

Sheila wondered if she'd said something wrong.

"The Kennedys play football," Arnie said.

"They play touch," Bernie put in as he left the room.

"That's on television. I bet they tackle off camera."

Alice sipped her drink. "Teddy wears a brace."

200

"Teddy's a pisher," Doris said.

"I didn't mean playing," Sheila said. "I love playing. I meant watching. What's the fascination of watching a bunch of men collide with each other?"

"It's a very intricate game." Arnie's tone was patronizing. May stopped spreading. She left a circle of alternating rounds on the plate and sat back. Sheila could hear Esther working with the pots in the kitchen. Bernie brought in some folding chairs and Phil helped set them up. He threw quick, unobtrusive glances at Sheila. She leaned forward to take an hors d'oeuvres and caught Edith covertly studying her.

"How have you been, Edith?" She offered her another round.

"Marvelous. Marvelous." She said it as though she was checking in.

"They just got back from Aruba," May told her.

"Aruba?"

"Aruba Aruba," Arnie said flatly. Alice laughed.

"Where's Aruba?"

"It's out of Miami."

"They're just starting to build it up," Bernie explained.

"It's not a bad hotel."

"Arnie thinks the Caribbean is a chain of hotels surrounded by water. We played golf in Daytona, then flew down to relax."

"It was off season."

"Is it near Cuba?" Sheila asked.

"I don't know. Arnie? Is it near Cuba?"

"About the same flying time. Why?"

"Just wondered. The blockade and all."

"That's all over," Arnie said sleepily.

"I was late finding out about it."

"Bernie? Is that Sally and Merv's car?" May asked quickly. Bernie shuffled into the hall. "They're here!"

May started spreading more hors d'oeuvres.

"Jonathon's with them!"

May was startled. "I didn't know they were bringing Jonathon." She shot a quick, helpless look at Sheila. "I'd better tell Esther to set another place." She went to the kitchen.

201

"Did he bring the camera?" Arnie called.

"He's got something in a shoulder case!"

"Your camera?" Edith asked. "What's he doing with your camera?"

Arnie shrugged. "He wanted to try it out when they went to Mexico. He's thinking of buying one for himself. It's a Leica," he explained to Jack.

Jack looked interested.

They could hear Merv greeting Bernie and May boisterously in the kitchen.

"He's not going to show slides, is he?" Doris asked suspiciously.

"I love slides," Alice said.

"I know. The last time I was at your house your brother spent two hours showing pictures of Puerto Rico."

"You didn't like them?"

"Who wants to see his wife in front of the toilet in the rain forest?"

Merv appeared at the archway, balding, redheaded, freckled, and energetic. He still wore his coat, and a camera and a large accessory case were strapped over it. He was small, with thick glasses. "Hello, everybody. Just wanted to check in before I got undressed. Make sure everybody's here. See if I wanted to stay for the orgy."

"Hello, Merv."

"Hello, Edith." He went over and kissed her. "Tonight's the night, baby. Get the key from Arnie. We'll watch the late show. You can work the remote control."

Edith laughed and pushed him away. He nodded to Alice and said, "Hello." Her drink was gone and she smiled back glassily.

"Go take your coat off, Mervin," Doris said. "You're making me overheated."

"Don't boss me around. I'm old enough to be your son." He kissed her on the cheek. "You're gorgeous." He jerked his head toward Edith. "When I'm finished with her it's you and me. Five-card stud." Doris pushed him away, too. "Here's your camera," he said to Arnie. "I only broke five attachments." He unstrapped the equipment into Arnie's lap. Arnie opened the case to examine it. Merv nodded to Jack. "How are you, you son of a gun? Still doing right by old John Philip?"

Jack smiled blankly. Alice laughed. "Sousa, Jack. Sousa." It was a little shrill.

Merv turned to Sheila. She thought she saw everyone's head turn away like characters in a Victorian melodrama. He examined her seriously from behind his bluff smile. Before she could smile back he was hugging her. "I'm so glad to see you, honey," he whispered. She was astonished at the gentleness and warmth. He let her go as suddenly as he had embraced her and turned to Phil. "It's all right. It's all right. I'm all talk, no action."

"Can I make you a drink?"

"The old man's got you tending bar? It's always the son-in-law who tends bar. You ought to organize. Bourbon and water. I'll get out of this coat so Doris can stop sweating." He almost tripped over Greta on his way out. She did not stir.

He passed Sally as he disappeared toward the closet. She touched his arm lightly like a talisman and he kissed the air in her direction. Sally was blond, with large blue eyes that sparkled vacantly as if she had bought them from a jeweler. Her face was set in a constant smile. A hollow-chested boy in glasses loomed behind her.

Sally looked around the room and smiled hello. Sheila braced herself for the change when her glance came to her. It never did. Sally managed to smile around the room without looking at anyone. She sat in the rocking chair. Jonathon sat on the arm.

"Jonathon's so big," Alice said. "Greta, you remember Jonathon, don't you?" She sat forward expectantly.

Greta looked up from the fire. "Hi."

"Hi."

She turned away.

So much for matchmaking, Sheila thought. She had an absurd image of Jonathon and Greta kissing—he, gangling and concave; she, hunched. Only their lips and toes would touch.

Phil came up beside her at the bar to mix more drinks. He touched her hair. She jerked away. "You all right?"

She nodded. "Just don't touch my hair. OK? It feels like you're fluffing me up."

He smiled tentatively.

She had thought she was doing fine, but Sally's arrival had rattled her. She hadn't even realized it was working on her until Phil's touch made her jump. She turned from him. "Sally? Jonathon? Can I get you a drink?"

Sally looked up at the boy helplessly. "Would you like anything?" she asked in a small voice.

"Are you going to have anything?"

"You decide."

He shook his head at Sheila. "No, thanks."

"Maybe I'll have a little Cherry Heering," Sally said. "That's very mild. Why don't you try a little, Jonny? It's very mild."

"OK."

Sheila took Alice's empty glass. "What were you drinking, Alice?"

She nodded and smiled brightly. "Fine."

Sheila turned to Jack. "Screwdriver," he told her.

"Heavy on the orange juice," she murmured to Phil as she gave him the glass.

"Greta?" Sheila decided to make a peace offering. "Do you have a drink?"

She shook her head, still staring into the fire.

"Can I get you one?" Sheila asked patiently.

"Bourbon."

"And?"

"Straight." She flipped her cigarette into the fire. Alice giggled. The girl's shoulders closed in.

Jack leaned forward. "Don't keep staring into the fire, honey. It'll hurt your eyes."

Bernie and May returned. He lifted Vikki onto his lap. She let him hold her a moment, then wriggled back to her color-forms. The conversation fragmented. Sheila sat in a folding chair near Doris, still trying to pinpoint exactly what had unnerved her so suddenly. The greeting had been less dif-

204

ficult than she expected. She had been bracing herself for the
gorgon's eye all morning. Now she had met it, four times at
least, and hadn't turned to stone. It was Sally who had thrown
her, flashing her smile around the room like a mirror, seeing
nobody. The scrutiny of the others was easy compared to
Sally's blankness. It made Sheila feel invisible.

She surveyed the group in her mother's living room like a
stranger. Everyone seemed relaxed. Sally had never taken her
into account. The others had simply satisified themselves that
Sheila was still sane, that she would do nothing dangerous,
then dismissed her. The five men worked out a schedule for
the football game. They would watch in shifts of two during
dinner. Edith and Sally compared vacation notes. May and
Alice caught up on relatives. Greta and Jonathon were concentrating on ignoring each other. Only Sheila and her
grandmother sat isolated. Sheila had thought that once the
greetings were over, the afternoon would melt into all the
other Woodview Thanksgivings she'd known, that she would
simply join the flow of talk and laughter. This time there was
no way in. She could not conceive of what she had brought to
the other times that gave her entry. What had she said to make
Edith laugh, or Sally nod? Whatever it was, she'd cut herself
off from it. She had no past she could share. Her future was
still hazy, and, besides—she felt a vague chill as she thought of
it—she could not remember these women ever talking of the
future. Their disregard worked on Sheila like a greater judgment than their scrutiny.

She took one of Doris' cigarettes absently. Both women
went for the lighter. Their hands touched and they murmured something embarrassed. For an instant she was fourteen, alone with Doris in the Paradise cardroom. Sheila
squeezed her grandmother's hand.

Doris said, "Some fun, huh kid?" and gave her the lighter.
She turned away. Sheila heard her murmur, "And I look
forward to it every year."

She turned back to the others, determined to find what
secret, unspoken agreement her personal act had violated.
She was not making it up. She was sure of that. Sally might

205

smile vacantly, and Alice had already drunk too much, but Edith was in control—and Edith had been avoiding her eyes from the moment Sheila first caught the woman studying her. Until now she had thought of her suicide only as an act of personal despair. But the people in her mother's house, not just the women, made her feel she had broken some unspoken, terrible law, had threatened some uneasy balance in the life of the whole small society. The punishment was exclusion.

Alice had joined Edith and Sally's conversation. "Aruba," she said. "I love those Spanish-sounding names. They always remind me of a South American I almost married. Rafael Alitos. Isn't that a wonderful name? Jack?" she called across the room. "Do you remember Rafael Alitos?" She did not wait for an answer. "He was a terribly sensitive and great pianist. I knew him at Juilliard before I met Jack." She smiled vaguely. "He's very famous in South America. He went right back after he graduated. Every time I hear a Spanish-sounding name I think I might be living in Buenos Aires this minute."

"Merv was the only man in my life," Sally said softly, with a trace of superiority.

"Isn't that wonderful?"

May laughed suddenly. "That would have made you Alice Alitos."

"Yes. That's right."

May stopped laughing. "It's just—it has a funny sound."

"Yes. I suppose it does." The women fell silent.

Vikki was on the floor in the far corner of the living room. Greta had worked her way toward her. The two of them lay on their stomachs and toyed with the colorform pieces spread around them. The older girl supported her cheek with one hand and occasionally wet her lips with her drink.

Jonathon handed Sally his drink.

"What's wrong, sweetheart? Don't you like it?" She put it on the end table beside her.

He shook his head. "I guess I don't like to drink."

She reached up and stroked his cheek. "You should nurse it like I do."

"How's school, Jonny?" Edith asked.

"Fine." His face flamed at being noticed.

"He's writing a special sports column for the town paper," Sally said proudly. "Why don't you tell them about it, honey? It's really wonderful. He covers all the football and basketball games. The editor is really so pleased with him. Isn't he?" She turned to the boy. "What was it he said to you?"

Jonathon mumbled something.

"What?"

"That he has the 'makings of a pro,' " Sally repeated.

"Do you like sports especially?" May asked.

"He loves it. It's really bringing him out."

"Do you remember a movie called *The Silent Melody*?" Alice asked Edith.

Edith stared back.

"It was about Beethoven. He was in it."

"Who?"

"Rafael Alitos. He played a young pianist and Beethoven had just gone deaf and was going to commit suicide but this young pianist—Rafael—comes to visit him and he plays the piano and it gives Beethoven hope."

"How could he hear it if he was deaf?" Doris asked.

Alice laughed. "Oh, Doris, you're such a realist. You always were." She stopped laughing. "It's his eyes," she said intensely. "He sees the light in Rafael's eyes and it gives him hope."

"Why didn't you marry him?" Sally asked.

"Oh"—Alice waved her hand vaguely—"I was so young. He was so young. I only knew he was a beautiful, sensitive artist. I had no idea he would be so successful. Besides, he didn't look like a pianist. He always wore business suits, and his skin was very smooth so he hardly ever had to shave." She laughed. "You should have seen Jack then, with his wild hair and his wild eyes. Do you remember, May?"

She nodded noncommittally.

"Well, when I saw *The Silent Melody*, there was Rafael looking as mad and romantic as I could ever have wanted Jack to be. Oh, this is silly. What am I carrying on about Rafael Alitos for?"

"Are you still talking about Rafael Alitos?" Jack asked from across the room.

Alice smiled back at him. "I just finished."

They had the attention of the men. Each one glanced at his wife. Sally's eyes grew bright.

"How ya doin', cookie?" Merv said.

She tapped the free arm of the chair. "Come sit with me. I feel lonely."

It broke the men's huddle. Bernie tried to take Vikki on his knee again.

Sally touched Merv's thigh as he sat beside her. "The men in my life," she said. She took a hand of each and settled back, beaming at the other women.

"I'd do anything for her," Merv said with mock intensity. "I'd even go straight."

"I didn't know you were queer," Arnie said. He laughed loudly. Alice joined him.

"I almost married a different man," Edith said. "A friend of Arnie's in medical school, as a matter of fact."

"Laurence Fedderman." Arnie said the name with her. "Here we go again."

Doris caught Sheila's eye. "What is this?" she asked in a low voice. "Jewish confession? Tell them to get instructions from your husband."

"At least you knew you wanted to be a doctor's wife," Arnie said. "Right?"

"Don't be so sensitive."

"She's just keeping the conversation going," Alice explained. May put a quieting hand on her sister-in-law's.

"And you could have had a caterer like me," Merv put in.

"You're a personnel administrator," Sally said.

"A personnel administrator for a chain of restaurants is a caterer."

Sally smiled. "Merv likes to pretend he's tough," she explained.

"Fedderman was going to be a dermatologist," Arnie continued indifferently. "And I was in pediatrics."

"You were going to be a pediatrician?" Bernie asked.

"He loved babies," Edith said dryly.

"Tell them why you didn't marry him." Arnie snorted and sank back drowsily.

Edith laughed. "I didn't want a businessman doctor. I wanted a dedicated doctor."

"Larry wasn't a businessman. He was a crook."

"—and Arnie was going to use his private practice to support a free clinic."

"I didn't know that about you," Sally said.

Arnie shrugged. "Neither did I. Only Edith did. She keeps telling me about it."

"That's because you keep forgetting. I ended up with a businessman after all. Fate."

"But not a crook. Those dermatologists make a fortune on pimples. I'm a damned good surgeon. I earn what I make. Besides, you do my billing."

Edith laughed again and turned to the others. "You know how that started? To save on expenses so we could open the clinic. The first year I was his receptionist, too. Remember that, May? When we first came to Woodview? That's how we met you and Bernie."

"My gall bladder."

"Imagine a gall bladder bringing such good friends together," Alice said.

"At the end of the first year we figured we saved about five thousand dollars. So we snitched a little to go to Europe. We figured we could look at the English system while we were over there, so it was all right. Remember, Arnie? The next year he got Mrs. Hardison, and I kept doing the billing so he wouldn't have to pay her as much."

"Is that how you got to Aruba?" Alice asked.

"He might as well have been a dermatologist."

"I'm a damned good surgeon."

"I hate the billing," Edith said between her teeth.

"Why do you do it?" The words were out before Sheila could stop them and the momentary silence that followed was sharper than the question. Everyone looked at Sheila. That did it, she thought. I was better off invisible. This time I really

209

will turn to stone. She could feel herself going numb under their eyes and the whole room start to recede.

Edith laughed and it sounded as though it came from far off. "For the clinic," she said.

Sheila had been growing restless since Edith started talking. She had never liked the woman. She had always resented her assurance, the way her voice inflected downward even on questions, her judgments on everything.

It was Edith Kaprow who had studied Sheila most expertly, as though she had some idea of exactly what to look for: Sheila was sure it was Edith who had somehow managed her ostracization; and, at the same time, it was Edith whom Sheila, herself, had been avoiding all afternoon. Even when she smiled and offered her an hors d'oeuvres and asked how she was, she'd been avoiding her. It was intuitive, like all her responses to the danger signals of the week. Edith, in some undefinable way, could explode the afternoon if she let her. Sheila could sense it coming when Edith started on the man she might have married. Sheila's question had sprung the response she'd been fearing. It was spontaneous. She'd had no time to shape it or soften the challenge behind it. And Edith had laughed and said, "For the clinic." There was no clinic. Edith Kaprow's joyless laugh told them all that she knew it—and whether or not there had ever really been one was beside the point. Edith's sharp judgmental voice, her sniping, and the quiet savage thrust that had released Sheila's question told them all that Edith had once believed in it, that at some unmarked point in time she could not believe in it any longer, and that she chose to proceed as though she still did. Sheila could almost hear what the woman's laughter had once sounded like, rich with faith in the future. Probably not even Edith herself could name the moment it first became tinged with despair. That time was buried forever, along with the time that must have come later when Edith recognized she had given up hope, yet chose to continue her husband's billing.

She's a suicide like me, Sheila thought, and realized she was staring at Edith with the same sharp, appraising look she'd been getting all day. She looked at all the others, one by one. They all are. The difference was that Sheila's act had a fixed point in time, and was over. The others had kept theirs secret, even to themselves, perhaps, and no one had found them in time to stop the pills from working.

Sheila felt herself recede further, but the process had reversed itself. It was they who were turning invisible, and only she—and Doris and Vikki, perhaps—had any substance. She felt like a spy in the land of the dead. She looked at the men with their sagging bodies, and the women, still trying to stay firm, with the confusion of loathing and sorrow, fear and compassion, the living always feel for the lost. She even saw Phil going soft as he sat with his shirt blousing out at the waist of his pants. For all the flesh, hard and soft, they were insubstantial. They were not judging or punishing her. She'd been unjust to Edith and the rest of them on that score. They were simply incapable of recognizing her. Her attempt to join them had failed. They were not unkind, after all. They were simply waiting for her to try again in a more acceptable way.

May said, "I think dinner's ready." There was a rush and chatter as they moved to the dining room. Sheila stood up to follow. Phil crossed the room to her against the flow.

"Do you want me to sit with Vikki?" His voice seemed to come from an echo chamber.

"What for?"

"To help her with the food." His familiar look of concern seemed like a cartoon to her. "You look pale."

"Do I?" Her lips trembled against laughter. Pale as a ghost? she wanted to ask, but she knew that would make him think she was losing her grip. She did not want to worry him. "I feel fine. Go on in. I'll wait for Grandma." She turned to Doris.

Doris worked herself up. "Your husband loves you," she said when they were alone. She collected all her earthly goods from the table. "Don't knock it."

"I don't."

"You like confusing him."

"It's self-defense."

"Don't give me that crap. I've been married, too."

211

"What should I do?"

"Pull yourself together."

"I'm trying."

"Try harder."

In the dining room Arnie had decided to get a picture before they disturbed the table.

"Everybody scrunch together," he said as he fumbled with a camera attachment.

"You handle that thing like an amateur," Merv said.

"Let's just wait till you get your slides back. Vikki, sit on your grandpa's lap. Greta? Why don't you sit in Jonny's lap?"

Everyone laughed.

Sally said, "Oh, Arnie," and clicked her tongue.

"Here's Sheila. Good. Sheila, you stand behind your father."

"Doris over here," Merv called. "On my lap."

She waved him away with the back of her hand.

"May and Phil on either side of Sheila. Gorgeous." He peered into the viewfinder. "Beautiful. Edith, push the turkey closer to Jack."

"Careful of the gravy," someone murmured.

"Good. Everybody ready? Get comfortable."

They all shifted. Sally licked her lips and held Jonathon's hand to her cheek.

May gave a cry.

"What is it?"

"Esther. We forgot Esther." There was a general buzz, then they called to the kitchen. Esther appeared at the door. "Come on, honey," Arnie said. "You've got to get in the picture." Esther knew better than to protest. "Stand next to Edith. No. Next to Sally. She's got blond hair."

Everyone fell back into position.

"Here we go now. One. Two. Three!" Nothing happened. Everyone let out a breath, then the bulb flashed.

Alice shrieked. "I was blinking!"

Arnie laughed. "I do that on purpose. I don't like it to look posed." He dismantled the camera as the group rearranged itself.

212

"That'll give Vikki and Greta something for their grand-children," Bernie said.

"If it comes out," Merv added.

Sheila sat between Vikki and Bernie. Phil was directly across from her.

"Are we boy-girl-boy-girl?"

"Oh, Sally," Edith said. "For Chrissake."

The serving plates moved around the table accompanied by small, surprised sounds.

Sheila served herself and Vikki from the heavy bowl. Doris sat next to Phil. There was a special plate for her with dietetic fruit, cottage cheese, and white meat. She watched all the food passing and lit a cigarette. For a moment Sheila almost forgave her father the secret chocolate.

The far end of the table had started eating. Arnie signaled to Phil and stood up with his plate.

Edith said, "You're not, Arnie."

"May doesn't mind. Do you?"

"No. Of course not."

"You see? Come on, Phil."

Phil looked at Sheila. May was reassuring Edith. "I want you to treat us like family. You know that, darling." Sheila pursed her lips and shook her head almost imperceptibly.

"I'll sit this quarter out, Arnie."

"Sheila, you don't mind, do you? You see—"

"Yes. I do," she interrupted quietly.

"Go on in yourself, though," Phil said quickly.

He stood uncertainly with his plate in his hand. "I thought we had it worked out. Merv? Jack? Hey, Jonny, how about you? You're not going to let the women stop you, are you? Want to watch the game?"

The boy pushed his chair back. It was partly a reflex of obedience, partly a gesture of pride at being asked.

"Merv?" Sally asked plaintively.

"Let him go. What does he want to hang around with a bunch of old fogies like us?"

Jonathon swept up his plate and silverware. He followed Arnie into the living room like an initiate after a priest. May

213

excused herself. "I'll get Esther to set up the television tables," she murmured.

The game clicked on in the living room.

"After dinner Doris is going to make a speech," Merv said.

Edith laughed to cover the sound of the football game. "You wouldn't want to hear what I've got to say."

"You couldn't shock me, gorgeous."

"Ha!"

"Isn't that what I've always said, Bernie? There's only two people in the world you don't screw around with—John Wayne and Doris."

Bernie smiled. "John Wayne you can screw around with."

"Vikki?" Merv called across the table. "You've been so quiet all day—"

"She's so good," Alice said, shaking her head.

"Nobody's been paying any attention to you."

"She's tired from the trip," May said.

"No, I'm not."

"You got any boyfriends, honey?"

Vikki stared at him, innocently baffled. Merv's smile turned clumsy under the logic of her gaze.

"Do you?"

"We live in New York," she answered seriously.

Everyone laughed. "Maybe you don't screw around with Vikki, either," Merv said good-naturedly.

Sheila smiled to herself. Maybe you don't, she thought.

"Has she got enough to eat?" Bernie asked.

Sheila nodded absently and surveyed the table. May sat perched on her chair at the far end, ready to leap up if anyone needed anything. Jack sat next to Edith. She talked across him to May. Doris sat next to Arnie's empty chair picking listlessly at her plate. She kept her cigarette going in the ashtray beside her. Alice was telling Phil and Sally about the man she met on the bus and the gift of light. She was having trouble with the Jello on her fork. She speared it daintily as she talked, but every time she brought the fork to her mouth it was empty. She did not seem to notice. Greta sat between her and an empty chair. Alice had managed to maneuver the girl next to

214

Jonathon. Greta ate silently, occasionally peering up at the rest of the table. Sheila could remember the times she had sat at company tables, open and baffled like Vikki at first, then gradually feeling more sullen and tight-lipped like Greta. Her feelings softened toward the girl as she recalled the foolish agony of her own adolescence. Of course, Sheila had been a bright young woman and Greta was stupid, but that only made her cousin's mask more transparent. Sheila had covered her own self-conscious confusion with precocity. She bantered with the grown-ups, delighted and astonished them, and scrupulously disregarded the faintly patronizing note in their laughter. Greta struck a different, more painful attitude. Yet the deeper the girl withdrew behind her hair and expressionless face, the more clearly Sheila saw herself. She saw the hostility that sprang from the desperate need to be noticed, and an unconscious sense of superiority. Every time Greta's eyes shot up at a callous joke from Merv or a vacuous comment from Alice, Sheila knew the girl was promising herself never to behave like that when she was finally old. She would modulate her laughter; she would remember how children hated questions that asked them to be cute; she would say and do the things that at sixteen she believed grown-ups should say and do—and that somehow no grown-ups she knew ever said and did. Sheila wondered if the girl was fighting against the same knowledge that had always gnawed at the back of her mind at those times, the knowledge that these people, too, must have been sixteen at dinner some time, and made the same promises—and wondering if their failure ensured her own.

"Don't eat so fast, honey," Jack said to her across the table. "It's not good for the bus ride."

Sheila looked away and started eating. The table talk had subsided and the noise of the silverware and china sounded like the rattle of delicate chains. The roar of the television crowd filtered through.

"Hey, if Arnie turns up the set a little we can all hear the game." Merv started to get up.

"I'll break his arm if he touches a switch," Doris said.

215

Sally guided him down with a gentle pressure on his forearm. "Hey, Vikki. Maybe you can get some pointers from Greta." Merv could not stand silence. "About getting a boy-friend, I mean." He did not notice the ripple of tension. "I bet you've got 'em standing in line, don't you?" He grinned, waiting for her to blush.

"Merv." Sally's voice was small.

"Leave it to Merv to keep things going," Edith said.

"Do you have a boyfriend?" It wasn't working, but Merv's solution to a joke that didn't work was to tell it differently —and louder. "What are you kids up to now? Going steady? Getting pinned? Petting?"

"How's the new house coming, Merv?" May asked. "Merv and Sally are building a beautiful new house," she told everyone.

"I'm really interested in what you kids are up to now." Alice's eyes began to fill. "I only get Jonny's side—and I have a feeling that he doesn't tell me half of it. Maybe you two could compare notes."

"Oh, Merv." Alice let out a soft wail as Greta pushed back her chair and left the table. She headed for the kitchen.

"What's wrong?" He turned to Alice. She had a napkin at her nose. He looked past her to Phil. "Did I say something wrong?"

Phil made a clumsy gesture of reassurance. "She'll be all right." He tried to make it sound manly and nonchalant, but it came out a mumble.

"I was only—"

"Mervin," Doris said. "Go watch the football game."

He lapsed into silence with Alice whimpering beside him. "I'm sorry. I'm so sorry." She glanced at Jack, who was eating slowly.

Sheila excused herself.

"Oh, yes," Alice said. "Talk to her, Sheila. Please talk to her."

"Sally?" May's voice was bright with new beginnings as Sheila left them. "Why don't you tell us about the new house?"

Esther was slicing a pineapple in the kitchen. The door to Poppa's room was closed.

"Is Dora Dazzling in there?"

Esther nodded without looking up.

Greta sat in Bernie's recliner, dumbly staring out the picture window. Her face was the same expressionless mask it had been all day.

Sheila closed the door behind her. Whatever the reasons, Sheila had chosen to pursue the girl. She might as well follow through. "Did Merv get to you?" she asked.

Greta shrugged. "He's a jerk."

Sheila nodded. "Sweet. But a jerk."

"What's so sweet about him?"

"Oh, for Christ's sake, Greta. That's like asking someone to explain a joke. If you don't get it, you don't get it."

She gave Sheila a dull look that was supposed to be defiant. "I didn't leave because of him. It's my mother. I hate it when she cries like that."

Sheila laughed. "I know what you mean."

"No, you don't."

"Of course not. You're the only person in the world with a mother."

"Why don't you leave me alone?"

"You said you wanted to talk to me."

"I changed my mind."

"So did I." There was a slight pause.

"So talk, then."

"Stop behaving like a stupid little sow. You're sixteen years old and screwing around with a married man. Both items disqualify you from sulking."

"I didn't ask you to follow me."

"True enough. But here we are. Saddled with each other. I can guarantee, if I go back in there now, after such a short time, somebody else will be in here after me to see if you're all right. Take your pick. Anybody you'd rather have than me?"

"Why can't you leave me alone?"

"I was asking myself the same question when I followed you

217

out. I don't like you very much. You might have picked that up."

Greta grunted.

"So I wondered why I chose to leave all that scintillating company to come in here." She took Bernie's binoculars from the table beside the recliner and focused them out the window. "Did you ever look through these things? There's a couple of sparrows hanging around my father's feeder." She offered them to her.

"What's that supposed to be? Psychology?"

"Forget it. I'll look myself. You had your chance before I came in, anyway. I suppose it never occurred to you to get interested in anything." She brought them back to her own face. The two sparrows were picking around the feeder. Sheila could see their beaks working. "I'll tell you why I followed you. Since I came home from the hospital I've made it a policy not to let things eat at me." She lowered the glasses. "You said you wanted to talk to me about suicide before and I got sore. I thought this would be a good chance to set the record straight. For myself."

"You didn't have to get sore," she mumbled.

"I'm not interested in joining any clubs where girls sit around and tell each other how miserable they are—and how terrible all 'those others' are to them—and I have a feeling that was just the kind of invitation you were extending."

"You were wrong."

"I'm glad to hear it. What did you want, then?"

Greta's face went tight. "I don't know anymore. I just thought—" Her voice went small and high. "I said that about suicide because I didn't know what else to say to you. I never know what to say to you. I'm sorry I just—" Her chin trembled. There was a pimple on the end of it that worked in and out. It didn't make it any easier for Sheila. "I know I'm dumb and you're so smart."

Sheila gave an ironic, embarrassed laugh.

"You are. My father's always telling me about how smart you are. He always says, 'Sheila's so smart. Sheila's so good. Why can't you be like Sheila?' "

"You must hate my guts."

Greta shook her head. "I just want you to like me." Her eyes and nose were running.

Sheila found a box of Kleenex. Greta took one and blew her nose. She dropped the used Kleenex on the table.

"Lennie says I shouldn't worry so much about what other people think of me. That he likes me and that's all that should matter."

"Is Lennie the guy who—"

Greta nodded. "Only he's not married," she said quickly. It sounded as though she had made the point countless times. She paused, then continued more weakly. "Well, he might as well not be. He's getting a divorce."

"Uh-huh."

"It's not what you think."

Sheila made an innocent hands-off gesture.

"He likes me." She nodded toward the door. "They say he's not good enough for me. I don't know what they expect. . . ."

"Maybe just someone who isn't fifteen years older than you and married."

"He's a musician. Doesn't that count for anything?" There was a hint of desperation in the way the girl said it. "I can't be like you. I used to try. I really did." She could not meet Sheila's eyes. She lowered her own and stared at Sheila's stomach as she spoke. "I used to watch you every Thanksgiving and try to see how you could make everybody so happy. Aunt May and Uncle Bernie were always so proud and you never even seemed to notice. You would say funny things and you could always ask somebody a question that would make them notice you and they were always these simple questions that I could never think of. Then when you would ask them I would be so ashamed because they were so simple and I should have been able to ask them too. But I could never think of one until after you said it. You would even ask me questions and I would be so surprised I couldn't answer and that would make me feel even more dumb. On the bus home my mother and father would talk about how lucky Uncle Bernie and Aunt May were

219

and about how you got scholarships and married a rich man and how blond he was—"

"How what?"

Greta shrugged. "My mother thought that was very important, that he was so blond. And they talked about how lucky you were because you had wanted to be a lawyer and you married the son of a judge so you could really be interested in your husband's work, and how happy your mother and father were because they had always cared about things like that, too." She pulled her feet up on the recliner and sat cross-legged, picking at lint on her skirt. Her thighs underneath were white and soft. "Every time on the bus I wanted to ask them what I should do to make them feel lucky like that. But I couldn't. . . . I was too ashamed."

"Ashamed?"

"You never had to ask, did you?"

Sheila's face tingled.

"So I have to guess. I try and I try. Remember in the car when my mother said that about how we used to do Yoga together? I tried so hard but I could never do it right."

"Maybe if you'd kept trying."

"I wanted to, but she said I was getting in the way of her meditation, so she gave me a book and said I should work on it by myself. I didn't want to do it for myself in the first place." She paused. "And I tried to be sensitive and wise like my mother and use big words, but she would laugh at me and tell me what a word really meant. Sometimes it was very close, but she would never notice. She wouldn't even notice how hard I was trying. It's always so close like that—and each time I think this time they'll notice. This time it will be perfect, but it's never right." She pushed back some hair from the side of her face.

If only the girl had a sense of humor. It would have been so much easier if they could share the absurdity of Alice Kahn, of Greta's image of Sheila as a woman blessed, and the inexplicable importance of her husband's blondness. The girl absently scratched her calf. No. Laughter was out of the question.

"When I first started going with Lennie I couldn't tell them

220

about it. He liked me. He really liked me—and that was a funny thing because he had a reputation around school for not liking anything."

"Around school? I thought he was in his thirties."

Greta nodded. "But everyone knows him. His gas station is right across from the school so everyone always goes over to get sodas from the machine and he's always very nasty. But one day he just started talking nicely to me and that was how it started. He told me once I was the only thing he ever liked and he was almost ashamed at the way he wanted to keep me his secret because of that. And I told him he was the only person who ever liked me so he was kind of my secret, too—and then he admitted he had one other secret and he pulled out his guitar and played for me. I was so thrilled because that meant everything would be all right if he was a musician. Then my mother and father would like him, too, and they could be proud of me for falling in love with a musician the way Aunt May and Uncle Bernie were proud of you for marrying a lawyer. So I finally told them and that was the end of my secret."

"You make it sound as though that were the only secret you ever had."

Greta shrugged. "That was when I really knew how dumb I am. When I gave it away myself like that."

Sheila wandered around the room, thumbing magazines, rearranging pencils and paperweights, but as Greta talked she listened more sharply. Sheila's angry response to her lifelessness and self-absorption, her frustration with Greta's uncanny ability to set herself up for humiliation in any circumstance had not really been directed at her cousin at all. Every time she looked at Greta it was like looking at herself three months before in a fun house mirror. She saw her own disinterest, her own hostility and self-hatred distorted by the lumpish, hulking body of the girl. Near the car, when they first arrived, Greta had darkly assumed some connection between them. It startled Sheila into rage, but there was a connection. She had followed her cousin into Poppa's room to cut through the distortion and find the point of contact.

221

She turned to Greta. "What happened then?"

"When?"

"After you told them?"

"I slept with him."

"You hadn't before?"

She shook her head. "They wouldn't let me see him any-more, so I had to sneak out at night and meet him at the garage. We'd stay in the back seat of whatever car was on the rack." She paused. "I didn't even like it," she murmured. "But at least it was another secret." She looked up at Sheila. "You won't tell them, will you?"

"You think they don't know?"

"Not for sure. They don't know for sure."

Sheila shook her head. "I won't say anything." She hesitated. "But—"

"What?" Greta's eyes turned anxious.

"If you don't even like what—"

"It's something."

"Greta. . . . You can't operate that way," she said softly.

"It'll work out."

"You know it won't."

"It's got to."

Sheila sat in the swivel chair near her. She spun around and stared out at the gray day through the picture window. She and Greta were faintly mirrored in the glass, like a cross-fade in a movie.

"How do you do it?" the girl asked softly from behind her.

"Do what?"

"How do you satisfy them all?"

Sheila laughed incredulously. "Are you still looking to me for answers? I tried to commit suicide, for Chrissake." She stopped laughing and turned her chair back to face her.

Greta studied her seriously. "Is that how?"

Sheila stood up.

"Is it?" the girl insisted.

"If it is, it's not worth it."

"No?"

"No!" Sheila said sharply. "Besides, you'll never please

222

them all. There would always be one who would hate you for it."

"Who?"

"Me."

"Would you?" she asked, hopeful.

"I already have, you idiot. You think suicide is only razor blades or ropes or windows? You think I committed suicide in the fifteen or twenty minutes I pushed those goddamned pills down my throat? I'd been killing myself for fifteen years. Just like you."

Greta shook her head. "That's not true. You were always so good."

"Like you want to be?"

"Yes. Yes," she said desperately.

"We're both such fucking good girls," Sheila said between her teeth.

"What should I do?"

"Be bad."

"How?"

"I wish I knew."

"You're talking crazy."

"That's what happens when you go all the way, cookie. If you come back, you come back crazy."

The door opened and Jack Kahn poked his head in. "Anybody home?" He came in with a plate and silverware. "I brought your food," he said gently to Greta.

Sheila watched her face go dead.

"Are you all right?" he asked tentatively. He brought the food to the side table and pushed aside the binoculars and used Kleenex. "Mommy was worried." He put the plate down and turned to Sheila. "You can go back in, honey." He smiled sadly at her. There were spaces between all his teeth. "Thanks." He kissed Sheila's forehead and sat in the swivel chair to watch Greta. The girl took the plate on her lap and hunched over it. "Not too fast, baby. Let it digest." She pushed back her hair to keep it out of the food.

In the dining room they were starting on pie and coffee. Sheila's half-finished dinner was still at her place. Jonathon

223

had returned. Phil glanced at his wife quickly when she came in. Alice eyed her hopefully. Sheila refused to meet either look. Bernie and Merv were talking real estate.

"I saved your food," Vikki said happily.

"Thanks. How are you doing?" she asked confidentially.

"I'm bored."

"After you eat you get Nanny to teach you how to play gin."

Doris was listening to May and Edith exchange heart-attack stories. She saw Sheila and Vikki look toward her.

"Edith knows every coronary and bleeding ulcer in Woodview," she said.

Edith laughed. "It's my husband's business."

Doris raised her eyebrows. "My husband was a picklemaker. Did you ever hear me talk cucumbers?"

May said, "Things are different, now, Momma. Wives take an interest in their husbands' work."

Doris snorted.

Sheila finished eating and helped May and Esther clear the table. The others moved into the living room as the first of the afterdinner guests arrived. Arnie moved upstairs to the black and white set in the bedroom. Jack came out of Poppa's room with Greta's empty plate. He gave it to May.

"She'll be all right," he said sadly to Sheila.

"What's all right?" Sheila asked.

"The Fines and the Resnicks are here, Jack. Why don't you go into the living room?"

Sheila and May kept passing each other as they collected dishes. May smiled shyly each time as though she were acknowledging a distant acquaintance. They met at the sink.

"Freddie?" she said quietly. "I just want you to know I think you're being wonderful. Daddy and I are very proud of you."

Sheila smiled wryly and nodded.

Doris and Vikki passed through the kitchen on the way to Poppa's room. Doris carried a pack of cards. "The living room is filling up."

"Maybe we ought to go in," May said anxiously. "Esther can take care of the rest."

"If anybody wants us we'll be in there," Doris announced.

224

Sheila grinned at Vikki. "You here, Greta?" Doris asked as she closed the door. "You'll play, too. Don't give me that 'kids' crap."

People spilled out of the living room into the hallway. Bernie was at the front door for greetings. There was traffic on the stairs. Some of the men had joined Arnie. They came down periodically to visit and announce the score. Others brought coats up to lay on the bed in the guest room. May said, "Hello, hello," as soon as she hit the hall, and moved to the first group who noticed.

Sheila stood at the living room archway unobserved. Phil was at the bar working feverishly. At first she thought she knew no one, then faces took on histories until it seemed as though her mother had collected for her the fifteen years they had lived in Woodview.

For the first time Sheila felt nervous. Her legs went weak; her arms trembled up to the shoulder. Greeting the dinner guests one at a time she'd been able to move cautiously. Now the swirl of bodies, the confusion of faces from her past overwhelmed her. It made her feel lightheaded. She stood at the threshold of the living room as though it were the rim of a whirlpool, unable to choose whether to plunge or to let it pull her in. Her heart beat over the noise of the chatter and ice. She was on the edge of submission again.

"Sheila!" It was Gertrude Rosenfeld, the rabbi's wife. She recognized Sheila and grabbed her wrist. "Darling, you look wonderful." She kissed her cheek and propelled her to a cluster of women.

Each face detached itself from the group for an instant as Sheila identified it, then faded back. There was the mother of a childhood friend, the wife of a contractor who did work for Bernie, the president of May's Hadassah chapter. The last time Sheila had seen them was the summer Vikki was born; before that was the wedding; before that was the first Thanksgiving she came home from college. They were always there to help May celebrate Sheila's decisions. They looked, appraised, and kissed.

Someone in another part of the room called, "Sheila!" She

turned. "You look wonderful, darling." Sheila spun from cluster to cluster for the rest of the afternoon. It was like a ride she remembered from Steeplechase where she slid down a chute to a field of whirling disks. She would spin from one to the other, each turning in a different direction, until one mercifully flipped her out through the cushioned exit.

Edith Kaprow stood near the window. Sheila caught intermittent glimpses of her, looking tall and imperious, behind the shifting crowd. When she was hidden her laughter cut through the noise.

Sally had returned to the rocking chair, still flanked by Jonathon and Merv, still holding their hands. She smiled up at whoever stood in front of her, while Merv perched with his back half toward her, talking business to a man at the sofa.

Once Sheila found herself near the bar. A friend of Bernie's, a Woodview judge, was talking to Phil. Phil had stopped tending bar and leaned, smiling wearily, against the side of the fireplace. "I understand you've got some prospects," the man was saying. "Something about a friend of the family in Connecticut?" Sheila frowned. She had just time enough to wonder how anyone here knew of something she'd only barely heard of before she was whirled away.

Women grasped her hands, men took her by the shoulders from behind, kissed her cheeks, her lips, her neck; they circled her waist from the side to hand her a drink, from the front to hug her, from the back to surprise her. She forced herself not to stiffen at the ease of the men who handled her with fatherly affection or the desperately warm pressure of the women's hands.

The voices and shrieks of surprise grew louder. Edith's laughter turned sharper. Once, as Sibyl Fine was leaving to refill her drink and all the others seemed to shift around her, Sheila thought she understood how the old Greek heroes must have felt when they made their trips to the underworld. All of her past swirled about her, she could recognize each of them, love some, question others, but none could really touch her. That was why they all tried so hard. The crowd in her

226

mother's house grew thicker, jollier, and she felt more and more like a visitor from another world.

Her father beckoned from the archway. She circled around Harriet Melman, shifting direction to greet Feda Rempel, paused only a moment, then threaded through to Bernie.

"The game's over. Arnie and Edith are taking Doris home."

"So soon?" She never felt she had enough time with her grandmother.

"It's getting late. She's tired."

Doris was waiting in the kitchen for Bernie to bring her coat.

"Grandma?" She touched cheeks with her quickly. She wanted to hug the old woman but she knew better. Doris would only shove her away and mutter. "I wanted to have more time with you, but—" She tossed her head toward the living room.

"Let that be a lesson to you. You make a jerk out of yourself, that's what happens."

"Never again." Sheila smiled and met her eyes directly.

Doris nodded once. "Your daughter's all right. She's got no card sense but she's got a head. You've quit treating her like a piece of glass. That's good."

"I didn't realize you'd noticed."

"That you did or you quit?"

"Both, I guess."

"For some things you don't need a college education. She won't break."

"I know."

"Neither will you."

Bernie came back with her coat. He handed it to Sheila and started back to the living room. "I'll get Jack and Alice."

"Bernie." Doris stopped him at the doorway. She made a wincing face that said, "Let it go."

"They'll be upset if you leave without—"

"They'll live."

Arnie found her as Sheila finished getting the coat on. "Ready, Doris? Edith's already in the car."

227

"I'm coming." She pulled the coat tight in front of her. "I'll be glad to get back to a normal routine again." She shook her head as though she were trying to think if she'd left something—or if something hadn't happened that was supposed to. "Every year there's something. . . ." she muttered.

May arrived in time for good-byes. Sheila helped Doris out to the car and guided her in. "I'll see you again soon, Grandma."

"Not if you catch pneumonia. Get back in the house."

The crowd started thinning when Sheila returned. The men who had been with Arnie came down, stayed long enough to be civil, then hustled off their wives. The women explained about baby-sitters, long drives, heart conditions. Merv and Sally took Jack and his family to the bus. Greta waited in the car while they all kissed. Jack and Merv held Alice firmly as they guided her to the driveway.

Phil was still with Judge Spizer in the living room. Bernie had joined them. Sheila signaled to him but he did not notice. She approached the group.

"Oh, Sheila." Judge Spizer put a protective arm around her shoulder and brought her into the circle. "Phil's been singing an old familiar song for me. That last year is the toughest. Don't I remember?"

"You want the women's chorus?"

The judge laughed. "Don't I remember that, too. Judithe had it worse than me. I remember. And that was during the Depression, too. But I've been telling Phil—and I'll tell you, too. It has its rewards."

"That's comforting."

"I've told him to take the job in Connecticut."

Sheila glanced at Phil. He kept his smile but he shifted uneasily against the mantelpiece.

"I don't think it's a sure enough offer yet," she said softly. "For such a definite decision."

"Sounds like it to me."

Phil had been keeping a hawk's eye on Sheila all day, but he did not seem to notice the puzzled look she threw him now.

"Come on, Carl," Bernie said. "Who could have given you advice at twenty-three?"

"Twenty-eight," Sheila reminded automatically.

"There were always people willing. I thank God for them now. It might have taken me thirty years to hear them, but once I did I was glad they took the trouble." He sighed a little dramatically. "That's what getting old is all about. Giving advice just when you've gotten wise enough to be able to take some." He inclined his head toward Sheila. "Don't be nervous about moving to Connecticut. It will all work out. I remember how nervous Judithe was about moving to a small town like Woodview from Philadelphia. Making new friends; adjusting, entertaining. Well, it worked out just fine. Just fine. And it has its rewards." He still had his hand clamped firmly on Sheila's shoulder. It was setting her teeth on edge.

"Phil? I think we'd better start thinking about leaving." He nodded without meeting her eyes. "We have a trip back to New York," she explained to the judge. "And the holiday traffic—"

"Of course, my dear."

"I'll see if I can find Vikki and get her into pajamas for the trip." Sheila waited for the judge to release her.

"I'll go," Phil said.

"No," she said quickly. "I'll take care of it." The hand did not fall away until she started to move.

"That's a hell of a girl you've got there," she heard the judge say as she left. "Going to be quite an asset. Judithe would have said the same thing. Did you ever meet Mrs. Spizer?"

"No, sir." Sheila hated when Phil called men sir. It was a holdover from his servile, prep school days.

"She's been gone twelve years, Carl," Bernie said.

"That long? I suppose you're right."

Sheila found Vikki in Poppa's room. "How did your game go?"

"OK. Nanny had to hold the cards for me."

"What about her own cards?"

"She held them, too."

Sheila laughed. "I bet she played both hands, too."

229

Vikki nodded. "I won."

Sheila found Vikki's pajamas. She told her to change and returned to the living room. There were only three or four people preparing to say good-bye. May and Bernie saw them off. Sheila started to relax as she heard the last of them dribble from the door. Her face fell back in position. The sides of her mouth and eyes ached from smiling. She had not realized how stiffly she'd been holding herself, how exhausting a job it was to maintain her sense of her own humanity against the stares, the shrieks, the affectionate, demanding embraces. She collected Vikki's colorforms, ribbons, dolls, sweaters. She was pulling the child's snowsuit out of the hall closet when two hands clamped down on her shoulders. It was too sudden. "Goddammit!" She whirled and flung out her arm. The back of her hand connected with Phil's face. She cried out on top of it, "I'm sorry!" But the anger that had spun her around was still in it. May and Bernie had just turned back from the front door.

"You frightened her," May said.

"I'm sorry," Phil murmured.

"She's tired."

Sheila closed her eyes and held the snowsuit to her tightly. "It's all right. It's all right, everyone." She laughed nervously. "I've just been touched so much today, I think there must be depressions all over my skin." She opened her eyes. "Did I hurt you?"

He shook his head.

She slid past him. "Let me see how Vikki's doing." She went quickly and hoped they had not seen how much pleasure she'd felt in the moment of startled freedom.

It was already dark by the time they were ready to get into the car. Phil carried Vikki bundled in a blanket. The cold night air was sharp and damp. Bernie and May had slipped on coats to come out with them.

"I already started the motor for you," Bernie said as they crossed the driveway. "The car should be warm. Vikki will have to sleep in front with you two."

"It's warmer in the front, anyway," May put in.

Sheila laughed. "Don't be silly. There's more room in the back."

"I don't know."

They found the back loaded with grocery boxes.

"What's this?"

"Just some stuff I thought you might be able to use."

"Like what?"

"Oh, you know. Little treats. Salmon and oysters and lox. A little pickled herring. Towels—"

"Towels?"

"There was a fire sale," May explained. "Daddy was able to pick up a carton of towels—"

"A carton. . . ."

"We kept some for ourselves," he assured her.

"A carton of towels?" she repeated incredulously.

"It was a very good buy."

"A carton of towels?"

"And a roasting pan," May said. "I noticed you didn't have one. . . ."

"A carton of towels and a roasting pan?" She turned to Phil. "We've got a carton of towels and a roasting pan in the back seat of the car. And little treats. Oysters and lox. So Vikki has to sleep in the front." Bernie had passed the limit. She could not even resent it; she could not feel threatened. The insanity was too glaring. She had a vivid image of her father working all afternoon to fill the cartons, absolutely insensible of what he was doing. She could see him, every time it occurred to him that his daughter had survived, or a new guest arrived—she could see him strolling into the kitchen to drop another tin in the box. Sardines, pickled herring, salmon. "Put Vikki in the front for now. We'll put all this in the trunk. Then schlep it all upstairs when we get to New York." They hauled the cartons out and transferred them to the trunk. "A carton of towels and a roasting pan. Twenty below, twelve o'clock at night, double-parked on a New York street, we're going to be taking a carton of towels and a roasting pan up in the elevator." When the back seat was clear, Vikki climbed over and rolled up again in the blanket.

The good-byes were brief. It was too cold for sustained ones and Bernie and May were worried about a draft on Vikki. They pecked and hugged and hustled Sheila into the warmth of the car. Phil backed out of the driveway. Bernie and May stood waving into the headlights. The car swung onto the street and pulled away. Sheila looked back once. They were still there, shadows now, still waving.

She put her head back on the seat and closed her eyes.

"Tired?" Phil asked gently.

The image of Bernie and May waving from the darkness lingered in front of her closed eyes. "Exhausted." What do they do now? she thought to herself. After the taillights of their rented car disappeared, what did they look at? Her mother would help Esther collect glasses and snack plates from all over the house. Bernie would take some Sanka and go upstairs to watch television. But who were they? Her ridiculous, evasive mother, her bemused, temperamental father. She felt as though all her life it had been her job to protect them from the realities that she alone could handle. Even the way she let them pamper her was a way she had found of pampering them, of helping them retain an illusion of innocence. The three of them had never had to face each other as human, fallible beings. They had spent God knows how many years playing some kind of cockamamy choose-up game of round robin, with Sheila keeping May a child while May kept Bernie while Bernie kept Sheila. Oh, God, she could remember her own arrogance with them so well, coming home on vacations with book lists. "You mean you've never read *The Idiot*? You've got to. *It is so gorgeous.*" Or dragging them to the Thalia when they came to the city. "*Children of Paradise* is playing *in the uncut version*. Of course you'll understand it. What's not to understand?" Always enthusiastic, always mystified by their reticence, but the enthusiasm was never as ingenuous as all that, and the mystification always faintly supercilious. It was a wonderful variation. She could put them in their place as naïfs. They could encourage her own intolerable callowness. Everyone could still be everyone else's baby.

232

No wonder they were puzzled when Sheila called time out and they had to drop hands. Then they had to admit they'd been fooling all along—but only for the other's sake. They'd become so used to disguising their own vulnerability, their own human needs, they did not know how to begin to know each other as grown-ups. So Bernie just kept filling cartons and May kept apologizing for Bernie and Sheila still could not imagine who they were when she was gone.

She would have loved to sit down with her mother to sort out the day, to describe her own amazement and curious relief when she understood that her own suicide was only different in kind from Edith's and Alice's and Sally's. She could still feel the idiotic awkwardness as they cleared the table, the number of times she had looked at her mother trying to find a way to say something—anything—that would free them to talk like two loving women, the number of times she had lowered her own eyes and smiled absently when May caught her looking.

Something about her time with Greta had been haunting her since it happened. She longed for someone to tell about it.

It had started when Greta talked about the mess she was making as her "secret." The word had startled Sheila then, even as it dug into her mind again now. The girl would never have been able to comprehend that Sheila, too, had had her secrets, that every woman who was with them that day had had some secret, and that just as Greta had given up her first and settled for something less—something that carried no pleasure or dignity, something that had nothing in common with the original dream except its privacy—Sheila and all the other women had compromised their secrets.

She opened her eyes and stared out at the shadows of the trees on the Parkway. She pulled the top of her coat tighter to her.

They never started out as secrets, either. They started as youthful certainties, as open and vulnerable as Greta's assurance that someday, when someone liked her, all the misery and confusion would make sense. It was only when the certainty came into doubt that they turned it into a secret, guarding it more and more jealously until it did not even matter

233

what the secret was as long as they had something to guard to keep them alive. That was where Greta was now. There was no way to warn her of the rest of the process, when the secret that had once sustained her would become a more and more intolerable burden until, like Edith's, it again became an open, bitter issue or, like Sheila's, it disappeared. There was no way to explain that her only chance was, not to cling to the secret, but to rediscover its source, to reopen the certainty, no matter how risky that might be, to make it vulnerable once again, no matter how painful that might be. She knew for sure now that that was the only course for herself. She was grateful to Greta for giving her a way to name the object of her own search. She had to rediscover her own secret. It was the unidentifiable weight that had dropped at her suicide, the thing that had once been open, certain, perhaps a little frightening. She had to find it again, reassume it, and this time push it forward, up and out until she was once again sustaining it, and not depending on it to sustain her. But what was it? Greta's secret was firmly grounded in the particulars of her banal, adolescent love affair, Edith's in her poisonous reminders of the clinic, Alice's in her inane assertions of the spirit. Even Sally's dream of power was there, for anyone who wanted to look, in her passive, mindless control of her men.

Where was hers? It must be there, as obvious as that of all the others, waiting to be released. Why couldn't she let go and recognize it? She felt on the verge of discovery. It was not the first time. How many times she could remember the long painful talks with Phil where he would sit there, intolerably patient, asking, "What do you want? If you could just tell me what it is you want maybe I could help." And she would pace, with the name of something on the tip of her tongue that always came out in the end as the same old lie. "I don't know. It's all right. It's my period." But it was never her period. It wasn't all right and she did know. She just couldn't find its name, as absurdly simple as it was. Her brain had become deft enough at leaping to empty ideas, all those fruitless generalizations her brilliant mind allowed her to put between herself and the simple truth. Identity, purpose, meaning, a future.

234

She could juggle all those till she and Phil were exhausted. She knew intuitively that the juggling still took less energy, was less terrifying than the naming would be.

This time, though, it was different. This time she was determined to stay with it.

"Is she asleep?" Phil asked softly.

Sheila shifted around to look. The light from the oncoming cars flickered across Vikki's face.

"Down for the count," she whispered.

Phil was intent on the road. She wondered if she could explain it to him. He would not be able to look at her while he was driving. That might make it easier. She knew she would not be able to speak if he were looking at her. She was still troubled at his silence about Fred Ryan's offer and stung at the idea that he had talked to Judge Spizer about it in more detail than he had talked to her. She had assumed the offer was a vague one and that since he had never brought it up after that first night he was not considering it seriously. The judge assumed the offer was firm. He advised Phil to take it. On what information? That was a bitter question. It rose in her throat whenever she looked at Phil. It was there, she knew, behind the accidental slap in her parents' closet and it was there now as she watched the lights play over his face the way they played over Vikki's.

She could not ask. It was important that he offer her an explanation without her having to ask. Yet the question was there whenever their eyes met and it got in the way of anything else she wanted to say.

"What are you thinking about?"

She gave a voiceless little laugh. "That's what I was trying to figure out."

They were being careful not to wake Vikki. Sheila snuggled deeper into her coat. Their whispering together gave her a lovely, nostalgic feeling of intimacy. For an instant she could remember what it was like to love him when she thought love was uncomplicated.

"Phil?" she spoke mainly to hear herself whisper again.

"Hmm?"

235

The important questions collided in her throat. "How was the day for you?"

He smiled. "OK."

"Was I. . . . Was I all right?" Goddammit, that was not what she wanted to ask.

"You were great. I don't know how you did it."

"What did you talk with my folks about?" she asked cautiously.

"When?"

"When I went to get Grandma."

"What makes you think I talked with them?"

"You were alone with them for a good long time. Didn't you?"

"A little. With your father."

"What about?"

He shrugged. "Nothing much."

"Me?" She wished she could stop bringing it back to herself that way.

"A little."

She waited for him to offer more, but he lapsed back into silence. She was on her own.

Part Two

---·—∞—·---

Swinging Out

6

Sheila

November 26-
December 15

THE NEXT day Phil went off to the library. Sheila encouraged it. She encouraged him to use the weekend to catch up, too. She wanted to be alone. She was still pursuing the one idea she had carried away from her mother's house. Since her failure to talk with him in the car, Phil was only a distraction. She was like a woman possessed. She could think of nothing else and nothing else had value except as a possible clue. Everything in her world had taken on a new and tremulous life. She was convinced that her secret was there for her, lurking in the most commonplace objects. Even more than her secret, she was convinced that the certainty which had preceded the secret was there and available if only she could look in the right way. In the morning when she read the paper she watched for a paragraph that would leap out at her and match with words the still nameless object of her search. While she was cleaning she would stop and scan the room. She would try to pierce through each object and force it to offer up its hidden significance. Yet she knew that it did not even need a piercing look; it was simpler than that: All she had to do was stand back and see it, not shimmering, but obvious and commonplace on the surface of everything. The quilt and the matching curtains, the night table and lamp, the desk with the books arranged on it, the closet door, half ajar, with her yellow robe on the hook inside, the throw rug, the alarm clock, the television set. She could look and look but she could not find what she had to do to see. So she gritted her teeth and went to the next room or talked to Vikki and listened even to her daughter's words as though she were listening to an oracle. She was on the scent of her own certainty. At times the idea thrilled, at others it terrified her, but she refused to let go.

Phil had told her the Monday appointment with Dr. Rankin was all right, after all, so she hadn't changed it. The first thing she thought of that morning was whether to talk to him about her search. She decided not to. She liked Rankin. Before her suicide she had always been suspicious of psychiatrists. They carried a quality of judgment with them as though they sat there with a pad and pencil waiting to pounce when you gave yourself away. "I always get the feeling they're trying to look up your nose," she had said once to Diana. Rankin was not like that. He was easy to be with. He did not moralize. He had a sense of humor, a little heavy, maybe, but a sense of humor. Still, when it came to trusting him with her search, she balked. Her instinct told her it would not be safe until she had named her object herself.

The session went smoothly. She could talk freely about Thanksgiving, about the scene with Greta and her love for Doris, even her disappointment in Phil and her doubts about Frederick Ryan's offer of a job. She could talk freely about anything now that she'd focused so sharply on the one thing she would not discuss. It was only on the subway going home that she wondered if she had done the right thing. She believed that she already knew what she looked for, that she'd been carrying it around for a long time, and that she'd only let go completely that one time. If that was true, she might also know it was something that would, after all, make Rankin judge her. Maybe she knew it was something bad. That startled her. She literally lurched when it hit her. Son of a bitch. I'm feeling guilty. She grinned. She must have looked idiotic to the others in the car. It was all she could do to keep from

240

giggling. Maybe Rankin was helping her after all. She was feeling guilty. That wasn't the way it was supposed to work, was it? She grinned all the way to 116th Street.

She suspected that when it happened it would happen out of left field. She went through her daily routines watching from the corner of her eye. She held herself ready, determined to act as soon as the realization came. The last thing in the world she expected was that she would act first and realize after.

It was Wednesday morning. There was absolutely nothing different in the organization of her day. She had seen Phil off and waked Vikki, fed her, and taken her to nursery school. They walked quickly down Amsterdam Avenue. It was cold. The nursery school was just across 116th Street. Sheila brought Vikki into the hallway. The children were lined up in front of Mrs. Haynes, who sat on a stool in the draft with a coat over her shoulders. As they approached her, one by one, she flashed a light in their mouths, inspected their throats, and passed them on. Some of the more impatient ones opened their mouths and kept them wide until their turn. The mothers hovered at the side waiting to be released when their own passed inspection. Sheila waved good-bye to Vikki as soon as she was cleared.

Diana was to start two weeks of shooting on a new job the next day, so they had agreed to get together for lunch with the kids. Sheila planned to shop at the A & P while Vikki was in school.

She started toward the corner, but turned instead and crossed in the middle of the street. There was traffic, but she made her way through it with ease. She pushed through the doors of the Law School Building easily, too. She noted that public doors always worked hard for her. As she pushed through the second set she remembered how different it had been that afternoon more than a month before when all the objects outside had imposed their wills on her and it had been she who had given way.

The secretary in Dean Colquist's office was pleasant. So was Sheila.

"I'd like to see Dean Colquist."

"Have you an appointment?"

"I'm a little late. My name is Sheila Gaynor."

She scanned an appointment book. "I don't see your name. . . . Miss—"

"Mrs. That's because I'm very late."

The woman looked baffled. She picked up the phone and buzzed. "Mrs. Gaynor is here to see you. She says she missed an appointment—" She put down the phone and pointed toward the door. "He's only got a couple of minutes before his next appointment." She looked around the empty office. "But they seem to be late, too."

Sheila smiled. "If they're as late as I am we've got years. Thanks. This won't take long."

It didn't. Sheila went in and explained to Dean Colquist. Her voice was cool, her words crisp and to the point. She was not surprised. The sentences must have been shaping themselves for days. She had graduated from Barnard six years before with a fellowship to law school. She had never used it. She wanted to reapply for admission and reapply for the fellowship. Dean Colquist could not give her any encouragement. There was a general tendency to look askance at applications from married women. Many of them simply didn't realize how demanding the study was. It was only the most exceptional. . . . Sheila had been through high-powered admissions procedures before. The more exclusive the school, she had learned, the more charmingly hopeless the admissions officer made it sound. She told him she understood the difficulties. She simply wanted to know how the most exceptional cases proceeded. What was the status of her old application and was she still eligible for the fellowship? Dean Colquist could not tell her offhand, but he would look through her files and bring it up with the admissions committee if she wanted. The name on the files was Sheila Kahn. He wrote it down. In the meantime, if she wanted to move through the regular procedure his secretary had application forms. . . .

Sheila thanked him and left.

She did not start shaking until she was back on the street. It

252

was impossible to tell the moment she realized what she was doing. She was not even sure she had yet. It was like riding the breakers at Atlantic Beach. She was moving up on the crest, shooting forward while the current pulled back from beneath.

She could feel the weight of the application forms in her bag as she walked back up Amsterdam Avenue. She'd been right. It was absurdly simple after all. She wanted to practice law. "I want to practice law." She said it over to herself, amazed at how easy it was to say now, and how hard it had been, how long it had taken to find the words. All she had done was to follow the impulse she'd had every morning when she dropped Vikki. She would come out on the street with a feeling that there was something important she had to do. She would hesitate, then remember the laundry, the cleaning, the ironing, an appointment with the dentist. That would become the important thing—she would make it the important thing, though she never really believed it. Then she would walk to the corner, cross with the green, and push back up Amsterdam to the apartment. This time she hadn't. This time, without trying to nail it in words she'd followed the impulse, cut through the middle and, only after she'd found herself in Dean Colquist's office, found that the words were there.

She wanted to practice law. She could even trace it back to its innocent, vulnerable certainty. High school in Woodview. She read a biography of Clarence Darrow. While all the other girls dreamed of Joan of Arc or Marilyn Monroe, she dreamed of Darrow. She had no need to be worshipped. But to be able to fight for new ways of seeing, to change people's minds, to defend what at first glance seemed indefensible, and be able to spend a lifetime doing it—that would be something. The next summer her father had the television on all day. She saw her parents' impotent rage at the Army-McCarthy hearings and, at the same time she shared the rage, only half understanding it, she knew she need not feel impotent. She knew she would practice law.

She could tell when she'd started to doubt the certainty and guard it. It was when she announced it to May and Bernie.

243

They nodded. They told her it was a good thing to dream about, and not to be disappointed if. . . .

Sheila got the shopping cart from the apartment and went downstairs to the A & P. She remembered the nightmare of paralysis in front of the cans of corn. Of course she hadn't been able to decide. Years before she'd lost her faith in her own decisions. She could trace them all now, a straight line of self-betrayals that took her farther and farther away from her certainty until she had lost their source—and herself in the process. It was still there when she chose Barnard and chose to study government, but those decisions were safe. A woman's school near a men's campus. Everyone went to college. It was right to declare your dreams in the shape of a major—and even if you didn't follow through, your chances for happiness were still so much surer. The secret was still there when she met Phil, but it started to take a new shape. His. Her mother and father were wrong. She need never worry about disappointment. Even if she never practiced law, the man she loved would. She had wanted her life to be the law. Her choice of a husband ensured it. And once they were married her choice of a child ensured her husband. And once she was a mother her choice of a full and passionate commitment ensured her child. By that time the thread was lost and the secret buried beyond her reach. All that was left was a vague and angry sense of betrayal that had to be buried as well to survive. Every choice had promised safety on the other side. The alternatives were a risk. She had played it safe. She did the right thing, the same thing all her friends had done, and her mother and her friends, and maybe even Doris and her friends. Each time she'd convinced herself she was acting freely, sanely, realistically, but every decision was a capitulation; each took her farther from herself. There had been no safety on the other side of those choices, none of the happiness they promised, only the deeper, more terrible doubt that always comes from compromise and demands for further capitulation. No wonder she finally could not choose a can of corn. She had no reason to trust her ability to make any decisions without selling herself out. No wonder she'd finally given up completely that October afternoon when she felt all the objects working their will on her and she had already killed her own will to fight back.

Now it turned out that she hadn't killed it. It had simply retreated to gather strength, then lay in ambush. She gave a short, voiceless laugh. Like Fidel, she thought. I've been carrying on my very own private guerrilla war. "Señora Gaynor reporting. The troops are ready to march on Havana." They'd just completed their first reconnaissance.

Her fingers and eyes itched to get to work on the applications. It took all her willpower not to dig into her bag and pull the forms out to study in the middle of the A & P. She loaded the cart quickly. At the checkout counter she fingered the folded papers while she waited to pay.

Back upstairs she unloaded the packages, grabbed the applications, and went to the bedroom. She cleared the books on the desk and spread out the forms and instructions, ironing them with the tips of her fingers.

She took a deep breath. It caught in the middle and she pressed her hands against her eyes. Oh, God, she thought, trembling. I thought I'd never be happy again. She gave herself time to calm down but she did not wait for her hands to steady. The papers rattled when she picked them up. There was a box of Kleenex on the desk. She blew her nose and got to work.

She sifted through all the routine stuff. Biographical data, transcripts, law board scores, an essay on goals, recommendations. She stopped at the recommendations. They called for three. She thought of Leo Kauffman and wondered if she hadn't already been heading toward this the day last week when she approached him on the street. She had forgotten that he had been responsible in the first place for her fellowship. He was an enormously influential man, the kind who was able to back up his recommendations with a pleasant personal phone call. With him behind her the other two recommendations hardly mattered. She could ask any of her old teachers who were still around. There was simply no question that he would back her again, especially after the lunch. . . . Her heart sank. She remembered the lie she had told him. She closed her eyes and shook her head. She'd been right again. She'd kept telling herself her secret was out there, staring her in the face, if only she could see it. And there it was, in the lie. She played with the edge of the recommendation form. It might have been comforting to know she'd been right, but it didn't much matter if she'd also cut off her best chance for success. How could she ask Professor Kauffman to recommend her when she'd already told him she was in her third year? She felt the whole scheme start to dissolve inside her. She put down the form and stared out the window.

Maybe it was lucky. It might be better to give it up now before she put too much faith in her plan and let herself in for a bigger fall later. She could take this one. If it happened later it would be even more painful. The disappointment spread through her with a familiar, poisonous sweetness. She'd had her kicks in the excitement of the morning; she'd been sure and hopeful and barreled in like all the other times. Now she could pay for it, chuck the whole thing, and learn to act a little more realistically next time. It was almost a relief. She pulled the papers together sadly and got up from the desk. She went to lie down. At least she'd got the shopping done in a hurry. There was time for a nap before lunch. She sat on the edge of her bed and pulled off her shoes. She held one in her hand and stared numbly around the room, remembering how she had felt when she came in. The last thing she expected was to end up napping.

Her wedding picture sat on the dresser in the gold frame Bernie and May had sent. She and Phil smiled at her, young, self-conscious, and so sure. Her grip on the shoe tightened. She stood up and threw it blindly. It missed the picture and fell between the dresser and the desk. "I'm not taking any fucking nap," she said between her teeth.

She padded to the living room, banging the wall in the hallway with the side of her fist. She circled the room, found a

246

cigarette, lit it, and went back to the bedroom. She stared at the doorway and looked at the desk. There was no reason to go in. She returned to the living room, flicked her ash in a tray, emptied the tray in the kitchen, and brought it back to the living room. A minute later she was back at her bedroom door.

The disappointment had lost its sweetness sooner than usual. Now there was only the bitter residue of anger. She would have to give up something else, make it more final, to remind herself of how good and brave she was to be disappointed. She went to the desk and picked up the forms, to start tearing them. The relief, the secret leaping of her heart when she'd realized it was hopeless came home to her full force. She'd welcomed the disappointment. She'd wanted the whole affair to be hopeless. How much easier to nurse the bitterness inside, to be sure of that, to be justified in it, than to break through and leave herself open to action that guaranteed nothing. It was all so neat. The circumstances were always there—just as she knew the name of her certainty had always been there and available—the circumstances were always there to help excuse her from commitment. Every other time she had leaped at them and loved them for giving her something outside herself to blame while she loathed herself for choosing them. Not this time. She put the forms back on the desk. She wasn't letting herself off so easy this time. She would go to Leo Kauffman, admit the lie, and start from there. If he would not help there had to be others who would. There was no more comfort for her in her despair. It was time to start meeting the obstacles head-on, to make them problems and not excuses.

She sorted the forms again and forgot her nap. Her energy returned, not euphoric this time, but grimly determined. She found Phil's yellow legal pad and started roughing out her biography.

The phone rang.

"Where the hell are you?" It was Diana.

"I thought we were meeting at noon."

247

"It's one o'clock."

She glanced at the clock. "Son of a bitch." She'd forgotten what it was like to get lost in time like that.

"We waited at the school half an hour. Then I brought the kids home. Are you all right?"

"I'm fine. Oh, Jesus, Diana, I'm sorry."

"What happened?"

"I can't explain. But I'm all right," she said quickly. "I really am. I'll be right over. Was Vikki worried?"

"I don't think so. I told her you said you might be late. They're in playing now."

"I'll be right over."

She did not tell Diana about her new plan. It bothered her afterward even more than it had bothered her that she didn't tell Rankin about her search. Her reluctance felt like a betrayal of their friendship. She let Diana talk about the show she was doing, how she had maneuvered the role, what she would do with it, where it could lead. Sheila said nothing about her own new plan and wondered why. Diana would have two weeks of shooting for sure, maybe three. The women agreed to hold off their Christmas shopping until she was finished. Then they would make it a jaunt, the way they used to when they were roommates. Sheila loved the holiday season downtown. She hadn't had the fun of hustling out of the cold into department stores, bucking the crowds, and smelling the starchy merchandise, perfumes, and pine scents for years.

Diana said, "It'll give you something to look forward to." Sheila smiled. Her friend's cheer was transparent and Sheila was touched. Five hours before she might have needed something to look forward to. It was an odd sensation seeing Diana talk to another Sheila. She almost told Diana then about what had happened. She didn't.

She didn't tell Phil, either. With him, at least, she knew why. Explaining to Phil was the most frightening prospect of all. She went over all the ways he might respond. There were none that might not threaten her own conviction. She'd been that route with him so many times before. She could not risk it.

As soon as she thought of her plan on his terms all the old doubts flooded in. She asked herself if she wasn't just indulging another fantasy, evading her real responsibilities, setting impossible goals. She did not know if she were more apprehensive of Phil's dismissing it or his taking it seriously. If he dismissed it she was afraid she would not be able to find the words—or the courage—that could convince him she was serious. In the past, when he tossed aside something important to her she would end up choking and inarticulate. He would use it to prove that she hadn't really thought it through and she would pull herself together and prove her maturity and sense by admitting it was just another vague notion after all. If he took her seriously, she'd be in for another one of those long, intimate talks where they finally got to what was really bothering her, she would have a good cry and he would be there to support and make love to her.

But those other times were, after all, just notions. She knew that now because she wanted to practice law and that was not a notion. And Phil had been right in the long talks. Those weren't the things that were really bothering her. This was. She wanted to practice law. She'd wanted it all along.

So she worked on her applications secretly, in every free moment she had. She finished her biography and statement of goals and her faith in the rightness and, even more, the possibility, grew. As she came closer and gathered strength the other reasons for secrecy forced themselves on her. Since that first morning when she returned and looked at Phil asleep beside her, Sheila had begun to change. She did not love Phil in the same desperate way she had before. Over the next two weeks, as the work on her applications absorbed her and the prospects of success grew in her mind, she understood more and more clearly how different her love was. Phil was no longer the center of her life. All her hope, all the possibility for a coherent future, no longer resided in him. She could see him dispassionately. When he came home late from the bookstore, exhausted and irritable, she could still respect his refusal to use his family's wealth, but now, at the same time, she could also see that his pride was foolish. Even more, she could recognize how that very need to affirm his own independence and strength had always demanded that she give up hers. She could think about that first year of their marriage when she pleaded with him to let her get some kind of job to help save money and maybe even allow him to get started earlier. He was hurt at the offer and asked, angrily, if she did not think him capable of supporting her. Now she could admit that every decision of his which she had admired as a matter of principle was as much a matter of vanity. He was self-indulgent, a little pompous, and for all his logical genius, incredibly naive and vulnerable. And now that she could admit all those terrible things she could love him more deeply, more consciously, than she ever had before. She had been so afraid to look before because she was afraid they were growing old too quickly. Seeing him now as he was, she was made aware of how young they both still were.

Her new love for Phil was as surprising as all the other discoveries she was making, as wondrous as her new future, as real as her new strength. It was no longer a fiction because she was no longer a fiction. This new kind of love grew more and more precious to her every day. She kept her plan secret because she did not want to lose it.

Sheila let two weeks pass before she contacted Leo Kauffman. Once she had all her other material ready she phoned his office. The secretary recognized her name.

"Miss Kahn? Professor Kauffman's been trying to find you."

"To find me?"

"He's leaving on sabbatical at the end of the semester. He said he wanted to see you before he left. The alumni office has no listing for you. . . ."

"I haven't kept in contact."

"Well, he'll be delighted you called. I'll put you down for next Wednesday morning."

That was a week away.

The weather turned colder. Christmas exploded in the streets and store windows. They raised the big tree on the campus sundial. Phil grew tense as the holiday approached.

250

He found more reasons to be away from the apartment. When he was there he was guarded and distracted. It happened every year as the end of the semester approached. Neither of them ever brought up Frederick Ryan's offer. Sheila was no longer hurt by that. Whatever Phil had said to Judge Spizer and Bernie was probably only some first aid for his dignity and confidence. She knew, really, that he would never leave the city, certainly not to move closer to Northfield. At any other time she would have been panicked by Phil's mood. Now she was too preoccupied.

Diana finished shooting and called to keep the shopping appointment. Wednesday was best. They could drop the kids at school and arrange for Estelle Donado to take them for lunch and the afternoon. That would give them the whole day. Sheila told her she had a morning appointment.

"What kind of appointment?"

"I can't talk about it yet."

"Can't you change it? It'll kill half the day."

"No."

"Sweetheart, you really need the spree."

"I can't change the appointment."

"Are you having an affair?"

Sheila laughed. "With who? The maintenance man?"

"I can't think of anything else that would keep you from shopping."

"I'll meet you at one o'clock at the Birdcage. And this time I won't be late. I promise."

"Can't you tell me what it's all about?"

"I will. Soon. Promise."

"I can't imagine—"

"I know. Isn't that a kicker?"

She wrestled with her demons for the rest of the week, questioning her motives, her ability, her sanity. Every day another opportunity to fall back on the old evasions leaped forward. Vikki came down with a fever over the weekend. She asked herself what she would do if it happened while she was taking exams. Phil's mood turned blacker and she wondered if her own distraction wasn't the cause. Then she remembered

251

her elation when she first discovered the name of her secret, the way she had unmasked her own, poisonous desire for disappointment, and her determination returned.

She kept the applications tucked away in the box of towels Bernie had given her. She had not yet typed out her rough draft. Every day she took them out, made small corrections. On some days they read like the most brilliant legal prose she'd ever seen; on others she was sure it was gobbledygook. It was maddening, especially now when she believed that if she failed it would be her responsibility. She was cutting loose from the luxury of circumstances.

On Tuesday night, while Phil was at the bookstore and Vikki was asleep, she typed out the applications. At first she had tried writing what she thought Leo Kauffman and the admissions committee would want to read. It came out inane, unconvincing. She did not know what they wanted. Besides, she'd already found out where that kind of lying could lead. She had chosen to be honest. She talked about service. She quoted Holmes and Warren and, yes, Darrow. She could see Phil smiling paternally and explaining that this was an application, not a valedictory speech. She asked him what would be more effective? She saw him grin and wave noncommittally. "If you can't do it on your own," she heard him say, "you'd better not try. No one helps anybody else in law school." He disappeared. She stared after him a moment, then returned to her typing.

Professor Kauffman was putting up a kettle of water when she arrived the next morning. Sheila stood at the door fingering her bag. It made her feel like an undergraduate again, watching him putter around the hot plate, setting out cups and saucers and servers. He was more stooped than she remembered. The back of his jacket rose up higher on his neck. His wiry hair, once salt and pepper, was completely white. She hadn't really noticed that at the Faculty Club. The familiar world of his office brought it home.

His face was a small oval and his glasses thick. When he smiled he looked like a benign mole.

"Miss Kahn. How are you? Come in. Sit down. I was just

252

putting up coffee." He ushered her in and she sat in a dilapidated armchair.

He wheeled his own chair out from behind the desk and sat opposite her.

"Let's sit and talk while the water boils." He surveyed her amiably. "I was delighted when Miss Haviland told me you called. I hoped I'd get a chance to see you before I went off. It's my sabbatical." He made a wry face. "My fourth. Can you imagine that?"

"Where are you going?"

"North Africa."

Sheila's eyes widened. "Not Algeria."

He nodded. "Think that's too dangerous for an old man like me?"

"I think it's too dangerous for anyone."

"Well, I have friends there. . . ."

"You're not going to work for the—"

"Research. You know sabbaticals are for research. I've always wanted to look at colonial governments. The other three times we went to Sweden. Elaine couldn't take the heat." He tilted his chair back. "But I did enough talking about me the last time we met. You've got something on your mind." He put his hands behind his head and waited to hear Sheila out. His jacket was unbuttoned and the straps of his suspenders showed.

There was a long pause. It had been one thing to tear into Dean Colquist's office and set her outrageous plan going. It was another having to admit the lie. It would have helped if she weren't so fond of him.

"Oh, my," he said gently. "It's something serious."

Sheila nodded. She'd promised herself she would not cry and the back of her jaw worked hard to honor it. She pushed back one wave and fished in her bag for a Kleenex. She had to shove aside the application forms to find it. "OK," she said finally. "First of all I've got a confession to make." She glanced up at him. His eyes were steady and interested. "When we had lunch the other day I told you I was finishing law school. It was a lie. I never went." He nodded once as a mildly amused acknowledgment. She waited for more, but he went back to listening. "I guess it wasn't so earthshaking after all."

"Don't be disappointed." The sides of his mouth twitched.

"Believe me. I'm not."

"What *have* you been doing?"

She shrugged. "Not much of anything."

"Well, that's a hell of a waste, isn't it?"

"I'm married."

He nodded. "I thought so."

"Why?"

"When a woman keeps a pair of white gloves on all through a perfectly fine lunch, even at the risk of soiling them with salad dressing, she's hiding either a third-degree burn or a wedding ring. Is your marriage in difficulty?"

"No," she said quickly. "I mean, yes. I mean, not in the usual way. We still love each other. Very much. I think. At least I do. But—"

"It's not enough." He helped her finish.

She stared at him. "You've been through this before."

"An awful lot of brilliant women have gone through Barnard."

She looked down at her hands and started to pull off her gloves. "I married Philip Gaynor. I don't know if you remember him. I made him take a course with you."

He shook his head. "But that's all right. All those Columbia pre-law men start to look alike after a while. Three-piece suits, tight necks, a slight backward tilt to their walk. . . ." The kettle whistled. "Go on. Go on." He got up to make the coffee.

"We've been married almost six years." She paused. "He's the one who's finishing law school."

"How do you take your coffee?"

"Cream no sugar."

"Do you mind the powdered cream?"

"No. It's fine."

"Do you have any children?"

"A little girl."

"Lovely. What's her name?"

"Vikki. She's five."

He smiled. "I remember that age. Believe it or not. How do you plan to take care of her and go to law school at the same time?"

"What?"

"I said, how are you planning to take care of her and go to law school at the same time? It's a terribly demanding routine. You must know that if your husband is going through it now. And I certainly know the way you throw yourself into things." He brought the coffee to her. "See if that's all right. I never know how much of that stuff to put in."

Sheila was still staring at him. "You know about—"

"I've been trying to reach you for over a week. You seem to have made some kind of impression on John Colquist." He raised his hand to stop her from jumping to conclusions. "I don't know what kind of impression, but some kind. He pulled out your files and saw my old recommendations in them and called to ask about you. I must admit I was puzzled at first."

"I bet you were."

"But it gradually fit together. I couldn't tell John much, of course. I didn't tell him anything about having seen you. I did tell him what I knew about you as a student—and that I'd try to get in contact again and be back to him. That's why I'm so glad to see you." He sipped his coffee. Sheila was too flooded with relief to touch hers. "Why do you want to go back to school?"

"I want to practice."

"What does your husband think?"

She started to speak, then stopped and shook her head. "I was just about to lie to you again. It's a hard habit to break." She clasped her hands and raised her head. "Phil doesn't know about it yet."

"Don't you think—"

"Yes, I do. But, nothing's going to stop me from what I want to do now. So not telling Phil is only putting off another possible and painful decison—it's not putting off asking permission."

"You sound determined."

255

"I am."

"But are you serious?"

"I'll make it through."

"I have absolutely no doubt that you will."

"Then why do you ask if I'm serious?"

"Because 'making it through' isn't what counts. A young woman like you discovers that she's always wanted to be something more than a wife and mother. A lawyer, say. She's brilliant, competitive, constantly searching for new ways to prove herself." Sheila started to speak. "Let me finish. So she digs in—at whatever cost—and becomes a lawyer. She works hard, harder than some of the cynical young men around, does splendidly, passes the bar. She's ready to go. She's proven she can do it. And that turns out to be what she was really after—the proof. She's a lawyer. Now she can go back to her family—or start to build a new one—because she's proven she can be other things if she chooses." He paused. "I call that determined, but not serious. If you really want to be a lawyer you've got to be willing to follow through."

"I never said I wanted to be a lawyer. I said I wanted to practice law."

"So you did." They looked hard at each other for a long time. "Why?"

"The same reason you're going to Algeria. It's a chance to do something instead of sitting around reading the *Times* and sputtering."

He smiled. "Change the world?"

"I don't have to. The world *is* changing. All I want is to be there, helping. You remember the other day when I met you and we watched the buses load and I was so excited? Six years ago I would have been excited by the glamor and the heroism of it all. But you know what excited me the other day? The idea that behind those buses was the law. That people like you—and my husband and his friends—could make those damned things roll. It was just starting to dawn on me that I could be helping make things like that happen, too. That I *should* be. And that everytime I've given up my chance to practice law I've been selfish." She gave a short laugh. "And

what's so incredible is that it's always looked like a sacrifice."
She paused. "You know, it's a funny thing. My husband used
to tell me I was prophetic. I was always seeing movements and
ideas two years ahead of time. This past couple of years,
though, I haven't. I've been asleep. It may even have been
some huge shift that jolted me awake. But a couple of months
ago I got up and started looking around again. And it's"—she
paused again, frowning—"this is the first time I've tried to put
it in words. . . . It's . . . something's going on that's bigger than
any of the single people that are making single things happen.
Does that make sense? Savio in Berkeley and King and the
other blacks. Even Kennedy. They're all only symptoms. And
there's a sense—you can feel it all over—there's a sense that
behind them there's this work that has to get done."

"There always has been."

She nodded. "I know. I know that. But this time it's different. You know what it is?" She stopped suddenly. "I never
thought of it this way before, but you know what it is? When I
graduated from here six years ago I knew I had an education
because I knew what attitude I should have about everything.
And that was enough. Now it's not. That's what you can feel
starting all over the place. The idea that attitudes aren't worth
a damn anymore until you do something about them. Test
them. It's going to be bigger than anything I can even imagine
right now. And I want in."

"I hope you're right. It's a feeling I always have before my
sabbaticals, too. Then I come back and nothing's really
changed too much."

"This time it will. Besides, it hasn't stopped you."

He shrugged. "Of course, you know things might be just the
same now as they always were. It might just be you who's
different."

"What difference would that make?"

Professor Kauffman put his hands together and brought
them up to his lips. "And your family?" She did not respond.
"Do you think that's none of my business?"

"Yes, I do."

"You may be right."

It was twelve thirty by the time she left. They talked about the hidden pressures she might expect in law school and the difficulties of finding positions later. He asked what field she might want to specialize in.

"Labor law."

He raised his eyebrows.

"My mother worked to get the ILGWU going. I wouldn't mind picking up where she left off."

John Colquist was out of town until Friday. Professor Kauffman said he would give him a call as soon as he was back. He put up a warning hand. He couldn't promise anything. Sheila said she understood.

The Birdcage was jammed with shoppers. Diana had managed to find a chair in the corner and save one for Sheila. She was reading *Backstage*, with the pages folded so no one could tell what it was. She wore a boatneck sweater and plaid skirt. Her hair was pulled back in a ponytail, her face clear of makeup. Diana had a talent for making the most casual clothes look like a costume.

Sheila paid her dollar and a quarter, took a chit, and went in.

"You're really doing the old roommate bit, aren't you?" Sheila said as she slid into the chair. It was shaped like an old-fashioned school desk.

Diana laughed and put aside her paper. "Isn't it fun? You know what I found this morning? My old purple bathrobe with the white piping. I wore it all around the house to get in the mood."

"Have you been waiting long?"

"No. But I'm starved."

They ordered sandwiches. The waitress took their chits and set a tray for each of them.

"I got most of my shopping done this morning, except for Donna. I figured we could brave the toy departments together. Look what I got for Joe." She opened some boxes and pulled out two tapered shirts and a heavy medallion. "I found this incredible kept-men's store off Fifty-sixth Street. It's run

258

by these two piss-elegant fags. Do you think Joe will wear it? He's so square about clothes. Maybe I'll take you over and we can find something for Phil."

Sheila laughed and shook her head. "You know better. I'm just going to get him a white turtleneck and a blazer."

"Oh, shit, Sheila. That's what they're all wearing. I was at a party the other night when we finished shooting and it looked like a convention of U-boat commanders."

"How was the show?"

She made a face. "You think *The Criminals* was a winner? This one's a pilot about a one-armed detective. I played a karate instructor so I got a chance to wear these black belt robes and go 'hong' and 'hawng' a lot." She sighed. "If I'd known eight years ago that I'd be working like this now I probably would have been ecstatic. I'm not knocking it, either," she said quickly. "There are still plenty of actresses who'd give their right eye to be doing what I'm doing. And they're probably better than me, too. But what the hell, I've got a face and a body that keep me from having to struggle." She shrugged and laughed it off. "Who am I kidding? I used to go around screaming I wanted to do *The Seagull* because every other ingenue went around pulling her hair back and exposing her cheekbones and screaming she wanted to do it. I really just want to keep busy and I'm doing that. I'm in demand. So what the hell?" She sat forward. "Now, where have you been all morning?"

Sheila grinned.

"Great. I ask a simple, friendly question and I get Enigmatic Emma. I've been racking my brains. Your doctor's appointment is on Monday—and besides, you would have told me that. You're not having an affair because you did tell me that and you never lie." Diana paused. "Now that you're here I can tell you I had some scary ideas, too."

Sheila looked surprised. "Did you think I might—"

"It crossed my mind. Listen, cookie, I haven't been able to figure out what's going on inside your head for a couple of weeks. You are a very weird lady."

"Am I?"

259

"First you're Olivia Overdose. Then you leave your child, your best friend, and her child stranded at nursery school without any explanation. Then you suddenly start having secret appointments and end up waltzing in here looking more gorgeous and bright and scrubbed than I've seen since you walked into our room at orientation week."

"I do look good, don't I?"

"You *are* having an affair," Diana said with finality.

Sheila waved it away.

"Then stop sparkling your eyes and tell me where you were this morning."

Sheila had no qualms now about telling her.

"I'm going back to law school."

"You jest."

Sheila shook her head.

"Well, tell me all about it, for Chrissake. When did you decide? How did you get Phil to agree? How are you going to work it out? Why didn't you tell me sooner? Why didn't Vikki say anything? That's incredible." She waved her hands. "Wait a minute. Wait a minute. Let me see how that feels." She sat back nonchalantly and started an imaginary conversation. " 'My ex-roommate—she's a lawyer now. . . . Sheila Gaynor. You remember her. My roommate. Terribly bright. She's a lawyer now, you know. . . .' " Diana sat up. "Great. It sounds great."

Sheila laughed.

"All right. Tell me all about it."

Their sandwiches came. Diana's excitement buoyed Sheila. She told everything that had happened from Thanksgiving to her morning with Professor Kauffman. "I can't tell you what it feels like," Sheila said finally.

"You don't have to. Look at you. It's sensational. Here I've been breaking my butt trying to figure out ways to help you up out of what you've been through and all the time you've been taking care of it yourself in your own cool, quiet way."

"It hasn't been so cool."

Diana shook her head in admiration and Sheila's face flamed. She felt stupid now for not having told her friend sooner. "You may be weird, but you're incredibly tough. Did you have a lot of trouble with Phil?"

Sheila took the toothpick out of her sandwich.

"I haven't told him yet."

"Uh-oh."

"It won't be a problem. I trust him."

"What does your doctor say?"

She shook her head.

"You haven't told him either?"

"You and Professor Kauffman are the only ones who know."

Diana tried to hide her deflation.

"What's the matter?"

She shook her head. "I thought it was all set. I'm sorry. I shouldn't have got so excited."

"It *is* all set. I've made my mind up. That's what's important."

"I understand that," she said quickly.

Sheila smiled to reassure her. "It's OK. I'm not going to flip out if you have reservations. I'm just telling you you don't have to."

"I believe it." Diana lowered her eyes.

"You lie like a housemother."

"Well, what do you want me to say? You come in here so up, you're like a different person. I don't want to bring you down."

"I know that. I'm a big girl. You don't think Phil is going to buy the whole business and you're wondering if it's really as healthy as it all seems if I haven't even talked to Dr. Rankin about it. Right?"

She made a noncommittal gesture.

"You can be honest with me."

Diana nodded. "I'm just not sure you're being realistic." Sheila smiled at the word and closed her eyes. "I mean, a woman with the kinds of resources you have—your brain, and your warmth and energy—there are a million other ways you could find to readjust."

"I'm not trying to readjust," Sheila said quietly.

261

"Oh, you know what I mean," Diana remarked off-handedly. "I don't mean 'readjust' like they talk about it in Problem Articles in the *Journal*. I mean something more serious. Finding something to do with yourself. Using your energy. Changing your environment. Getting the hell out of the house and being creative."

"You make it sound so selfish," she said, puzzled.

Diana leaned forward and touched Sheila's wrist. "You've got a right to be selfish. You've been through enough."

"I'm not going back to school to get out of the house."

"I know. I know." It was supposed to sound supportive. "I know what you're doing. I just wonder if there are better ways to do it," she said cautiously. "That's all. Jesus, with your credentials you could probably snap up a job tomorrow without going through all the crap of law school. I mean, do you have any idea how that's going to disrupt Phil and Vikki? If you found a job at least you could afford full-time help. You know how badly they need legal secretaries now? And you'd be a knockout."

Sheila flushed. "I'm going to practice law. I know what I'm getting into."

"You don't think it's too soon?"

"Too soon?"

"After the pills."

"The pills were because I waited too long."

Sheila watched her shape a question, start, then discard it. "What?"

Diana shook her head.

"No, seriously, what were you going to ask?"

Diana stared at her briefly. "How's your sex life?"

"Oh, for God's sake."

"It's not such a lousy question."

"It's beside the point."

Diana looked harder at her.

"Oh, stop it, Dee. It's too easy."

"What are you going to do? Become a big-time corporation lawyer? A judge? Go into politics? Cookie, I know those big-time professional women. I've been there with casting directors and agents and producers. Monsters. They're all monsters. They're either monsters or dykes and that's not you. The dykes at least have a normal sex life. But the monsters are maneaters."

"What about you?" Sheila asked softly.

"I'm different."

She nodded slowly. "I guess that's why I thought I could talk to you."

"Well, what did you want me to do? Help you kid yourself and make believe there was nothing in the way?"

"Why are you getting so upset?"

"Look." Diana lowered her voice. "I think what you're planning is sensational. I really do. To have something like that to look forward to? I know what that's all about. How important it is to have something to get you from one week to the next." Sheila's teeth clenched. "All I'm asking you to think about is whether you're making the dream too big. That's all. I mean, Jesus, where would I be if I started out wanting my own series?" Diana gave a short laugh. "And Joe? And Donna? You take a little bit at a time, honey. Then maybe you end up with it all. That's all I'm saying. We're not like other women. We can have it all if we want it. I mean, one of the things I've always envied about you is the way you've been with Phil and Vikki. I'm always making a mess of it because of my work and I only go for small potatoes. But you want to go for the big time. Have you really thought about what you might have to give up? If you play it right you don't have to give up anything. But you're risking your whole life."

"I've already done that," Sheila said flatly.

Diana lapsed into silence. Sheila watched her pick at her coleslaw. Over the past three weeks she had been exuberant, frightened, angry, expectant. This was the first time she had felt so saddened. She thought she was ready to meet the challenge her decision would make to her life with Phil. The challenge to her friendship took her by surprise.

"Dee?" Her voice was ineffably gentle.

"Hmm?"

"Don't think about telling Phil."

263

Her head shot up. Her eyes flashed. "Do you think I would—"

"I don't know anymore."

"That's a hell of a thing—"

Sheila nodded and looked away from her. "Were you thinking about it?"

"If I were it would have been for your own good. You really are acting crazy."

"You know I'm not." She smiled sadly and picked up Diana's copy of *Backstage*.

"What kind of a friend would I be if I sat here and supported your fantasies?"

"You've supported all my others."

"What's that supposed to mean?"

Sheila looked down and played with the newspaper absently. "You don't want me to change. You need me the way I was."

"That's the biggest crock of—"

"No. It's not. Look, it's not your fault, either. And it's not Phil's or my mother's or father's or Vikki's or anyone's but mine. Whatever any of you needed from me, I've been the one who's been looking crooked. You remember, good old Sheila Kahn, dedicated to service." She grinned at Diana. "Mary Missionary. Right? It's in my blood. But somewhere along the line I got things confused. In college I started out *doing* things for other people, but all of a sudden I found myself *being* for them, instead. *Being* a good daughter so my parents could feel like good parents, being a good wife so Phil could feel like a good husband—and helpless so he could feel competent." She shrugged. "And crazy, so he could feel sane." She stopped.

"And for me?"

"Ordinary so you could feel special." Sheila looked hard and tenderly at her friend. "How many times you've told me about your work and I've sat there, thrilled for you and loving you and feeling the envy like grit in my teeth. I know how you felt now because for the first time I did it myself—to you. I sprang my career on you on the heels of your one-armed detective and I guess now I knew what I was doing. It was a wonderful, cruel feeling—and I'll never do it again. It's too expensive—and unnecessary."

There was a long silence. Diana slipped the paper out of Sheila's hands. "You haven't started eating," she said quietly.

"I know. I've been shooting my mouth off."

Diana stuffed the paper in her bag. "A couple of new plays are casting," she said absently. "I wonder if I should call my agent about them. He only thinks of me for television."

Sheila bit into her sandwich. "You want to call him now?"

She glanced at her watch. "He's never back until two. Maybe I should go see him instead." She nodded toward Sheila's tray. "But then we won't have time for shopping."

Sheila nodded. "It's OK. I don't have that much to do."

"I could pick up that last couple of things for Donna quickly at Schwarz. He's right around the corner."

"Go ahead," she said softly. "I screwed it up by being so late, anyway."

"You're sure you don't mind?"

"No. It's OK. Really."

Diana collected her things. "Look," she said brightly. "Here's the name of that men's store." She wrote on a napkin. "It really is fabulous."

Sheila took it and Diana prepared to leave.

"Good luck with your agent."

She gave an embarrassed little wave of her hand. "Oh, him. . . . It'll just be the same old crap." She stood above Sheila tentatively.

"I hope not."

Diana leaned down quickly and kissed her cheek. Sheila watched her thread through the little chair-desks with her arms full of packages, then looked down at the napkin. She was surprised at how dear and familiar the handwriting was, how many times she had recognized it in notes tacked on the door, left on her desk, slipped in her mailbox. She would miss that.

7

Phil

December 19- Christmas, 1962

PHIL WOKE up at ten. Sheila had already gone. The night before she had told him she was going shopping with Diana. Estelle was taking Vikki. The apartment would be empty. He decided to cut class and use the day to catch up on studying, for he liked working at home much more than in the library. When Sheila and Vikki were in and out it was impossible, but a long stretch of time like this was an opportunity to work in comfort. He could bring coffee to his desk instead of running downstairs to the machines; if he felt drowsy he could pop into the bathroom and douse his face; and there was no danger of distracting conversations.

He had told Sheila to set the alarm for ten. With the holidays approaching the bookstore was hectic. At school his instructors were spurting ahead to cover all the material they'd missed. He was exhausted.

He lay on his back listening to the stillness in the apartment. He could not remember the last time the bed had felt so empty. He was used to waking up alone, but the space beside him always seemed filled with Sheila's morning footsteps, the click of her cup and saucer, the water running in the kitchen sink. He stretched himself across the mattress and wondered if he could afford another hour of sleep. That would defeat the whole purpose of the day. He had worried about getting up late in the middle of the week in the first place. Breaking discipline was always dangerous. Even the decision to work at home felt a little like playing hooky. At least when he nodded off over his books at the library he was nodding in the right place.

He slipped out of bed and padded to the kitchen. Sheila had left a bowl and spoon set for him and a box of cold cereal. He put up coffee water and glanced around the counter to see if she'd left a note.

He brushed his teeth while the water came to a boil and decided to work in his pajamas and robe. The sheets and the blanket on the bed were only slightly rumpled. He threw the quilt over them.

When he came back to the kitchen he checked again to see if he'd missed a note. Sheila had left the kitchen clean. She'd even dried the dishes and put them away instead of letting them sit in the sink drainer. That was a kind of note, he supposed, to let him know she was all right.

He ate some cereal, a little surprised at how loud the crunching sounded, then dropped the bowl in the sink. Sheila always asked him to fill his snack bowls and milk glasses with water. It kept the stuff from sticking to the sides. He left the bowl dry and took his coffee to the bedroom. It splashed over the sides of the saucer and left a trail down the hallway. He. went back to the kitchen and avoided looking at the sink as he searched for the paper towels. She'd just better not say anything about it, he thought. He realized he had wakened irritable. As he worked his way down the hall, sopping up the mess, he imagined what he would say if Sheila called him on it. She had nothing to complain about after all the times he'd come home and found lights burning in every room. Sure, she was getting better at remembering things like that. He still couldn't count on it, though, and he didn't know which was worse—having her remember once in a while or at least being sure that nothing was getting done. It was driving him crazy. He would come home to a clean, smoothly running apartment for three nights. The knot in his stomach that happened every time he opened the front door would loosen. Just as he'd start to believe everything was under control something would happen. The living room would be cluttered with toys because Vikki had a friend over; Vikki would be crying because Sheila insisted that she clean up the mess. Dinner would be late because Sheila had gotten involved in something and lost track of time. All little things. But they added up. And he had enough on his mind without having to worry about the routine at home. Besides, it was natural for him to tighten. He still had heard nothing from her on Rankin. He had no idea of how well she was. Everytime they hit a snag in the routine it might be a sign she was slipping back. How did she think it felt to come home from a discouraging interview to a hall full of laundry or a screaming kid? How much longer did she expect him to carry her and Vikki on his back on top of everything else? If she wanted her dishes filled with water she ought to be around to fill them instead of running out shopping and leaving him alone with a box of cold cereal and no note.

He'd played the scene out in three different keys by the time he worked his way down the hall. He brought the wet towels back to the kitchen and dropped them in the garbage. He had been finding himself in the middle of these imaginary fights a lot lately. Most of them were with Sheila, some with his mother, or Renata, or Paul. The theme was always the same. Why did they have to depend on him? How did he get elected the crisis center? Didn't they realize how much pressure was on him? It usually happened just before he started studying. He would catch himself at it and force his concentration back on his books.

He started back to them now. Before he left the kitchen he splashed some water in the bowl.

The peculiar thing was that they all were making fewer demands on him now than they ever had before. He had not spoken with anyone from Northfield since before Sheila's illness. Sheila, herself, seemed busy and happy. Vikki grew more self-sufficient every day. Sheila had not asked him to take their daughter for the day since she came home. She did not even seem to mind when he spent the weekends in the library. Yet it was just at those times, when he was most free, that the angry scenes would happen in his head.

Before, when Sheila needed him, he had no trouble stifling resentment. He never begrudged her the hours he'd spent in the hospital—even when they grew difficult and the two of them did little more than stare out the window together. He would return to the law school refreshed, able to handle the public pressures because they were somehow balanced by the private ones.

The confusion had really begun the night before they left for Woodview, when he realized he would have to give up his concern and find a new way to express his love. He had still found nothing to take its place. Sheila was determined to ask for nothing.

He spent fifteen minutes arranging his books and pads. He was used to finding the desk exactly as he left it, but Sheila had been using it lately. Every time he sat down he had to reorder everything. There was an ashtray filled with butts. He brought it to the kitchen and emptied it in the garbage. It made him conscious of the stale smell when he returned to the bedroom. He opened the window. It was cold out. He would let the room air for a while, then shut it. He pulled his robe tighter, arranged it over his lap, and sat down. The draft hit him on the neck and chest. He had already laid out his text for constitutional law, opened to the right page. He assumed a position of concentration and took a sip of coffee without looking at the cup. That convinced him he was studying.

He had barely read down a page before the chill from the window became too much. He closed it. The coffee had turned cold. He went to the kitchen to heat it up. On the way back he was careful not to splash. He could not afford to waste more time. He sat down again and realized he had to piss. He stayed at the desk, determined not to relieve himself until he'd read through at least one case. It would give him something to work against. He tightened his crotch. Now that his attention was divided he could get something accomplished.

By noon he had only read through a few cases and made

notes on them. He was ready for lunch. He'd had a late breakfast but his body was on clock time. Maybe he needed the impetus of the others to get his rhythm going again. He considered shaving and dressing and going down to the lunchroom. If he did that, though, he'd be wasting the opportunity of the empty apartment. He shoved out from the desk and went to make himself a quick sandwich.

Sheila had left the *Times* on the floor just inside the front door. He brought it to the kitchen table and scanned it over his coffee. KENNEDY CONFERS WITH MACMILLAN TO NARROW RIFTS . . . PRESIDENT AND BRITON PLAN TO VIEW POST-CUBA STANCE. . . . He could not concentrate beyond the headlines. He flipped the pages aimlessly. Unimportant articles caught his attention. Three men buried under soft cement at a Tennessee rocket center. Salt air corroding the bars at Alcatraz. He didn't have to think about those. They weren't the kinds of things they discussed in the lunchroom. The others—the ones about Algeria and the Congo—were too demanding.

It was always like this when the holidays approached. The hurdles would loom up ahead. His energy would flag, then he'd pull himself together for the jump and before he knew it he'd be over. A little resting time, then the new set appeared in the distance. Each time he'd think, If only I get past this one. This time he knew there'd be just one more. One more semester and he'd be through. There was a little comfort in knowing that at least it had an end.

In some ways Phil liked the pattern. He really was cut out for the law. He liked the neatness of it all. They set out the tasks; he did them; they were finished; he could go on to others. Nothing ever hung over. It would be the same later. He would work on a case, see it through, get a ruling, and travel on. When he performed well they'd tell him. There would always be something tangible there to confirm him—a grade, a ruling, a raise.

Yet this time knowing the end was in sight made it harder. It made him more acutely aware of how long he'd been running, how tired he was. He'd been told enough times that he had the skill to make it as a lawyer. He was beginning to believe it. They were testing something else now, his endurance. That was new. He had no way to tell if he'd pass this one. He couldn't until he'd already made it or failed. That was what preoccupied him now. The speculating made it hard to concentrate. Of course, that could be part of the test, too. A hidden one. Those were the more terrifying.

He made another cup of coffee and wondered if any of the others thought the way he did. He would have liked to ask, but those weren't the kinds of questions he brought to his friends. Friendship in law school ran by a set of rules as strict and tradition-bound as any competitive sport. The skill lay in keeping frank and good-humored but never vulnerable. He could talk cases and torts, news and politics, sports and sex, as long as he didn't betray his position, give up whatever edge he might have, or threaten the others. Sheila was always puzzled by his friends. The first year he was in law school he would tell her about the lunchroom talk. Once she said, "It doesn't sound like you talk to each other at all. More like you sit around rattling spears." She asked him if he had ever had any close friends, really close friends, the way she had Diana. He was annoyed and named college drinking partners, tennis partners, basketball players, handball partners. She'd been puzzled again. "Do all men measure friendship by how much sweat they can work up together?"

When he was at the law school he had no doubt about what he was doing there. Everything supported him. There were the scheduled class hours, dependable rituals, other men he could count on to think in predictable ways. He knew who he was on 116th Street. Sheila had a way of cutting the ground out from under him. Lately she had been asking more and more about the law school. Her questions, her genuine astonishment at some of the absurdities, had a subtle way of unnerving him. They wrenched him back three years to the time he was just beginning. He had asked the same questions. Why the outdated curriculum? If it was a place that prepared him to practice law, why did he end up cramming for the bar exam? Why the cynicism of the *Law Review*? It had taken him three years to feel comfortable with the answers. Now she was asking him to justify it all again.

That was why he could not find his way to opening up Fred Ryan's offer with Sheila. It all made sense when he thought about it at law school. He had talked it over with some of the men in the lunchroom. He could count on them to look at the alternatives as objectively as he. Even Judge Spizer in Woodview had agreed. The job was available. It was attractive. It had a future. The realistic decision would be to take it. He could account for it without even having to touch his secret love for Frederick Ryan. With Sheila it would be unavoidable. She would bring it into the open somehow, and once it was out all his other secret desires would follow. It was stupid to be ashamed of his dreams. He wasn't when he was at the law school. It was only through Sheila's eyes that they somehow embarrassed him, the idealistic as well as the selfish ones. She had that uncanny knack for making reason look like expediency; maturity like compromise.

He refilled his coffee cup and returned to the desk.

He had been working a long time when the phone rang.

"Philip? It's Eleanor Ryan. How are you?"

"Hello." He was always embarrassed when people found him at home during the day.

"Fred and I are flying up to Northfield early for Christmas. Todd's going to close up the house and follow in a few days. We wondered if you and Sheila would like to drive up with him."

Phil hesitated.

Mrs. Ryan's voice was rich with amusement. "It won't represent a commitment."

"I wasn't thinking that," he said quickly. Then, to prove it. "Thank you. Yes. We'd like it."

"Splendid. Todd will pick you up on Monday, then. A little after noon."

Sheila's appointment with Rankin was at two.

"Will that be all right? You don't have classes on Monday, do you?"

272

"No. No. It'll be all right." He would work something out. "Monday at two is fine."

There was a short pause. "Did I say two? I'm sorry. I meant a little after noon."

"Fine."

"Would two be more convenient?"

"No. No. That's all right."

"How's Sheila?"

"Just fine."

"I'm glad to hear that. I'll look forward to seeing all of you."

"Good. Thank you." He hung up and went back to his books.

Eleanor Ryan was the only person from Northfield who knew about Sheila. There had been no reason not to tell her about Sheila's appointment, but he had been unable to say it, and too slow to invent a lie. He was always ashamed when he had to adjust his decisions to Sheila, especially with the Ryans. They might take it the wrong way, imagine he was less of a man.

He forced his eyes down to his book. It was no good. His concentration was shot. He went to the living room and sat in the recliner. He was doing something wrong. All he wanted was to be on top of things and keep his dignity. It seemed so simple, but it was all always going out of control. Maybe he was trying too hard. Maybe if he just let go for a little. He pushed back on the recliner. He shut his eyes and tried to force his shoulders down. They resisted. His thighs tightened. His elbows pushed against the arms of the chair. Even now he felt as though he were being watched, that his aptitude for relaxation was being judged, his chance for success at it being measured.

He opened his eyes and stared at the sofa. He had not thought of his father-in-law since he came home. The conversation in the toolshed had hung in the back of his mind, but he refused to bring it to consciousness. In the half-light, tired, old, and shy, Bernie had touched off confused emotions in Phil. The kind of love he felt then was very different from the kind he felt for Frederick Ryan, and much more frightening.

273

Bernie Kahn had stood at his side, almost touching shoulders, and admitted he was as bewildered as Phil. He had grasped Phil firmly on the back of the neck and said, "Relax." It was the gentlest touch he had ever felt from a man. There was no judgment in it. Bernie made no demands. He simply acknowledged that they shared the same, incomprehensible love, that they were both less than perfect, less than guiltless. And that it was all right. Bernie had told his own story with as much compassion for himself as May Kahn. He talked without mystery. His words were as simple, his gaze as direct, as if Phil were as old as he. Phil had never felt so young. Frederick Ryan's demands were easy compared to Bernie's tolerance, his tender assumption that they both shared the same, unmeasurable condition. Yet Bernie Kahn was a failure. At fifty he was still powerless, vulnerable, subject to humiliations inconceivable to a man like Frederick Ryan. Phil could love Ryan, secure that he would stay eternally different and inaccessible. His new, more chaotic feelings for Bernie were much harder to handle.

Phil ran his hand across his cheek. His beard was thicker than he thought. Perhaps if he shaved he could whip himself back into shape, keep his attention on his books. He went to the bathroom, stripping off his robe on the way. He hung it on the bathroom door and took off his pajama top. Phil always avoided looking too closely in the mirror. He did not particularly like the freckles that covered his shoulders or the way his chest and stomach were going soft. He kept his muscles flexed and his stomach pulled in whenever he worked at the sink, in case he should happen to glance up. His arms were still solid from handball and sometimes the veins on the back of his hands stood out. That was reassuring.

He kept his shaving equipment carefully arranged on a shelf beside the sink. He still used a brush and lather. He had tried to switch to an electric razor once, but he never really felt clean with it. Besides, his father had always used a brush and lather. It made Phil feel more like a family man. He worked the brush over his face. The lather made his teeth look brown and darkened his hair. He rinsed the brush before picking up

274

the razor. Clumps of black hair stuck out from under the blade. Sheila could never remember to change it after she did her legs and armpits. There was nothing worse than the pull of a used blade. He washed it, threw it away, and opened a fresh one.

The water was running hard. It always cut him off from all the other sounds in the apartment. Today there were none. He turned off the tap for a moment to listen. He wondered if this were the same kind of silence Sheila had listened to on the afternoon she took his pills. Phil had spent a lot of time trying to understand why she had attempted suicide. He had never tried to imagine what it must have felt like. The stillness in the apartment, his frustration at not being able to work, the odd feeling of abandonment that had hovered over him since he woke, all came together for an instant to give him some inkling. He held the fresh blade between his fingers. He stared at it, wondering just how much more it would take to draw the edge over his wrist. It was inconceivable. He brought it closer, testing. The blade and his wrist became abstract objects with wills of their own. He laid the flat edge against his skin. Sheila's heart must have been beating loudly. Her body must have been wound up like this. There must have been something more, though. All it would take was a single, swift flip of the wrist. She had managed to sit down and swallow pill after pill. How had she managed to get her hand to her mouth that many times? He glanced up at the mirror. His eyes and the soap on his face made him look like a stranger. He snatched the blade back and loaded the razor quickly, nicking his thumb in the process. The lather had gone dry. He moistened it with the brush and shaved quickly.

The front door opened while he was drying his face. He heard the rustle of packages and Sheila tiptoeing down the hall.

"Phil?"

He had wanted to be engrossed in his books when she came home.

"I'm in here."

She appeared at the bathroom door.

275

"I just took a break to get cleaned up." He tried not to make it sound like an excuse.

"I was afraid I'd disturb you. Were you able to get a lot done?"

He nodded and hung up his towel. "Worked all morning."

"Good. I was so afraid you'd be too tired."

"No. It was fine. I was going to go back in after I shaved."

"Don't let me get in your way." She put her hands on his chest and kissed him. He flexed his muscles.

"Your hands are cold."

"It's gorgeous out." She rubbed her hands together to warm them. "I'll leave Vikki with Estelle so there's no noise in the house."

"Maybe I should go to the library."

"Not if you're comfortable here."

"What time is it? You're home early."

"Around three. Diana pooped out. She had to see her agent about something, so I just picked up a couple of things for Vikki and came home. It's going to be another simple Christmas," she said apologetically.

"You know I don't care about stuff like that."

She took off her coat and went down the hall. "I still don't know what to get for your family," she called from the closet. "We'll have to talk about it. I can pick something up before my doctor's appointment."

Phil hesitated. "OK. We'll talk about it later."

"You going to go right back to work or do you want a cup of coffee?"

"I was going to—"

"Why don't you have a cup? You can afford it if you've been working since ten." She came back and kissed him again. "When's the last time we've been alone like this?" She touched his cheek. "I like kissing you after you shave." She put her arms around him and pressed tight. It took him by surprise. "Oh, Phil, I love you." There was a peculiar urgency in the way she said it. "And I'm so happy. It's all going to be all right. I know it." Her wool dress scratched his skin. Her hair smelled cool from the outside. He kissed it distractedly. "I can't wait till

276

this damned semester is over and then this damned year. I'm so sick of getting by."

"I guess I'll get dressed," he said softly.

She nodded, her head still against his chest. "Let's make love."

"What?"

She grinned up at him. "Before you get dressed. If you've got time for a cup of coffee, you've got time for a screw. We haven't made love in the light since Vikki was born."

He wasn't used to such an open invitation.

"Come on," she said. "I know you must be as horny as I am." Her eyes sparkled mischievously. Phil checked an impulse to reach for his pajama top. Their lovemaking had been sporadic and tense since Sheila came home from the hospital. He wanted to respond but was not sure what response would be right. He was afraid that might be a danger signal. It was certainly not usual. Rejecting her might be dangerous, too.

She put her hands on his chest. "They're warm now, aren't they?"

He nodded.

"You're so tight."

"It must be all the work," he said lamely.

"I'll give you a massage."

"I don't—"

She put her arms around his neck and whispered in his ear. "It's called foreplay, darling."

She took his hand and led him to the bedroom. "Lie down on your stomach. Wait a minute." She turned her back to him. "Unzip me."

"Sheila, I don't know if we should—"

"It'll do us both good."

"You sound so clinical," he said irritably.

She turned back to him. Her face had changed. "Do you really not want to?"

"It's not that. . . ."

"I didn't mean to be pushy."

"You weren't," he said quickly. "Honestly. I guess I'm just so distracted." He nodded toward the desk.

277

She searched his face seriously. "I put you in a bind."

"No. Well, yes," he said, flustered. "But it's all right."

Her shoulders dropped and she lowered her eyes. The two flaps of her unzipped dress hung down like dog ears. "I'm sorry."

"It's all right."

"I'll slip out of this into something more comfortable and leave you alone." She said it easily, without recrimination.

"You're not upset?"

She smiled up at him as she stepped out of the dress. "A little disappointed, that's all. I've been feeling very sexy all day. Look at me. I'm wearing a slip and my padded bra and the whole shmeer. I figured getting done up like this, it shouldn't be a total loss." She pulled off the slip and unhooked the bra. Phil glanced toward the window. Sheila held the bra around her and went to pull down the shade. The room turned brown.

Phil watched her from beside the bed. She worked the bra off and shook out her hair once. Phil could always tell when she was really unconcerned and when she was forcing it. She knew he was watching her. He remembered what it had been like before they were married. They both felt so grown-up, then, making love in the afternoon, both of them undressing with the same studied nonchalance.

She disappeared into the shadow of the closet.

"Sheila?" he called in after her.

"You want to flip on the light for a second? I'm trying to find a decent—"

"Maybe there's time for just a little rubdown."

She reappeared. Even in the dim light he could see her smiling. "Do you want to set the alarm?"

He started out of the room.

"Where are you going?"

"To put the chain on."

He heard her laugh softly as he went to the front door. It made him nervous. Phil took his lovemaking very seriously. Sometimes, especially when they were first married, Sheila would get fits of the giggles when they got into bed. He would envy her ability to be so freewheeling. He would try to join in the hilarity. She could laugh and make love at the same time, but it would render him incapable and they would both have to calm down before he could concentrate. He did not want that to happen now. Before he had seen her undressing in the dim room he'd been tentative because he was not sure it would be right for her. That was only part of it. He was just as afraid, with the state of mind he was in, he would not be able to perform. The rush of nostalgia reassured him it would be all right. He committed himself—and she made a joke.

The bed lamps were on when he came back. Sheila had slipped out of her panties.

"We never look at each other anymore," she said. Her eyes were still dancing. Phil kissed her to show he was serious. She put her arms around his neck and pressed against him. It was reassuring. She worked his shoulders with her fingers. "You're one huge knot," she whispered. "Lie down."

He lay on his stomach and left room for her to sit beside him. She straddled him instead. Her knees hugged his waist and she kneaded his shoulders slowly. "How does that feel?"

"Great." His voice was muffled in the pillow. He started to relax. She reached under his pajamas. He jumped. "Just making sure you're comfortable."

"Quit clowning, will you?"

"Sorry." She kissed him on the back of the neck. "I was just being bawdy. I'll be sexy instead. OK?"

She went back to work on his shoulders. Her strength surprised him. The touch was firm. The fingers and palms pressed him into submission. His body loosened the way he had tried to force it to loosen in the recliner. He closed his eyes. Sheila worked her way down. She pulled down his pajama bottoms to get at the lower back. Phil lifted his arms and rested his cheek on his hands. The knots unraveled under the warmth and the pressure. He felt looser than he had in months, but he could not give in completely. His attention kept going to his groin. He wasn't responding. He would not be able to relax until he did. He pumped his muscles surreptitiously to test himself. He started to tighten.

"Stay loose," Sheila said. Her voice was very low.

It was too late. Phil's mind was already working. He cast around for excuses, but was feeling too pressured. He was not used to the break in the routine. He was too preoccupied to get out of himself. Maybe if he imagined he was someone else. He had done that before, but did not like it. It always felt somehow like cheating. Sheila's hands became more insistent. She stopped for a moment to pull his pajamas down farther. She put her cheek against his back.

Phil thought of Frederick Ryan. He imagined himself a young version, in the massage room of the athletic club. He let one arm drop to the side of the bed. His body turned small and wiry. Sheila's hands became the black masseur's. It worked. He felt himself stir and press against the mattress. He gave himself time to elaborate. He imagined all the cases that were in his head, the young men he could help make careers, his wife at home entertaining one of them. He'd just come back from New Haven and stopped at the club for a rubdown to help him relax. His time was his own. It was all right now. He started to move, but did not feel sure enough yet to give up the fantasy.

Phil turned on his side with his eyes closed. Sheila slid off gently and resettled next to him. He put his thin arms around her. His body was hard and tight, not a wasted ounce of fat, quick and precise on the handball court. He kissed her, proud of his power. His hand traveled down her back and side. He traced the ghost of a young Eleanor Ryan over her body.

Sheila gripped his wrist and led his hand down her stomach. Eleanor Ryan wouldn't do that. He tried to resist but she forced it. She guided his fingers into a massaging rhythm. She was moist. That excited him, but it was Sheila exciting him and he did not want to give up his own transformation. He struggled against it, trying to stay small, wiry, and quick. His own thicker body became insistent. Sheila let go of his hand and followed his arm to the shoulder. She pulled air through her teeth. It was Sheila's sound, unmistakably hers, and he tried not to listen. She rolled on her back and pulled him over her.

Her grip was strong, and her nails dug into his back. He tried to make it his decision. She wrapped her legs around him. It traced the reality of his own body. Phil had to keep his eyes shut tight to hang on to the images he'd summoned. He did not need them anymore, but he still wanted them. Sheila had never been so active, so insistent on her own body. He tried to break the grip of her legs. The struggle excited her. She dug deeper into his back, bit at his neck and shoulders. He wanted to let go now but he was frightened. If he lost his image of young power and gave in to Sheila nothing would be left of him. Sheila's rhythm turned faster. He tried to hold back until he'd made a decision. She would not let him. Her heels pressed his back. She cried out and shuddered. She lay still a moment, her breath rippling, then slid her feet down past his buttocks and wrapped her legs over his thighs. She thrust up against him more slowly. His brain swung between his fantasy and the reality of her body until it was spinning behind his closed eyes. His stomach tightened. He let go, still suspended.

When Phil opened his eyes she was smiling up at him.

He told Sheila about the ride to Northfield at dinner.

"I've never been on the Thruway in a limousine," she said. "Who pays the tolls?"

There was no difficulty about canceling the appointment with Rankin. They had only got up to slips of the tongue, anyway. It would be weeks before all the dirty stuff started.

Phil was relieved, but a little apprehensive about her attitude. "I thought you were taking your sessions more seriously," he said casually.

Sheila shrugged. "It's expensive enough, I know. Actually I don't think I'll be with him much longer." It surprised him. "He just wants to make sure I've readjusted." She rolled the r out. "Besides"—she made a grave face—"I think I took care of one of those 'deeply rooted problems' this afternoon." She laughed. Phil's face tingled.

He had agreed to work in the bookstore all day Saturday and Sunday. On Saturday afternoon Sheila appeared with

Vikki. They'd come downtown to see the store windows and thought they'd surprise him for lunch. They went to Chock Full o' Nuts at Vikki's request.

"You're born with taste or you're not." Sheila sighed. They stood near the wall waiting for a threesome to open up. "She gets it from me. Remember how it worked in college? Boys would date Diana and there was never any question. They took a taxi. They called for me and asked if I had any tokens."

They were all in wonderful spirits. Sheila's face was rosy from walking. Vikki was still searching out every Christmas decoration she could find. Phil was genuinely happy to see them. The bookstore had been frantic all morning but he welcomed the work. It took his mind off school.

They found stools and ordered. Sheila grinned at him. He looked at her questioningly. "I feel like a family," she said.

He smiled back. It did feel good and he was delighted with Sheila. She had taken him by surprise when she told him she might not be seeing Rankin much longer. His first impulse was to phone and demand an official progress report. Instead he had talked around it at the lunchroom the next day and came away with a new and reassuring perspective. It all made perfect sense. He was almost ashamed that he hadn't seen it before. Sheila was a woman who had had thousands of dollars poured into her education. When she finished she discovered what she really wanted was a family. It was no wonder she felt guilty. If only she could realize that the education was good in itself, that she did not have to prove herself anymore, to pay back the investment in any other way than living as she was now, she could relax. She seemed to be coming around to that on her own. He was angry at himself for being so insensitive. He understood now, though, and he could help.

It clinched his decision to accept Fred Ryan's offer. It would be as much for her as himself. Away from the pressure of the city and all the imaginary demands that living near Barnard must be making, she would be free to enjoy him and Vikki and their life together. She would be in a society that demanded an education without judging how it was used. He could feel them all knitting together again.

They finished eating and walked Phil back to the bookstore. Sheila slipped her arm through his.

Todd was at the apartment promptly at twelve.

Light snow dusted the sides of the Thruway. It got deeper as they moved north. In Northfield ploughed banks lined the streets.

Nothing ever changed in Northfield. The town had been incorporated in 1790, when the Harmons, the Langleys, and the Freemans were the leading families, all farmers. Constance Gaynor was a Harmon. Eleanor Ryan was a Langley.

The house was a short ride beyond the center of town, hidden from the main road by a small pine grove. The Northfield Episcopal Church nearby was built by the youngest son of Thomas Harmon in 1860. They passed the church and pulled into the quarter-mile driveway through the trees.

Snow lay in great clumps on the pine branches, one of which spilled over and showered down as they pulled up to the front door. The house was an old, white, Federalist mansion with two acres of open land behind. Fifty yards beyond was the carriage house and a stable. Philip Gaynor had owned two Morgan horses, and Phil could still remember watching his mother and father ride off in the sulky on Sunday afternoons and the excitement of the late-summer horse shows in Litchfield and Farmington. His mother sold the horses when Philip Gaynor died, and closed the carriage house. There were signs of workmen there now. Lumber lay stacked in the snow, partly covered by drop cloths. Deep tire tracks ran around to the back. When they got out of the car Phil could see a parked pickup truck.

Constance Gaynor came to the front door pulling a sweater around her shoulders. Phil's mother was a tall, tweedy woman. She had been a first-rate skier and tennis player when she was young. She still played, but now it was more to keep in condition than to win. Her hair was light like Phil's, pulled back in a swirl.

Phil watched Sheila and Vikki meet her as he helped Todd unload the trunk. The two women touched cheeks. It was the first time he did not worry about Sheila's arrival in Northfield. His mother signaled hello to him and he waved back a box. "I'll be right in," he called. She put her arm around Vikki and led her inside.

They were still in the hallway taking off their coats and chattering pleasantly when he and Todd pushed through the front door. Phil dropped a suitcase to shake hands and touch cheeks with his mother.

"Hello, Philip. Merry Christmas." She touched his cheek with her fingers. "It's good to see you." She had the rich, cordial voice of a professional hostess. Even Phil could never be sure when it was automatic and when there was genuine warmth. It had gotten her over a lot of difficult times with Sheila. Today it seemed genuine. She had been easy with Sheila when he came in. He smiled confidently into her eyes.

Todd stood behind him with an armful of gifts. "Hello, Todd." She let go of Phil's hand and started toward the living room. Todd followed. "How are you? Did you have an easy trip? You can put those under the tree." She returned. "Just leave your coats and bags near the bench. Paul will put them away. He's just gone out back to get some more firewood. I have tea and coffee ready in the living room." She smiled at Vikki and rumpled her hair. "Hot chocolate for you."

They followed his mother into the living room. There was a low fire going. Vikki ran to the tree with Sheila close behind.

"Isn't it gorgeous?"

"It's so big!" Vikki said.

"Paul cut it down a few days ago. I think it's the fullest tree we've ever had. We had to take two feet off the top to clear the ceiling." She laughed at Phil. "It was your brother overdoing again. Are you drinking coffee or tea these days?"

"Coffee."

"And Sheila—I know you take coffee."

"Yes, thank you."

She settled behind a service and started pouring. "There are three ornaments on the table. We left one for each of you. Why don't you put them on now and come have something?"

Phil joined Sheila and Vikki. He hung his ornament

quickly. Sheila circled the tree once with her ball, then stood on tiptoe and hung it opposite his. He put his arm around her briefly and she leaned her head against him. Vikki hooked hers on a lower branch, then took it off to reconsider.

"We had such fun trimming it. Ed and Renata were over with the boys. And Eleanor and Fred made some mulled wine. We wished you could have been with us. Perhaps next year." She smiled at Phil and Sheila.

"How is Renata?" he asked quickly.

"Terribly busy. The wedding's less than a month away." She called to Vikki. "You're going to have two cousins very soon. Big boys." Phil and Sheila took their coffee. "That's the hardest part. Adjusting to two teen-age grandchildren. You'll meet them tonight. Renata gets on with them splendidly. I'm not surprised. After all her experience with Paul." Vikki came to join them. "Ah. You made your decision, did you? Where did you put your ornament?" She patted the sofa beside her. "Come sit next to me and point it out."

"I can't see it from here."

"It's in among all the others, is it? That means you made a good choice." She handed Vikki her chocolate and a napkin.

"There are a lot of presents."

"Aren't there? I don't think we've had so many gifts under the tree since your grandfather was alive. That's because the family's getting bigger again. It's like a new beginning."

"I saw my great-grandmother."

"Did you? At Thanksgiving?"

"She has orange hair and she gave me a dollar."

"How is your family?" Constance asked Sheila.

"Fine, thanks. They send their regards."

Phil settled back. He had never seen Sheila and his mother so comfortable with each other. On all the other visits he had to stay between them and mediate the conversation. His mother would treat Sheila with cool charm. Sheila would respond sharply, or sullenly, or, worst of all, with desperate brightness. Today there was none of it. Both behaved as though there had been a secret reconciliation. Phil could relax. All he had to do was keep the conversation clear of

Fred Ryan's offer. He was no longer worried about telling Sheila; he just hadn't found the chance.

Paul Gaynor swung through the door to the dining room with an armload of wood. His face brightened when he saw them. "I thought I heard a car."

Phil started out of his chair.

"Stay there. Stay there. I can handle it all." He crossed the room to the fireplace. A log fell from the top of the pile.

"Paul!"

Phil went to pick it up.

"It's all right. I'll get it." He dumped the wood near the fireplace. Phil handed him the log as he stacked the others. "Thanks. Did it dirty the rug?"

"Just a little snow."

"I'll clean it up," he said to Constance.

"You tried to take too much."

"I'll clean it up."

He finished stacking the logs and stood up. "Now I can greet you." He shook hands with Phil and kissed Sheila's cheek.

Paul was shorter than his brother, with a round face that made him look even younger than he was. His cheeks were red from the cold. Phil had inherited his mother's blond hair and fair skin. Paul was the image of his father, dark, with bright blue eyes and a heavy black rim outlining his pupils. He would have been dazzlingly handsome if his face could break free of its baby fat. When he was sixteen everyone waited expectantly. Now he was twenty-one. There was the possibility that he might move right into middle age without the revelation. He wore work clothes—old brown corduroy pants, a lumber jacket, and work boots.

He kneeled down next to Vikki. "You remember your old Uncle Paul," he said, kissing her.

"Hi."

"What have you got there?"

"Hot chocolate."

He looked up at Constance. "Is there any more? I'd love some."

"Go take your boots off first. Then come join us."

He got up and started out. "I'll just leave them in the hall and bring them up later."

"Paul's been working with the men in the carriage house."

"What's going on there?" Sheila asked.

"We only worked half a day because of Christmas Eve," Paul called in from the hall.

"Are you opening it up again?" Phil asked.

"We're turning it into a house!" Paul was determined to stay in the conversation. They heard him drop his boots on the hall floor.

"A house?" Phil gave his mother a puzzled look.

"For you and Sheila," Paul called.

Phil stiffened.

"A house for us?" Vikki asked.

Sheila laughed. "He was joking, honey."

His mother shot a look at Phil.

"No, I'm not."

"Paul, I hate shouting between rooms," Constance said. Then, to Sheila, "It's going to be a guest house."

Paul returned in his heavy socks. "It's great working with the men." He fell into the armchair opposite Phil. "I'm learning all sorts of stuff."

"Paul is thinking about going into contracting," Constance explained.

"I wanted to see how well I could get along with the workmen and all that. That's why I'm—" He jerked his head toward the carriage house.

"Here's your chocolate."

He leaned forward to take it and slapped his brother's knee on the way. "Well, how are you doing, you son of a gun?"

Phil felt very old whenever he saw Paul. His brother always seemed to be trying on a new personality with him. Four years earlier, when Paul was a freshman at Dartmouth, he had come to Phil as a young intellectual. He was going to study philosophy. "Ideas are the only reality," he said in an intense voice that must have been one of his instructors'. When he dropped out he became a radical. He planned to move South.

287

It wasn't enough to take bus rides, you had to live among them, show you were putting yourself on the line. A bronchial infection killed his plans. He became a cynic. Once a month he would come into the city and stay with Phil and Sheila explaining he was working on a deal. Now he was a hearty man of the people. All the changes gave Phil a sense of his own stability. Paul's eagerness, the way he always seemed to watch his older brother from the corner of his eye, checking for a response to his new personality, forced Phil to turn cool, noncommittal, considered. Phil's whole body moved up and back to keep disengaged from each new enthusiasm. He had always felt a deep and protective love for his younger brother. He was sure of it when he was not with Paul. When they came face to face, though, he would lose it. He could never find a way to respond to Paul's onslaughts of energy, his naked pleas for approval.

"You're starting to look a little soft," Paul said. He sat forward in the armchair as Phil settled farther back. "Once you're out of the mill you ought to get some exercise. I tell you, there's nothing like it. All the physical work I'm doing. I'm turning hard as a rock."

"You're looking great," Phil murmured.

"If I could just lay off the beer. I could, I suppose. But it's a good thing to split a sixpack with the men. Kind of breaks the ice. You know what I mean? And I tell you, you've got to be a regular guy with those men." He shook his head appreciatively. "They really are beautiful people. They can see through a phony in a second. They're so"—he searched for the word—"real. You know what I mean? They know what's what. They don't take any bullshit from anybody—"

"Paul!"

"Sorry." He grinned apologetically, but with a tinge of pride. "I guess I've got used to being with the men. And they're *craftsmen*," he continued. "Not just workmen. They take real pride in their work. Just to see them sling around that wood, it's like a dance, a goddamn ballet."

"All right, Paul."

"Look, Mother, I'm sorry." He turned to her sharply. "That's the way I talk. That's me. You'll just have to put up

288

with it." He looked back at Phil. "She gets upset because I talk that way in front of the boys. They're . . . what? . . . Fifteen? Sixteen? You'd think they never heard language like that."

"No, Paul," Constance said dryly. "You use it as though *you'd* never heard it before."

"What did he say?" Vikki asked Sheila.

"It's not important, honey." She made a face to say, "I'll explain later."

"It's a matter of principle."

"Paul," Phil said quietly. His brother was setting himself up for a new humiliation. Phil made a confidential, man-to-man gesture to calm him. It always worked. Paul withdrew into his hot chocolate.

Vikki finished hers and handed the cup to Sheila.

"Just put it on the table, honey."

"You certainly finished that quickly."

"It was good."

"Your father used to like hot chocolate, too. Do you remember, Philip? He hated the marshmallow, though. That's why I didn't put any on yours."

"I like marshmallow."

Paul laughed. Constance smiled and hugged her granddaughter lightly. "Next time I'll remember that."

"What's all this about contracting?" Sheila asked. "The last time we saw you you were going to start a vanity press."

"That deal fell through. It was going to be a partnership, but I got shafted. Just as well." He turned to Phil. "I couldn't see myself in that world, anyway. You know me. I'm too down to earth for all that wheeling and dealing."

"And contractors don't wheel and deal," Sheila said, amused.

"It's not the same kind of thing," he said vaguely. "At least you're working with something solid. You know what I mean?"

She smiled. "No."

He turned back to Phil. "I've got a design for the letterhead all worked up. I'll show it to you later. This is one deal I'm going into on my own." He paused for a response. "Ronstein wanted to buy in on it, you know. But I've been burned once—and that's enough for me." This time he waited long enough to force Phil to speak.

"Isn't contracting an awfully big—"

Paul waved it away. "Not for me. I'm learning the ropes out there. It all looked mysterious at first. But you know me. I've got a business head. I was talking about it with Freddie Stevenson the other day—"

"Young Fred? Is he here?" Phil asked.

"Up for the holidays. Great guy. We were playing billiards and chewing the fat—" Constance rattled her saucer. "There's nothing wrong with that."

"No," she said vaguely. "I suppose not."

"Anyway, he thinks I know what I'm doing."

There was an uncomfortable silence.

"Could I play in the snow?" Vikki asked Sheila.

"Sure."

Phil sat forward, happy to have a chance to shift his attention. "I bet you're ready for my old sled."

Sheila's face brightened. "What a sensational idea!"

"Do you think we could find it?"

"Paul? Do you know where it is?" Constance asked.

"Out in the stable, I think."

"That whole huge hill all to yourself," Sheila said excitedly. "I used to dream about hills like that. All we had was Prospect Park and that was like belly-whopping in a traffic jam." She put down her coffee. "Let's go change into playclothes and find it. Would you mind, Mother Gaynor?"

"Mind?"

"I mean, we've just arrived and everything."

Constance laughed. "I think it's a splendid idea."

Sheila looked at Paul. "Have you got an old ski jacket or something I could wear?"

"You can use my pea coat."

"Great."

"Help them up with the luggage, Paul, will you?" Constance said.

"Oh, that's all right. I can handle it."

"Not at all. Paul doesn't mind."

"Can I finish my chocolate, first?"

"Really, Mother Gaynor. It's all right. It's only two light bags. We'll go up now." She motioned to Vikki.

"Be sure your mother lets you have a chance on the sled," Constance called after them.

Sheila turned at the door and smiled. "Don't worry about that."

"Sheila's in wonderful spirits," Constance said when they were gone.

Phil grinned. "Everything's working out fine."

"Has there been trouble?"

"No. No. It's just that"—he gave a short laugh—"it's just been a rough three years, that's all."

His mother nodded. "Vikki's growing into a sturdy young girl. I like that."

"I know."

"She's coming out of herself." Constance smiled at him but there was an inquiry behind it. She wanted to talk about his decision. He glanced at Paul. His brother was still brooding over his cup. Phil and his mother seemed to spend their lives shooting signals to each other about him.

"If you've finished with your chocolate," Constance began.

"I haven't."

"I wish you would," she said, unruffled. "I'd like you to find that sled."

"I will. I will." He looked at Phil. "Anyway, I'll show it to you later."

"What?"

"The letterhead design. I'd really appreciate any suggestions."

"Oh, sure."

"Of course, the way things are going I might just decide to stay where I am. Just join the union and become a master carpenter." He waited again. "What do you think of that?"

Phil nodded as though he were considering it seriously.

"What does that mean?"

"What?"

"That—" He imitated the nod. "Yes? No? It's a great idea? It stinks? Jesus, you know how hard it is to talk to you?"

"I don't know what to say, Paul. If that's what you want. . . ."

"But what do you think? You must think something, for Chrissake."

Phil made a helpless gesture. "It doesn't matter what I think. It's what you—"

"It matters."

"Then it's OK." Phil looked down at his own cup. His brother had a knack for setting him off, throwing his own decisions in Phil's lap like that and begging him to pass judgment. It turned Phil cruel and inaccessible. Each time, Paul would end up hurt and Phil vaguely guilty at his inability to give his brother whatever it was that he wanted. What did he, himself, want from Fred Ryan? He frowned and wondered why he should connect the two. They weren't the same. Paul was a kid—and Phil was no Fred Ryan. Yet he couldn't dismiss it. Maybe that was a part of what it meant to be a hero like him, the worst part. It was a trap to know that someone he didn't admire needed his admiration so urgently.

"Paul, please go and find the sled," Constance said quietly.

"I haven't finished."

"There'll be more when you come back."

"A man can't even sit in his own living room—"

"It's not your living room. It's mine. It will be yours when I die." Her voice was like a stiletto.

Paul colored.

"I want some time alone with Philip."

"You think I didn't know that?" he murmured.

She threw Phil a despairing look.

"You going to work for the old man?" He put down his cup and saucer. "Freddie thinks you'll be making a mistake."

"I didn't say I was yet."

"The carriage house is for you."

"Paul."

"She says it's a guest house, but that's a crock."

"All right, Paul."

292

"Freddie clued me in on the whole deal. You've been out from under for three years. I admire that, but I didn't expect it to last." He shrugged. "It'll be nice to have company."

"Go find the sled," Phil said.

"I'm going." He pushed himself out of his chair. "Glad I left my boots downstairs."

Constance watched him move slowly into the hall. Her eyes were cold and angry. When she turned back to Phil he glimpsed a sadness he'd never seen. He'd never before been with his mother in a losing situation.

"I'm sorry," she said. She kept her voice low so it would not reach the hall.

Phil nodded that he understood.

"The wedding is very difficult for him. It's all for the best, though. Once he's adjusted—"

"It'll work out."

She lowered her eyes. "More coffee?"

"No, thanks."

She put her own cup on the tray. "Why don't you help me bring all this into the kitchen? I gave Annie the day off. She's having Christmas Eve with her family and coming tomorrow to help with brunch."

She collected the china and swept up the tray. Phil followed her into the kitchen. It was a huge room with a stone fireplace. The round, oak table nearby had been in the same place since the first American Harmon built it. All the counters were oak, too. Annie kept them in a high polish. The picture window behind the sink was the only change since the room was built. It looked out on the snow-covered field behind the house.

Constance set the tray near the sink. She turned on the water.

"You still haven't got a dishwasher?"

"I've tried. Annie refuses. She says she doesn't trust them. If she had her way she'd be beating our clothes on rocks."

Phil was always a little shocked when he saw his mother wash dishes or run a vacuum cleaner. She was as capable as any housewife or domestic, yet she approached the chores with a man's detachment, as necessary tasks but not ones that defined her. She would have been able to do them, and do them well, in an evening gown.

"Why don't you take a towel and dry?" She rinsed the cups. "Fred Ryan thinks a great deal of you," she said after a moment.

"Does he?"

"He's looking forward to seeing you tomorrow. We'll all be meeting at the church, then coming back here for brunch." Constance Gaynor's hands had always been beautiful. Phil watched her long fingers play over the china. They moved efficiently, but not as swiftly as he remembered, and he wondered if she might be arthritic. "Are you going to accept his offer?"

"Do you think I should?"

She glanced at him. "What an odd question to ask me. You've always prided yourself on making your own decisions."

He smiled. It had been a long time since Phil talked about himself with his mother. Their last serious conversation had happened almost five years before when he told her he would not take money for law school. Before that it was about Sheila. He was surprised at how easily they could reassume their habitual attitudes with each other. Constance always treated their exchanges like public debates. Her face and her voice turned impassively pleasant. Phil responded with caution. Constance demanded they speak only of substance. Phil would circle the point, trying to find his way through her public stance to the private motives behind. He was always convinced there were hidden implications. Since he was a child he'd carried around an uneasy suspicion that Constance Gaynor manipulated him, and all the others, with surfaces. Too many times, when he was younger, she would guide him to eminently reasonable decisions. They always worked out for the best, but Phil would be left with a vague idea that he'd betrayed his first impulse. That had happened when he thought about leaving Northfield Prep after his first year because he was bored. He stayed and ended up with his choice

294

of Ivy League colleges. It happened when he thought of quitting the tennis team because the coach was turning the game joyless; he stayed and won the Connecticut State Championship. It happened when he had the chance to work on a cruise ship for a year before he went to college; he went straight to Columbia, his father's school, met Sheila, and had Vikki just before they tightened up on draft deferments. She would be pleased that he was going to accept Fred Ryan's offer, but he wanted to make sure the decision was his before he told her.

"Is the carriage house for us, Mother?"

"If you want it."

"If we don't?"

"I'm giving it to Paul. He can use it for a home and office."

"Do you really believe that business about contracting?"

"I've been willing to back him before. I'll back him this time, too. He needs someone to believe in him."

"Then it's not even his own money."

"You know Paul doesn't have his own money, Philip. How would he?"

"Why don't you throw him out on his own?"

"He's not as capable as you. He'd never survive." She worked silently on the teapot.

"I'm going to take the job with Fred Ryan."

"It's a sensible decision."

"But we won't live in the carriage house."

She nodded once. "Have you any idea of the real estate in this area?"

"We probably won't live in Northfield." He laughed self-consciously. "The offices are in Hartford, you know. And I'm not going in at an executive rank."

"Fine. Then Paul will get the carriage house. At least for the present. It will be good for his self-esteem." She turned off the water. "I'm very pleased that you're going to accept, Philip." She dried her hands and looked into his eyes. "We've missed you." She gave him a brief, warm smile.

He concentrated on his drying. It was out. He was committed. He'd been waiting for a long time to offer someone a clear

295

decision. It was the only way he could find out if it was the right one. He'd expected to feel relief and certainty, but his mother's response was ambiguous. It seemed to have nothing to do with him. He told himself it was foolish to expect to know all the consequences from one brief smile.

He finished drying. Constance put the service away. Phil looked out at the snow. Its brilliance made the field look smaller than it did in summer.

"I'm puzzled about Sheila," she said.

"She's fine." His mother's face was spotted with glare when he turned to her. He could just see her head nod.

"Your wife is not the most adaptable young woman I've met. I would have expected her to be much more resistant."

He blinked and looked away.

"You don't see us very much. There have been changes."

"And there was no resistance at all?" she asked skeptically.

He did not answer.

"Philip?" His eyes had cleared. She studied him closely, her head cocked a little to the side. She frowned. "You haven't told her yet."

"It's going to be all right."

"You haven't," she said incredulously.

"It's a little complicated, Mother. And very private."

"I can't imagine what you're thinking of."

"She's been ill."

"Well, I'm not sure this kind of surprise is the ideal thing for healing tissue."

"It's going to be all right." He did not mean to sound defensive. "I'm planning to tell her this afternoon."

"And if she *is* resistant?"

"It will be all right. I understand Sheila. Look, Mother, we've had a very difficult winter. I'm not going into details because I frankly don't want to give you a chance to crow about it—even to yourself."

"Don't sell me short."

"The point is that we've both grown up through it. I know what my wife wants and needs."

"What's that?"

296

He started to speak but realized he didn't have the words. He'd been carrying his new, clear vision of Sheila inside him for three days. This was the first time he'd had to articulate it. All the ways he'd said it in his head tasted weak in his mouth. "Freedom"—he blurted out, finally—"from responsibility." She stared at him coolly. "You think your wife wants that." "I'm not going to tangle with you about Sheila." "Of course not," she said flatly. There was a slight pause. "I thought there was something odd in the way she laughed off Paul's news about the carriage house. And the way you jumped at it." She looked at him closely. "Are you very sure of her?"

"Very." He said it with finality, then frowned. It made him sound like a conspirator.

"Fred is expecting a definite answer tomorrow."

"I know that."

"I'd like to know that it's cleared up by then." She laughed softly. "You know how this family is about certainty."

He folded his arms and leaned àgainst the counter. "You make it sound as if I'm accepting your offer, not Fred Ryan's."

"Don't be coy with me, Philip," she said impatiently. "You know perfectly well I had a hand in the business."

"You've got your hand in a lot of places." That familiar sense of betrayal started creeping up on him.

"In family places, yes. You all mean a great deal to me. You seem to think there's something wrong with the idea that I suggested Fred offer you a job, that the position must be tainted. It's absurd."

"And what about Renata?"

"I had a great deal to do with that, too, certainly. When your father was alive I had a whole career to look after. Since he's gone I've had only a family and your welfare is the most important thing I have. Since you were fifteen I've worked as hard at that as I did for my husband before. I have planned, I have made decisions in all my children's interests, always in good faith and, always, whether you want to believe it or not, out of love. I've done what I can." She leveled her eyes at him. "And you, of all my children, know that I've *only* done what I can. You've still been free agents. I may have made mistakes, but I've never connived. I've never lied. I've never been underhanded in any way. When you've made decisions that were very different from mine, I've respected them, honored them as gracefully as I could, and still never given up your welfare as my primary concern. Certainly I introduced your sister to Ed Ronstein and encouraged a relationship, but it was she who agreed to marry him. I set the stage for Fred Ryan's offer of a position, too, but it's you who have decided to accept it. I've really had quite enough of young men who insist on casting themselves in the role of victim, Philip. I expected better of you."

"I don't see myself as a victim."

"Don't you?"

The door swung open. Sheila and Vikki burst in, buttoning up their coats.

"Here they are," Sheila said. Paul's pea coat was too big on her. She pushed up the sleeves to keep them from flopping over her hands. Constance's face went automatically bright.

"All ready?"

"Where's the sled?" Vikki asked.

"Paul's in the stable finding it."

"Let's go out and meet him, honey. Phil? You want to come along?"

"Why don't you, Philip?"

"I'll have to change."

"We'll meet you."

"You can have a look at the carriage house while you're out there."

"Marvelous." Phil watched Sheila and Vikki bustle out the back door. "I'll go up," he said. He avoided his mother's eyes.

The closet in his old room was still full of clothes from his college days. He put on dungarees and a flannel shirt. The pants were snug. He left the shirt untucked.

Constance was putting on her coat when he came down again.

298

"I'm going into town to pick up a few things for tonight, Philip. I won't be long." She reached into the closet. "Here's your old ski jacket. You might want to use it."

"Thanks."

She took her handbag from the hall table.

"Mother?"

"Yes, Philip." She searched the bag for her car keys.

"I'll have that business taken care of before you come back." She glanced up at him. "I'd be very pleased."

There was a hill that fell away from the back of the carriage house. Phil remembered how he and Renata would roll down it in summer. Paul, Sheila, and Vikki were at the top as he came to meet them. They had found the sled. Sheila lay down on it and Vikki jumped on her mother's back.

They were shouting and laughing. "Hold on, honey," Sheila said. "Give us a push, Paul." Paul bent over and shoved them off. "Here we go! Hang on! Keep your legs up so your feet don't drag! Here comes Daddy!" They were already on the way. Sheila called to him as they slid down. He waved back.

Paul had on a heavy wool shirt and gloves. He stamped from one foot to the other as he watched them.

"Where's your coat?" Phil asked as he met him.

He waved it away. "None of the men wear coats in weather like this."

The sled hit the bottom of the hill. Sheila and Vikki tumbled over into the snow. Their laughter floated up to them. Phil smiled. "It was a good idea, wasn't it?"

Sheila waved. They both waved back.

"You want a turn?" she called.

"Sure!" It felt funny to shout with Paul standing next to him.

"Hey, Phil. I'm sorry I was such an asshole before." They both watched Sheila and Vikki trudge back toward them.

"That's OK."

"I mean, I'm really sorry."

"Don't sweat it."

299

He nodded. "I know. I wish I could stop trying so hard." He was shivering. "Like you." Phil colored. "How do you make it so easy?"

"You're cold."

"It's OK."

The women made happy, gulping noises as they struggled toward them.

"Oh, that's so sensational," Sheila called as they approached. "You know how long it's been since I've done that? Have to get used to it all over again. Did you see the spill? Vikki wants to go on alone this time. Can you wait awhile, Phil?"

He laughed. "You think you can steer by yourself?"

"It's fun! I got snow on my face." Both their cheeks were red and wet. Their breath came in short, quick puffs. "I want to go on with Uncle Paul later."

Paul's face lit up. "You sure?" he said, laughing.

"It looks like Daddy's never going to get a turn."

"Do you want a turn?" Vikki asked.

"That's OK, honey. I tell you what. Why don't you and Uncle Paul play out here for a while, and Mommy and I will look around in the carriage house?"

"Oh, let's stay out a little longer, Phil."

"This is a good time. You'll get more turns on the sled, I promise."

"One ride wasn't very much."

"Please, Sheila?"

She flapped her arms. "OK."

They watched Vikki take one ride down by herself. Sheila's face was radiant. She pressed against Phil.

"You don't mind, do you?" Phil said to Paul.

He shook his head. "Unless you want me to give you a tour. I can point out the workmanship and everything—"

"Vikki would be disappointed."

"I guess so."

"Thanks." Vikki waved from the bottom of the hill.

The inside of the carriage house was a maze of skeleton

rooms. A large table saw stood near the front door. Sawdust and beer cans covered the floor nearby.

"They've ripped out every wall in the place," Sheila said, surprised. Her voice echoed. "She really is doing a job. Can you figure out what's what? This must be a kind of living room." She went to the space with the saw and turned around, trying to assign rooms. "Jesus, do you realize this guest house is going to be twice as big as my parents' house-house?" She noticed a ladder. "There's an upstairs, too." She went to it and looked up.

"Better not," Phil said.

"What?"

"Better not go up. I don't know if it's safe."

"It must be safe if they've got a ladder here."

"Well, let's look around down here first, anyway."

She went back to him. "It's chilly, you know? I didn't notice the cold outside, but it's really chilly in here. And listen to my footsteps. The echo makes me sound like a truckdriver. Can you figure the layout? If this is the living room, this must be some kind of dining room."

They moved from space to space. Bits of plaster crunched underfoot. Phil followed behind Sheila as she explored all the jogs and alcoves. She made curious, puzzled noises. "Pantry . . . kitchen . . . closet. . . . This must be a bathroom. . . . Phil? What could this big room be? That's the living room. That's the dining room. You think she's going to have a downstairs bedroom?"

"Maybe it's a study."

"A study in a guest house?"

"It may not be a guest house. She's thinking of giving it to Paul." Sheila threw him a puzzled look. "For a home and office."

"That doesn't sound much like your mother." She slipped between two studs and giggled. "Do you realize there's going to be a wall there one of these days and I just walked through it?" She knocked on a beam absently, then threw him a serious nod. It was a caricature of Paul. "Good workmanship." He

301

smiled. "Anyway, it's not like her to jump into a thing like this without knowing what she's going to do with it. Let's look around upstairs. Maybe we can figure it out from that." She started back to the ladder.

"Sheila?"

She stopped.

"I don't really want to look around."

"But you're the one who—"

"I know. I just wanted to get a chance to talk with you."

"Is anything wrong?"

"No. No."

Her face turned serious. "Don't tell me I've done something wrong."

"It's nothing like that."

"I thought it was going so well this time."

"It is."

She looked at him more closely. "But you're upset."

"Do I look upset?"

She gave a short, nervous laugh. "Well, you're scratching your sleeve a lot and it's a heavy coat."

He jerked his hand down and put his fists in his pockets.

"Phil?"

"It's nothing to get worried about."

"Why don't you tell me, then. So I can stop worrying."

He nodded. In all his thoughts about the future this was the moment he'd kept leaping over. He was not prepared for the reality of her waiting face, the mixture of curiosity and caution in her eyes. He knew he couldn't wait too long or indulge in any elaborate introduction. That would look as though he wasn't absolutely sure his decision was right. At the same time he couldn't simply blurt it out. In the pause before he spoke he paid for all the opportunities he'd passed up.

She stood near a sawhorse on the other side of the room. He went to it and half sat against it. She watched him without moving.

"We've got to discuss some plans for next year."

"Now?"

"I know I haven't talked with you about all this before, but

. . . there were reasons for that. . . ." It was only vaguely accusing. "Maybe I should have. But, anyway, we can talk about it now, if you like."

"About what?"

"I'm taking a job with Fred Ryan for next year."

He brushed the floor with his toe and made a little design in the plaster dust. "It's really been stupid the way we just haven't been able to get together to talk about anything." He found the light tone he'd been searching for. "It's been so damned hectic with the end of the semester and . . . you and everything."

"There's been time."

He raised his shoulders. "Maybe there has."

"What's going on, Phil?"

She stood very still, watching him closely and waiting.

"You remember a long time ago I mentioned that Fred Ryan had made a tentative offer to me."

She nodded slowly.

He smiled. "I wasn't sure if you would. It was just about the time you came home from the hospital. . . ."

"Don't keep bringing up the hospital. That's over."

"I know." He jumped on it. "Everything's really been going so well." He held up his open hands. "You see? I haven't even had time to tell you that—and how proud I am of you."

"That's not what you're telling me now."

"It is, in a way. I didn't really take the offer seriously at first. Mainly because I wasn't sure you'd be able to make the adjustment."

"You said the job was in Connecticut."

He nodded. "Now I'm sure."

"Sure of what?"

"It's a good offer, Sheila. Good for you, too. It'll get you out of the pressure of the city. Give you and Vikki a chance to breathe. . . ."

She shot a look around them. Her eyes widened in recognition. "Here?" She almost whispered it.

"No." He reassured her quickly. "I told her—"

"Your mother knew about it?" Her face registered all of it.

303

"I just told her."

"Told her what? How could you tell her anything if we've never talked about it?"

"Can we talk about it now, then?"

She shook her head slowly. "You can't take that job."

He checked an impulse to answer angrily. "Don't you think that's a little unreasonable? I know you're hurt that we didn't discuss it before. And I'm sorry. It was a mistake."

"Oh, boy, was it a mistake!"

"I'm trying to make up for it now." His teeth were slightly clenched. "You haven't heard anything about it yet. Can you come over and sit down or something?"

"No. I'm rooted to the spot."

"Sheila, please."

She stepped back and leaned against a stud. "OK. Let's talk."

He assumed a controlled, reasonable tone. "The job's a good one. It's going to pay well and it's got a future. Fred Ryan wants me in Connecticut because I'm familiar with the tobacco industry. He trusts me. Thinks I can do my best work here. That's not a small thing."

"What's not?"

"To be trusted by a man like him."

She looked at him curiously.

"I know how you feel about the Ryans," he said quickly. "And I know how you'd feel about living in Connecticut. That's why I didn't really take it seriously at first."

"What changed your mind?"

"It's been a hell of a year. You know all the interviews I've been having."

"Not that many."

"There are some you don't know about."

"There's a lot I don't know about."

"Maybe so." He paused. "Do you know what it's like to sit there in one of those interview rooms with those guys? I mean, they're all sitting there behind this desk with your file in front of them and you know they have no respect for you because you're there with your hat in your hand. They all ask the same questions but they all want different answers and while they're sizing you up, you have to size them up and figure out what answer this one wants. Does he want you to be humble or aggressive or a regular guy? You try one tactic and if you're not sure it's right you work in another one to test it out, and when it's all over you know he hasn't once seen who you really are. And by that time you're standing in the hall and he's still sitting inside making a decision about your whole future. Then there's always somebody else standing out in the hall waiting to go in and he's sizing you up, too. So you act casual and in control as though you winged it. You know what that's like? And you know what's worst of all? When you're finally alone you tell yourself that you're really a million times better than the man who interviewed you, anyway—but you can't be sure if you really believe it or if you're just saying it to keep yourself glued together—because you still don't have a job, and he does." He could not look at Sheila while he spoke. The humiliation of the job interviews were his own private ordeal. A week before he would never have dreamed of telling anyone, especially Sheila. "Fred Ryan offered me a job," he continued after a pause. "*He* offered it to *me*. I didn't have to beg. And he did it because he knows who I am. He never looked at my files. You know what that did for my self-respect?"

"You worry too much about your self-respect," she said softly.

He shrugged.

"Why didn't you take the job right away?"

"He gave me till Christmas. Besides, I had to consider you."

"Did you ever consider talking to me while you were considering me?"

"I tried that first night, Sheila. Remember? I brought it up, but you just laughed it off."

"So you never brought it up again. It sounds to me like your mind was pretty well made up even while you were considering me. Were you afraid I might change it?"

"That's not fair. I've been pulled apart about this thing for a long time. . . ."

305

"You weren't afraid to bring it up with my father or Judge Spizer."

He nodded. "I've handled it badly. I know. But it's going to work out. I'm sure of that."

"It's not that easy."

"Trust me."

"No good." She paused. "Oh, shit, Phil, we've both screwed this thing up so badly."

"What do you mean?"

"How long is it since we've talked to each other about *anything*?"

"We've talked."

She shook her head. "We've circled around a lot. That's all. Just . . . circled around." She gave a short laugh. "You know what's funny? I mean, you know what's really funny? I can't even get mad at you for not talking to me about it. How do you like that? You know why not? Because while you've been busy finding reasons not to consult me, I've been finding reasons not to consult you. It's what they taught me in every government class I ever took. Unilateral decisions are dangerous." She let out a deep breath. "You just can't take that job."

"Look . . . honey, I know it's a whole new prospect you have to start working with and it's thrown you off balance—but you're going to have much less trouble adjusting than you think. . . ."

"Oh, Christ! I think if I hear that word one more time I'll start ripping these studs out. Like Samson. I'll bring the whole fucking house down. I can 'adjust.' Of course I can 'adjust.' I can adjust to anything I damn well want to. I don't want to adjust to this. . . ."

"I told you we're not going to live here. I already turned my mother down. . . ."

"I don't mean this house. I mean this life. I mean Connecticut and Eleanor Ryan and Renata and your mother. I'm not going to turn into another one of those lawyer's wives who've adjusted themselves out of existence—and who have to manipulate other people's lives to convince themselves they're

306

still around. Phil, I've already applied to Columbia Law School. I want to start in September. I want to pick up where I left off."

It was her turn to look away while he put it together. Phil sat very still. He had a feeling his face looked like his mother's the day he told her he would take no money for law school. Her mind must have been racing in the same way, not able to tell how seriously to take him, searching for the best way to help him give up his whim without giving up his dignity.

"Now tell me we've talked to each other," Sheila said drily. "I've asked for the fellowship I had when I graduated. Professor Kauffman's helping me. The chances look very good."

"I don't understand." She had slipped her hands through her floppy sleeves like a mandarin. Phil had never noticed the way the space beneath her chin moved in and out when she swallowed, or how wide her mouth was.

"I wanted to wait until everything was sure before I told you. That was *my* excuse." She shrugged. "Anyway, I was counting on more time to get you ready."

"Law school?" He was still trying to make sense of the news.

She nodded. "That's why we've got to stay in the city. If I'd known you were thinking of . . . this. . . ." She gestured to the room. "I'd have handled the whole thing differently. But you've always talked about working in New York. I just took it for granted everything would gel."

"Why do you want to go to law school?" He gave a half-incredulous laugh. "Why would anybody want to go to law school that didn't have to?"

"I have to."

"What for?"

"Because I want to practice law."

"I'm going to practice. You don't have to."

"I want to."

Phil studied her closely a moment. "Have you told anyone else about it?"

"Only Professor Kauffman . . . and Diana." Sheila looked up

at him sharply. She flushed. "Oh, Phil." She shook her head slowly. It was a mixture of warning and disappointment. "You don't want to know if I told anyone. You want to know if I told Rankin."

"Did you?"

"Don't do that, Phil."

He held her eyes. His instinct had been right. She'd been feeling pressured in just the way he imagined. That was why she'd avoided telling him and Doctor Rankin. It was a desperate attempt to live up to everything she thought she had to. He wondered how long she'd been carrying around a futile, secret plan like that, afraid to let it out to anyone who might threaten it. A wave of compassion took him by surprise. "Honey," he said softly.

"Don't, Phil." Her voice was sharp. "That's dangerous."

"I'm sorry, honey. It's just not realistic." Now that he understood he knew he had to be gentle, but firm. "I understand how you feel. I really do—and you're right. Whatever we do next year, I'm going to be damned sure we can arrange for a way to get you doing something constructive. It's something we should have done a long time ago. It's been my fault. I've been so damned selfish and absorbed. I never really picked up the signals." He shook his head. "But not law school. I mean, you can't be thinking clearly. You've seen what it's like. It's not the kind of thing you go into like a part-time job. You must know that." He gave a small, tender laugh. "That's probably why you never told me about it before. You knew I'd say what you really knew all along." Phil was moving cautiously. He knew how hard it was for her every time she came to him with some extravagant plan and he made her look at it calmly, without illusions. He could never tell if it was more painful for her to give up the dream or for him to watch her. It was a cruel and tender process that would go on all their lives. In a moment she would grow angry. She would level accusations at him, and as he let her work out her frustration and disappointment, she would work the dream out with it. It was like a periodic fever. In an odd way he took it as a sign she was all right, that things were back the way they were before the suicide. He was more convinced than ever his own decision was right.

"Phil, I think you'd better listen a little more carefully." There was an unfamiliar coldness in her voice. He leaned forward and met her eyes. "No, honey, I didn't say you should look like you're listening. I said you should listen. I've made a decision about something I want to do for the rest of my life and it's very important for both of us that you understand it. It's a decision that's going to change our whole lives."

He smiled. "You see? And this is the first time you've even mentioned it."

She held still a moment, then nodded. "You handled it badly. I handled it badly. Now we've both apologized and here we are. I'm going to law school this fall. Not because I'm looking for a part-time job, not because I want to get out of the house, but because I'm going to practice law."

"What about Vikki?"

"We can arrange something for her. I'm not as worried about that kind of thing as I used to be."

"And money?"

"There's not a problem you can throw at me that I haven't already thrown at myself. And a million others that wouldn't even occur to you. They're all real. They're all going to make it hard—and I'll meet every one of them, because this is something I'm going to do."

"Can I ask you a question?"

She nodded.

"Why Columbia?"

"You know all the reasons." She looked at him cautiously. "Why do you ask that?"

He made a half-dismissing gesture.

"No. What were you thinking?"

He shrugged. "Are you sure it's not just the old competitive thing?"

"What competitive thing?"

"Come on, honey," he said gently. "You know you always

309

used to feel as though you were in competition with me. We used to fight about it all the time."

"No good, Phil. No more of that. No more turning it all back on me, no more rooting around for incriminating motives."

"You're getting angry."

"I've got to make you understand how dangerous this is."

"Becoming irrational isn't going to help."

She drew a sharp breath and stared at him incredulously. "You know that's a lie," she whispered. "I'm making sense. Jesus, maybe I've always been making sense."

"Honey, I think you'd better get away from this for a little while and then we can both talk with clear heads."

"Our marriage is at stake."

"That's melodramatic."

"Phil . . . I'm trying very hard to like you right now and you're not helping me. I'm going back to the house—but please try to hear me, really hear me. You can't take a job with Fred Ryan in Connecticut. Even if I had no plans of my own I'd be telling you the same thing. It's too incredibly poisonous. I think I'd even be able to take it if you worked for him in New York, but not here. Can you ask him to put you in the New York office?"

He shook his head. "He wants me here."

"He? Or your mother?"

"I know the tobacco industry."

"And you want to be a lawyer for the tobacco industry?"

"There's a future in it."

"What kind?"

"A real one, honey. Not an idealistic storefront dream."

"I take it back. Not even in New York. You're already starting to sound like him."

"Is that such a bad thing?"

Her eyes clouded. "You want a discourse on the dangers of selling out?" she asked wearily.

"That's adolescent."

She nodded and pushed herself off from the stud. She ran her hand down it absently, then made a fist and pounded it

310

lightly once. "Don't take the job," she said simply and started out.

"Sheila?"

She shrugged her back as she made her way to the front door. "We can't afford it."

Phil stared after her a moment, then got up from the sawhorse. He kicked it angrily. Every time he was sure things were under control something like this happened. Half an hour before it had all looked easy. He'd been looking forward to telling Ryan he would take the job. His future would be decided; all the cogs would slip into place. Whatever the compromises, whatever dreams he had to give up, at least he would have the certainty of an ordered future. He had never felt so clearheaded and mature. Now Sheila had to fuzzy the edges. He zipped up his ski jacket and dug his fists into the pockets. She'd fooled him. He'd taken all her new energy as a sign of health, that somehow their mutual love had pulled her through the confusion of the last three months and now they could start fresh, but it was only a new fantasy that had been sustaining her and the same old subtle evasion of her commitment to him and Vikki. He wandered through the studs aimlessly, stinging with disappointment. She made everything so much harder than it had to be.

He came to a window looking out on the hill. Vikki was gone and the sun hung low. The snow had lost its brilliance. He stared out at it a long time until Paul called from the house. Renata and Ed had arrived.

They were all in the living room. Sheila and Vikki had changed back out of their playclothes. Paul was still in his work pants and socks. Renata sat on the edge of the sofa talking up to Vikki. She held both Vikki's hands as the child told about the sledding.

"Hello, everybody."

Renata turned happily, but her voice barely rose above a whisper. "Phil." She got up.

He remembered how Eleanor Ryan had looked coming toward him across the living room in New York. Renata had

311

assumed the same grace and authority. Her face shown with the same warmth, only less brightly. She was thin, with lines in her neck that always made her look twenty years older. Her hair was pulled back and held in place with a large silver barrette. The wisp that always hung over her forehead was gone. Renata's eyes were set a little too close, her mouth was a little too sharp. When she was young she developed a habit of holding her face expressionless as though to keep from calling attention to it. For the first time Phil was aware she was older. Her plainness did not seem to matter as much.

As they hugged lightly, she said, "I'm so glad to see you."

He looked hard and warmly at her, tentatively searching for signs of unhappiness. She smiled back. Her face was suffused with a dim glow.

"Where's Mother?"

"She's not back yet," Paul said. He was working at the fire again.

Renata pulled at Phil's hand. "Come meet Ed."

He was at the bar, mixing drinks. Two teen-age boys wearing prep school blazers stood stiffly beside him.

"Ed!" Her voice startled Phil. He'd never heard it so loud. It was sharp, too, as though she had not yet learned to force it past her habitual whisper. The man at the bar did not respond. Renata touched his shoulder. He turned, smiling. He looked at Phil, then closely at Renata. "This is my brother Philip," she said in a softer voice.

"Hello, Phil." They shook hands cordially. He was a little shorter than Phil, barrel-chested, with a large shock of pure white hair. His face was smooth and red. It wasn't so bad after all. The man had obviously kept himself fit. His handshake was firm, his eyes alert, as he looked back and forth between Phil and Renata. He put his arms around the two boys. "I want you to meet my sons. This is Carl. This is Thomas." The two boys shook Phil's hand and bowed stiffly.

"How do you do, sir."

"Well, I'm just in the middle of fixing drinks. Can I make one for you?" He looked at Phil intently.

"Scotch and soda's fine."

312

"Coming up." He mixed the drinks.

Sheila sat at the far side of the living room. Phil brought her a drink. She smiled up at him with the same open brightness that had been there before they'd gone to the carriage house, but her eyes had turned impenetrable. Renata, Ed, and Paul sat around the coffee table.

"Why don't you move over with us?"

She nodded, still smiling, and joined the others. Phil watched her uncertainly. Her response had been too compliant, her smile too quick.

"That's a beautiful girl you've got there," Ed said to Phil. He turned to Sheila. "Renata's told us all about you. We feel as if we know you already."

Sheila laughed. "Oh, dear. That means we can't surprise you."

He liked that. "I'm not much for surprises." He sat with his arm stretched along the top of the sofa behind Renata.

"You do look wonderful," she said softly.

Phil sat on the arm of Sheila's chair. She shifted away to make room. "Well, now I want to hear about all your plans." The two women smiled into each other's eyes. It had always been Renata, of all her husband's family, to whom Sheila felt closest. The two women had hit it off from the very first and Phil was astonished at how much they were able to communicate without words. They were seldom alone together, yet after each visit to Northfield Sheila would reveal things about Renata to Phil that he might have known from a lifetime of intimacy but never realized. It was only after he'd known Sheila, in fact, that he began to value his sister.

"Everything's working out splendidly," Renata said. Ed leaned forward. She turned her face to him. "Everything's working out fine," she repeated.

He grinned and nodded. "The wedding's only a month off."

Renata laughed softly. "It's going to be very quiet and informal. But I do want you to be there."

Paul clinked the ice in his glass. "How did you like the carriage house?"

"Great," Phil said.

"Everything looked very plumb," Sheila said.

Paul stared a moment, then nodded. "We use a leveler for that." He threw an understanding look at Ronstein.

"And this is your daughter?" Vikki sat crosslegged near the Christmas tree, examining the wrapped presents. "We've got some surprises for you tonight, honey," he called. Vikki did not respond. "I guess she didn't hear me." They laughed good-naturedly. "Kids—" He threw an appreciative look at his own. They were still at the bar, drinking Cokes, formal and unobtrusive. "You can come join us if you want, boys."

"We're fine, sir."

"Suit yourselves."

"Are these all your children?" Sheila asked. He was still looking at the boys.

"He's got a married daughter in Wisconsin," Renata answered for him. She put her drink on a coaster as Ed turned back to them. "I wonder if I ought to see about dinner."

"I think you can relax," Ed said. "I'm sure your mother's got everything under control. Rennie's been a busy lady for the last couple of months, keeping two households going."

Renata blushed. "Only since the boys came home, really." The front door opened. "Here's Mother."

Constance hurried into the living room with her coat still on. "I saw your car. Hello. I'm terribly sorry I'm late. Paul, I left some packages in the hall. Will you take them into the kitchen?" She went directly to Ed and Renata. "How are you, Ed?" He stood up and they shook hands warmly. It made Phil vaguely uncomfortable. "Carl. Tom." Constance went to the bar. "I'm so glad to see you." The boys shook hands and bowed.

"Connie, you look beautiful."

She turned to Ed. "I look harried right now. Mrs. Loring kept me half an hour making plans for the Historical Society house tour." She took off her coat and brought it to the hall. "Can you imagine that? On Christmas Eve—and the tour isn't until June. But what could I do? Her children are married and

314

gone. It's all she has, poor thing. She's got to make it last from year to year."

Ed remained standing. His welcoming smile stayed on his face a little too long.

"How was the sledding?" Constance asked.

"We didn't stay out long enough," Vikki said.

"I thought you had almost two hours."

"Uncle Paul got cold."

"Well, maybe tomorrow. Maybe the boys would like to try it."

"Yes, ma'am."

"Phil and Sheila saw the carriage house," Paul said.

"How did you like it?" Phil wondered if Sheila caught the missed beat before she asked it. "Of course it's so hard to tell anything with the maze of open walls."

"It looks exciting," Sheila said.

Constance laughed. "It's all so peculiar. At my age I should be pulling everything in instead of expanding. It's an exhausting way to stay young."

"You'll never get old," Ed said.

"You're a romantic."

Phil had never seen his mother tear into hostessing with such energy. It seemed as though she'd dropped ten years when she came into the room and found them all there.

"Will you give me half an hour to get dinner set?"

Renata started to get up but Constance waved her down. "You are on vacation tonight. Get Ed to make you another drink and relax. I'm in training for when I have to really go it alone. But Vikki can help me if she'd like to."

Vikki scrambled up.

"She's a stupendous lettuce shredder," Sheila said.

"Just what I need."

Sheila and Constance smiled at each other, and Constance left. Sheila turned back to Renata and Ed, and in the moment of transition Phil thought he saw her face go dead.

He joined Paul and Ed while Sheila and Renata exchanged news. The men discussed contracting. Ed did most of the talking. He seemed more comfortable when he did not have to strain to hear. Phil's attention kept shifting between the men's conversation and the women's. He wondered how the two women could sit so close to them, yet manage to maintain such privacy. Their words were inaudible; only the murmur of their voices reached him under Ed's. It had a quality of intimacy and intelligence. Sheila leaned back against the corner of the sofa, occasionally turning to flick her cigarette ash in the tray on the end table. Renata's pale hands lay still in her lap.

Vikki announced dinner. Renata touched Ed lightly to signal him.

In the dining room Carl and Tom stood by their chairs at the far end of the table while the others shuffled for places. Phil and Ed met at the head.

"Do you want to carve?" Ed asked.

"No. That's all right." Phil moved to a chair between Vikki and Renata. It was the first time he understood that his older sister was marrying.

Constance came in with the roast and set it near Ed. Renata nodded to the boys and all the men sat.

Sheila and Constance kept the conversation going all through dinner. At any other time Phil would have been delighted. Sheila was impressive when she was at her best. Her questions and her delighted and sharp responses made everyone around her feel interesting. She made Phil proud, and confirmed the rightness of the risk he had taken in marrying her. She could never be simply another lawyer's wife. She would always be an original.

Now, though, he was uneasy. There was too sharp a difference between the woman who had seemed so desperate in the carriage house and the one who sparkled with his family. What he was seeing had to be a mask. Its very impenetrability might be a sign that it covered something desperate and dangerous. He watched her closely as she questioned Ronstein, always full-face, coped with Paul, met Constance as an ally, helped Vikki, and even engaged the two boys and managed to find hints of humanity in their stiffness.

Constance watched her closely, too. Phil knew his mother

was not convinced. She might have been if he were able to support Sheila's performance, but every time his mother threw him a questioning glance he turned away.

It was another ordeal. He had been looking forward to a Christmas Eve free of tension, one in which he could enjoy his family in a way he had not been able to in years. He was coming back to the fold. He had found a solution to the conflict that had marred all the other gatherings, but there was no way to enjoy it. He felt cheated.

Sheila, Renata, and Vikki helped Constance clear the table. The men went back to the living room to wait for coffee. It was almost dark outside. Paul turned on the tree lights and stoked up the fire. Alone with the men, Phil could feel safe and clearheaded, but the women took a little too long to join them. He began to worry that Sheila might tell his mother what had happened, that a scene might have exploded. He grew restless. The promise of the fire and the tree only sharpened his disappointment.

Ronstein offered cigars. "Can I interest anyone in some brandy?" He pulled a hearing aid from his jacket. "Might as well really make myself at home now." He plugged it into his ear and adjusted the box.

"I'll have a little cognac," Paul said.

"Phil?"

He nodded. The women returned with coffee and dessert trays. Phil looked for signs of a confrontation.

"—the only Harmon who wasn't married in the Northfield Episcopal Church was my great aunt Serena," Constance said over her shoulder as they came in. "I never heard too much about her."

"She was a sculptress." Renata set her tray down and began pouring. She did not have to ask how any of them took it.

"Renata is the family historian. I don't know how she's accumulated so much information."

Renata smiled up at Sheila. "She ran away to London after reading D. H. Lawrence."

"Where on earth did you find that out?"

Renata laughed. Phil could not remember hearing his sister

317

laugh like that before. He was fascinated by the change in her. He had expected to see her preparing for the marriage with the same quiet resignation with which she had taken over the household duties in her mother's house, disappearing further into herself, her voice turning softer, her face a little more controlled. Instead she seemed to move out and take her place with the other women. At dinner he had been surprised at her quiet authority when she directed the boys, the ease with which she joined in Sheila's and Constance's conversation. It was all very muted, like the glow he had noticed when she greeted him, but unmistakable. She was too old and too conscious for the excitement of a young bride, and still too young to have given up all memory of her hope for it.

Phil remembered what Eleanor Ryan had said when she first told him about the marriage. His sister knew how to compromise, how to face what it was that she didn't have and then will her refusal of it. He looked from Renata to Ed. The marriage would work. His mother had managed to put the family back together and keep it going. The Gaynors were realists.

"Can we open the presents now?" Vikki asked.

"Vikki." Sheila gave her an admonishing look.

Constance laughed. "Don't be silly, Sheila. She has every right to be impatient."

"I'm excited myself," Renata said.

"I tell you what. Why doesn't Vikki be Santa Claus this year? You give out the presents. The names are on the little cards."

"I can't read."

"Tom will help you," Renata said.

Both boys got down on one knee, trying to hide their own enthusiasm. They picked through the presents. The first was for Paul from Constance, a large package. Vikki brought it to him and stood by while he opened it.

It was an attaché case with his initials in gold. Everyone murmured admiration.

"Thank you, Mother."

"I thought it would be useful."

"It will be."

318

Vikki went for more supplies. Phil's father had started the tradition of opening presents one at a time. It was the only way to give each gift its value, he had explained. Besides, it helped the children learn discipline and made the celebration last longer. It worked well when Paul, Phil, and Renata were younger, but as they got older it had the peculiar effect of killing the excitement. The gifts, themselves, would fade into the routine of unwrapping and admiring. Everyone would run out of original ways to say thank you, and the response of the others to each new display turned mechanical. The addition of Ronstein and his two sons drew it out even longer. There were a few highlights, a puppet theater for Vikki from Paul, an expensive doll dressed in red velvet from Constance, a lacrosse set for the boys; a Ming vase for Constance from Ed. Ed and Phil had both given nightgown and peignoir sets to their women; at the end, Carl and Tom wheeled in a tricycle for Vikki from Ed. The rest was an assortment of slightly daring shirts, new books, interesting jewelry, and sandalwood boxes. The living room was strewn with crumpled paper.

"We can stow it all in the fire," Paul said. Carl and Tom collected it. Vikki wanted Phil to set up the theater right away but there wasn't time. She started to cry. Sheila picked her up.

"That is crankiness," she said lightly. "And the end of a very big day. I think it's bedtime. Will you all excuse us?"

She took Vikki upstairs.

Phil had not been aware of how tense he was until Sheila left. He felt his whole body relax. It disturbed him. He'd thought the business of splitting himself between Sheila and the rest of his family was over. It looked as though it would be different this time. For all the others it might have looked like it was, but he knew she was not resigned to joining them in the way she would have to next year. If only she could learn from Renata. His sister and mother sat opposite each other admiring the peignoir. There was something beautiful and radiant about the way Renata was cautiously learning to hope again after she had learned so well to give it up. There was a sense of justice in it, too, for Phil. Her soft, restrained happiness was a reward for resignation. He liked to believe it was at the point

319

that she'd given up all faith in the future that this had happened. That was what real maturity was all about—giving up dreams of the impossible in order to have what was real. It certainly was what Renata had done. It was what he would do tomorrow when he accepted Fred Ryan's offer. And it was what he had to help Sheila do.

Carl and Tom disappeared into the game room to play billiards. Paul followed a while later. "Anybody want to join us?" he asked Phil and Ronstein.

"Maybe a little later."

"Watch out for the boys," Ed said proudly. "They're hustlers."

Sheila returned. Phil tightened.

"Everything all right?"

"Fine. She kept insisting she wasn't tired, until she hit the pillow." Sheila stifled a yawn. "Oh, excuse me. I guess none of us is used to this country air."

"It looks as though you might make it an early night yourself," Constance said.

"Let me stay with you all a little longer." She laughed. "That sounded like Vikki, didn't it."

"Stay with us," Renata said.

She nodded and looked at Phil. He smiled back distractedly. He wanted to join Paul and the boys but could not leave Sheila alone with the others. He felt as though he were spending all his energy either monitoring her or finding ways to keep her out of the way. It could not go on too much longer.

Ed offered her a brandy.

"No, thanks. It will put me right out." She went to Renata and touched her hand lightly as she sat next to her.

Ed talked tobacco with Phil. He had a way of splitting Phil off from the women every time they were all together.

"I'm just giving you the general picture, though," Ed said. "Fred will probably fill in the details pretty quickly. I can promise you this. You're not going to have much time to settle in before things start popping."

Phil looked quickly at Sheila. He could not tell if she had heard.

320

"There are still some things in the air," he murmured. There had been no time for his mother to tell Ed about his decision. That meant he, and Ryan too, had taken it for granted. Phil did not like that. He speculated for a moment on what would happen if he turned the offer down. Sheila had given him a good reason. It might even be a good thing to let her try to follow through on her plan. He suspected she blamed him for the failure of all her other schemes. Maybe if he let her follow through on this one she would learn from its failure. But as soon as he thought about turning Ryan down, a great void opened before him. He could not tell how many more humiliating interviews, how much more uncertainty —or how much more compromise it might finally mean. If he were younger, perhaps, it might be a real possibility. But he was already almost twenty-nine. He didn't have time for the luxury of grand gestures. Besides, if he refused, he'd have only Paul, young Fred, and Sheila to support his decision.

Ronstein was explaining the connection between tobacco and the advertising industry. Phil wondered if it would be worth it just to see the surprise on Ronstein's face and Ryan's. It would certainly force them to reconsider him. His mother would be furious. He looked down at his brandy. Now that the thought had surfaced he couldn't shake it. She'd been right about one thing. He had to admit it. Since the time Ryan made the offer he'd never seriously thought of refusing. His agonizing had really been over the best way to justify taking it.

He glanced at Sheila, who was listening delightedly as Renata ran down the Harmon genealogy. His wife would take it as a personal victory. He did not know if that would be good for her.

Constance moved to the armchair. She sat back comfortably, sipping her second cup of coffee. For the first time Phil thought that perhaps the decision really was in his hands, that he really was the free agent his mother always claimed he was. He really could say no to Fred Ryan if he chose. The idea was frightening and exhilarating.

Sheila was having trouble holding back yawns. "This is

terrible," she said on the tail of one. "I just can't keep my eyes open. I think I'd better go up."

"Oh, dear, I've been chattering, haven't I?" Renata said.

"You know better than that."

"Every time there's a major event in the family I spout like this." She laughed. "It's awful."

"I love it." Sheila touched her cheek gently. "Besides, this time you're the major event."

Renata blushed. "I wasn't even thinking of that," she said, flustered.

There was a pause. Phil sat forward a little too quickly.

"That's OK, honey," Sheila said. "You can stay down longer if you want." He nodded uncertainly. "I'm going to take up my new nightgown, though. Ed"—she shook hands—"say goodnight to the boys. I'm sorry I'm such a poop-out." She went to Constance. "Goodnight, Mother Gaynor."

"Goodnight, dear. Sleep well. We'll all be going to early communion. If you and Vikki are still asleep, Annie will be here to give you breakfast. The Ryans will be joining us for lunch."

She glanced at Phil. "I know."

Phil stayed in the living room a little while after Sheila was gone, then made his way to the game room. The boys had taken off their blazers and loosened their ties. Their sleeves were rolled up to the elbow. They were intent on the game. Carl was lining up a shot when Phil came in.

"Come on, motherfucker," he murmured, then noticed Phil. He straightened up. "Hello, sir." His body went stiff again; he assumed the same formal smile he'd worn through dinner. "Would you like to play?"

Phil felt very old. "That's all right. I just thought I'd watch." He perched on a stool near the table and looked on. Ed came in.

"We'll have to be going soon, boys."

"Yes, sir."

He clapped Phil on the shoulder. "Did they whip you?'"

They left shortly after. The boys bowed and thanked Constance.

322

"We'll see you tomorrow," Ed said at the door. "Fred's looking forward to it." He shook his head. "The man never rests. I guess that's what put him where he is." He extended his hand. "Good to meet you, finally. And tell your wife goodnight. She's a charmer." He turned to Renata and kissed her. "See *you* tomorrow, too." It sounded like a playful order. Phil realized he was trying to be tender. Renata nodded. "Sleep well."

"You, too."

Phil said goodnight to Renata as soon as the others were gone. He managed to get upstairs before Constance could find him alone.

Sheila was asleep. She wore the light-blue nightgown. The peignoir lay across the foot of the bed. The small light on the night table beside her was on. She lay on her side with one bare shoulder showing. The soft light made her look incredibly delicate.

He slipped into his pajamas noiselessly, then sat down beside her. There was one small beauty mark on her back. He touched her shoulder gently. She turned in her sleep. Now he was alone with her he could give in to his love. All the anger and disappointment of the carriage house, the anxiety he felt when she was with the others drained from him. Lying there with only the thin strap of the nightgown covering her, she seemed so fragile, so pliant and utterly uncomplicated. If only she could find the way to always rest as she was resting now, if he could help her give up the foolish and impossible challenges she was always giving herself, she would glow with the same warmth and luster that her shoulder glowed with now in the lamplight.

He brushed her cheek with his lips. She stirred. Phil turned off the light and got into bed.

"Phil?" She was still half asleep.

"Goodnight, honey."

She rolled over and put her arms around him. He kissed her. She tightened her grip until she clung to him fiercely. "Oh, Phil, please," she whispered. "Please listen to me."

"You're still asleep," he said tenderly.

323

She released him and rolled over. He fell asleep quickly.

It had snowed during the night. An inch or two of fresh powder covered everything. They drove the short distance to church, Paul at the wheel, Constance and Renata in the back. Sheila and Vikki had still been asleep when they left. The stinging cold and clean smell of new snow and pine took Phil back to the Christmas mornings when his father was still alive. For the short ride to the church he was fourteen again. They cut through the tree-lined drive and he had the peculiar sensation of thrilling to the pines as a man while he took them for granted as a boy.

They had got a late start. Paul had discovered he had no clean white shirt. Annie had not arrived yet, so Renata had to iron one for him quickly. Constance kept her reprimands minimal. She did not want a scene that might wake Sheila or Vikki. Phil was afraid the service had already started. It was bad enough that they'd have to come in after everyone else was seated. Their pew was right up in front beside the Ryans. He hated walking down the aisle under the eyes of all North- field, and the idea of interrupting the service as well was mortifying.

Paul dropped them in front of the church and took the car off to park. They stripped off their coats and boots in the vestibule. The church was full but the service had not yet begun. Phil followed his mother and sister down the aisle. He looked straight ahead with a neutral, acknowledging smile in case he should happen to meet an eye. The Ryans were al- ready there. Eleanor Ryan sat between her husband and grandson. Ed and his boys had a pew directly behind. Renata split off from her mother and joined them. Phil reached across and shook hands with Ronstein.

"Good morning. Merry Christmas," Phil whispered.

The boys nodded. "Sir!"

"Merry Christmas."

The priest appeared just as Phil slipped in beside his mother. He reached across her to shake hands with the Ryans. Young Fred was farthest away. He had to reach, too.

324

"Fred. Merry Christmas," he whispered.

Young Fred grinned at him. He looked as slicked down and young as Phil felt. Only his red-rimmed eyes betrayed him.

"Phil. How's the handball?"

Phil reddened. He laughed softly and did not answer.

"Merry Christmas, Philip." Eleanor Ryan shook hands with him.

"Merry Christmas."

The priest spoke as Phil turned to Fred Ryan. *"The Lord is in his holy temple...."*

"Hello, Phil. Merry Christmas."

"Merry Christmas, sir."

"... let all the earth keep silence before him."

They shook hands and Phil settled back.

"Behold I bring you good tidings of great joy, which shall be to all people. For unto us is born this day in the city of David a Saviour, which is Christ the Lord."

Paul arrived as they knelt for the Lord's Prayer.

"Our Father...."

He slipped in beside Phil. "I had a bitch of a time parking."

"... Thy kingdom come...." Phil said it insistently, to silence Paul. They stood.

"Alleluia. Unto us a child is born; O come let us adore him. Alleluia."

The small Northfield choir sang the *Venite*. Phil glanced across his mother. Fred Ryan followed the hymn in the prayer book impassively. There was no reason to expect any sign from him. The day might be important to Phil, but to Ryan it was another Christmas, with some minor business to take care of along the way. Ryan's presence threw things into perspective. Being near the man, Phil could see his own decision in a new and larger context; his own petty conflicts faded into the reality of Ryan's empire; his wavering of the night before had been egotism and fantasy. Phil's caution slowly turned to gratitude.

Ryan never moved under his gaze. Phil's mind wandered distractedly between Ryan, the choir, Sheila, his mother. He projected scenes, tallied possibilities, replayed yesterday's events while Frederick Ryan remained motionless, intent on prayer. His ability to concentrate on the task at hand was another sign of the man's genius.

The sermon was short, based on Luke II: "And it came to pass in those days, that there went out a decree from Caesar Augustus. . . ." The subject was obedience. The priest spoke briefly of tyranny, the slaughter of the innocents, the miracle of God's justice and mercy in sending his Son to be born and to give meaning to the act of submission.

The cloth on the communion table was very old. Alma Harmon had woven it while her brother built the church. The priest brought out the bread and wine. He prayed for the state of Christ's church and called for the congregation to take Holy Communion.

"Ye who do truly and earnestly repent you of your sins, and are in love and charity with your neighbors, and intend to lead a new life, following the commandments of God, and walking from henceforth in his holy ways; Draw near with faith, and take this holy Sacrament to your comfort; and make your humble confession to Almighty God, devoutly kneeling."

Phil knelt for the general confession and absolution.

"Therefore with Angels and Archangels, and with all the company of heaven, we laud and magnify thy glorious Name; evermore praising thee, and saying, Holy, holy, holy, Lord God of hosts, Heaven and earth are full of thy glory: Glory be to thee, O Lord Most High. Amen.' "

There was a general shuffle. Constance, Paul, and Phil approached the railing. They knelt beside the Ryans. Renata, Ed, and the two boys joined them.

As he knelt, waiting for the bread and wine, all doubt dropped away. He took the wafer and wine. The priest moved to Paul. Phil lowered his head. He could feel the presence of the others kneeling beside him. All the history of this church, the worn, red velvet covering on the altar rail, the taste of the wafer and wine, the starched smell and the rustle of the priest's robe, the order of the service, the bowed heads of the others whom he knew and understood so well, all fell together

326

and confirmed him. He was one of them. He had a place there.

Constance and Paul rose on either side of him and started back to their pew. Phil stayed a moment longer, then joined them.

Outside he would tell Fred Ryan he was taking the job.

8

Sheila

Christmas, 1962-
January 6, 1963

SHEILA WAS awake before they left for church. She had felt the mattress give when Phil slid out of bed and she lay with her eyes closed while he crept around the room, easing drawers open, silencing the change in his pants and the hangers in the closet. She listened until the door snapped shut, then turned over and sat up. Whispers and quick footsteps slid through from the other side. They were being quiet for her and Vikki; their cautious voices came through more clearly than if they had been speaking normally. Even Renata's soft voice was distinguishable.

"It's all right, Mother. I don't mind."

"You should. He's old enough to take care of these things himself."

"OK. I'm sorry."

"Keep your voice down. What are you going to do when your sister's not around anymore? I won't be as understanding, I can promise you that."

Sheila stared at the closed door and wondered why it was always the eavesdropper who felt self-conscious. She was embarrassed for them all. They were like any other stupid, petty family. She'd known that for a good, long time, of course, but hearing them now as they struggled to keep it a secret and thought they were succeeding only brought it home. She looked back on her first vision of the Gaynor family. How dazzled she'd been by Constance Gaynor's authority, by the elegance of the house and the effortless entertainment. And Phil, golden-haired and shining as the oldest male. As soon as they arrived for a visit the orderly routine would revolve around him. It was like visiting an old English country house in a Victorian novel. She felt like a commoner, wide-eyed and tremulous, welcomed on the strength of some innate nobility she'd never known she possessed. But she was twenty then, still only one of "Philip's interesting friends," a whimsical curiosity. Now she was one of them, at least partly. She was still on the other side of the door and her mother-in-law still ordered Paul to keep his voice down.

Sheila arranged the pillow behind her and sat back against the headboard. She would have liked to brush her teeth, but she was not about to leave the room until they were gone. The day before had been hard enough. It would take all her energy to pick it up again. She'd carried it off. She had given the right amount of attention to her infant brother-in-law, the two priggish boys and their fatuous father; she'd waltzed around with Constance. Not even Renata could have suspected the alternating panic and numbness underneath. She wondered if Phil knew. Maybe he was going through the same ordeal. She was usually able to read him in familiar situations, but these were new circumstances and she could not be sure he even understood that much.

Their marriage was falling apart.

Her stomach started churning again. She stared hard at the bedroom door, praying for Phil to have forgotten something and come back in. She tried to will him back so she could hold him and make him understand what was happening. She'd bungled it badly yesterday. In the carriage house even she hadn't realized just how serious the situation was. She'd allowed herself the old luxury of anger. She'd known enough not to let it out this time but she hadn't trusted herself enough to keep it under control indefinitely and she'd run before she

329

had made him really understand. It was only afterward that it hit with full force. That was why she had been so desperately pleasant with all the others. Somewhere in the back of her mind was the crazy idea that she would be on stronger ground if she could prove herself to Phil. If she could make him believe she was as capable as any of the other women, that she could carry off the role of the young lawyer's wife, that she could be as attractive and dazzling an asset as he needed her to be, it would somehow make her own needs more valid for him. She had entered into a desperate bargain all on her own. If she gave him what he needed, then certainly he could reciprocate.

What if he didn't? The mess that had opened up in the carriage house was intolerable. The two of them had been creeping around each other the way Phil had crept around the room that morning, each making his own future, each sure the other was still asleep. She would have liked to believe it was all a stupid coincidence. It wasn't. The two of them had been moving farther and farther apart for over a year. It was coincidence that they'd been able to hold together for as long as they did, not that the rupture had finally shown. Phil had been locked into a routine that kept him from seeing. There had been nothing important enough to Sheila to make her look. Now there was.

It would all be easy if she did not love him. Yesterday in the carriage house he had been insufferable—obtuse and patronizing. She had wanted to lay into him with a sawhorse. But that didn't make the idea of living without him any the less unthinkable. She was frantic to make him see how their survival depended on his turning down Fred Ryan's offer and her going to law school. Maybe it wasn't pure love, whatever that was, that made her so panicky at the thought of losing him. She needed him. She knew what his body felt like; she knew every change that had happened to it over the past seven years. She knew all his contradictions, his selfishness and generosity, his need for order, his facility with abstractions and his infantile intolerance of human ambiguity—the very

330

intolerance that made him incapable of comprehending her own contradictions. She would not give up any of that.

The noise on the other side of the door stopped. Sheila swung out of bed and went to the window. The car was gone. She went into action quickly. She brushed her teeth, stripped the bed and remade it, brushed her hair. She worked vigorously, throwing her whole body into every action to stay on top of the trembling. The new nightgown caressed her legs and slid against her stomach. She was used to wearing Phil's old pajamas. The nightgown made her feel like an actress dealing with a new and complicated costume. She went to the closet to dress. Phil's clothes filled one whole rack. When they were first married and Phil was away she would go into the closet and bury her face in his shirts. She did it again today but they did not smell of him. Constance had stored them in cedar. She dressed quickly and went downstairs.

Vikki was already up, sitting on the living room floor in her pajamas and robe. She played with the doll Constance had given her.

"Hi, sweetheart." Sheila's voice was cheerful but unsteady. "Could you set up the theater?"

"Have you had breakfast yet?"

She nodded. "Annie's here. Could you set up the theater?"

"Let me get a cup of coffee first. You go upstairs and get dressed. By the time you're ready we can get to work."

Vikki took the doll and started upstairs.

"Why don't you put on the red sweater and slacks outfit Aunt Renata gave you?"

Vikki looked at the doll. "Then we'll match."

Sheila laughed. "You'll clash. But it doesn't matter." She found the box, and hugged the child tightly before giving it to her. "I love you," Sheila said.

"I know."

She nuzzled her daughter's neck. Vikki did not smell of Phil either.

Annie was in the dining room setting the brunch table. She greeted Sheila and offered breakfast.

331

"I just want a cup of coffee."

"There's a fresh pot on the counter."

Annie had started a low fire. Sheila took her coffee and sat at the oak table near it. She lit a cigarette. Her hands were still shaking. If only she could be sure Phil would not say anything to Ryan before she had a chance to talk to him again. He had to realize it was that important.

The two of them had been caught so off balance. She tried to think it out rationally, in a way Phil would have approved. He had every right to think this was another whim, she told herself. He had no proof it was any different from all the other times when she'd left the final decision on her impractical schemes in his hands and come around to see it his way. She was asking too much to have him take this one on faith. She hadn't yet brought him through the process of her own revelations to help him understand the difference this time. The burden of proof was still on her. It was up to her to marshal her evidence. She tried. She went through the explanations in her head coolly. She went back to the suicide and her own painful search for its root. She made whole sentences in her mind, precise, pointed, utterly unmistakable. Yet all the time she laid it out so rationally in her head, another, wordless impulse flooded up from below. He would never understand. They were breaking up. She was losing him. It took all her effort to keep the two trains of thought from colliding. She started to ache behind the eyes. He had to give her time to explain.

"Are you all right, Mrs. Gaynor?"

Sheila jumped. Annie had just come in. "Yes. I'm all right." She smiled distractedly but she could not control her lips.

"You're white as a ghost."

". . . a little tired."

"You're sure I can't get you anything?"

Sheila nodded. The panic in her stomach had turned to nausea. She tightened her throat to keep it down and the coffee turned bitter behind her tongue.

"It's nine o'clock. The others should be back in an hour, depending on how long the minister talks. The Ryans are coming to brunch." Annie sliced up a side of bacon as she

332

chattered. If Sheila hadn't been there she would have hummed. "They're the nicest people. I don't think I've ever heard an unpleasant word from either of them. And she's so well-bred, if you understand me. Of course, it's not for me to pass on other people's breeding and if I didn't think so highly of her I wouldn't. At least, I wouldn't *say* it, even if I thought it. That's one thing my mother taught me that I'll never forget. 'If you can't say anything nice about someone, don't say anything at all.' She was right, too. I've always followed that rule and it's never gotten me into trouble. Of course, that grandson of theirs. That's a different story—"

Sheila's mouth went suddenly dry. She pushed her chair back with a clatter.

Annie ran to her. "You're not feeling right."

Sheila rushed through the door. She slammed into the bathroom and steadied herself with one hand against the sink, pressing the other against her stomach as though holding her dress out of the way. The vomit burned her throat and splattered into the toilet. She belched it all up until the spasms went dry. Her stomach subsided. She held still a moment to make sure. The ache in her forehead faded; the sweat turned cold. She flushed the toilet.

Annie called in. "Mrs. Gaynor? Are you all right?"

Sheila washed her face and rinsed her mouth.

"Mrs. Gaynor?"

"Yes. Thank you." She leaned back against the wall. "I'm all right, now." She closed her eyes, took a couple of deep breaths, and checked her dress to make sure it was unstained.

Annie was still standing by the door. "You gave me a fright."

"I'm sorry."

"I'll make you some tea and toast. That'll settle you."

Sheila nodded. "Thank you." She followed behind Annie. How's that for breeding? she thought wryly.

She felt better. Along with everything else she seemed to have heaved up the panic. Her stomach was calmer and the trembling in her hands as she held the teacup was only aftermath. It had taken her by surprise. I'm not the vomiting type, she wanted to reassure Annie.

Vikki came in wearing her new clothes. The labels and washing instructions still hung from them. "I'm ready."

Sheila grinned.

"Your mother's not feeling well, dearie. . . ."

"It's all right, Annie. Really. Come here, honey. You look like a sales rack at Ohrbach's."

Annie found a pair of scissors and Sheila snipped the threads.

"There." She took one more sip of tea. "Now let's get to work."

They brought the theater upstairs so the living room would be clean for guests. It took a while to assemble. Sheila worked slowly and sent Vikki scurrying down to Annie as they discovered they needed tools, a screwdriver, pliers, batteries for the little stage lights. Sheila was grateful for the complicated process. It took all her concentration, and she only glanced at her watch a couple of times. Once, while waiting for Vikki to return with some Vaseline for the pulleys, a wild hope struck her that Phil had understood everything. Perhaps he was turning down the job that very moment. The idea that it was possible sent a surge of joy through her. For an instant she believed it. He would not have to consult with her about that choice. It would mean that he had, after all, heard her yesterday, that he had pieced together even the things she hadn't said and hoped for their future. It was an outside possibility, but as long as she was still here alone with Vikki it was real.

The hope sustained her until she heard them downstairs. Their voices were fresh and cheerful from the cold. They snapped her back to reality. He hadn't refused. The most she could hope for was time.

"Daddy's here," Vikki said.

Sheila's hands trembled again.

Vikki sprang to her feet. "Let's show him."

"I still have this pulley to adjust. . . ." she said weakly, but Vikki was gone.

Sheila sat on the floor peering up underneath the little stage opening. Her fingers turned clumsy as she tried to work the

334

string through the greased pulley, but she had the curtain working by the time she heard Phil and Vikki.

"We made it ourselves," Vikki said as they came down the hall. "It's bigger than I thought. And the curtain's supposed to go up and down."

"Well, let's see it. Let's see it."

Vikki pulled him by the hand. He was still in his coat.

"Is it ready?" Vikki said.

Sheila nodded. She pulled the string. The curtain gathered in short, jerky stages.

"It works!" Vikki shouted. "See?"

"I'll show you how to do it yourself a little later."

"Now."

"There are guests downstairs. We should say hello first."

"I want to show Uncle Paul." Vikki raced out again before her mother could stop her.

Phil stayed behind. He smiled down at her. "Did you have a nice morning?"

She nodded. "You?"

"Fine. We all walked home from church."

She looked up under the stage and worked the curtain again. "How are the Ryans?"

"Fine. They're downstairs waiting. . . ."

There was a long pause. "Phil, I want to talk to you again before you say anything to him."

"I already did."

The string slipped. Sheila worked her finger into the pulley again.

"I took the job."

"Don't tell me that."

"I want you to know before we go downstairs."

She shook her head. "Don't tell me that, Phil." Her jaw was tight.

"I gave it a lot of thought."

"Not enough." She tied off the string and sat back against the bed, then stared up at him with hard eyes. All the fear, all the hope of the morning was drained from her. Only rage was left.

335

The door burst open. Vikki pulled Paul into the room. "Show him, Mommy!"

Sheila got to her feet. "Get Daddy to show him. I'm finished entertaining his family."

She pushed past Paul and Phil and went to the bedroom. Phil followed her. She wheeled when the door opened.

"Sheila, I don't want a repeat of yesterday."

"You schmuck!" She could not stop her voice from breaking.

He closed the door. "Would you rather I hadn't told you? Let you find it out from them?" He kept his voice low the way the others had that morning.

"You jumped at it. You couldn't wait."

"I made a decision."

"Before church? After? During the fucking service?"

"We were walking home—"

"You couldn't wait," she repeated angrily. "Not even an hour to let me finish explaining."

"Was there really any more to be said?"

"There was plenty, you prick."

"He wanted an answer today. It looked like the only time we'd have alone."

"You could have asked Mommy. She'd have given you time off."

"All right, Sheila!" For the first time his tone matched hers. She flinched automatically. "I'm not putting up with any more of this self-indulgent crap. I made a practical decision. I'm a man with a wife and a daughter to support."

"Does that feel good when you say that? Does it make you feel like a big old grown-up? Does it excuse you?"

"You've put enough of a burden on me this last couple of months. I'm not taking any more of it."

"Not even an *hour*?"

"It would be the same old scene, you know that. It is now."

"No. It's not."

"Maybe you're right. This time I'm not indulging you."

"Indulging. . . ." She stared at him in disbelief. "Is that what you thought you were doing? Yesterday, too? *Indulging* me?"

336

He lowered his voice. "Look, I'm tired of all this. I've been operating as carefully as I can. I've made all the allowances I could."

"Allowances?"

"You've been sick."

"Allowances? Indulging? What is this?"

"I've taken the job as much for you as myself."

"How? You don't even know who I am."

"When you're thinking clearly—"

"I am thinking clearly, goddamnit. Don't pull that bullshit with me anymore. You stand there talking about allowances and indulging me as though I were some kind of half-brained simp and you tell me *I'm* not thinking clearly. How clear is your head if that's who you think you're talking to?"

"You know I don't think that."

"You think whatever's convenient for you to think. You don't think at all. You rationalize. And call it logic. You took the job for me," she echoed him contemptuously. "You took the job because that old man snapped his fingers and your mother shoved you from behind. And while you were trotting over it was convenient for you to think you were doing it for me." She paused and spoke more softly. "You're never going to humiliate me like that again. Indulging . . . allowing . . . using me to justify your own compromises."

"If it's law school you're worried about—"

"It was law school. Now it's you. That you could have gone ahead and told him. After yesterday."

"He was expecting an answer."

"Who is *he*? Jesus Christ, Phil, don't you even hear what you're saying? He wanted. He expected. You're saying all that to *me*. As though I didn't tell you what I wanted. What I expected. Why didn't you tell *him* that? Are you afraid of him?"

"You know better."

"I thought I did. All I know is when Fred Ryan wants it's realistic. When I do it's self-indulgent."

"I can't talk to you when you're like this, Sheila."

"I tell you what, then. Talk to him. Tell him you've

reconsidered. Tell him no, the way you've told me a hundred times. And lay it out for him as logically and realistically as you've laid it out for me. OK? You can do it. You've got the material. Explain how you knocked yourself out—and me, too—for five years because you didn't want your mother running your life and how it would all be meaningless —meaningless, Phil—if you moved right back into it now. Tell him you just can't see yourself changing your brother's diapers and watching your sister sit there being grateful for crumbs. Explain how you can't see putting all your training, all your talent into something as stupid and selfish as tobacco. Tell him what's happened to me and how your marriage depends on our staying where we are. Because it does, Phil. You won't be lying if you tell him that. You lay it all out, and you explain that you're only being realistic. And then you kiss him and tell him you're proud of him and you know he's mature enough to understand it's all for the best. And you just watch him adjust."

"I want to work for him."

Sheila paused. "Well, at least we're moving into honest territory," she said softly.

"He's a great man."

"He's a moxie with style. It's only idiots like you who make him important."

Phil leaned back against the door and looked at Sheila for a long time. He pressed his lips tight. "Fifteen minutes." He gave a short laugh and shook his head. "For fifteen minutes I felt really good. You know? While we were walking home. I'd told him I was taking the job. Everything was simple, uncomplicated. I could say good-bye to all those rotten interviews, all that. . . . I didn't have to work to make the decision right. It was right. It is. We made plans. I had control. I had a future. I'm not saying no to that."

"And Sheila will come around. I suppose that's how you took care of the complicated part: 'I can sell her the old maturity line.' "

"I thought I could trust you."

338

There was a pause. Sheila looked at Phil closely. "Is this what you've really wanted all along?"

He closed his eyes briefly. "You never get what you really want."

"You always get it," she said sharply. "That's when you find out what it was in the first place. And this is it for you."

"I want a little security. For you and Vikki."

"Don't slip that cog again. Leave us out of it. I'm talking about you. Do you really want this?"

"I want some control over my life," he said tightly.

"And you want things simple and uncomplicated at the same time? Are you kidding? You take control of your own life and nothing is simple anymore."

"I'm willing to take that chance, then."

"By working for Ryan? That isn't taking control. That's giving it all up. I tell you, maybe for a while it'll seem like everything's turned simple. He'll be there with a nod and a good, firm handshake to reassure you. He may even tell you you're a 'hell of a good lawyer' once in a while. And when he's not around your mother will be there—or Ronstein. They'll all tell you how right you are, how simple and uncomplicated and safe it all is. And it'll *seem* like you've taken control. But watch out." He started to interrupt but she wouldn't let him. "I've been there. I've been giving up control all my life and pretending I was taking it. I swear to God, Phil, nothing felt simpler, more secure than when I gave up my control to those pills. I didn't even take them. How do you like that? I let them take me. And nothing ever felt righter. Safer."

"It's not the same thing."

"It's exactly the same thing. Believe me. I've become an expert on suicide. There are grades and varieties."

"I am not a suicide."

"I didn't think so, either. You had me fooled. You're a man, and I wasn't on to the male varieties till I came up here."

"I don't know what you're talking about."

"Women commit suicide for men. Men commit suicide for each other. You for Ryan, Paul for you, those two evil boys for

339

their father. And everybody busily, busily reassuring everyone else that they're right, that it's realistic, that the lies and the torture you put each other through don't exist—or that they can be gotten free of tomorrow. That's suicide."

"And what am I supposed to do, Sheila? Let *you* decide for me?"

"What? And 'unman' you?" She laughed ironically. "Look at you. Those narrow little eyes and that tight mouth. 'Ballbreaker.' That's what you're thinking. Right?"

He kept silent.

"Boy, do I know that look. You can't count the number of faces I've seen it on. And what a trump it is. It still scares me. Automatically. I used to commit a little suicide every time I saw it."

"What about it, then?"

"I'm not after your balls," she said. "Even if I were, who could get in there while you guys are so busy crunching away at each other's? Looking over your shoulders blaming it on us. You're the ones who make a mystique out of that little item, not us." She shook her head. "I'm not taking the responsibility for that kind of suicide, either. The decision's still yours. I'm just laying out the alternatives."

"And giving ultimatums."

"You know what I'm doing? You know what I'm really doing? I'm asking you to marry me."

"Come on, Sheila."

"No. I'm serious." She sat down at the foot of the bed. She nodded. The words had taken her by surprise. She worked it out as she spoke. "Get this, Phil. I'm asking you to marry me, like you asked me six years ago. No—not just like. When you asked me, we both took it for granted I'd give up everything that was real to me for everything that was real to you. We took it for granted. Both of us. Well, we were wrong." She shrugged. "This time it's your decision. But if you say yes, it means giving up all your lies about what's realistic, all your compromises. That's the difference. I'm not expecting you to give up anything valuable. And I'm not taking it for granted

340

you'll give it up just to be able to tell the world you're my husband."

"What about love, Sheila?"

She closed her eyes. "I wouldn't be proposing if I didn't love you."

"You're asking me to make a choice."

"The same one you want me to make."

He stared at her in confusion. "What's happened to you? What's happened to everything I loved? All the softness, all the warmth and sweetness."

"It's still there. You just have to work at finding it. The way I'm going to have to work at finding your strength, and independence. Maybe we can give each other pointers."

There was a long silence.

"Will you marry me, Phil?"

"If I said no?"

She looked down at her hands. "It would be harder for you than for me. I'm used to giving things up." She got up from the bed. Her heart was beating fast. So this is what it's like, she thought. This is what all the panic was about this morning. She'd been right. It was terrifying. She was on the other side of it now. There was no turning back. "I'll leave the big suitcase for you and Vikki."

"You're not leaving?"

"There's no sense to my staying around. I wouldn't be very good company for all those people down there. I'm not going to give a repeat performance of last night for you and we've both got some heavy thinking to do." She swung the suitcase onto the bed and began to pack.

"Where are you going?"

"Back to the apartment."

"I can't let you go back alone."

"Don't worry about another attempt. There's not a chance."

"What should I say to the others?"

She stopped in the middle of folding a dress. "That's something you're going to have to work out for yourself."

She concentrated on the packing, gliding between the closet and the bed, careful not to look at him.

341

"It's a gesture, Sheila. That's all it is."

"No." She shook her head.

"It's like everything else you've started and never finished."

"No. It's not."

"You've said that before."

"It's not. I swear it."

"Prove it."

She turned to him sharply. "What?"

He held her eyes. "Prove it." Phil lowered his voice. "Not just to me. To teachers, to every other student, to interviewers, to juries, to judges. That's what you're letting yourself in for. You ready for that?"

She shook her head blankly. "What are you saying?"

"It all looks so easy. You see me go off every morning with my books packed and a schedule to follow, and you figure, 'Shit, I can do that. Anybody with half a brain can do that.' But you've never had to feel yourself being sized up—"

She gave a short laugh.

"No. Not like that. That's easy."

"You think so?"

"You can afford to get angry when men size you up like that. How about when they're looking to see if you can do the job—and everything depends on convincing them you can? And you can't afford to get angry." He paused and lowered his voice. "You've never had to be responsible for proving yourself every day. They're always looking to see if you can do the job, Sheila—today's job. Right now. And if you do it, you know what it gets you? The chance to do something else tomorrow, to prove it again."

"I know it'll be hard. . . ."

"But will you *like* it?"

"Do you?"

"I have to *love* it."

"No. You can fight it."

"Not as long as I'm responsible for you and Vikki—"

"Don't use us like that."

"I'm responsible for you and *to* you—and to my mother and

342

Paul, even to May and Bernie. Don't tell me I'm using you. You've never had to be responsible like that. You never will."

"What about being responsible to yourself?"

"That's a luxury I can't afford," he said softly. "Not anymore. I can't pick up and run."

"I'm not running away." Her voice wavered. "I want you to come with me."

"Why?" he asked sharply. "Why should I? Here's your chance for a rehearsal. Prove it to me. It should be easy. Prove you're serious."

"I can't until—"

"That won't be good enough. Until what? Until you get a job? Until you get a case? Why should they take a chance on you? And what do you do about food for your family in the meantime?"

"My life does depend on this, Phil."

"What about mine? What about my chance to prove all those things? I've got it now. After wading through crap for three years. And you want me to give it up. All because you had another spurt of energy."

"I know," she said desperately. "I know what I'm asking. I know what it's like."

"Not until you've been there."

"Then let me!" She was leaning over the suitcase, braced against the sides. That was a mistake. She didn't mean to ask permission. She pulled herself up and met his eyes. "Go away, Phil."

"You know I'm right."

"It's not a rehearsal anymore. You really want proof."

"Should I take it on faith?"

"I did." There was a long silence. "I'll get Paul to drive me to the bus. Nobody'll miss him."

She used the packing to look away. When she turned back he was gone.

Her body went limp. She finished packing. A single, voiceless sob surprised her and she stood trembling, afraid to trace it to its source. Her toothbrush was in the bathroom. The

343

noise from downstairs grew louder when she opened the door to the hall. She could make out Fred Ryan's gravelly voice, Renata's laughter. Sheila tiptoed quickly into the bathroom as though she were afraid to disturb them, found her toothbrush, and started back.

"Sheila?" Constance Gaynor was in her bedroom. "Is that you?"

She froze in the hall. "Hello. Yes." She managed to make it natural. "How was church?"

"I just came up to find a sweater. Are you going to join us?" Constance appeared at the door, arranging a sweater over her shoulders.

Sheila paused, then shook her head slowly. "No. I'm not."

Her mother-in-law could still frighten her. Constance stood at the threshold of her bedroom, composed and cordial, still connected with the sounds downstairs.

Her casual, public smile faded.

"Do you think Paul could give me a lift to the bus station?"

"You're leaving?"

She nodded.

"Can we talk about it a moment?" Constance asked softly.

"I'd rather not."

"I understand that. But don't you think we should?"

"You have guests."

"Renata will take care of them. Come in." Constance went back into the room without waiting for a response. Sheila hesitated, then followed.

She'd never seen the inside of Constance's bedroom.

There was a sitting area near the dressing table with a small chaise and armchair. The room was plain, almost ascetic, with a textured, cream-colored wallpaper and blue-gray curtains. There were photographs everywhere, eight-by-tens in standing frames on the bureau and night table, collages on the walls, a miniature album the size of a single snapshot on the table near the chaise. A larger one, with thick cardboard pages of daguerreotype prints, lay open on an antique music stand.

"Why don't you close the door?" Constance said. "And come sit down."

Sheila obeyed. It was a morning of closed doors.

The pictures made the air feel heavy. Phil, Paul, and Renata surrounded her, alone, in groups, posed, candid, infants, children, teen-agers. There were no pictures of Constance.

The woman sat on the chaise, waiting. Sheila went to the armchair. She twirled her toothbrush, then tapped it against her hand.

"Philip's handled this very stupidly, hasn't he?" Constance began.

Sheila kept silent.

"It's not my place to apologize for him."

"No. It's not."

"He told me yesterday you knew nothing about his plans. I thought that very dangerous." There was an almost imperceptible pause. "And odd."

Sheila dropped the toothbrush on the table. Her elbows rested on the arm of the chair. She folded her hands. "What is it you want to know, Mother Gaynor?" She always tried to fight turning sullen in uncertain situations. Today she made no effort.

Constance proceeded as though she was unaware. Her body was relaxed. She regarded Sheila with open interest. She could have been carrying on the conversation downstairs.

"I want to know why Philip didn't speak to you before yesterday."

"Hasn't he told you?"

"Very little. Even if he had, I would still be interested in hearing your side."

"You're an incredible woman."

"I pride myself on frankness."

"I know."

"If everyone met on the same terms there'd be a great deal less misunderstanding."

"As long as we could be sure we were being honest at the same time."

"You think I'm meddling."

"Not at all. You seem to have as much invested in this thing as I do."

"That may be true. Are you considering divorce?"

Sheila tightened.

"Would you believe I was being honest if I told you I care about your marriage?"

"It's important to your son's career."

"That's a great deal of it. Our part of Connecticut is still a very small and very traditional world. Divorce is still looked on as a sign of instability—a rather ominous kind of failure."

Sheila gave a short, bitter laugh. "I always thought Phil's marriage was considered that."

Constance disregarded it. "I also believe that Philip loves you."

Sheila flushed.

"He's changed in some splendid ways over the last few years. He's far more sensitive, less intolerant." She laughed softly. "I could understand from the first why he was so taken with you. I was more puzzled about what you saw in him. He really was insufferable. Brash, selfish, terribly priggish. That was all my fault. You've been a good influence. I don't know if you were even aware of it. You have always brought out the best in him. I've liked you for that. I wouldn't want him to lose it."

"What makes you think I was responsible?"

Constance smiled. "Don't be ashamed of your accomplishment. It's proof that you'll make a good lawyer's wife."

"I've never worried about that," she said bitterly. "I've never worried about succeeding at anything that didn't really matter."

"Don't underestimate the work." Constance sat back. "Did you realize you were beginning a career when you married Philip?"

"I never thought of it that way."

"No, I suppose not. Neither did I." She studied Sheila briefly. "Ever since I spoke to Philip yesterday I've been trying to think back to what Judge Gaynor and I were like at your

346

age. Of course, I was dreadfully spoiled, which was one big difference between you and me."

Sheila looked up startled.

"You seem surprised. Don't say you can't imagine me spoiled."

"It's not that." Sheila was flustered. "I always . . . took it for granted that you thought I was."

"Spoiled? You?" Constance was amused. "That's the last thing in the world. . . . No, I was a cynic by the age of sixteen. I had everything I wanted, except a sense of values. I expected everything to be given to me. My only redeeming feature was that I accepted it all graciously. I've always thought just the opposite of you." She held her lips back from a smile. "You've always seemed to me to have nothing but values. I'm not saying I approved. I suppose I would have preferred an immoderately spoiled daughter-in-law to an immoderately idealistic one. They're easier to manage. You've misunderstood me if you thought I saw you as spoiled. I wonder why we always have to wait for the crises to clear up things like that."

Sheila unfolded her hands. The woman's openness was seductive.

"At any rate, I had no idea, either, of how much work it would take to be a lawyer's wife. I also knew my husband less well than you know yours. Philip—*my* Philip—was a turkeycock. A young man from East Hartford, ambitious—what do they call it now?—'on the make'? Incredibly attractive, though. If you can imagine all of Paul's potential realized. . . ."

Sheila's eyes wandered to the photograph.

"It was a shocking marriage. But I was willful. I wanted him and I got him. My parents were furious. I ascribed it to snobbery and preened myself, I suppose, on being modern. I took it for granted that marrying me was all Philip needed to make him successful. It took me a long time to realize that underneath all the strutting he didn't even want to be successful. He thought he could remain an insurance lawyer and spend his life marveling at how an insignificant insurance lawyer could have married into the Harmons." She smiled. "That would have proved my parents right. It wasn't till then

347

that I realized what a career I'd taken on. In certain ways you're luckier. At least your husband will help you make him successful. But it will still be work."

"I know."

"No, you don't," she said sharply. "Up until now you've both been playing at it."

"Do you think so?" Sheila asked ironically.

"Certainly Philip has. Working his way through law school is one of the greatest luxuries he's ever permitted himself. He's been playing at being a self-made man the way his father played at being successful—without really committing himself to it. That's why I've disapproved of it."

"Is it?"

"You think I want to control him."

"Yes."

Constance looked at her, puzzled. "You and Philip both tend to underestimate me terribly. I've disapproved because it was thoroughly dishonest. He's the son of a respected Connecticut judge and a rather wealthy mother. To spend five years as he has is as dangerous and wasteful an evasion as my other son's fantasy of joining the union."

"And me?"

"Once Philip moves into his rightful place with Fred Ryan you'll discover that his career demands an exhausting commitment. It's not just the entertaining. It's the way you will have to represent him everywhere, the way you will have to learn everything you can about the world he moves through, to educate yourself, and then keep that education hidden so you can use it to serve him."

"What about myself?"

"That will be yourself." She paused. "That's what I meant when I said you were both still playing," she continued softly. "You're still holding on to the separation between yourselves and your commitment." She smiled. "Perhaps that's why you're both having difficulty now. The leap is frightening."

"It was a lot easier underestimating you," Sheila said quietly.

Constance inclined her head. Sheila thought she could even

348

feel warmth in the response. "That's another luxury you're going to have to give up." There was a pause. "But you still haven't answered my question. Why didn't Philip consult you?"

Sheila paused. "He's told you nothing about the last few months, then?"

"Only that you've had a difficult time."

"That's a fair account. I tried to commit suicide last October."

Constance closed her eyes for an instant. "I see."

"An hour ago I wouldn't have believed that you did."

"But you do now."

She nodded.

"And Philip? Does he see?"

"Not yet. He still thinks it's his fault." Sheila looked up at her. "It's not, you know."

Constance acknowledged the reassurance. "That's not what you quarreled about this morning, though."

She shrugged. "I told him he couldn't take the job with Fred Ryan."

"For what reasons?"

She hesitated, still unsure of how vulnerable to make herself. "I'm going back to law school in September."

Constance raised her head slightly. "And Philip knew that?"

She reddened and shook her head. "Not till yesterday."

"Then he's not the only one who handled things stupidly."

"No, he's not."

"And your plans can't be altered. Everything is arranged."

"I'm waiting to hear from Columbia now."

"And you're aware of all the difficulties."

She nodded, but Constance's presence, her very understanding, raised even more doubts than Phil had about how well she knew them.

"This all came out of your . . . illness?"

"I wish people would stop calling it an illness. I tried to commit suicide. That's not something you contract—and it's not communicable."

"But the decision came out of it."

349

"Yes."

"You'd be asking Philip to interrupt his own career for yours—at a terribly perilous moment in his."

"I did it for him."

Constance sighed. "You're only able to say that because of his self-indulgence. If he'd had the strength to begin school immediately and move right in where he belonged, you'd both be launched already. You wouldn't feel your career was interrupted. Rather that it was just beginning."

"You mean a career like yours?"

She nodded.

"I don't think so. It would have meant giving up too much. And I'm not too hot on renunciation."

"You seem willing to give up a great deal right now."

"I don't want to give up anything," she said tightly. "Not anything of value anyway."

"Do you love Philip?"

"Yes. But I don't love what he'd become working for Fred Ryan."

"Fred's not a monster."

"That doesn't make me like what happens to Phil when he's around Ryan."

Constance smoothed the upholstery on the chaise absently. "So you've told Philip you're leaving," she said after a moment.

"I'll be in the apartment when he comes home."

"You're asking him to follow you."

"No."

"Testing your power."

"That's not a game I'm interested in."

"And do you think running away will resolve anything?"

"We both need time to think."

"Thinking things out in private is never very helpful, Sheila. You don't give yourself a chance to meet the real challenges. I think you know that. I suggest you stay. It will show Philip you're willing to work at a solution." She hesitated. "If you are."

Sheila looked away. She did not respond immediately.

350

When she did her voice was low and determined. "When do I find out if he's willing to work at it, Mother Gaynor? When did you find out your husband was willing to work at a solution?"

"He never was," she said simply. "Oh, I resented that at first. Just as you do now. But I came to welcome it."

Sheila looked up quickly.

"It made my task so clear, you see. It defined my province. Once I came to understand that, as I'm afraid you're going to have to understand it, I stopped wasting my energy."

"That's not for me."

"It has its rewards."

"No. It has its *gifts*. I know about those. I was brought up on surprise packages—prizes for expecting nothing. Those aren't rewards."

Constance lowered her eyes. "Have you thought about what will happen if you fail?"

She did not respond.

"What if you discover you've made the wrong choice?"

"I'll have to live with that."

"And Vikki and Philip will have to live with it, too. Are you willing to take the responsibility for that?"

"I think so."

"How will you be sure? After not taking the responsibility for your other decisions. You'll have failed at your marriage, failed at your work. What will be left? Will you ever be able to be sure you did everything you could?"

Sheila studied her, trying to gather strength. "Do you know I thought you would jump at the possibility of a divorce."

"I told you—"

"I know. Connecticut's a small world. I'm not convinced. You're too good. You could handle that. Especially with the Ryans. They never thought the marriage was right any more than you did."

"You're a talented young woman. You could be trained."

"There's more."

Constance raised her eyebrows and spread her hands. "There is," Sheila insisted.

"I don't believe in 'hidden motives.' "

351

"What happens if I succeed?"

"I'd be very happy for you."

"That's the first time you've been less than open with me."

Constance pursed her lips. "Perhaps."

"You think failure is inevitable."

"I think you're making a mistake. I certainly haven't tried to hide that. I think you'll be happier—"

"Like you."

"Yes."

Sheila stared at her. "You all need to be so sure you're right. You'd sell your souls for that reassurance."

"Really, Sheila." She made a dismissing gesture.

"And how reassuring for you if I became another successful lawyer's wife. How—confirming. That's why he's lost his nerve. He's afraid to be wrong. And somewhere in the back of his head he thinks you and Ryan *know*. What will happen when he finds out that you're all depending on him to prove *you're* right—as much as he's depending on you? And I'm just not that comforting, am I?" She sat forward. "You want to know why Phil never told me about the job before yesterday? He was afraid I'd raise doubts. But, I mean about all of this. All of you . . . all of it."

"And you? Why didn't you tell him?"

"I—" she didn't finish.

"Are you going to stay?"

She shook her head.

"That's very foolish. He needs you."

"If I stay everything falls into place for him," she said, but her voice had lost its assurance. "Sheila becomes difficult but flexible, and even the difficulty is reassuring. I've been propping him up too long by being difficult."

"And you don't think you're being difficult now?"

"Now I'm serious."

"Can you trust him to see the difference?"

"Can you trust him not to?" Sheila paused. "I'm sorry," she said more softly. "I didn't mean that to sound—"

"Never apologize for a direct hit," Constance said wryly.

352

"It's a sign of weakness. And you're going to need all the strength you can find." She stood up. "I'll get Paul."

She left Sheila alone.

The woman had touched nerves. The jolts of fear that shot though Sheila were as real and astonishing as pain. Constance had talked about failure and evasion in ways that were real to Sheila and she felt herself falling back into the void. If only Constance had been a hypocrite or a monster. She could have dealt with that. Until now she had seen the woman through a blur of attitudes and assumptions. Sheila could feel her eyes refocusing to match her mother-in-law's acute vision. The reality of the woman was powerful. For an instant she wanted to run and call her back, to ask Constance to teach her how to survive.

Vikki drove with them to the bus station. On the way Sheila explained. She and Daddy had quarreled. They both needed time alone to think things out. She thought Vikki would have more fun in Northfield with all the people around.

"You shouldn't tell her all that," Paul said.

"What should I do, Paul? Lie?" She put her arm around Vikki and held her tight, partly to reassure the child, partly to find comfort and strength. "Would you want that, sweetheart?"

Vikki nestled against her.

Before they arrived Vikki shot a look at Paul. She got on her knees to whisper in Sheila's ear.

"Are you going back to the hospital?"

Sheila closed her eyes. "Oh, sweetheart." She said it with tenderness, and relief that Vikki had been able to ask. Sheila took her by the shoulders and looked directly into her eyes. She shook her head. "I'll never go away from you like that again." She stroked her cheek once. "Do you believe that?"

Vikki nodded.

Sheila pulled her close. "These big heavy coats don't give us much chance to hug, do they?" She laughed softly.

The child shook her head.

353

Sheila kissed her. "I'm very proud of you," she whispered.

It was Christmas day, and the bus was nearly empty. Sheila stared blankly out the window. Red sun glinted off the snow, then off the glass in the office buildings as they approached the city.

The apartment felt as if she'd been gone for a month. The radiators hissed in the empty rooms. The air smelled of rusty water. Sheila dropped the *Times* on the kitchen table and went to the bedroom to unpack.

It was after four. She'd had nothing to eat but that morning's tea and toast. Her head ached from hunger. She left the bag on the bed—it would give her something to do after she ate—and went to the kitchen. She scrambled some eggs and toasted an English muffin. Sheila worked with her usual speed, then realized she had no need for efficiency. She ate without tasting and sat over coffee, watching the courtyard grow dark through the kitchen window.

She'd wanted the time to think, but her mind kept jumping to inconsequentials. She would try to concentrate on herself and Phil and find herself replaying scenes from childhood, wondering about friends she hadn't thought of since high school. She forced her attention back, but a moment later she was trying to remember the details of her bedroom in Brooklyn.

She got up to make another cup of coffee. The apartment was pitch-black. She turned on the kitchen light. It made a mirror of the window. For a fraction of an instant she felt a terror she hadn't felt since childhood, alone at night and sure there was someone at the window. It made her remember how she could never decide which was more frightening, being alone in the dark or alone in the light with the dark outside.

She made the coffee and took it into the living room, flicking all the lights on the way.

They were getting a taste of what it would be like. Phil was probably learning how it felt to manage in public without her. She was lonely. And frightened. Of course, Vikki would be there. Her jaw tightened. No, she would never use Vikki to fill

354

her loneliness. She had to promise herself that now, as soon as the thought surfaced.

She sat in the recliner. It was built for Phil, and Sheila could never get comfortable in it the way he did. She had to curl her legs under her and push with one shoulder to get it back. She lay like that, with her cheek against the back, for a long time, staring at her coffee. Her anger had returned, but this time not fiery but hard and cold, like a gem she could hold to the light and study. More than anything else it was the thought that he had never taken her seriously, the humiliation of that moment when she realized that all the times before when she had come to him filled with excitement and possibility her hopes had been doomed from the start. That made her eyes flash even now. He'd been patronizing her all along. What was worse, she had nothing to fight it with except her anger. If only she'd already been sure of a place at Columbia she wouldn't have needed her anger. He was right. She had nothing, no tangible evidence, only ideas and her own vision of the pattern their lives had followed, one that Phil either could not or would not share. His mother, too, had known she had nothing to show. Sheila wondered if the woman's intolerable composure didn't come from some secret anger as hard and polished as her own. Constance must have known that kind of impotence, that nightmare where she could feel herself turning invisible and she would shout for help while people stood around her and smiled as though they could still see her.

Sitting there in that hideous room surrounded by those frozen faces, Sheila had met the woman's challenges; they could only come from a woman who had been there. Constance understood in a way Phil never could, but even as Sheila met her questions about law school and her love for Phil, she felt the whole plan slipping away. The fact that Constance did understand made the idea of her own career feel weak. Her mother-in-law's silences, an occasionally raised eyebrow, her charged smile, forced Sheila to admit difficulties to herself far greater than the first flush of enthusiasm had allowed her to. It was not just a question of arranging to take care of Vikki and Phil for the next three years of study. The struggle would only begin afterward, as she tried to carve out a place for herself in a very hostile and suspicious world.

She had to admit, too, that somewhere in the back of her mind she'd been relying on Phil and his career to help her, even at the same time she was jeopardizing it. She was risking her marriage while she still did not know whether they would accept her—and so much hinged on a fellowship. She rolled her head on the back of the recliner.

The doubts flooded up. She still needed something, some kind of understanding to make her sure; something to help her face her loneliness, to help her confront the doubt that would challenge her every day, the doubt that every decision, every face, every failure and success would generate—the kind of doubt and loneliness that made her shiver at that very moment and wrap herself in her own arms.

She sat forward and let the recliner swing up. If she called Northfield, just to reassure Vikki, Phil could take it as a signal. No. She would be honest. She would admit she needed his help. Phil's voice and assurance would cut through the loneliness and doubt that was building all around her as real, as absolute as the darkness outside in the courtyard.

Sheila took a sip of coffee and went to the kitchen, planning her words and tone. At the door she stared at the wall phone. She had to be sure that Phil knew she loved him. There was so much that had been left unsaid. While she was still staring the phone rang. It was to her ear before she had time to prepare herself.

"Hello?" She did not even try to hide the relief.

"Hello, darling." It was May Kahn.

Sheila's heart sank. "Oh, hello, Mom."

"How are you?"

"Just fine." Sheila forced herself to be bright. "How did you know we were home?" She bit her lip at the lie.

"We called Northfield, darling," May said quietly. "Phil told us."

"Oh." There was a pause. "Is something wrong?"

"Grandma's in the hospital."

356

"Oh, no."

"Do you think you could—"

"Yes."

"I'm sorry."

"Yes, yes, yes," Sheila said impatiently. "I'll be there as soon as I can. What happened?"

"She went into shock."

Those goddamned chocolates, Sheila thought.

"It's nobody's fault," May said as though she had heard her. "It happens. And at her age, you never know what's—"

"How is she?"

"She asked for you."

"How is she?"

"You never know in these things, darling. Her heart—"

"Is she dying?"

"I think so."

"All right, Mom." Her voice cracked. The tears she'd been fighting all day filled her eyes and throat. "I'm coming. I'm not even unpacked." She hung up before May could say more. Sheila sat on the kitchen stool and released the sobs—for Doris, for Phil, for herself and Vikki. She perched with her legs crossed and her arms wrapped around her waist and rocked with it. Her shoulders heaved and the cries crowded through her throat, one on top of the other.

She hadn't finished when the phone rang again. This time it was Phil.

"Honey?" His voice was shaky.

"Hello."

"Your mother called here."

"I know."

"She reached you? Are you all right?"

"Yes, I'm all right."

"You don't sound—"

"That's because I'm crying." Another wave of sobs took control.

"Should I come home?"

"Oh, Phil, don't ask me questions now. For Christ's sake don't ask me questions."

357

"All right. All right, honey," he said softly. "Try to get hold of yourself."

"Oh, Phil." Her voice cracked and sputtered. "I love her so much."

"I know."

"I'm going to Woodview tonight. Tell Vikki what's happening. Tell her the truth."

"OK."

"You call me there tomorrow so I can talk to her. I don't want her coming back to an empty apartment with you unless she knows where I am."

"All right." He hesitated. "Sheila? Honey?"

"Later, Phil. I've got to go."

"All right."

She hung up.

Bernie met her at the Woodview station. Sheila had finished her crying while she repacked. She could tell there were still traces of it from the way her father looked at her. His own face was tired.

"Hello, cookie." She kissed his cheek as she got in the car. "We don't usually see you again so soon," he said jokingly.

"How is she?"

He shrugged.

They said nothing more until they were home. May was waiting with coffee and cake. She looked better than Bernie, more functional, but she started to talk brightly as soon as she saw Sheila—and did not stop until they went to bed. It was mainly about Doris and what had happened. May did not have enough control to keep her account in sequence; sometimes she would leap to entirely different subjects. Twice she asked about her and Phil, why Phil was alone in Northfield with Vikki, but before Sheila could respond she was back to Doris. Bernie kept eating coffee cake and buttering pieces for May and Sheila, until May interrupted herself. "Bernie, please. I've been eating on the run all day. It's making me nauseous." So he just buttered for Sheila.

May's story was disconnected but Sheila put it together. It

358

had started a week ago, before the holiday. Doris was late coming down for the poker game so the women knew something was wrong. They sent Millie Levith up. The gin game always started a half hour later. Millie found Doris in insulin shock. They rushed her to the hospital. She came out of coma. Everything looked as though it would be all right. That was why they hadn't called Sheila. Old people go into the hospital all the time. Yesterday she'd had a heart attack.

Jack and Alice would be coming tomorrow. Edith was being marvelous. She was at the house every day, helping May keep them going.

Sheila asked when she could see Doris.

"Tomorrow morning. She was quiet when we left her."

"Too quiet," Bernie said.

"Don't talk like that. Your mother's a horse. A woman who smoked three packs of cigarettes every day and was never sick in her life?"

Bernie looked at Sheila. "They'll call us if anything happens tonight."

They set Sheila up on the day bed in Poppa's room. It was after two in the morning by the time May and Bernie had finished puttering with the sheets and pillows. Sheila expected a restless night, but she fell asleep quickly and slept soundly.

The sunlight streamed through the picture window when May woke her. "What time is it?"

"Nine o'clock."

Sheila shot out of bed. "So late."

"The visiting hours aren't till two. We called the hospital. She's still asleep. But she's better. Jack and Alice are going straight over when they get in."

"That's all she needs to wake up to," Sheila said as she dressed. "Tears and mysticism."

They had a quick breakfast. Phil called with Vikki just before they left. Sheila told him she'd be staying in Woodview as long as they needed her. If she was still there when classes started he should bring Vikki down. Phil put her on the phone so Sheila could explain the plans.

359

"I'm not worried," Vikki said. She sounded like an adult reassuring a nervous child.

"Good, sweetheart."

"Aunt Renata showed me how the theater works. I'm making a play."

"I want to see it when I get home."

"Mommy?"

"Yes, darling?"

"Do you think I should give back the dollar?"

Sheila paused. "No, darling." It took all her will to control her voice. "Nanny wants you to have it."

She let Bernie and May talk to her briefly before they hung up.

Doris was still asleep when they got to the hospital. They found Jack and Alice in the solarium. Jack sat gloomily with his hands clasped between his knees. Alice was reading *Newsweek*.

"Have you seen the doctor?" May said after they had all kissed.

Jack shook his head. "He hasn't come around yet. The nurse says she talked a little this morning."

"Wonderful."

"What room is she in?" Sheila asked.

May told her the number. "You can't see her yet, though."

"I know. I'll just talk to the nurse."

"They're so busy, darling. . . ."

"I know." Sheila smiled to herself. Her mother had trained her to be so considerate. Both of them were always the best patients on the floor. Now May wanted to be the best visitor.

The door to Doris' room was closed. Sheila glanced both ways down the hall, then slipped in.

She was shocked by the oxygen tent. Doris lay beneath it, almost indistinguishable. There was a nurse in the chair near the window. She started up. Sheila made a firm, quieting gesture and tiptoed closer until she could make out her grandmother's face. The nurse remained poised until she was sure Sheila would not disturb the patient. Doris lay on her back, her mouth half opened. The sheet on her breast moved

360

up and down slowly. The skin beneath her eyes hung in loose folds as though her whole face was deflating. Her hair lay crumpled on the pillow. It seemed detached from the tight gray roots at her forehead and temples. They had strapped an intravenous needle to the old woman's arm.

Sheila stared at her for a long time, trying to reconcile the inert, wasting body with the squat, imperious woman she had watched leave the cardroom of the Paradise Hotel only a month before. It wasn't possible to change so quickly. Even more impossible to hope that she could ever recover a semblance of that proud, ridiculous body. She was dying. Sheila stood with her arms hanging limp at her sides trying to comprehend that even as she stood there her grandmother was slipping away through time. The Doris she knew was already lost to her. She'd disappeared in her absence. All she had left was this grotesque souvenir, vague reminders of her grandmother's face, remnants that seemed to grow more distant and distorted with each moment. It didn't even breathe like Doris; her hands had never been still the way they were now. They were always in motion, arranging cards, pulling out cigarettes, fumbling with a pocketbook.

Sheila did not know how long she'd been there when she realized that the eyes were open. Doris was looking up at her through the veil of the tent. The two of them remained unblinking for a long time. Doris slowly turned her free hand palm upward, and raised her eyebrows and shoulders as if to say, "Don't ask *me* how I got here."

Sheila smiled back through tight, trembling lips.

"She's awake," she said softly to the nurse. "Let me talk to her."

"I don't know. . . ."

"Please."

"She shouldn't be disturbed. . . ."

"Oh, please," Sheila said. "If I possibly can. I'm her granddaughter. She asked for me."

The nurse got up reluctantly and disappeared into the tent for an interminable time. "I think it'll be all right," she said when she reappeared. "Don't excite her, though."

"I understand."

The nurse arranged a small flap on the tent and set a chair for Sheila. She sat with her face close to Doris'.

"Hello, Grandma," she whispered.

"You're gorgeous." The old woman's voice was weak, but still flecked with rasp.

"You're not," Sheila said tenderly. "You look terrible."

"What did you expect? Carole Landis?"

Inside with her, Sheila could make out bits of color in the skin. Her breath was sour but she did not care.

"I only found out you were sick last night."

Doris made a resigned face. "Your father thinks he's in the FBI. Everything's a secret."

"Vikki and Phil send their love."

"They're not here?"

Sheila shook her head.

"Then how serious could it be? Right?"

"Jack and Alice are here."

"They'll make it serious."

Sheila laughed cautiously. They were silent a long time, simply looking into each other's eyes with open, unembarrassed tenderness.

Doris' eyes turned serious. "I'll tell you a secret."

"What's that?"

"I'm dying."

"Grandma. . . ."

She closed her eyes to signal no nonsense. "You know how I know?"

"How?"

"I don't feel like a daughter anymore."

Sheila stared. Doris nodded slowly.

"Is that something? It took this to convince me I'm grown up." She raised her hand. Sheila took it. "You know what I mean?"

Sheila nodded.

"Don't you be so stupid."

"You're not stupid."

"Don't argue. It's not good for me."

"All right. You're stupid."

"Be grown up."

"I will." Sheila leaned in to her. "Grandma, I have something to tell you."

"You're pregnant."

She shook her head. "I'm going back to law school. I'm going to practice law."

Doris' face barely changed, but her eyes glowed dimly. "You want that?"

"Very much."

The woman's lips tightened with pride. She made a weak movement of her head toward the nurse. "Tell her to get my pocketbook."

Sheila smiled and shook her head. "Grandma. . . ."

"Tell her."

Sheila turned toward the nurse. "She wants her pocketbook."

The nurse brought it. "Not too much longer," she said quietly. Sheila nodded and turned back to Doris.

"Open it up."

Sheila obeyed.

"You see the zipper?"

"Yes."

"Open it." There was a tattered, unsealed envelope inside it. "That's for you. From poker."

Sheila started to protest, then realized it would be no use. She opened the envelope. There were three thousand-dollar bills and six hundreds.

"There should be a quarter in the corner."

There was.

Sheila looked at the money incredulously, then at Doris.

"I always carried it. Nobody knew. It gave me confidence."

"From poker?"

Doris nodded.

"Grandma, I can't take it."

"Do I need it?"

The nurse approached them. "I think—"

"All right," Sheila said. She leaned closer in to Doris. "Grandma, I love you." She kissed her cheek.

Doris tightened her grip on Sheila's hand. "I wish it were more."

"I'll make you proud of me."

"Make Vikki proud."

Sheila nodded. "All right." Doris' face turned puzzled. "What is it?"

She shook her head weakly. "I don't know. Whenever I leave some place. It's like something didn't happen that I expected." She shrugged and closed her eyes, but her face remained troubled.

Sheila left to rejoin the others.

Doris went into coma that afternoon. She died two days later. Sheila and May were in the cafeteria while Bernie sat with her. May was the first to see him come in. Sheila saw her mother's eye go instinctively to the wall clock. The two women got up and met him. They embraced and went to the waiting room where it was all right to cry softly.

It was Friday, the twenty-eighth. They had to look it up when they got home. No one was sure. Sheila had arrived Tuesday night, but the hours between then and now had fused. The lights burned in the house all night. Someone was always up, working in the kitchen, going, coming, making something to help them sleep—or keep them awake. They worked as though it were day and talked in nighttime whispers.

Sheila had never been through the routine before. It seemed familiar to the others. She learned from them. She learned to live with the disorder that death imposed on the house, to find the small ways to fight it even while she recognized its triumph over them all. Their consciousness of days and hours faded, but Sheila made sure the guest towels in the bathroom were always clean; Alice dusted the books; Bernie emptied the ashtrays in the car.

Once it was over the sense of order returned with a vengeance. Everything went on schedule. From the moment May glanced at the clock, times became exact. The funeral would be Sunday. They were to be at the chapel at nine thirty. The service would start at ten thirty. The drive to the cemetery took a half hour. They would be there at eleven forty-five. The funeral directors knew that the house must be ready for the visitors by one.

Sheila called Phil and told him to come on Sunday morning. She would meet them in the chapel. He asked how she was in a familiar tone of concern. She told him she was tired. Vikki was at Diana's.

"What should I tell her?" Phil said.

"Tell her Nanny died."

"Just like that? She's five years old. She'll be frightened."

"I'm twenty-seven. I'm frightened, too. Tell her Nanny died."

"Sheila," he said, before he hung up. "I love you. We can work things out."

She paused wearily. "I love you, too. It should help."

May made four strategic phone calls. By Saturday morning everyone knew who had to. The house would be full on Sunday afternoon.

They were the first to arrive at the chapel. Sheila had not packed anything black. She wore a dark-blue suit. One of the assistants at the funeral home pinned a black ribbon on it, said something in Hebrew, and slashed the ribbon with a razor.

The room filled quickly. There were faces she hadn't seen for years, cousins they had left behind in Brooklyn and the Bronx. Older, fatter, they brought memories of hallways with tan stucco walls and elevators with diamond-shaped windows. Everyone from Woodview came, Edith and Arnie Kaprow, Merv and Sally, women she recognized from the Paradise looking frightened and grateful for something different to do on a Sunday.

Phil arrived with Vikki. He was wearing a dark gray suit with a vest. The cut and his blond hair made him conspicuous. He had dressed Vikki in a brown jumper. She held Phil's hand

and walked close against his leg through the crowd. Her eyes were very serious. She saw Sheila halfway across the room. Once the child found her, she kept her eyes fixed until she was in her arms.

Sheila scooped her up and held very tight. The inside of Vikki's knees felt warm and smooth.

"Oh, darling, I'm so glad to see you," Sheila whispered into her ear.

Sheila kissed Phil. An assistant gave him a *yarmulke*.

May kissed his cheek. He went to Bernie and the two men embraced. Sheila watched, astonished. She could not have conceived Phil capable of such an action of warmth. He shook hands with Alice. Jack was alone in a corner. He'd already begun crying. Phil returned to Sheila.

"Should I take her?" He extended his arms toward Vikki.

"You are getting awfully heavy. Should Daddy hold you for a while?"

"I can stand."

"That's my girl." She eased her down.

"Hold my hand."

They held fast while people approached to murmur condolences, touch cheeks, hug. Vikki watched silently, her face impassive. May and Bernie broke away to come to them. Bernie knelt down in the crowd.

"Hello, princess." His eyes were filled but he was in control.

Vikki stared at him, unsure of how to respond. She seemed to sense the extra weight of importance she carried and she did not want to fail him. She let him guide her into his arms and kissed him cautiously on the neck.

The directors cleared the room until only Bernie's family and Jack's remained. Greta stood beside Jack, her hand on his shoulder while he cried, her face more determinedly a sleepwalker's than ever.

Bernie took Jack by the shoulders and lifted him up. "Come on, Jack," he said. "We're the sons."

Jack stumbled into the chapel with Bernie.

Phil went to Sheila. "They've got the coffin laid out," he said in a low voice. "Should I take Vikki in the other way?"

366

Sheila shook her head and picked her up.

"Are you sure?"

"My father did that with me at Aunt Sophie's funeral. I dreamed about what was in the box for years." She turned to Vikki. "We're going to see Grandma for the last time," she said softly.

They had retouched Doris' hair at the roots, but the colors didn't quite match. The skin that had lain in folds in the hospital looked stretched and waxen.

Alice was in front of them. "She looks like she's asleep."

Sheila and Vikki looked up at her, Sheila astonished that people still said such things, Vikki startled at hearing the lie for the first time. Vikki looked at Sheila, then back at Doris.

"She doesn't, does she?" Sheila whispered.

Vikki shook her head almost imperceptibly and buried it in Sheila's shoulder. Sheila rubbed her arm gently. They should have put a cigarette in her mouth, she thought.

The chapel service was short. The rabbi had not known Doris. He'd got the names of the immediate family from the funeral home.

". . . beloved mother of Bernard and Jack . . . grandmother of Sheila and"—he stumbled at the unfamiliar name—"Greta. . . ." But when he said the prayers, he named her, "Doris, daughter of Laban ben Israel."

At the far end of the aisle Jack sobbed. Vikki's head shot toward him when Bernie began to cry, too. May sniffed and straightened her back.

The rabbi talked of a rich life of service to family and friends. He noted the size of the crowd that had come to pay their respects. A community, he said.

Alice had said it, too. All day yesterday the phone had been ringing. "Well, she had a full life," she had repeated with a mechanical sigh into the mouthpiece. Each time Sheila would think through her teeth the way she thought now, That's a lie. She closed her eyes. The tears that seeped through surprised her. It's the waste, she thought. The mind and the energy. The vile, disgraceful waste. She remembered her grandmother's face on the pillow, bewildered with disappointment, never understanding that it was not what hadn't happened that had betrayed her, but what she had left undone. Rage and frustration and unbearable compassion filled Sheila. It was not the fact of her grandmother's death, but the half-spent life that had brought her to it, the evasion of the knowledge that it would finally come to this that had kept her from taking her life into her own hands, the fear that had kept her a daughter to the brink of her death.

This was the evidence she'd been looking for when the others had assaulted her with threats of reality and almost broken her will. Far more than the foolish and beautiful money, this was her grandmother's legacy. This knowledge, the relentless, undeniable truth that it would come to this. And the rage at the waste.

Phil pressed his handkerchief into Sheila's hands. She wiped her eyes.

The cemetery was cold. The earth was crusted with frost. Jack and Bernie said Kaddish. As Sheila watched them lower the box the horror of her own suicide consumed her. Her fists clenched against every grotesque denial of life, every compromise with the truth, every death-dealing choice as large as hers, or as trivial as her Aunt Alice's lies.

The rabbi told them not to look back as they left.

The living room was ready when they returned. The funeral home had left boxes for *shivah* and flowers. For the next seven days they would sit on the boxes. There would be a stream of people. The living room would echo with bright conversation. Everyone would eat fruit from the baskets that came wrapped in yellow cellophane.

The afternoon started in murmurs. Edith Kaprow's was the first voice to break through with animation. In the hallway Merv laughed tentatively at something. Soon the room was filled with greetings, conversation, the click of ice. The front door slammed more loudly at each arrival and departure.

Sheila found her way through the crowd to Phil.

"Tired?" he asked.

"I don't have time." She offered him a bowl of raisins and nuts she was holding.

368

He shook his head.

"It's called *rozhinki-mit-mandlin*. Like a Chunky bar without the chocolate."

He smiled up at her.

"Are you staying tonight?"

He looked away. "I think I should."

Sheila tightened. "You want to talk," she said quietly.

"I don't know. I don't know if it's fair to you—with Doris and all."

"My grandmother's dead two days. I've had time."

"To adjust?" the irony was gentle.

"Yes," she said seriously. "To this. It's necessary."

He stared up at her a long time. "Then I want to talk."

She took a deep breath. "OK."

She worked with trembling hands for the rest of the afternoon. His face had told her, like the faces of the doctors around Doris, unconsciously serious and sympathetic. He had made a decision—and he understood, at last, how important it was. That was something.

May noticed the change in her. In the kitchen, alone for a moment, she asked what was wrong. Sheila shook her head.

For the rest of the afternoon she made her way back and forth between May's anxious eyes and Phil's.

At four, as though a bell had rung, the guests left.

Sheila went to Poppa's room to lie down. She stretched out on her back and listened to May in the kitchen. She smiled. Her mother tiptoed while she clattered the dishes.

The afternoon light was fading. She watched the shadows deepen in the room, then closed her eyes. The noise in the kitchen stopped. She could not be sure if May had really finished or if she, herself, was dozing.

The door opened a crack and Phil peered in toward the bed.

"I'm awake," she said. She snapped on the reading light.

"Did I wake you?"

"I was just dozing."

He slipped in and closed the door carefully behind him.

Sheila remained on her back. She could feel her heart

369

through her whole body. The two of them looked at each other, unsmiling, for a long time.

"Is that the only light?"

"There's a wall switch behind you."

Phil flipped it on. Sheila squinted and shaded her eyes.

"Does it bother you?"

"It's all right."

She'd been too preoccupied all day to notice how tired his own face was. Behind the starched shirt and the three-piece suit his eyes looked washed out, his cheeks haggard. "You don't look like you've slept much."

"I haven't." He paused. "Everyone in Northfield sends condolences."

She nodded acknowledgment. "How was it for you?"

"Hard."

"Did you say anything more to Ryan?"

He shook his head. She put one arm over her eyes. "Oh, Phil," she said sadly.

"I need time, Sheila." He slipped beside her. She let him take her hand. "I love you."

"I don't know what that means anymore when you say it." She withdrew her hand. "I don't even know if you do." She sat up and slid back against the wall. "I can't go with you to Connecticut," she said. "Do you understand that?"

He looked down at his hands and nodded.

"I don't want to lose you but it's not my choice anymore. It's up to you now."

He gave a short laugh. "I thought after Christmas I was going to be finished making choices."

"I know how you feel. That's what I thought when I married you."

"It's got to stop sometime."

"For my grandmother it just stopped."

"Sheila. . . ." He faltered, then opened his hands in a helpless gesture.

"I guess I threw a lot at you at once."

"We threw a lot at each other. But I'm the hotshot lawyer. I'm supposed to be able to think on my feet."

370

"It wasn't a test."

"Everything's a test for me."

"That's a hell of a way to live."

"You're telling me. Ever since Tuesday I've been wasting my energy finding ways to justify myself." He reddened. "All I could think about was how many other guys were going through the same thing I was. And whether six years was a *normal* time for a divorce." His face got redder as he spoke. "I even tried to figure a way to find out how many state and federal judges were divorced. And while I was in Northfield I didn't even think there was anything wrong in thinking that way. I didn't even blush at it," he said ruefully.

"You're blushing now."

"It's my law training. Always looking for precedents."

She was beginning to remember why she loved him. Honesty was always so painful for him, so much more than for her.

"I even worked up a whole list of absolutely convincing reasons for you to come with me to Connecticut. How you're not strong enough yet. How Vikki needs you—and how I do. How you don't really want it, anyway. How maybe you could start easy with a couple of night courses in Connecticut."

"Old home week."

"Yeah. I realized it wasn't going to be that easy when I saw you this morning." He covered his face with his hands. "Sheila, you looked so beautiful. When I came into the chapel you were standing there . . . so sure of yourself and . . . beautiful. And when you picked up Vikki. . . . I had hoped you'd be falling apart."

She nodded. "That's always made it easier."

"I knew I was kidding myself. I have no business asking you to come to Connecticut with me."

"You have no business going yourself."

"If I only knew that for sure."

"Don't you?"

"When I'm with you I'm sure. When I'm with them I'm just as sure it's right to go." She had never heard his voice so anguished.

He dropped his hands from his face, but he could not look

at her. There was a long silence. "I think we should separate for a while."

Sheila gripped her knees tighter.

"I have to go off by myself. Not with them . . . not with you."

"Stop waiting for signs."

"I'm not. Don't underestimate me. You know where that—" He stopped himself.

They compared notes, Sheila thought. She smiled and shook her head sadly.

"I need to think for myself."

"I thought that was a luxury you couldn't afford."

He smiled wryly. "You've made it a necessity. How about that? Maybe I can even learn from you how to do it." He paused. "I need time, though. I'm sorry, Sheila. It's the way I'm made."

"Don't say that!" Her intensity pulled him up short. "For Christ's sake stop thinking like that. Don't you understand that's exactly what's got us into this mess in the first place? Neither of us is *made* any way. We make ourselves." She slapped her knees and looked up at the ceiling. "How many ways do I have to find to make you understand that?" She leveled her eyes at him. "Five years ago we thought we were married because a rabbi and a priest and a flock of strangers told us we were. And we thought we loved each other because we were married. And we felt so secure and safe that it never occurred to us that it needed working at. All because they told us. We figured we were made for each other, that love was something out there somewhere that had happened to us, so we could trust it to keep us going. Only while we sat there on our asses thinking we were 'made that way' we ended up making ourselves strangers, killing ourselves." She looked at him intensely. "No more of that, Phil. We can't get away with it."

"I do love you."

"Not unless you work at it. Every inch of the way."

"What about you?"

"I asked you to marry me last week. I want to work at it."

"But not enough to come to Connecticut."

372

"I don't want to work at loving the person you'll make yourself there. And you wouldn't want me there."

He paused. "I need some time."

"What then?"

"I don't know. I *think* I'll know what's right."

"What's right or wrong isn't out there somewhere, either, Phil. You can't sit around and wait for it to happen to you —not from Ryan or Ronstein or your mother or me."

"I know that."

She shook her head. "You'll need more time. Then more. You'll waste your whole life waiting for letters of confirmation."

His eyes seemed utterly exhausted, his face more haggard than when he first came in. He looked around the room distractedly. That was how it started for all of them, Sheila thought—all the people who sell themselves for reassurance. The eyes start to shift, checking for it. They turn guarded and end up haunted. She shook her head. Wasteful! Wasteful! she thought furiously.

"Everything's so new," he said.

She leaned her head back and closed her eyes. "It's new for me, too." she said wearily. "Believe it. I've found out some things in the last three months a lot more terrifying than anything you've picked up in the last week. The morning I woke up in the hospital I found out I was on my own and that I really was responsible for everything I did, every blink of my eyelashes, every lie I told myself, every evasion, every corner I cut. And that morning when I sailed into Colquist's office I found out I was free, that as long as I was alive I was able to choose and do, and that it was up to me to make what I chose and did right. And no one, not you or Rankin, or my father, or your mother, or anyone else, could make it right by telling me. You know what it means if you put all that together?" Her eyes were still closed, but she smiled as though she was looking at him. "It means I found out I have a soul." She paused. "And I almost threw it away."

She opened her eyes. Phil's hands hung loose between his knees. He stared down at them.

"That's why I can't promise you anything if you stay with me, Phil. No assurances—except to work at loving you. And I know, darling—I do know what I'm asking you to give up."

He sat quiet for a time. When he spoke his voice was low. "I doubt that you do. That is not an evil world, Sheila. It provides useful things—valid things. I'm not as sure as you are that it can't provide freedom."

"You'll end up paralyzed."

He opened his hands.

"Sooner or later you use up your share of escape clauses."

He nodded.

"That's what they call hell."

He closed his eyes.

Sheila held still. He moved to get up, then turned back to her. "Sheila. . . ."

"You see? You can't even make it off the bed." She swung her legs over the side and stood above him.

"I think I ought to go back tonight."

Sheila touched his hair and face softly. "You need a shave. I can never tell just from looking at you. She tilted his face up. "I'll be here a week, Phil. Will you be home when I get there?"

He did not answer.

She shook her head sadly. "Have you heard anything I've said?"

"All of it."

"And still you can't—"

"I don't know."

"It's up to you. You understand that? The decision is yours."

He kissed her cupped hand.

They stood close, facing each other.

"Sheila?"

She shook her head. "No assurances. Even together we're going to be on our own."

"Is that the way to work at love?"

"The only way."

374

He closed his eyes and smiled sadly. "And we never know for sure."

"You're getting the idea."

That night May asked Sheila what had happened. She told her mother as much as she could.

"It'll be hard, darling."

"It's hard already."

May shook her head. "I don't know . . . everything at once. . . ."

After the full seven days, Sheila and Vikki took a crowded bus back. Vikki fell asleep on Sheila's lap.

Sheila was frightened as she had never been frightened in her life. She was sad. She was angry at the number of ways people found to torture themselves in the name of necessity. But she was not in doubt.

They had had snow during the week of mourning. There were still traces of it on the flat, brown fields. Sheila leaned back against the headrest and watched them pass. Vikki stirred in her lap.

They'd been standing there, she and Phil, teetering on the edge of the moment so long. That was the place where doubt ate away at your feet. He was still there, grabbing behind him at safety ropes hooked to nothing. It filled her with rage and compassion. She had reached forward, swung out, holding tight to the void. She hung there now, exhilarated by the terror, consumed by a loathing for death.

It was hand over hand from now on.